Praise for Gerald Seymour

'A first-rate thriller with all the strengths of his recent work: audacity, believability, impeccable pacing, [and] a rich, diverse ensemble of supporting characters.' *The Sunday Times* on NO MORTAL THING

'Seymour expertly marshals his plot as Jago inches ever closer to the heart of darkness. A thoroughly engrossing thriller.' *Mail on Sunday* on NO MORTAL THING

'Gerald Seymour produces the most intelligent writing in the thriller genre.' *Financial Times* on VAGABOND

'Seymour is, quite simply, one of the finest thriller writers in England, every bit the equal of Frederick Forsyth and Robert Harris.' *Daily Mail* on THE CORPORAL'S WIFE

'Gerald Seymour is the grand-master of the contemporary thriller.' Major Chris Hunter, author of *Extreme Risk* on DENIABLE DEATH

'Seymour is not one to cut corners. He does his research, thinks hard about his story and gives us richly imagined novels that bristle with authenticity.' *Washington Post* on THE COLLABORATOR

'The finest thriller writer in the world today.' *Daily Telegraph* on THE UNTOUCHABLE

'A superb feat of storytelling by a master of his craft.' *Sunday Telegraph* on THE UNKNOWN SOLDIER

NO
MORTAL
THING

Gerald Seymour

HODDER

First published in Great Britain in 2016 by Hodder & Stoughton
An imprint of Hodder & Stoughton
An Hachette UK company

First published in paperback in 2016

1

Copyright © Gerald Seymour 2016

A CIP catalogue record for this title is available from the British Library

B Format Paperback ISBN 978 1 444 75865 8
A Format Paperback ISBN 978 1 473 62690 4
eBook ISBN 978 1 444 75866 5

Printed and bound by Clays Ltd, St Ives plc

Hodder & Stoughton policy is to use papers that are natural, renewable
and recyclable products and made from wood grown in sustainable
forests. The logging and manufacturing processes are expected to
conform to the environmental regulations of the country of origin.

Hodder & Stoughton Ltd
Carmelite House
50 Victoria Embankment
London EC4Y 0DZ

www.hodder.co.uk

For the many friends I rely on when I stray into areas beyond my experience – they know who they are – and whose patience, kindness and advice I value greatly.

PROLOGUE

The boy kissed his cheeks, first the right, then the left, and Bernardo smiled. He felt a sort of happiness at the love shown him by the boy, and the respect.

He had told him that afternoon what he wanted of him. The boy was Marcantonio, his grandson. Bernardo was now seventy-four years old and owned a wealth of experience from the life he had lived, but there were matters – at present – that were beyond his powers to achieve. A few years back, ten certainly, he would not have required the assistance of his grandson, but he did now. He was slightly built, maintained a good head of hair and his arms were muscled. His stomach was without flabby rolls, and his eyesight was good. His hands were broad, and calloused from the work he did in the garden at the back of his home. But he had lost a little of his strength and his breath was shorter. He had asked his grandson to do what he would have preferred to do himself. Some four years ago he had realised he could no longer strangle a man with his bare hands when his victim had writhed and kicked and he had had to call the boy to finish the job.

His grandson grinned, then hugged him once more, touched his arm and turned on the step at the kitchen door.

A few years before, Bernardo had taken Marcantonio to a car park by the beach on the Ionian coast where they had met a man he supplied with cocaine. It had been a familiar story, a cash-flow shortage, a contract broken. There was no indication as to when the debt would be paid. The man would have believed he was dealing with an elderly *padrino*, once strong but now in failing health and with only a teenage boy in support. The man had had, in the car park and evident from the glow of the cigarettes in the darkness, an escort of three. As instructed, the boy had ambled towards the second car, taken the pistol from the back of his belt and used it to smash the windscreen. He had poked his arm inside and had held the pistol tight against the front passenger's temple. No one had challenged him. From the interior lights on the dashboard they would have seen his face, its expression, and prayed to the Madonna. He had reached inside the car and started to squeeze the fleshy throat.

In his youth, Bernardo had been able to kill, by strangulation, in less than three minutes. He had walked the few paces across the car park, relieved his grandson of the pistol, then gestured with a jerk of his head towards the man's car. His grandson, still at school and shaving only once a week, had gone and done the work. A minute, perhaps. One guttural croak, one last kick inside the footwell, then silence. He had thought it similar to taking the boy to a brothel, in Locri, Siderno or at Brancaleone, to lose his virginity, a rite of passage he had facilitated the year before.

The escort had gone and the body had been buried in scrub above the beach. Bernardo had driven his own car, a nine-year-old Fiat Panda City-Van, up into the foothills of the mountains while Marcantonio had driven the victim's. After they had set fire to it, they had gone home, grandfather and grandson showing less emotion than if they had been to a football match. The boy had made no fuss, shown no excitement. It had been a job well done.

Now Bernardo stood by the door. The winter was over but it was still cold. Marcantonio paused, half turned, then gave a little wave. The light came from behind Bernardo and caught the scar – the only blemish in his grandson's smooth skin. There had been a dispute with a shoemaker in the village; drink might have given the man more courage than was good for him because he was rude about the principal family. Marcantonio and a gang of *picciotti* had gone to his house and beaten him, then wrecked the main room. They had been leaving when a child, who had followed them out, picked up a stone and flung it after them. It had struck Marcantonio's chin, had needed two stitches. They would have taken revenge but a *carabinieri* car had happened on the scene. Marcantonio, a handkerchief pressed to the wound, and his fellows had slid away into the darkness. The shoemaker's family were gone by the morning, their possessions loaded into a lorry, with an escort to see them out of the village.

Further down the track that led away from the house, a car engine coughed into life.

They had talked about it in the kitchen, the radio on, and the television at the other end of the room. They had sat opposite each other at the table, their heads close. Mamma had been behind him, mixing the sauce that would go with the pasta she would serve after they had eaten slices of cured ham and spiced sausage. The boy did not interrupt but sometimes gazed out of the window at the fading view of the wooded crags behind the house and the distant peaks of the Aspromonte mountains. Bernardo had said what should be done, how and where. Then he had questioned the boy: did he understand? There had been a nod. Mamma did not comment. He did not require her opinion so she was quiet. She, though, had packed Marcantonio's grip. The sports holdall had bulged with clothes, trainers, a well-filled washbag, and a framed picture, protected with bubble wrap, of the Madonna at the shrine of Polsi, in a steep-sided valley to the south-west. The boy smoked at the table, which irritated Bernardo's chest but he said nothing. The boy was his future: he had killed five times already in his life, would do so twice that evening. At the end, the boy had not answered him but the delicate fingers of his right hand rested reassuringly on Bernardo's wrist: the old man worried too much . . .

When Marcantonio had stood up, thin and sleek, Mamma had wiped her hands decisively on her apron, enveloped him in her arms, crushing him close to her, then abruptly released him. The radio had been switched off and the TV had been turned down. She had laid the table and Bernardo had poured wine from the Crotone region: a good measure for himself, another for Mamma, but half a glass for the boy, who had tasks to fulfil that evening. The bag went into Stefano's car.

Exhaust fumes spilled from the old Lancia, and the headlights captured the path that led to the vegetable garden, the chicken coops, the shed, whose roof was unstable, and the dry stone walls, which bulged outwards. The first buds were on the trees and the branches swayed in the wind. The last autumn leaves scurried over the path and whipped against the shed door. The boy walked to the car and did not look back.

His elder son, Rocco, was Marcantonio's father, married to Teresa. She was at home, a kilometre down the track. She had not been asked to attend the last meal before her son's long journey. Rocco had not been there because he was detained in the maximum-security gaol at Novara in the north, subject to the brutal regime of Article 41*bis*, by which the authorities could hold men in isolation from fellow prisoners. The problem confronting the family was not with Rocco and Teresa, but with Bernardo's younger son, Domenico, husband of Annunziata and father to Nando and Salvo. It involved *honour*, and could not be ignored or shelved. Domenico was in gaol at Ascoli, also subject to Article 41*bis*.

The problem centred on Annunziata's behaviour. Some women took hard the imprisonment of their husbands – sent down for twenty years or more. A few took to drink, and some suffered nervous collapse. One or two sought a lover . . . which was unacceptable. Bernardo, the *padrino*, leader of the Cancello clan, had condemned his daughter-in-law. A simple enough solution. He could not kill her himself and, shut in their cells, neither could his sons. And it was beneath his dignity to order lesser men to carry out killings when the issue nudged at the very centre of his power. She was a fine-looking girl, Annunziata. She had worn well after the birth of her children. Slim waist, a brittle smile, which seemed always to show that her thoughts were elsewhere. Her clothes, bought in Milan or Rome, were not suitable for the village or her home, which was three hundred metres down the track from Rocco and Teresa's. If it were known that his son, in gaol, had been betrayed by his wife, it would reflect on the whole family and gnaw at their power.

He heard the car door slam, and Stefano – at the wheel – began the three-point turn. God's truth, he would miss the boy.

Stefano was two years younger than Bernardo, and had been at his side from the day that Bernardo's father had been shot dead in the covered market at Locri. He would take Marcantonio to the first targets. The man who had sex with his daughter-in-law was the owner of a small picture gallery in Catanzaro. Bernardo had learned of a beach hut to the south of Soverato, where the pair met, copulated, ate a picnic and drank wine, then locked up and went their separate ways. The man was always there first, and his arrival would coincide with Marcantonio's. Marcantonio would have with him a sharpened kitchen knife and a lump-hammer. The man first, then Annunziata . . .

The car went away down the hill. Stefano always drove slowly. Bernardo saw the headlights bounce from the trees. He knew each of those trees, and every metre of the stone walls flanking the lane. He went back inside and closed the door. The house, expanded now, had been his father's and his grandfather's. He was in the kitchen.

He had seen a photograph of the gallery owner. A short man, he had a beard, which was carefully trimmed. From the photograph, Bernardo reckoned that he took time each morning to tidy it. Within two hours the dark hair would be blood red. Stefano would rip the man's trousers down to his knees, and Marcantonio would use the knife to slice off his penis, then force it into his victim's mouth. He would hit the man with the heavy hammer, one blow or two, to stop the struggling, then leave him in the beach hut. It might be weeks before he was found. The job would be done quickly, any shrieks carried away on the wind – they might sound like the cries of gulls. He imagined it all and felt only satisfaction.

Mamma was at the sink, washing up, even though they had a dishwasher. She washed his and her clothes by hand, too, and didn't use the German washing-machine built into the kitchen units. Their daughter, Giulietta, was with Nando and Salvo, as she was every time Annunziata went out at night. Each Tuesday, Giulietta took care of the children and was like a mother to them. She would not have her own. She was ugly, he thought, especially with the large-framed spectacles she wore. She knew that by midnight the children would have no mother, and approved. Giulietta was skilled with a computer. She knew how to deal with passwords and cut-outs.

Bernardo should not have been in the house. He had been conceived and born, in the big bed at the front with the view down the track towards the centre of the village. His boys and Giulietta had been born in it too. It was the bed in which Mamma slept, when Bernardo slipped away to the narrow divan in his hiding place, where he felt safest. It hurt him that he could not be in his own bed, with Mamma's heavy hips against him.

He checked through the window. The car lights had gone. By now Annunziata would have left for the coast. He felt his age in his bones, especially his knees.

Bernardo was of the older generation of clan leaders and enjoyed the discipline of tradition in language, behaviour, or in the drawing up of agreements where a man's word was his bond the spoken word pledged a deal. Tradition applied also to methods of killing. A favourite of this group of clans, a loosely tied association known as the 'Ndrangheta of Calabria in the extreme south of Italy, was the *lupara bianca*. The *lupara* was the sawn-off shotgun used by goatherds against wolves, but *lupara bianca* meant something different. Marcantonio had been told that in particular circumstances a body should never be found and no announcement of a death would follow. Bernardo had determined that Annunziata would suffer *lupara bianca*. He glanced at his watch. Soon the gallery owner would open the beach hut, spread the rugs, light the candle and open the wine.

He had nothing to read. There were no submissions from bankers, accountants or investment managers that he could pore over. He fidgeted. Bernardo, a clan leader, held information in his head: he kept no compromising documents in a safe at his home.

He and Mamma had been married for forty-three years: she had not waited for his death to replace her coloured clothing with black blouses and stockings, skirts and cardigans. Marcantonio was Mamma's creation. She had shaped and moulded him from the time he had sat on her knee.

Annunziata would receive no mercy from her nephew. She was from a clan family herself, had come no more than twenty kilometres to her new home. Now she might have travelled a thousand kilometres but her own people would not have saved her. She had broken the disciplines that were valued by her own and her husband's family. Her eyes showed a challenging haughtiness, as if she thought herself superior to the peasant society into which she had married. Marcantonio would pinion her while Stefano bound her legs and arms. They would show her the corpse of the gallery owner and push her head down so that she could see the blood in his beard and what filled his mouth. She, too, would be allowed to scream.

Bernardo went outside and filled a watering can from the tap, then the plastic jug that held the chickens' feed. He moved warily, his three dogs close to him, their ears back as they listened for disturbance. They would hear if a fox was close enough to threaten the chickens. He was between a line of trees and the sheets that Mamma had hung out, which would not dry that evening.

He had called for a *lupara bianca*. A family in a village higher in the mountains owed him a favour, and tonight he would call it in. It was about disposal and disappearance. Several families kept pigs, which would eat anything, alive or dead. But the family that owed him the favour owned a tank of strengthened steel. It was available to him, he had been told, and might contain sulphuric acid or the chemical that unblocked clogged drains. That was where Annunziata was going tonight ... The chickens hustled towards him. Each had a name and he cooed at them. He was bonded to each fowl and the dogs that were close to his heels. The last unwanted litter of puppies had been put into a sack two years before and Marcantonio had carried it, oblivious of the squeals from inside, to the stream below the house.

The family had relations in Berlin, the German capital. Marcantonio would spend a useful period – several months – out of sight, far from the *carabinieri*. He could learn the arts of cleaning money and evaluating potential investments. Questions would be asked after the boy's aunt had disappeared and an inquiry launched, but he would be far away. He had said to his grandson that he must be discreet in the city and not attract attention.

When they went to the building, with the woman tied and weeping, knowing already that pleas for her life were in vain, Stefano and Marcantonio would carry her inside. Then Annunziata might see the tank and smell its contents. She would know that, by morning, she would be sludge at the base. He would almost have guaranteed that she would be alive as she went into the liquid, eased down so that she did not splash them. She would go in slowly, probably feet first. Who in that part of the mountains would report hearing screams in the middle of the night? No one. When the next visit to Domenico was due, Mamma would go to Ascoli with Giulietta. Although their conversation would be monitored with microphones and cameras, he would be told. It was possible to give serious news to a prisoner held under Article 41*bis*, and Domenico would be glad to hear that his wife had been punished for her treachery. She would go in alive.

Afterwards, Stefano would drive fast to Lamezia airport. There was a late flight to Rome, which met a connection to Berlin's Tempelhof. Bernardo had never been outside Italy – never outside Calabria. He tipped the last of the feed onto the ground and the chickens scurried and pecked around him. The dogs sat quietly. God's truth, he would miss the boy, yearn for him to return.

Now it was time for him to go to his bunker, sneak away like a rat to its den ... He saw again the grin that had played on his grandson's lips and hoped the boy would heed his advice. A camouflaged door opened. His torch showed a tunnel made from concrete pipes. He went to bed.

I

He could have flapped a hand and distracted the fly. It was on the branch of a pruned rose, close to a carefully constructed spider's web. It was a trap – and a work of art. Jago Browne had time to kill, more than twenty minutes, and had settled on a bench. The autumn sunlight was low and at that hour of the morning the frost had not dispersed. The grass around the tidy beds was whitened, the earth sparkled, and the web's intricate lines were highlighted in silver. The fly was doomed – it seemed unaware of the danger. It took off, then seemed to charge the patterned fibres of the web.

He was in the park because he was early for his appointment. He should have been sipping coffee with the *Frauboss*, as he thought of Wilhelmina, and glancing with her through the file, checking the client's complaint and the level of the bank's error. She had thought it would reflect well if she – the team leader in Sales Investment – was accompanied by a smartly presented young man from her office: it would demonstrate their commitment that the bank was taking the error seriously. His presence would underline the importance of this client's account to the bank. He fancied, also, that it was an opportunity to drill him in the standard of care that the bank demanded of its employees. Earlier this morning Jago's mobile had rung. Wilhelmina had had to cry off: the nanny was sick, the elder child had damaged an ankle so couldn't go to school, and her husband was abroad on United Nations business, saving the planet with a climate-control programme. Jago was to keep the appointment. She had lectured him on to his manner and the apology he would offer on the bank's behalf. He glanced at his watch. He had no need to hurry.

The fly hurried to escape. Its legs and wings flailed and, with each quick movement, the web seemed stronger. It thrashed. Jago had known cobwebs. His mother had dusted them away in the one-time family home; staff used poles topped with feathers to clear them from office ceilings. He had never before sat outside on an autumn morning and marvelled at one. He couldn't see the spider. He thought of the energy it would have taken to build the web, and the elements it had secreted in its body to do so. The fly fought for its freedom. If Jago had waved a hand when the fly was first close to the web, it would have been safe. He was between Charlottenburg and Savignyplatz, among pleasant, well-restored streets. The park was manicured, with bins for dog mess, cigarette ends, plastic and newspapers. It was a good environment for a client, a place where old Berlin wealth had survived.

An elderly woman now sat opposite Jago. His attention had been on the fly and he hadn't seen her arrive. Well preserved and well dressed, an expensive overcoat, a cashmere scarf and decent shoes – from two different pairs. There would be money there, an opportunity for a salesman from the bank. He had his business cards in his wallet and brochures in his briefcase . . . But the fly took his attention away from the woman who might need an investment portfolio. The fly struggled.

A girl came out of a pizzeria, to the right of the elderly woman. Jago Browne was twenty-six, single and unattached, though Hannelore and Magda, who worked alongside him, might have wished otherwise. Her dark hair was piled high and she wore a shapeless cardigan under a broad apron. Her skirt's hem was level with the apron's. She swept the pavement outside the pizzeria with a stiff brush, punishing the slabs. The forehead above the pretty face was cut with furrows. She was interesting, but . . . The fly was not long for this world.

He looked at his watch. Five more minutes. The apartment block where the client lived was at the far end of the square. The old lady opposite eyed him but didn't encourage conversation. He thought she would be in her middle eighties. He had been in Berlin long enough, seven months, to know the principal dates and events. The fall of the Wall, the Kennedy speech, the defeat and the flooding of the destroyed streets by hungry men of the Red Army . . . She would have been, then, fifteen, probably in the first flush of beauty, hidden in cellars in the hope that an infantry platoon, an artillery team or a tank crew wouldn't find her. She stared at and through him.

An open sports car pulled up outside the pizzeria, but the death of the fly consumed his attention. One last movement of the wings and legs, then a convulsion. Life extinguished or hope gone? Jago didn't know. Now he saw the spider. Cunning little sod. It had stayed back, against the angle of the main trunk of the rosebush and a stump to which part of the web was hooked. He supposed it needed to hide in case a hungry sparrow or robin passed by. Now it came out and tracked fast over its web. A resourceful killing machine closed on its meal. Whatever sustenance there was on the body of a fly was likely to be more nourishing than a scrap of meat or cheese swept off the pavement in front of the pizzeria. He looked at the web more keenly and realised that what he had taken for fragments of old leaves were the husks of previous victims. He'd learned something. The spider might not be hungry. It was a killing machine and fed regardless of need. That was its nature. It reached the fly and seemed to try to cover it, belly on back. It was smaller than the fly, but had the intellect to plan the trap, the engineering skill to build the web and would eat when opportunity arose.

Jago pondered. He wondered what he might have done.

Jago glanced again at his watch, then unfastened the clasp on his case, checked that the papers were beneath his laptop and closed it. Time for a quick cigarette. He lit it, dragged the smoke into his throat and wheezed a little. The old woman leaned towards him and asked, in a gravelly voice, if he would, please, offer her a cigarette. He did so. Would he, please, light it for her? The flame lit her eyes, a cough convulsed her, and he won a wintry grin. She told him that her doctor forbade her to smoke, that her children thought the habit disgusting, that her grandchildren were nicotine-Nazis.

Jago Browne, on a bank's sales team, reflected that the fly – by keeping him there – might have inched him towards a possible client . . . He mouthed, silently, the first sentence of what he would say to the client.

'A thousand euro a month, is what it will be.'

He blustered an answer but his words were indistinct. It was the third time he had told the man the figure. The face had gone pale and glistened.

A smile curled Marcantonio's lips. 'You understand? I can't make it any clearer. A thousand euro each month. For that you'll have total protection and your business will prosper.'

The man's face was sheened with sweat. There was no heat in the pizzeria, not enough sunshine yet on the windows for warmth and Marcantonio's cousin filled the open doorway. Marcantonio posed as a friend, almost a business associate. He was there because he was bored.

'A thousand euro a month. I don't negotiate. You'll pay in advance and I'll come tomorrow to collect. A thousand to start with, but when your business is doing well, it'll attract more attention from rivals so my fee will go up. For now, though, a thousand a month.'

The man jabbered something. Marcantonio couldn't understand him. The pizzeria had been open for two weeks in a fashionable quarter of the city. The rent would be high but the rewards, potentially, were good. The man seemed as timid as a rabbit cornered by dogs.

Marcantonio had been in Berlin just over six months. Home – the village, his grandfather – seemed increasingly distant. His cousin in the doorway, Alberto, was a long-term resident in the city and his minder – his subordinate in the clan's pecking order. He had collected rents from properties owned by the family, cleaned sums paid in Hamburg and Rotterdam, and inspected proposed leisure or business sites on the Baltic coast and in the Ruhr district. Old habits died hard and boredom irked Marcantonio. He knew how to create fear.

'Without protection, you risk a petrol bomb through the windows and then fire. Same time tomorrow.'

A girl hovered at the back by the cash desk. She wasn't as dark as girls in Calabria and the high Aspromonte villages. He saw hatred in her eyes. She hadn't spoken. He hadn't addressed a word to her. No reason why he should have. Where Marcantonio came from, the women and girls kept silent and were obedient. Any who were not went into the tank as Annunziata had. To ease the boredom, Marcantonio wanted to set up his own ring of protected businesses, draw an income and see eyes blink in fear, smell the sweat and hear the gabbled answers. This would be the first, and already he felt better. His car was outside. In Berlin he drove an Audi R8. Sometimes, on the open roads, going south or west out of the city, he laughed at the thought of his grandfather and Stefano in the City-Van, the engine chugging when it climbed hills. He was not supposed to draw attention to himself . . .

The man slumped, shaking into a chair as Marcantonio strolled to the door. Marcantonio had been polite and specific. His behaviour could not have been faulted. He went outside, lit a cigarette and began to walk towards where the Audi was parked. It was capable of acceleration to speeds above 160 k.p.h. on the *Autobahns*.

His arm was grabbed.

He turned. The girl's fingers were locked into the fabric of his windcheater. Alberto had spun and was ploughing towards her.

She hissed, 'We won't pay you *pizzo*. This is not Naples, Palermo or Reggio. We don't pay thieves. You're scum. Don't come back.'

Alberto caught her shoulder and tried to pull her back, but her grip on Marcantonio's arm was too tight. Her nails came up towards his face. He saw them as they came for his eyes. He hit her with the back of his hand. She reeled away, freeing him, and screamed.

The elderly woman's face showed no change of expression, but she would have heard the scream. He swung round and saw the girl who had been sweeping the pavement at the entrance to the pizzeria. She reeled away from the guy and would have fallen if a bigger man hadn't held her upright, making her a better target.

She spat at the one who had hit her, and kicked the shin of the man who held her arms. The two men were speaking Italian – Jago had learned some in his sessions at the language laboratory in Prenzlauer. The boy hit her again with a clenched fist, first her head, then her stomach. Her nose bled. Now he kneed her in the back.

What to do?

Jago was wearing one of his two work suits; the bank expected him to be formally dressed. That day, with a client to visit and an error to be corrected, he needed to be at his best. The elderly woman had disappeared.

Different for Jago.

How different? Quite different . . . the scream had been anger but the punch to the stomach had squeezed the air from her and she had first wheezed, then coughed, then choked on a squeal, and there had been another gasp as the knee went into her back.

A man was at the door to the pizzeria. He didn't move – as if he had decided that intervention would gain him nothing. At work Jago Browne was assessed on his ability to 'care for clients', his 'dedication' to his employer, his 'work ethic' and 'attention to detail'. For that he received a touch north of four thousand euros per month, plus bonuses. He was not paid to rescue distressed girls.

Now she was writhing on the pavement. Cars went by but none slowed. A woman pushed a pram towards the girl and manoeuvred it round her. A couple stepped off the pavement into the gutter to avoid her.

Jago took a step forward, than another. The man who had hit her was smartly dressed: designer jeans, windcheater, lightweight maroon pullover and polished shoes. His hair was well cut. The look on his face was part pleasure and part about the need to exercise power: he had been challenged by a lesser creature. He called a few words to the man in the doorway, who cringed. Something about 'tomorrow' and 'coming back', a warning to be 'very careful'. Then he headed towards the parked sports car.

The older man, the one who had held and kneed her, passed her, following the first. Her arm came out and she grabbed his ankle. He pitched forward, then went down hard onto the pavement. He swore. The first man came back as the second stood up. They circled her, then launched the attack. They kicked her . . . People passed them, looking away.

Jago started to run. He shouted, in German, 'Stop that. Leave her alone!'

This was a criminal assault. He expected them not to yell back at him but to walk away. Where he had been brought up, in East London, kids carried knives after dark and only an idiot would intervene in a fight. An even bigger idiot would stay behind as a witness when the police arrived. But this was Berlin, and not just any part of Berlin: it was the Charlottenburg and Savignyplatz area. He went forward – it was about bloody time that the guy in the doorway shifted himself, but he didn't.

Both men kicked the girl's backside and belly. She was shouting at them, struggling to get the words out and trying to claw their ankles but they danced out of her reach. Neither had yet turned towards him.

'Stop that! Stop it, for God's sake.'

He was armed with his leather briefcase, a self-indulgent purchase during his first week in the German capital. A church clock chimed, telling him he was now late for his appointment. He couldn't turn back. They hadn't run to the car. He was drawn in, as people were towards a cliff's edge. Logic had clouded, and the red mist came down. He reached her, crouched over her.

They watched him. He looked into the face of the younger man. Nothing was said but Jago saw his expression. It said, *Who the fuck do you think you are?* Or *None of your business.* Superior, dismissive. His heart was pounding and he had lost the calm that the bank's Human Resources people looked for in young people they employed. The girl looked up into his eyes, and the two men peered down at him. There was a moment of quiet before he spluttered, 'Go away, you bastards! Leave her alone. Scum—'

The older one hauled him upright. Jago's eyes were close to the younger face. He could see the clean skin and the immaculate hair, could smell the deodorant and the mint on the breath. He noted the scar on the right side of the chin. The heel of the hand came up fast, no warning, and caught his upper teeth, lip and nose. His eyes watered as pain shot through him. He was dropped. When he could see again, the sports car was reversing into the traffic flow. They didn't look at him. He wasn't important enough, he realised, for them to glance back and see how he had reacted.

She didn't thank him, or ask how he was. She pulled herself onto her hands and knees, then half upright. The man in the doorway come to help her, and the two of them went inside. Jago used his handkerchief to wipe away the blood that was streaming from his nose.

He steadied himself, then walked down the pavement towards the client's apartment block.

The messenger had come across Europe and far to the south, delivered and gone. Giulietta had met him. Then the dutiful daughter, whom he could not marry off but was precious to him for her understanding of the technology he would never master, had brought it to him. Bernardo danced.

It had been a good summer, warm, with little rain. There were corners of his garden, tucked out of sight or shielded by trees, where he had been able to sit and allow the sunlight to filter onto his legs, hips and back. The weather had been good for his arthritis. Dancing, therefore, was easier than it would have been had he attempted it in the spring. The single sheet of cigarette paper had been brought by hand from Rome, not entrusted to BlackBerry instant messaging or Skype. A man had flown from Ciampino, Rome, to Lamezia, where he had been picked up by a cousin and driven to Locri, which was overlooked by the village where Bernardo lived. Every week on that day, Giulietta went to the local covered market to buy vegetables – she hardly needed them because Bernardo grew enough for the family. Today the sliver of paper had been slid into her hand. She had brought it to him, then whispered in his ear what verbal message the courier could take back on the next flight.

His dance was almost a jig. He was sure he wasn't being watched by strangers to the village. Enough of the *picciotti* scrambled regularly over the rocks and along the goat trails on the steep-sided hills above his home, checking for ROS teams. The message was confirmation. A man had been located. A traitor had been identified as living in Rome, his address pinpointed. It confirmed the instruction Bernardo had sent back with the courier to those who now watched the target and would carry out the sentence of death. The killing would be publicised and no tears would be shed in the villages around Bernardo's home. His dance steps were in the tradition of the Aspromonte mountains.

It would be good for his sons to learn that the man who had put them in their cells was dead.

He would have liked his grandson to kill the turncoat with a knife, face to face, seeing the fear build, or with a pistol, sidling close, then shouting a name. It wouldn't be the name given to the rat by the Servizio Centrale di Protezione, but his old name, bestowed at his baptism. He would start and turn, then face the last few seconds of his life. It had been almost as great a disgrace to Bernardo as any that had befallen him. A *pentito* on the fringes of his clan, a former man of honour who knew some of the clan's secrets, had taken seventeen men to the *aula bunker* in Reggio where, in the subterranean fortified courthouse, he had given the evidence that had sentenced them with Bernardo's sons, to long, life-destroying sentences. He grinned to himself.

Two treats awaited Mamma for her birthday. The death of a rat and, a more joyous gift, the return of his grandson for the celebration. He would not stay long, but Bernardo would see the boy he had missed so much. His organisation was sealed in blood and by the family ties. The greater the trust, the closer the blood. None was closer to Bernardo than his grandson . . . and the reports that came from Germany were not good. He shrugged.

His lettuces had flourished. The tomatoes were good, and the vines had done well. The olive groves he owned were lower in the valley, and the crop was excellent; the harvest was almost complete. He lived a fine life. The imprisonment of his sons was the price the family had paid for its success. He had little to worry him and the children of the 'disappeared' Annunziata had moved in with Rocco's wife, but they were often in his own kitchen and Mamma was firm but loving. A large cargo was at sea. A rat had been identified and would be dead within the week. Marcantonio would soon be home, and as the day approached, he had noticed a softening in his wife's stern features. And he had, he supposed, come to terms with the hidden bunker that had become his second home.

Giulietta told him each month what she estimated the inner family, where the blood line was strongest, to be worth. She would list the value of investments and would murmur a figure in his ear. Each time she did that, her voice shook and her cheeks flushed. They were worth, Giulietta told him, in excess of four hundred million euros. She was like her father and mother – and there was nothing in the modest room at her parents' home where she lived that stank of wealth. For her, it was about power.

Giulietta was a fine daughter, almost as good as another son. She worshipped at the same altar as himself: wealth was power. Power was the ability to buy. Any man had his price. There were two important men in his life: the first was a clerk in the Palace of Justice, and the second worked as a civilian at the Questura; sometimes as he went about his work he heard gossip and saw screens used by men and women of the Squadra Mobile. From those two men, Bernardo had discovered that he was under investigation and that his liberty depended on him sleeping in the buried container and being always watchful, always suspicious. He could do that without difficulty. He was a peasant by nature, a *contadino*. The peasant, mindful of enemies, looked for what was best in the future. It was easy for him to be an optimist, and the news that day had been gratifying.

It was a fine morning. The skies above the village were cloudless. He believed himself secure.

'If he's there, wouldn't we see him?'

They had seen chickens, dogs and Mamma – but not their target.

'He's as cunning as an old vixen.'

Fabio said, 'He's seventy-four. What sort of life can he be living? He's somewhere in a hole in the ground, no daylight, can't walk down the track to see his family. What's he hanging onto – if he's there?'

A rueful grin from Ciccio. 'He's there.'

Their heads were together. They spoke in the faintest of whispers. Their appearance differed only to their wives and the *maresciallo* who commanded the surveillance unit. Fabio was two centimetres taller than Ciccio and his feet a size smaller than his friend's; there was fractionally more brown in Ciccio's hair, and a trace of ginger in Fabio's beard. They had been together, a bonded partnership, for four years and took leave together from the Raggrupamento Operativo Speciale barracks outside Reggio Calabria. They holidayed in the same hotels or beach apartments, and their wives endured their relationship. It was under strain, had probably run its course, but neither would yet speak of fracture. That morning domestic life was far in the background. They had come to the hide that overlooked a part of the house seven hours earlier, at dead of night.

'It's a fucked-up life,' Fabio said.

'The price he pays for being the boss . . .' Ciccio managed a slight shrug.

They wore British-manufactured gillie suits, German-made socks under their Italian boots, and the 'scope was Chinese. The smell was their own. It would get worse. They had done a week's reconnaissance in August when they had found this cleft between two mammoth rocks. It was not perfect because, below them, the trees had not yet shed their leaves and the view of the house was partially obscured. They could see the wide turning point of the track and any car that came up it but not the door. At the back, the kitchen door was masked from them but they could identify anyone who took three or four paces away from it and kept to the right of the yard. If that person, usually Mamma – Maria Cancello, aged sixty-three and wearing her age poorly – went to the left, a conifer allowed them a fleeting glimpse. She kept a line of washing up alongside a path leading away from the yard, up rough steps to a shed, of which they could see the back wall and all of the roof. Windows on the far side of the house were hidden from them but if lights were on in the master bedroom or the one adjacent to it, where the daughter slept, they saw the occupants. If they had come nearer to the house they would have been at greater risk of discovery by the dogs that were always with Mamma or the daughter. If they had been further back, higher and able to see over the tree canopy, they would have endangered themselves – there were herdsmen's tracks where the slopes were gentler and every day *picciotti* came with dogs. They had brought with them survival rations, plastic bottles for urine, tinfoil strips to wrap faeces, and would take their rubbish out with them. The hide was 'protected': a man would have to scramble, clinging to rocks, roots and branches, as he descended into the space between the big boulders. They must not leave a trail of scuffed earth, dislodged stones or crushed lichen when they came and went. When they were not there, another ROS team kept a watch on the house but from higher and further back. As Fabio said, often enough, 'They can't see anything.'

As Ciccio said, frequently, 'They're just clocking up overtime and might as well be in Cosenza or in bed.'

They thought themselves the best, took pride in their work, but hadn't yet located their target, the *padrino* of the Cancello clan. It hardly mattered to them where they were and who they were searching for: there was no shortage of photographs on the most-wanted lists. 'Scorpion Fly' was a long investigation and a prosecutor in the Palace of Justice had emphasised its importance. Scarce resources had been committed to it.

Both knew most of what there was to learn about the scorpion fly: *Panorpa communis*. The male's wingspan averaged thirty-five millimetres, and it trailed what seemed to be a scorpion's sting from its rear. In fact, it was two tiny hooks with which the male held tight to the female during mating. It was a member of the Heteroptera family.

They captured them, when they could, for a cousin of Ciccio's, an entomologist. When they laid hands on one it went into a small plastic jar. It was a poor morning for scorpion flies.

'If he's there, in a hole, how would that make life worthwhile?' Fabio asked.

Two driven men, hating corruption and the virus of organised crime endemic in their society, little cogs in a big wheel, watched the limited view of the house and saw Mamma wave away her daughter. What kept them alert was the hope that they would identify the target, find his hole and call in the arrest squad. They knew about the missing daughter-in-law, Annunziata, and of a grandson who seemed to have left home. 'Hope' was a candle flame and often it guttered.

On the ground floor of a drab house in an uncared-for quarter of Reggio Calabria, a photocopier needed replacing – it was painfully slow to operate – but there were insufficient funds for a new one. Consolata cursed. Paper churned at snail's pace into the tray. The printed sheets would be stuffed into plastic sleeves, then tacked to telegraph poles. In the committee meeting, everyone had argued against her.

'We can't frighten people, Consolata. It's not up to us to hector them into action. They must be persuaded.'

'Your suggestion, Consolata, of sticking our posters in the windows of businesses that we can only *suspect* of paying *pizzo* is ludicrous. We have to take people with us, not confront them.'

'We'll stay on the high ground, Consolata. We don't stoop to their level.'

'We know change is slow, Consolata, but it's coming. Last year thousands marched on the Corso Giuseppe Garibaldi. Thousands.'

'You must be patient, Consolata. Not this generation, but the next – perhaps – will reject the 'Ndrangheta state. Have faith.'

It was early in the morning, she wasn't yet dosed up on coffee and had 'turned the other cheek', which was rare for her: she had torn up the page of notes she had made to justify 'direct action' going to the edge of violence, or beyond. She had proposed, too, that those who tacitly supported the taking of the *pizzo*, a percentage of the profits made by legitimate business, should be confronted and shamed . . . A deep breath. She had disappointed the committee – they would have expected her to fight, argue and then be destroyed by their arguments. She had ducked her head, almost with good grace, but Consolata burned with fury.

The pages continued to flop out of the photocopier. Soon the ink would run out.

Life, she believed, had passed her by. She was thirty-one, and reasonably slim. Her hair was medium length and naturally blonde, which was unusual in Calabria. She came to work in trainers and jeans, a T-shirt and a light loose jacket. No jewellery and no makeup. She was from the town of Archi, a few kilometres up the main road north from Reggio. Her parents were still there but she no longer lived with them. If circumstances had been different, she would have worked in a shop selling curtains and good-quality wallpaper. Her parents had owned the business, built it up and made a living from it. 'One day' they would have retired and she would have taken over. Then *they* had come. A figure had been fixed, which her father couldn't pay. A whispering campaign had followed, and trade evaporated. Questions had been asked – was her father a paedophile? Had he been questioned by the police over the molestation of children? There had been no violence, no threats. Then *they* had made an offer to buy out the business. A few months before the price would have seemed ridiculous, but the bank was now calling in the overdraft and *they* would have prompted that. The business had been, in effect, stolen. Her father now drove a delivery van in Messina across the strait, commuting there each day, and her mother cleaned bedrooms in a hotel fronting the Corso Vittorio Emanuele, near to the ruins of a Greek settlement, dating to eight centuries before the birth of Christ. Consolata would have said that a new dark age had replaced the glories of that civilisation.

Archi was the town of the de Stefano and Condello clans, the Imerti people and the Tegano family. It didn't matter which of them had decided to launder their money through a legitimate wallpaper and curtain business. One of them had and the business was gone. Consolata had been sixteen, in the year of supposed optimism, the new millennium, when her father had come from the bank, ashen with confusion. Now there were cut-price goods in the window and cocaine money was rinsed there.

The most significant bosses in Calabria lived in Archi. None would have known her name. None woke in the morning wondering what she was planning.

She had gone to university, to keep her mother happy, and had studied modern history. Then she had enrolled at a language laboratory and become an interpreter, but had seldom returned calls offering work. Now she was a volunteer with a group that denounced the plague of organised crime in their community. Four or five years before she could have left the toe end of the country, abandoning her parents, and flown to Germany, Belgium, France or Britain to put her language skills to use. She could have made a new life. She had not. Now it was too late – a window had closed. Her fervour for the group she had enrolled with was gone; her loathing of the target remained undiminished ... They had laughed at her ideas.

She would probably spend the whole morning coaxing the machine to cough up more posters.

Consolata's ambition had almost atrophied. She was, she believed, the typical cuckoo in the nest of optimists. When she stopped to let the copier cool, she rolled a cigarette. The nicotine improved her mood a little. Those she had been at school with or known at university were mostly married and pushing prams, had jobs or had flown to freedom. She soldiered on, knew her enemies but not her allies. She could see, through the glass window in the door, the committee: men and women satisfied that they were 'in the vanguard of changing attitudes', ignoring her. She was, they thought, a 'doubter', perhaps even a 'heretic'. Again, she started the machine. Again, it spluttered to life. Usually she said it to herself, but this time she shouted over the noise of the photocopier, 'Not one of those people knows my name. We're doing nothing. Until they know my name, we've failed.'

No one heard her, but more posters fell into the tray.

*   *   *

In her Charlottenburg apartment, the client said, 'I like you, Mr Browne, and I like your apology. I also like your explanation of the circumstances of the error, and that you have not attempted to deflect blame from yourself. I'm impressed, too, that you came to me, your client, before going to hospital for treatment to your face. You came here as a priority and ran through the performance of my portfolio. Now you must report to the police the assault against yourself and the young woman. The police are at Bismarckstrasse, to the north of Savignyplatz.'

Jago nodded. He thought her attitude to him was pretty gracious. He had come to her door looking a mess – his tie was askew, his hands dirty, his nose still bleeding and his hair all over the place. She had led him to the bathroom, then given him a towel and soap. When he had emerged, sheepish, she had offered him a slug of schnapps. He had refused, but she'd poured it anyway. Twice during his explanation, the phone had rung – the *FrauBoss*. The client had been fulsome in her praise of him and had made no mention of his 'adventure'.

'Promise you'll give a statement to the KrimPol on Bismarckstrasse, Mr Browne.'

She dripped money, but without ostentation. Her jewellery was discreet, her clothing simple but classic; her face and throat showed her age. Most of the pictures on the walls would have been valued at more than Jago's annual salary.

He started to retrieve the papers he had used for his presentation. The client had three accounts: one in Zürich with Credit Suisse, one with Deutsche in Frankfurt, the third with Jago's bank. Her money, targeted by the *FrauBoss*, was the stuff from which bonuses flowed.

Jago closed his briefcase. He had given her a brief description of what had happened on the pavement, just enough to account for his appearance and his reason for being four and half minutes late. Where he came from in East London, nobody went to the police to complain of a minor assault. He said softly, 'Hardly worth it.'

'But you should.'

'I'm sure they have better things to do.'

They stood up. There was a trace of perfume about her. Her eyes were watery and had lost youth's sharp lines. Her hand was on his arm and crabbed fingers clawed a grip on the material. 'Because you do not wish to be involved?'

He tried to laugh it off. 'Someone where I used to work, in London, would say when anything went wrong, "I expect worse things happen in Bosnia." I don't know much about Bosnia, or what happened there, but it's what he always said.'

'Was it at the new pizzeria?'

He didn't answer.

'Were they Italian?'

He grimaced.

'Perhaps you're an innocent, Mr Browne.'

He still had nothing to say.

'Of course the police should be involved. You should stand up as a witness, Mr Browne. In Germany, still in living memory, we made an art form of avoidance. Evil flourished and we did nothing. Evil of any sort should be confronted. I am an old lady. I speak out because I have nothing to lose by doing so. For the young it may be different. Perhaps your pride is hurt because you were knocked over. Perhaps you can put the attack behind you because your place of work is on the other side of the city. Can you?'

He worked on the old east side of Berlin and here he was on the old west side. He lived miles from here and might not need to come back. The chance of the *FrauBoss* allowing this client to drift from her orbit was slight. He smiled, as if he was about to leave, but she persisted. He felt her intensity through the grip of her fingers.

'There was a theologian, Martin Niemöller. He was imprisoned for many years but survived in a camp while many around him were hanged. He was ashamed that he had lived when so many brave men and women had been murdered. He wrote about those who, like himself, did not stand up to evil. When they had arrested the socialists, he didn't speak out because he wasn't a socialist. When it was the trade unionists, he did nothing because he was not a trade-union supporter. When it was the turn of the Jews he was silent because he wasn't a Jew. He wrote, 'And then they came for me, and there was no one left to speak for me.' That was the big evil, the mature oak. The little evil is the acorn, thriving unnoticed – crime on the streets. Did you see a woman sitting in the little park, as old as myself?'

'Yes.'

'And she wore odd shoes? Expensive but not matching?'

'Yes.'

'Did she see what happened?'

'Saw the start, then slipped away.'

'Her father was hanged in the last days of the war, at the Flossenburg camp. Eighteen days later the Americans arrived. The evil consumed her. She says her father would have been better to close his mouth, do nothing, look away, and live to bring her to adulthood. I hope, Mr Browne, that you will find time to visit the KrimPol detectives. The girl won't. Her elder brother is the manager of the pizzeria. He won't either. They are Italian and would say they know better.'

He apologised again for his lateness, his appearance, the absence of the *FrauBoss*, then thanked her for her patience, courtesy and the schnapps. He gave her his smile, which was already famous among the investment team (Sales).

The fresh air was bracing. He looked across the square and saw an everyday scene. He had been punched there, a girl had been kicked – and a spider had murdered a fly. For him it was about where he had been brought up, his mother, what had happened to him and to her. Walking briskly, he phoned in and said that all was well with the client. He could see into the pizzeria, where customers were drinking coffee. The man, the girl's brother, was behind the counter. He checked on his phone for directions.

2

A woman behind a reinforced glass panel had told him, via a microphone and loudspeaker, where he should sit but not how long he would have to wait.

When Jago Browne had got dressed that morning in his attic apartment, he had not considered that he would spend hours on a hard bench in a police station on Bismarckstrasse. Where he had been brought up, Canning Town in east London, the closest police station had been on the Barking road, a formidable red-brick fortress. He had never entered it, although half of the kids close to where he lived had. He supposed that, there, a waiting area existed like this one. It smelt of urine and disinfectant. When the door onto Bismarckstrasse opened, a gust of cool air dispersed it briefly.

He was with two girls, about twenty, both probably tarts. One cried convulsively and the other comforted her. There was a fidgeting junkie, who tried to make conversation with an elderly man, who was muttering about a lost dog. A stream of men and women came to the counter, offering ID cards – they were clocking in as a bail requirement. There was graffiti on the walls – not clever or witty. Jago assumed that it was *verboten* to scribble on the walls but the woman behind the barricade couldn't do much about it. It was a *Rauchen Verboten* area too, but there were small burn marks on the linoleum.

Police officers hurried through the waiting area. Some came off the street and tapped a code into an inner door; others came from inside and headed for Bismarckstrasse. They had in common, entering or leaving, a reluctance to glance at the flotsam waiting on the benches. He supposed that a pistol in a holster, a truncheon and a gas canister gave the officers confidence to ignore him and those around him.

The man who might have lost the dog was the first to break. He stood, shouted abuse at the woman beyond the glass, aimed a kick at the end of the bench and left. Jago might have followed – he nearly did. Then the woman called him forward. His spirits soared until she pushed a sheet of paper through the grille and told him to fill it in, then bring it back to her. Why had she waited forty-five minutes to do that? He had requested to see a detective following an assault and a possible instance of extortion on the square two streets away. He took the paper. He had asked Elke at the bank to tell the *FrauBoss* that he was running late.

Heavy stuff from the client and he wondered if he believed any of it. It could all have been fantasy: hangings, Jews, camps, odd shoes worn by an old lady. The spider was real death. He couldn't quite decide whether the client had been playing with him. He started on the form: name, address, work, complaint.

He was Jago Browne. Born 1989. His mother was Carmel. Her parents were semi-lapsed Catholics from the western edge of Belfast and had left in 1972 at the height of sectarian disturbances in the hope of finding a less traumatic life. One daughter, the apple of her parents' eyes. Just after her eighteenth birthday she'd gone to Cornwall with her two best chums for a week's camping. Might have been the draught cider, or ignorance or an act of rebellion: a one-night stand with a deck-hand off a Penzance–Newlyn trawler. A one-night stand followed by a one-morning stand that had drifted into a one-afternoon stand. She'd thought his name was Jago, but it might have been Jack. Anyway, 'Jago' was Cornish and she had fastened on it once the sickness started in the mornings. Her parents had pretty much dumped her, couldn't cope with their little jewel dropping their hopes and aspirations in the shit. That was his mother, and home was a council flat in a part of London where few wanted to be housed – Canning Town – but she was lucky to have a roof over her head. She was a fighter – and wanted love. Dave was the boyfriend who gave her a brother for Jago, and Benny had provided the sister. Neither Dave nor

Benny had lasted long. She was a single mum, with three kids and a maisonette, within a bullet's reach of the Beckton Arms. That was Jago Browne, and they didn't need his childhood history or his education.

His flat was built into the roof of an apartment block in the Kreuzberg district, between the Landwehrkanal and Leipziger-strasse, with an entry on Stresemannstrasse along which the old Berlin Wall had run. His workplace was a bank – the section dealing with private wealth management and advising on investments – in the old east sector, out beyond Alexanderplatz and the great tower. The boy from a sink estate in Canning Town had made it into the stellar world of international banking via a school that believed in merit, a university in the north-west, where he'd worked his brain raw, a merchant bank in the Bishopsgate area of the City of London, and on to Berlin. How had he done it? People liked him. Those who had stumbled across his path thought him 'worth a punt' or had felt good after giving him 'a helping hand'. He would have said that he'd been in the 'right place at the right time' so he was on a two-year exchange with the bank in Berlin, and a German youngster was coping with life in Bishopsgate. He added the bank's name to the form he was completing.

Under 'complaint', he put, 'To report extortion and criminal violence'. It was almost eleven o'clock. It would take him the best part of an hour to get across the city and its former dividing line, beyond Karl-Marx-Allee and to the top of Greifswalder Strasse. By the time he got there the whole morning would have gone. In the section, they all worked like beavers at the direction of the *FrauBoss*, and Elke had been back on his mobile to ask when they should expect him – as if he had a criminal's tag on his ankle. He pushed the sheet of paper through the grille. A uniformed woman took the girls to a side room.

Jago continued to wait. Earlier it had seemed a good idea but the excitement had palled. In Canning Town no one made witness statements. His act of defiance was to get out a cigarette, not light it but roll it between his lips. He'd give it five more minutes.

*　　　*　　　*

On an upper floor of the station, in a pinched office, a picture on the wall faced his desk. Each time he looked up it was straight ahead, there for him to feast on. The sun was at its height. The sea was pure blue. The beach was golden, and not many of the pebble banks showed. Bikini-clad girls lay on multi-coloured towels, stood on the sand, or among the slight waves. He had taken the photo himself. He gloried in it, bathed in its warmth. It made the greyest, coldest day in Berlin a little more acceptable.

He was an investigator, had passed the 'detective' course run by the national police college, was in the KriminalPolizei, but would never allow himself to be promoted to sergeant. If he looked away from his screen and ignored the picture, he had the window to look out of. There was a courtyard and a glimpse of the sky – it had clouded over, wasn't raining yet but soon would be. The picture was his joy . . . He sighed, then allowed himself a brief smile. Manfred Seitz, investigator of the KrimPol based at the station on Bismarckstrasse, smiled infrequently when others might see him do so. Sometimes in the presence of his wife, not often . . . He was given the shit by those who ran the KrimPol section that dealt with organised crime in that part of Berlin. He was a dinosaur. Most of them were young enough to be his kids but they had the status of 'sergeant' or 'lieutenant' and could instruct him on his duties, which events he should follow-up. He fielded the rubbish and was kept at a distance from any work that might offer a step up the promotion ladder. He didn't complain . . . There was a bank worker in Reception, with a scarred face, a foreigner reporting 'extortion'. No one was dead, and there had been no hospital admission. It was for him to handle.

Fred – everyone used the abbreviation – sipped the coffee he had brought to work in his Thermos. He did not patronise the canteen, thought it tiresome. He brought his own sandwiches, which Hilde made for him while he showered each morning – he went to the station before she left for the infant school – so he could avoid the gossip and back-biting at the lunch tables. He had been Fred to his parents and at school in the Baltic city of Rostock, and when he had joined the police. . . . His children used it – the daughter in Zürich and the son at college in Dresden. He thought it suited him, that it matched his appearance.

It was a quiet morning. The 'kids' had made arrests the previous day, Kurdish pickpockets, and were still celebrating. Fred Seitz was at that stage of his career – within three years of retirement – when he was too junior to appear before the cameras or brief the press, and too old to appear in court as a witness on whom a conviction that could lead to advancement might depend. He was in a rut. A last glance at the sea, the beach and the bikini girls. His screen showed a new report from a Nature Conservancy group handling the parkland to the east of Lübeck, across the estuary. His pipe was on the table with sweet-smelling ash in the cold bowl. He killed the screen, hitched his jacket onto his shoulder and closed his door. The kids were around a central table in the work area but did not want him in their midst so he had been awarded the partitioned small room as an office, space that should have gone to a team leader.

He took the staircase down two floors.

When Fred stood behind the woman at Reception he could see, distorted by the stains on the glass, the bank worker. A nice-looking boy, good build and features. He asked the woman and was told he had been there close to an hour. The 'kids' would have held it up: smart-arse idiots. She told him which interview room was empty.

He went through the security door.

He said briskly, 'I am sorry you have been kept waiting so long. Follow me, please . . .

'Do sit down.' He gave a suspicion of a smile, an empty pleasantry. 'Now, how can I help you? Excuse me, you are English? Do you speak German?'

Jago said, 'I have adequate German. You could have helped me a while ago by coming to find out why I was here. So, sometimes your language, sometimes mine.'

'A good compromise . . . and I apologise. Communications in the building are not always satisfactory . . . How can I help?'

'Are you always so cavalier with the time of people who bother to report a crime? Or is that bad for the clear-up figures?'

'I've already apologised . . .'

'There's a phrase in England that all those public utility companies – or the police – use when they keep you hanging on a phone and have likely failed you. 'We take your complaint very seriously.' But I'm a member of the public and, although I'm a foreigner, I'm registered here as a taxpayer. So I pay your salary – or a fraction of it.'

The smile widened, might even have been touched by genuine humour. In the corridor, before getting to the interview room, they had introduced themselves. The investigator, Fred Seitz, was tall and thin, the skin sagging below his cheekbones. His throat was scrawny and his jacket hung loose from angular shoulders. His scalp was discoloured and his hair cut short. Jago estimated him to be in his mid-fifties.

He told his story.

'Is that all you saw?'

'I've told it as I saw it.'

'And described accurately the injuries to you and the girl?'

'I believe so.'

The investigator had produced a notepad and pencil but had written only a line at the top of the page, then closed it. Now it had gone back into his pocket, with the pencil. He produced a pipe, which whistled as he sucked the stem. 'What do you expect me to do?'

'As a police officer, I expect you to investigate the assault, interview the girl concerned, follow that up, identify our assailant, then arrest and charge him.'

'Are you widely travelled, Mr Browne?'

'Not particularly.'

'But you are aware of the Italian diaspora – of course you are.'

Jago said sharply, 'I know many Italians live here. I have eyes in my head.'

'You have not visited Italy?'

'No. Does that make me an inferior witness to criminal acts?'

'I understand, Mr Browne, your irritation with my questions. I assure you they are relevant.'

'I've given you chapter and verse on a crime.'

'You want me to be honest?'

'Does honesty mean evasion, denial, what we call "sweeping under the carpet", too unimportant for you to—'

'Allow me to be *honest*. It's always good to speak the truth, even when it's unpalatable.'

The smile had broadened. The investigator had pushed back his chair and stood up. His police pistol, in a grubby holster, was against his hip, his shirt was not clean, he wore no tie and his trousers were crumpled. At the Plaistow police station, where they handled Canning Town, they would have been red-faced at his rudeness. He thought the man didn't give a damn.

'Mr Browne, in Germany we are a colony of Italy. Not of the Italian state but of the various arms of the Italian Mafia. They bring their customs, behaviour and daily habits inside our frontiers. Although they live in Germany they don't change their culture. It's a ghetto life. They exploit the lax legislation concerning criminal association and they do well – extremely well. In Germany, the principal representatives of the generic Mafia are the 'Ndrangheta. Have you heard of 'Ndrangheta, Mr Browne? It would help your understanding if you have.'

'I know nothing about them. Why should I?'

'Because you are a banker. It says here, above your signature, that you work in a bank. You can recite big numbers, understand spreadsheets and statistics . . .'

'I've reported what happened to me and a young woman. Have I wasted your time?'

If Fred Seitz was about to lose his cool he hid it well. 'They bring into our country billions of euros. *Billions*. They buy up hotels and apartment blocks, businesses and restaurants. A man who has no visible sign of income suddenly purchases a four-star hotel and pays ten million euros. We are swamped by them. It is the proceeds of cocaine money. Right at the bottom of the scale, their protection rackets are perpetrated on legitimate business

– not for billions or millions or even hundreds of thousands. They're Italians, and that is how they live. What am I supposed to do? Nothing – so I cannot justify spending much more of my time on it. Sorry, but that's the truth."

'You'll turn your back on it and walk away?' Jago felt the tiredness crushing him. He stood up and picked up his briefcase.

'Do you want my advice?'

He said he did.

'Does your employer know you're here?'

He shook his head.

The investigator said, 'I admire what you did. You intervened when many didn't. Pin a medal on yourself, but do it in private. You will note that I took no statement from you. As far as the legalities of this incident go, you played no part in it. What is it to do with you? Get a life – look the other way. The Italians and their gangster habits are not your priority. Do you smoke, Mr Browne? Would you like a cigarette?'

He did. Jago felt the need of one. The investigator must have liked him because *Rauchen Verboten* took a back seat. A window was opened on one side of a central pillar, then a second. Both had been locked but the other man used a straightened paper clip to unfasten them. He led and Jago followed. A leg out and over the window ledge and they could almost have kicked the heads of pedestrians on the Bismarckstrasse pavement. There was a cloud of smoke as the pipe was lit, then acrid fumes. Jago dragged on his cigarette. He thought it the work of an expert because there was a smoke detector in the centre of the interview-room ceiling. He was told that if you sat under a desk in the office and smoked close to the floor, the alarm would sound because it was well made, German manufactured. A flicker of a grin. When he had finished his cigarette he threw it onto the pavement while the investigator hammered the pipe bowl on the outer wall. Jago saw many marks on that stretch of wall where the paintwork was dented. It would have been a familiar routine. He brought his leg back inside.

'Will you follow this up?'

'I am away tomorrow evening for a few days' vacation with my wife. I will look at it when I return, perhaps. No promises. Thank you, Mr Browne, for coming. A last word. Forget it. No one will thank you if you do otherwise.'

The investigator showed him to the door.

He'd wasted his time. Jago Browne walked towards the S-bahn to go east and back to work.

'Get a life,' the man had said. 'Look the other way.'

Marcantonio paid cash. The two shirts, a hundred euros each, were wrapped by the sales assistant, and the girl slid glances at him. The shop was on the Ku'damm, small, smart and exclusive. He dressed well, though the knuckles of one fist were scratched and his right shoe was scuffed at the toecap. He never used a card, and the two hundred euros were from a wad of more than two thousand he carried in his hip pocket. The girl would have noticed the money. Most days he went to the shops on the Ku'damm. He preferred the range there to those on Potsdamer Platz or Friedrich-strasse. He shopped, sometimes with his minder and sometimes with the woman at the edge of his life, because on most days he had little else to do.

He had learned a little of what might be useful to him in his future life, if not as much as his grandfather would have wished. He found the company poor and the preoccupation with business contacts and investment opportunities tedious. Also, in Berlin he had no special status. He was not recognised, as he would have been in the village. It was as if, here, he was a probationer, having to prove himself worthy of respect, which was about the margins of percentages, buying and selling prices, what could be bought in property, square metres for how many euros . . . It bored him.

It was more interesting to shop, buy shirts and jeans. They would go into a cupboard at his apartment – when the door was opened there was often an avalanche of clothing, still in its cello-phane wrapping. Marcantonio did not, of course, give out his mobile number: difficult to do it because the device changed so often and he used a new number most weeks. If he wanted the girl, he would drive past at near to closing time, park on the kerb and hoot. She would come running. Many did, and the banknotes in his hip pocket were an encouragement. Sometimes he tipped lavishly with the absurd profits made from the sale of cocaine, or firearms, or immigrants without papers, or from the rents raised by apartment blocks and the profits from restaurants and hotels, and . . . So much money. It cascaded through his hands on a level not possible in Calabria. There, it was likely to be noticed and draw attention. Here, no eyebrow was raised. The girl's lashes fluttered, her blouse bulged, and her fingers were smooth over the wrapper, but he did not reward her. First, Marcantonio had no time to screw her as tomorrow his half-year of imprisonment in Berlin would be over and a little freedom beckoned. It was as if he was out 'on licence' – which his father and uncle would never know. He was going home to the village, and he would no longer need to change into a clean shirt halfway through each day. The second reason that Marcantonio did not tip the girl was that a nagging frustration diverted him.

The girl in the pizzeria. The girl with the brother who had stammered about his inability to pay. The girl who had come at him with her nails. That girl had clawed a place in his mind.

In the morning he would have the opportunity to go back to the pizzeria, as he had 'promised' he would, and collect the *pizzo*. They always paid. Tears, shouting, even threats of going to the authorities, but they always paid. Marcantonio had no need for an additional thousand euro a month, but the targeting of the pizzeria had made for entertainment. It was outside what was allowed, but few would know and fewer would care.

He took the wrapped shirts. He met the girl's eyes, allowed himself to smile and turned away. A woman had looked into his eyes on the last night he had been at home. She had been tied up and her clothes were torn because she had fought. He and Stefano had hoisted her up, and her legs had splashed into the stuff when they had begun to lower her. She had screamed in the night and would not have been heard. She, too, had challenged him. She had spat in his face, and then they had pushed her down. Her head had come up once more but she had been too weak and too much in shock to spit again. It would have been good to fuck her, his aunt by marriage, but he had not tried because she was part, temporarily, of the family.

After she had gone down into the tank he had carefully wiped all trace of the spittle from his face, and Stefano would have burned the clothes they had worn, and the clan who had provided the facilities for a *lupara bianca* would have removed anything left in the sludge. He would tell his grandfather what had happened.

The shop manager, tall, blond and aloof, stood behind the girl who had wrapped his shirts and taken his money. He was gazing at Marcantonio as if he were dog shit on a shoe. So German . . . but Marcantonio's people owned much of the country, used it like a goat they milked regularly. He could have bought that shop, that franchise, its stock and the girl, and would have regarded the outlay as small change.

He left. Time for lunch, some pasta – not as good as that prepared by his grandmother. It annoyed him that the girl that morning had not cowered in front of him. The next morning he would be back. He sauntered across the pavement to his car.

Bernardo slipped out of the kitchen door.

His route was skilfully prepared. Near to the door was a vine trellis, the leaves not yet shed, then a high wall. Beyond the wall was Mamma's washing line, always with double sheets and large towels on it, then a second section of wall, a vertical cliff face – the path led right against it, perhaps ten metres up – then a retaining wall beside the steps that led to the old shed.

Every man had a price, which was often surprisingly low. Sometimes favours were offered for nothing. A clerk in the Palace of Justice or at the Questura, in the headquarters of the *carabinieri* might cost a couple of hundred euros a month if he needed it for medical expenses, or he might supply information for free because he was screwing on the side and the truth would kill his elderly mother, or he gambled . . . There were so many reasons.

He knew he was under close investigation.

He took this route from the house each evening. He used neither telephone, nor computer, so he left no electronic trace. The ROS, the GICO and the Squadra Mobile worked on the principle that the best weapon in their hands was intercepts of messages, BlackBerry or email, so he denied them that chance. He would be vulnerable only to human surveillance, and their teams could not come to the village and sit in a closed van with spy-holes drilled into it. Strangers were not tolerated in their village. If electricity cables needed repair after a winter storm, local men did the work, not outsiders. His home could be watched only from the high ground behind it. There might be cameras there, or listening equipment, and it was possible even that men might be inserted in hiding places. Most of the *picciotti*, who owed him and his family total loyalty, had his blood in their veins: they regularly searched the upper slope with the dogs. But Bernardo was still careful.

A combination of the vine, the walls and the washing protected from any viewer or lens, and he used the route each day to go to and from his home. At the end of the path, beside the shed, there might, many years earlier, have been an earth slip beside the retaining wall. That was how it would appear to a stranger. Underneath the earth, stones and scrub was the steel cargo container, his refuge.

The retaining wall seemed solid. One stone could be removed to expose an electrical switch with a waterproof covering. When the switch was thrown a section of the wall eased quietly to the side. The first stone was then replaced and . . . He hated it. He had to get down on his old hands and knees and crawl through a tunnel of concrete pipes that, dimly lit, stretched ahead of him. Another switch closed the wall. He would have disappeared, no trace left of him. He could not stand or crouch in the tunnel, which was barely a metre high, but had to drag himself the five or six metres to the entrance in the iron side of the container, his other home.

The *pentito* had known the location and the timing of the meeting to which his sons, Rocco and Domenico, were travelling when they were blocked, pinioned, handcuffed, taken. He had not known of the hidden container. Twice in the last nine months Bernardo's home had been raided by the ROS teams – before

Annunziata had died and afterwards. If he had not been in the bunker, he would now be in a gaol cell in the north, isolated, his power diminishing. He moved forward, pads protecting his knees. Bernardo would have given up a great deal to sleep in his own bed, with his wife, but not his freedom.

He seemed to hear the voice, no spoken words, just a whimper. A child's voice. Recently he had heard it more often than he had last year. Extraordinary that he would be aware of it when his hearing was fading. He had first heard the sound thirty-six years before, then forgotten it. For decades he had been free of it, but he heard it again now that he had to go like a rat down the tunnel to his room.

But tomorrow night the boy would be home. A smile cracked his lined, weathered face as he reached the prefabricated door, opened it, straightened and stepped into his other home. It would be so good to have the boy back. Warmth again flowed in his veins, and a degree of happiness.

'Consolata reckons life is about confrontation.'

She had heard them discuss her.

'She wants drama – sirens, flashing lights. I just don't think she grasps the virtues of non-violence.'

She had her own room, with space for a single bed, a rack for her clothes, boxes for the rest of her possessions – shoes, underwear, books and one photograph.

'Consolata should leave our group.'

The photograph, framed in cheap plastic, showed her father and mother standing proudly outside their shop in Archi. It had been taken a year before they were approached and made an offer – take it or leave it – that amounted to grand theft. The photograph lay in a cardboard box, covered with books and papers on the regime of the 'Ndrangheta in Archi, Rosarno, at the port of Gioia Tauro and in Reggio Calabria, knickers, old trainers, T-shirts and more jeans. She had been a good student at her school, not obsessed with work but performing more than adequately – she was thought by the staff to have an anarchic streak, which they liked, and had run the shop on any Saturday morning when her parents could not be there. She knew the price of paint and wallpaper, and was imaginative on colour co-ordination. Everything had been predictable, unremarkable. Now the certainties had gone, picked up, tossed, scattered, but the scars remained. She had kept her past from the committee.

'She's with Massimo for the next two days. He's steady . . . a good influence.'

Later that night there was to be a meeting at the university. A prosecutor was due to speak. He would flatter them, talk up their influence and bolster morale. She had already decided not to attend, pleading a headache. It was that time in the afternoon when the squat went quiet. Some would read and others would smoke. Consolata couldn't be bothered to read and had no stomach for learning more on the influence of the clans, how their empire stretched from Calabria, their wealth, the bribery they practised and the virus of corruption. She punched the pillow. *They* didn't know her name and *they* were not aware of her efforts to sabotage them – if handing out leaflets and going to meetings qualified as sabotage. She didn't do drugs, and had no boyfriend to take to bed.

But she couldn't break away. Consolata couldn't see herself, with a packed duffel bag, going out into the dawn, leaving the front door to swing on its hinges, then trekking to the station for the journey to Reggio. She just couldn't believe herself capable of it. Massimo was a true believer: it would be torture to endure two days with him . . . And the city was quiet. When it was quiet that didn't mean 'Ndrangheta was too nervous to be about its business: on the contrary. It was how they liked it and how they functioned best. *They* did not know her name, and the chance that *they* would learn it soon seemed remote. She punched the pillow again and again.

If she had been going to the prosecutor's address at the university, she would have asked, 'How do you know when you're losing?'

And his answer, if he was truthful, would have been 'I know I'm losing if they ignore me.'

*   *   *

The question the prosecutor was never asked: 'Against the 'Ndrangheta, how do you know if you're winning?'

He was in the Lancia, wheels low on the tarmac because of the weight of the armour plating in the doors and the chassis. One of his boys drove fast from south to north across Reggio Calabria, and another held a machine-gun on his lap; three more were in the car behind, blue lights flashing. It was hard for him to concentrate because of the wail of the sirens. He was going to give a talk: it seemed important for him to be seen and to attempt to engage a younger generation. His address would not be brilliant but would satisfy his audience. He was a servant of the state, a work horse, and lived inside a fragile bubble of supposed protection. The name of the *padrino* of a remote village on the far side of the Aspromonte was at the top of his in-tray. Bernardo Cancello was uppermost in his mind, dogging and taunting him.

Had he been asked, and had he answered frankly, he would have said, 'When I'm hurting them they'll kill me. If I'm winning against them, I'm dead.'

To go from his office to any public engagement required that his full escort travel with him. Good boys – and sometimes a woman. If he was winning they would all be dead alongside him. His enemy was the criminal conspiracy of 'Ndrangheta, named from the Greek settlers of this far corner of Europe almost three millennia before. The word encompassed 'heroism' or 'virtue' and a member of the conspiracy – held together by family blood – was thought of as a 'brave man', not as a killer, not as a purveyor of life-destroying narcotics, not as a seller of the weapons that killed innocents in faraway wars, not as the provider of smuggled children brought into Europe to satisfy the lusts of perverts. He regarded them as the enemy and saw himself as something of a crusader. He liked to employ the old tags of 'good' and 'evil' when he was with schoolchildren and college students. Cocaine importation played well, but the weapons supplied to African warlords and the youngsters transported from Asia and the old Soviet satellite states for paedophiles played better. The beast, as he described it to audiences, was akin to an octopus, with many tentacles, hidden deep among subterranean rocks. Its arms could insert themselves into the smallest space.

He liked to quote the Englishman, Edmund Burke, and could quieten a lecture theatre when he intoned, "'All that is necessary for the triumph of evil is that good men do nothing".' Then he would tell them of the huge demonstrations against Cosa Nostra in neighbouring Palermo, just across the strait, after the murders of the magistrates Falcone and Borsellino, and they would applaud and imagine themselves chanting anti-Mafia slogans. Then would punch them collectively in the gut by saying that nothing changed, that Cosa Nostra would be broken by dedicated police work, not by kids marching. The point he made was that 'occasional antipathy' against organised crime meant little: commitment was required. It was a necessary part of his workload to deliver such addresses.

The prosecutor was surrounded by defeatism. He struggled against it. Sometimes he believed in minor successes; at others he was afflicted by minor catastrophes. He neither won nor lost. He had so few Holy Grail moments to treasure. Convictions, little triumphs, went hand in hand with men of great savagery being freed by the courts on technicalities. Close at hand there was corruption: a judge, a magistrate, a colleague, a senior officer in the *carabinieri*, a lowly clerk . . . Who knew where?

He was exhausted by the load he carried, and he believed that, for all his endeavours, the clans tolerated him. He lived with his guards, but his wife went shopping and took the kids to school unprotected. His protection was cosmetic. The day they wanted him, they would have him.

They went north and the cars were onto the Viale Manfroce. He had left his work piled on his desk in the office that had a door reinforced sufficiently to block high-velocity rounds or a hand grenade's blast. The last message in was for the Scorpion Fly file. The daughter and the wife had been seen, the grandchildren had come to the house and been seen. Each week the prosecutor had to fight tenaciously for a decent share of the finances allocated by Rome. It was a major investigation, and the family had considerable importance in the hinterland above the coastal towns of Locri and Brancaleone. The clan's leader was worth his place on the most-wanted lists, and the disappearance of the daughter-in-law – who had declined to be a *vedova bianca*, a white widow, and either discreet or chaste – was an added incentive . . . Without results his resources would be drained and the whispers would start that he had not used the precious money well. Hard times. He acknowledged it. He would tell the students that afternoon how remarkable it was that this obscure corner of Europe had a single claim to fame: that it was home to the continent's most renowned organised-crime group, which spread misery and dishonesty thousands of kilometres to the north of their city. He liked to tell them that.

How would he know if he was winning? He murmured, 'I don't know? It has never happened to me so I can't answer your question.'

His escort never interrupted him when he talked to himself. But the one in the front passenger seat eased aside the machine-gun, took a packet of cigarettes from his pocket, and extracted one, then lit it and passed it to him. He loved his guards as if they were good friends, loved them as much as he loved his work . . . But without results on the old fugitive he would be lost.

'My God, what happened to you?' He worked on the third floor of a modern block. The office space given to the sales section was small, cramped: they were on top of each other. 'Are you all right, Jago – have you been attacked?'

Heads turned. Questions speared at him.

From Hannelore, who liaised with the Frankfurt traders and had made a push for him at the summer party: 'Were you mugged?'

And Magda, who did pretty much the same as himself and had twice invited him to run with her in the Tiergarten: 'Did it happen on the S-bahn?'

And Renate, who was the fixer, kept the section's moving parts oiled, and whose rare mistake had sent him to the client to make a fulsome apology: 'Have those injuries been looked at?'

And Wilhelmina, the *FrauBoss*, who regarded him with suspicion and had done so from his first day: 'Where, when, why?'

Nothing from Friedrich, their analyst, who squinted at him, seeming to say silently that his appearance in that state was inappropriate.

He went to the *FrauBoss*. She pushed her papers aside, and the plastic tray on which she'd had her sandwich. He leaned against her desk. He said he had seen a young woman attacked near the client's address, that he had attempted to help her and . . .

Jago Browne was a success story, against the odds, from Canning Town in east London. He knew about street fights. All around the cul-de-sacs and alleyways near to the Beckton Arms there were teenage fights, thefts, knives shown and boots used. He would not have come through it without his mother's spirit. He reckoned she had fought for him more than for either of his siblings: Billy, whose father was a Polish roofer, and Georgina, who had come after the 'lodger', a Nigerian student, had moved on. Carmel Browne had nagged him, driven him, cracked a whip over him at junior school, had stood in his corner at the Royal Docks Community School, and had found the best teacher, the old-school Miss Robinson, to take him on as a 'work in progress'. And his mother – at Miss Robinson's demand – had taken him to an interview for St Bonaventure Catholic Comprehensive, the top-performing local school. He had been taken into Heath House, named after the Blessed Henry Heath, a martyr, held at Tyburn, 1643, then taken out for hanging, drawing and quartering. They had drilled into the pupils at the school that it was important to stick to 'principles'. Arthur Bell and John Forest were martyrs of the same period, also put to death hideously, also remembered by the school.

Jago had known his place in life because overlooking Canning Town, and the low-quality housing erected after the Blitz bombing had flattened the old terraces, was the triumphant glory of Canary Wharf; a world apart and a mile away. Canning Town only came to Canary Wharf to clean the soaring building and deliver their necessities. There was always an exception, though. A hero of capitalism trawled local schools for talent. A name had come up; the boy had interviewed well; his future was mapped out.

'And all of this happened before you saw the client?'

'Yes. It was why I was slightly late. I apologised.'

'When I telephoned, no mention was made of this.'

'The meeting was satisfactory, Wilhelmina. There seemed no need.'

'Or was she merely gracious?'

'I don't understand.'

The Bible they worked from, at Broadgate in the City, at Canary Wharf and at any bank in Berlin or Frankfurt that looked to attract corporate and personal business, was *KYC. Know Your Client.* The requirement for trust was stamped into their thinking, too. Risk was acceptable for the traders who made the big bucks and lived with the threat of burn-out and stress, not for the foot-soldiers in the sales teams, who were up close and personal with clients.

'Jago, was she merely being polite?'

'I don't think I upset her.'

'And afterwards you went to the police on Bismarckstrasse, and told an officer of this incident.'

'I told an investigator from KrimPol what had happened to me and the young woman.

'You made a statement? You listed your place of employment as this bank, named it and its address?'

'No.'

'No statement? How is that possible?'

He had confused her. Did she doubt his word? The frown had set on her forehead and her lips had narrowed. Her make-up had been generously applied even though her husband was abroad, and her eyes had the glint that seemed to identify a lie.

'Actually, Wilhelmina, I would have made a statement but the investigator refused to take one. His advice was that I "get a life. Forget it, because no one will thank you if you do otherwise." That's what I was told.'

Her features lightened and the her eyes softened. 'Very sensible.

May I explain, Jago, because you are young and enthusiastic and honourable? If the good name of the bank was in the media – papers, radio, internet – in connection with street crime, no one here would welcome it. Although you acted from instinct, and therefore cannot be blamed, it would be *negative* for the bank's name to be dragged into the courts.'

'I understand, Wilhelmina.'

'The good name of the bank, in difficult financial times, is of paramount importance. Perhaps, Jago, you would use the rest room to tidy yourself. Thank you.'

He pushed himself away from the desk. His own cubicle was minute but neat, with no decoration. Others had photos of loved ones or pets, or postcards fastened to the low walls beside their screens. He had nothing personal. He had already volunteered to do the Christmas Day shift – the Gulf markets would be open, as would Tel Aviv and parts of the Far East – and watch over the figures. Hannelore would have taken him to Stuttgart for Christmas with her parents. He kept a washbag in the low cupboard at his desk. He was reaching for it.

Wilhelmina's voice was quiet: 'Was the client upset because I didn't come myself?'

'She understood, Wilhelmina, that a really serious situation caused you to cry off the meeting, almost life and death.'

He went to wash. Had he spoken with irony or sarcasm? She wouldn't have noticed either. The entertainment was over and the team were busy again at their screens. She wouldn't have noticed his rudeness because she didn't know him well enough. Who did know him? Fewer people than he had fingers on one hand. That suited him. It was the way of the streets of Canning Town, where he came from and where old habits clung. When he had washed he would go back to work, and tomorrow would be another day. It would start with a seminar on sales tactics: a kick in the backside against complacency. The captain of finance, at Canary Wharf, who might have boasted about giving a chance to 'youngsters from the other side of the tracks', had said, 'Jago, I'd like to leave you with this. The two most important days of your life are the one on which you were born and the one when you find out *why* you were born. What is your destiny? Think about it.' He still didn't know the answer. He scrubbed his face, cleaned the cuts and looked in the mirror to gauge the success of the repairs. He did not see himself: he saw the girl, the curl of defiance on her face, and heard her scream. He had been challenged.

In a building behind a security fence, set back from Felixstowe docks, a phone rang. He answered it, heard serious excitement in the voice of the young woman who had called him. She had a 'customer' and his Class-A consignment. Her voice on the phone was shrill in his ear. 'You should get yourself down here, Carlo, it's a real nice one.'

He had been 'Carlo' since the overseas posting.

'Just finishing a coffee, if you don't mind.'

He'd heard the snort down the line from Dooley Terminal, where the lorries came and went, and the ferries were roll-on and roll-off. 'Bring me one, two sugars. I think it's a cracker.'

'I'll be there when it's convenient.'

'Thanks, Carlo.' She'd have known he'd be out of his office, in the main administration section of the Customs area, and heading fast for the dockside bay where the vehicles were subjected to a thorough search. Usually it was intelligence from abroad that dictated which were pulled aside and given the treatment, but it was always Christmas come early when the 'uniforms' were allowed to choose which to wave down and put through the wringer. She'd known he'd burn the rubber to get there fast.

He had gone to Rome, drugs liaison officer attached to the embassy, as Charlie. He had done four years there, should have been three but the replacement had suffered a last-ditch angina attack so the man in place had been asked to 'endure' another twelve months in the Eternal City. No complaints, almost fulsome gratitude to Human Resources at Her Majesty's Revenue and Customs. In Rome, immediately after arrival, he had become Carlo. He was Carlo with the guys in the Guardia, the Polizia, the *carabinieri* squads, throughout the embassy, and had brought it back with him to Felixstowe. He was a bit of a legend. It was whispered among the younger uniforms that Carlo had gone almost native in Italy.

A driver sat on a hard chair in an interview room and two guys watched him. His passport was Albanian, and the find was two kilos of smack. The current price of heroin, at this point in the chain, wavered around an estimation of its purity. What they had on the table might be worth anything between two hundred thousand and three hundred and fifty thousand pounds. It would have helped with the cultivation of the legend if Carlo had told her he didn't get out of bed in the morning for less than a million, and it took more than five kilos to stop him yawning. The uniforms had done well and wanted congratulating, so he did that, augmenting his popularity.

The driver didn't speak English – or German, French or Italian. It usually took four hours to get hold of an interpreter, and then the little bugger – shivering and pleading for a fag – would likely communicate in a dialect that stumped the translator. There was nothing in the cab that indicated the end destination, except a Europe-wide road map, with crosses in pencil on the page that had the M6 toll route round the east of Birmingham and might be a service station or an exit. Difficult – next to impossible – to let the Albanian head onwards and tail him to his rendezvous.

If the driver was allowed back on the road with a surveillance team attached to him, that would mean ten guys and girls tied down, maybe a dozen. For a million, anything was possible. For five million it was probable. For a third of a million it was pretty much a charge sheet, a trip to the docks police station where the holding cells were, a beer or a shiraz in the bar, and not much more. It would not have been right to pour cold water over them, and the girl was keen. Carlo had been keen once, a long time ago. Keenness, he reckoned, was likely to wear out, like the heel of a favourite shoe. If his keenness had slid it was because incentives were scarce. The cuts pared resources and the poaching of staff by the National Crime Agency removed the best and the hungriest.

He congratulated the team, gave them what they wanted to

hear. He didn't tell them that there was a container port on the coast of southern Italy, where formerly only mosquitoes had flourished, at which, on average, four thousand kilos of pure cocaine was seized each year, and that was the tip of the iceberg of what was brought through Gioia Tauro, far less than a quarter. He suggested they inform the press desk that the haul had a street value of half a million. He showed interest, was polite.

Four good years in Rome, and because he had achieved so much there it would have been thought he needed cutting down to size. The tag 'gone native' never helped a career. He had been posted two years before to Felixstowe, and his skills were wasted there: he was supposed to collect dross and filter it, then pass it, if relevant, to the investigation teams. No one thanked him for less than a million's worth in smack, coke or the recreational stuff.

He backed off. The driver eyed him. Where he used to work, the driver would have been labelled a *picciotto*, a foot-soldier, at the bottom of the food chain, expendable, replaceable, little more than a mule with a condom up the back passage full of resin. He had seen big players taken down in Italy, those with the rank of *padrino* or the title of *vangelista* or *santista*, and had played a part in their downfall. He had seen the faces of men numbed at the shock of arrest, with the cuffs tight on their wrists, and had felt the glow of achievement. Before that he'd done well on Green Lanes in north London, targeting the Turkish Mafia importers, and up in Liverpool where the heavy action was . . . but Rome had been the love affair.

But he was not in Rome now, at the embassy on Via Venti Settembre. Carlo was at Dooley Terminal in Felixstowe. He was short and squat, with a barrel chest, now aged fifty-three. His hair was thinning and silver, but his moustache was red – he coloured it.

'It's a good one. Thanks, guys. Appreciate you calling me.'

He went back to his office to push paper round his desk and on his screen, and killing time until he could go home.

Hi, Wilhelmina. Sorry, but feeling the after-effects, a bit sick. Seeing a doctor tomorrow morning. Apologies about your seminar. Best, Jago.

He sent the text.

Jago had waited until nearly midnight. He reckoned the *FrauBoss* would be asleep and wouldn't see it until morning, but he'd keep his mobile switched off anyway. He doubted he would be missed. He sat in the comfortable chair in his room, in the living area beyond the partition that shielded the bed, and sipped coffee. The room, under the sloping ceiling, was tidy. In ten minutes, Jago could have packed a bag, run the vacuum over the rugs, wiped a cloth across the draining-board, cleared the fridge and left traces that only a forensic search would have found. He was the star of the street where Carmel Browne lived, with his brother and sister, the one who had worked at Broadgate in the City and was now on an exchange with a renowned bank in the German capital. His progress had seemed effortless. Neighbours would have congratulated his mother on what he had achieved. She didn't love him, maybe no one did, but he slept well without love.

There was distant traffic and rain pattered on the skylight, but the quiet gathered mournfully around him. It was more than two years since he had been back to Canning Town. His mother, last he'd heard, cleaned service apartments for people patronising the ExCeL conference centre. Billy was a probationer – at Canary they'd call it an 'intern' – hardly paid on a market stall. Georgina worked at an Oxford Street shop, flogging shoes at discount prices. His success had cut the links and the contact. Last Christmas he'd sent a hamper to the maisonette by the Beckton Arms and taken himself to a guesthouse on the Devon coast. There, he had walked the cliffs and eaten solitary meals surrounded by lonely pensioners . . . He didn't know where he fitted in. He lit another cigarette. He didn't fit, and it was years since he had.

A dark February afternoon, in his school uniform, homework piled on the kitchen table. Jago was fourteen. There was no milk and Carmel was home from work, flustered and tired. Would he go down to Freemasons Road and get some? A suppressed protest, and Billy, aged nine, had piped up that he'd go. Georgina was too young for errands. Jago had gone, with bad grace, the money jangling in his pocket and Billy had skipped along beside him. He'd worn his school blazer and tie. They'd bought the milk. The kids had come out of the shadows. Some might have known him before he'd become 'a high achiever' and been moved on, but his smart blazer would have egged them on. The milk had been snatched. He'd been pushed and shoved, then punched. He'd gone down. The blazer had been a major investment for his mother, with the white shirts, the school tie and the pullover. The milk was over the pavement. Kicks were aimed at him and he was cursed in the gang *patois*. Blood was streaming off his face, and his phone had gone. He might have been about to take a bad kick, one that would do damage. But Billy, four years younger, had thrown himself across him and saved him from that kick. A car's headlights had lit the scene and the kids had drifted away. Half of the milk was still in the plastic bottle. They'd gone home. Billy had told Carmel. Jago supposed he had been challenged and had failed, but he was now a banker. Billy had been challenged, had passed the test and worked for a pittance on a market stall on the Barking road in all weathers.

He ground out the cigarette. It was a first: Jago Browne had never before taken a day off work sick, genuine or bogus. Nor, when at Lancaster, had he missed tutorials or lectures. The girl that morning had been pretty, but there had been beauty in her anger as she had spat at her attacker. Magnificent. All those years before, he had seen the same pride on Billy's face and the same anger on his mother's. It was about cliffs, the emptiness under them, the waves beating on sharp rocks far below, and how men and women were drawn to the edge, couldn't help themselves, and didn't know why they had been born.

Jago could have spent that evening with Hannelore or Magda. He might have been with either of them in one of the Turkish cafés in Kreuzberg, or with Renate. There was another girl further down the office, between the flags that hung from the ceiling, denoting the languages spoken, and the clocks that showed the time in San Francisco, Riyadh and Hong Kong. She sometimes eyed him over the low walls that divided them from each other and seemed to approve. He just hadn't seemed to have time. It might have been better to be with one of them, not crying off sick and not being pulled towards a cliff edge.

3

The web was tickled by a breeze and moved. What had been the body of the fly swayed gracefully, as if death had brought it some dignity. The manufacturer of the trap, the killer, was not to be seen.

He sat on the bench, waited and watched.

It was a morning almost like any other in the recent times of Jago Browne. From force of habit, although he was off sick, he wore his office suit, the one that went, dirty or spotless, to the dry cleaner round a corner from his attic apartment every Friday evening and was collected on Saturday. His shoes were polished and he wore a clean shirt with a nondescript tie. He had not brought his briefcase or laptop. The weather had closed in a little and cloud built to the east, over Spandau and Tegel. He had a formal raincoat – nothing as casual as an anorak – folded over his knees. Jago had no weapon. He didn't own one.

The lady was opposite him. She had been there when he had arrived, then had gone to the same bench and taken the same place on it as the previous day. She might have noticed that the young man facing her was dressed similarly to when she had first seen him and looked as if he was killing time before a business meeting. She might have caught little nuances of change. No checking of his watch and his eyes hovered mostly to his right. Perhaps she understood. That day she had brought her own cigarettes and a lighter with mother-of-pearl sides. She had already smoked two, but had not offered him one. She might have thought he was too preoccupied to engage in the chatter that would accompany the gift of a cigarette. She was well dressed again, and her shoes, almost new, still didn't match. Jago thought that each pair would have set her back a hundred and fifty euros.

He had a clear view of the pavement in front of the pizzeria. He could see the doors, and shadows moving inside. He hadn't yet seen the girl. Why was he there?

Difficult to summon up an answer. He didn't know yet the extent of his involvement. His mother had known where she was going and why on a darkening February evening eleven years before. Jago had been left in the kitchen. His mother's orders had been staccato, sharp, and he would have been an idiot to challenge them. He was to start his maths homework. He was to make Billy's tea. He was to help Georgina with her reading and get her something to eat. He had told his mother what the kids had been wearing, in which direction they had sauntered off. She already knew, of course, the make and style of his phone: she had saved hard to get him a decent model. The door had slammed after her. His mother was five foot two. She weighed under eight stone. She had no flesh on her, neither muscle nor fat – but she could summon up the temper of her Irish ancestry.

Among the few who knew and the fewer who cared in Canning Town, a little of a legend had been born. Various stories were peddled. One had it that Carmel had fastened the group's leader with her gaze, requested the return of the phone and been given it. Unlikely. Other versions roved over her finding the leader, slapping him a bit, standing on tiptoe, then kneeing him in the groin, head-butting him and taking the phone from his pocket. The most popular had her marching into the kid's home, pushing aside a shaken mother, going upstairs and bearding the bastard in his room, not needing to touch him because he cringed from her, then taking the phone from the bedside table and leaving. She had come home. She had checked that the phone worked, then put it down beside his maths book.

Which legend was fact and which fiction, Jago didn't know: it was never spoken of again. When he had closed his books, she had chucked a coat at him and taken him out. There was a sports club on Caxton Street. She had signed him up. No questions were asked: he was a teenager doing what his mother demanded. He had hated the humiliation and her for inflicting it, and had hated his brother for going to his rescue when he had been whimpering on the ground.

He could have trotted out all of that, if a shrink had been sharing the bench with him, to explain why he was there.

The door of the pizzeria stayed closed and no car had edged up to the kerb close to it. He saw the girl more clearly when she came to the window and wiped it vigorously. At the bank, Jago was under what they called '360-degree reporting'. He was subjected to a form of close surveillance, monitored. They wanted to know if he had the skills to sell the bank's product. It might be 'cold calling'. It might be spotting a business in a road back from Unter den Linden, or a main drag through the Turkish quarter of Kreuzberg, pushing in through the door and doing the talk. There was a story the *FrauBoss* liked to tell – a sandwich bar on Karl-Liebknecht-Strasse that always had a queue outside: she'd passed it often enough, and thought the owner looked sick. She had reckoned he was due to sell up and had gone in with the sales spiel. The investment was more than six million. Anyone could score if their eyes were open, and their brain was clear.

He looked away from the pizzeria to the woman with odd shoes, and wondered what his chat-up line might be, how to attract her and her wealth to the bank's stewardship. He should have known why he was there and what he hoped to achieve, what might be the consequence of failure or success. The woman breathed an aura of money. Something about a challenge, and something about a gesture.

She came down the stairs.

There was a dress code, of sorts, in the squat. Boys should not move about the rooms, the landing and stairs in their underwear: it was disrespectful to the girls. Consolata broke rules, written and unwritten.

Her feet were bare and she was wearing a skimpy cotton nightie, short and low-cut. The sun wasn't high enough to warm the inside of the building and she shivered but came down warily because there was no carpet or no lino on the stairs: she risked a painful splinter in a toe or the sole of her foot. She had no friends among the others and didn't think anyone would miss her if she went out through the door with her duffel bag on her shoulder. She was there because it emphasised her indifference to their attitude towards her – and because she had nowhere else to go.

She wandered into the communal area. In the inner room, a meeting had already started. On the table there were dirty plates and mugs, while the previous night's bowls, from dinner, were in the sink. The front was off the photocopier: there would have to be a committee meeting, then a canvassing of the membership, and finally they might agree to buy a new or second-hand one. Perhaps the Palace of Justice would help . . . She stubbed her big toe on the copier's metal cover and swore.

If Consolata had left a man asleep in her bed, she might have viewed the world with more charity. But there was no man – hadn't been for months – and the last had treated her as if she were a chattel, in the Calabrian way, on call when he wanted her. Before that there had been the *carabinieri* trooper: he had been good in bed, which she was not, and had thought of her as a trophy. She had wanted to talk about the 'war against corruption' and he about her cup-size and about the best kit he could buy for his work from survival magazine offers. Francesco had been amusing, and it had lasted fourteen weeks – Consolata had a good memory – before he had tired of her. She had seen his wedding notice in *Cronaca della Calabria*, with a picture of a smart, attractive woman – everything she was not, she had told herself. He had not hated the 'Ndrangheta families he spied on, but often said he had a decent job, was paid reasonably, and that there was camaraderie among the team. He'd shown her some of the disciplines of covert work, how to move and to lie motionless, and had boasted of his skill. Once he had let her wear his gillie suit and another time his flak-vest, with the armour plates. He had said she was good at covert movement and had an intuition for dead ground. Sometimes he had to ask her to show herself. She had cried when he ditched her, but in her room, not where he or anyone else would see.

She bit into an apple. Others must have risen as dawn broke – the heap of printed leaflets was double the size it had been when she had left the night before. They would have burned out the photocopier, not had the patience to coax it. Massimo was in the inner room at the table. He looked away, blushing, because she was almost naked. He wore heavy glasses and was attempting to grow, not yet successfully, a beard. They believed in non-violent opposition to the criminal culture, as she had when she'd joined. Perhaps not tomorrow, but victory was inevitable. At first she had been a true believer. The man at the head of the table, Piero, waved to her.

Was she still keen to picket? Would she picket the big villas in her nightdress?

Where did she think it most appropriate to stand with a placard? Outside the home of the de Stefano matriarch in Archi, down towards the coast and up the private road? At the hilltop villa of the Pesce family in Rosarno? Or perhaps she would go to San Luca, or Plati in the Aspromonte?

Laughter rippled around the table. She thought the other girls disapproved of her display of flesh, and that the boys' eyes stripped her. Piero told her when they would divide up the leaflets, and where she should go with Massimo. They would start in an hour. She knew no other life. The men who headed the families were demons, and their faces, from the newspapers, flickered in her mind. They didn't know who she was. She threw the apple core at the bin, missed and it rolled under the table. She left it where it was and went to dress.

He passed her a cigarette, which she took, and lit it.

Jago said, 'Forgive me for disturbing you. I hope you won't find this offensive. May I, please, give you my card and tell you what I do?'

Her face was wreathed in smoke. She looked sharply at him, then nodded.

Buried in his bunker, Bernardo – *padrino*, master of his family and of his village, a euro millionaire many times over – had only a minimal sense of time passing.

An air vent in the ceiling of the container rose through the stone, earth and undergrowth to surface beyond the decrepit shed, behind the roots of an aged rotting oak. An air-conditioner rumbled inside, but it was covered with blankets so the noise was muted. He had enough power to run a fridge, a cooker, a TV, on which he could watch DVDs, and a battery radio, with a discreet aerial that ran up the ventilation shaft to emerge at the lip. He had an electric blanket in the bed for the winter. It was his second home.

He eased himself out of bed.

That bed was a source of annoyance. Until he had been forced into the bunker – an informant had said that the Palace of Justice was targeting him – Bernardo had never made a bed or folded away his pyjamas, not even during his two brief spells in the San Pietro gaol while he had awaited trial. His grandmother had done it when he was a child, then his mother, and his wife had understood her role to perfection. Mamma, married to him the day after her twentieth birthday, was too stiff in her knees and hips – rheumatism or arthritis, but she refused to visit a doctor – to crawl down the concrete tubing into the container.

There was a picture of the Madonna, another of his grandson, and one of himself with his grandfather and father – if he died in his own bed, he would have done better than either of them. His grandfather had expired in the prison in Reggio, after a heart attack; his father had been blasted by a gunman with a sawn-off shotgun, acting on the instructions of the family of Siderno. One brother had been taken from his car by men from Plati, pinioned, then thrown alive down a vertical-sided gorge; the body had not been recovered for two years. A second brother was said to be in the foundations of the A3, the Highway to the Sun, north of Gioia Tauro. That was the price he had paid for his freedom.

If he didn't wash his dishes, he had nothing to eat off. There was a microwave to heat the food Mamma prepared, but he had to wash the ladles and spoons he used. He supposed he spent half of his day skulking inside his house, not exposing himself to any possible vantage points where a camera might be hidden, and the other half in the bunker, where the damp of autumn seemed to seep through the cold earth and the steel sides of the container. He slept there, slid furtively back to the house during daylight but never walked in the garden, soaking up the sunshine. To leave the property, he employed a variety of disguises and subterfuge. He remained free.

He dressed.

He had a wardrobe that swayed when he opened it. Marcantonio had brought it in pieces down the tunnel and assembled it, then the bed. The bed had been well made and was firm, but he would bring the young man down the next day or the day after and ask him to tighten the wardrobe's screws, do what he could not do himself. Stefano was no longer agile enough to come through on his hands and knees, while Giulietta had a phobia of confined spaces and came reluctantly. Bernardo had more money than he could count, but lived in a hole. According to Giulietta, he owned bedrooms in apartment blocks in Monaco and Nice, a four-star hotel on the Costa del Sol – it was in the process of expansion – shares in a resort in Brazil, then more bedrooms in service flats in Dortmund and beside the river in London. He had never slept in any of them and for almost a year hadn't slept beside Mamma. He pulled the sheets and the thin blanket into place and smoothed the pillow.

He found the socks he needed, and the shoes.

He used a battery-powered razor. A man of his status should have been able to go to the village barber, sit in a chair, then be shaved and treated with respect.

He combed his hair, which was well cut – Mamma did it in the house.

Bernardo did not appear from the tunnel when he wanted to leave his bunker. Mamma would come, or Stefano, with the corn for the chickens and call them near the hidden entrance. Then he could emerge.

A good day awaited him. The boy was coming back for Mamma's birthday. The *pentito* in Rome would be stalked and the plan made for a killing: he hoped that the man who had sent his sons to gaol would experience fear and pain. He ate some bread, and turned on the coffee machine. A freighter loaded with more containers was heading across the Mediterranean, *en route* from the Venezuelan Porto Cabello. It was two or three days from docking at Gioia Tauro and carried cargo for him.

His eyes might dampen when the boy arrived and – for all his inbred caution – he could not envisage any danger capable of fracturing his mood.

The girl, with her broom, had come out of the pizzeria. Jago didn't think she had looked towards him. She had swept the pavement, polished the outside of the window, then gone back inside. He had talked to the woman as he would have done on any cold call. It had passed the time and he felt less conspicuous. At the bank, sales staff worked in teams of two, a man and a woman; the man did the business and the woman offered reassurance. From force of habit, Jago said to his prospective client, 'I'd like you to meet my manager. She's a woman of integrity. We'd bring you the brochures on what we can offer. Your money would perform much better than where it is now. We'd be there for you.'

They watched her through the binoculars.

Ciccio might have been wrong – she might once have been beautiful – but he doubted it. They knew her as Maria Concello, but logged her on the electronic report sheet as 'Mike Charlie'. They saw her throw a cupful of corn beyond the front entrance to the house. There, they had a good eyeball on her. She would have been clucking for her chickens, which were locked up at night but let out at dawn by the handyman, Stefano – 'Sierra'. Ciccio was convinced she'd never been worth a second glance. The families used marriage to form alliances, and the strength of her family would have served as her dowry.

Quite soon, Giulietta – 'Golf Charlie' – would come up the track, and later the grandchildren, with their mother. The only target was 'Bravo Charlie': they had no recent photograph of him, but they would have recognised him, had he appeared, as an old man, lame on the left, with thick white hair. The *pentito* who had blown away the sons had said Bernardo still had his hair. His wife had a sharp face – jutting nose, a prominent chin, heavy grey eyebrows and a short, scrawny neck. She did not appear to have aged and thereby lost her looks.

She turned. Only a few chickens had come for their food. She went along the unfinished paving by the side wall and disappeared behind the trellis and the sheets that were already hanging on the line, flapping in a light wind. It was weeks since Fabio and Ciccio had observed how often they were washed, how long they spent drying on the line and how often they were left to stiffen in the sunshine or to be soaked in a rare storm. She appeared again, this time with fowls at her feet. She was close to the shed, a dog with her.

They took turns with the binoculars and both knew almost each wrinkle on her face – but they weren't interested in her.

Fabio and Ciccio were a major resource. There would have been a half-dozen prosecutors in Calabria who made representations to the colonel running the surveillance teams in the *carabinieri*. Each would emphasise the importance of their own investigation. The prosecutor who had commissioned Fabio and Ciccio would have had his back to the wall, and they would do what they could, but if Bravo Charlie didn't appear ... Ciccio whispered about the woman's ugliness and wondered whether she had ever been different.

Fabio logged her appearance, and they discussed their breakfast. As *carabinieri*, they had army survival rations: the breakfast was a chocolate bar, some sweet bread and a measure of cold coffee. For lunch they had a choice of *tortellini al ragù, pasta e fagioli* or *insalata di riso*. There had been times when the two men had almost fallen out over the choice of field rations.

They hated to fail. If they did not get an eyeball, *fare a occhio*, they would crawl away at the end of a long duty, file an interim brief, soak in the shower and go home to their women in the knowledge that their prosecutor's case was weakened.

A stick broke under a foot. A dog barked. Each was armed.

A major inquest would follow if they fired, wounded or killed. Every morning, close to that time, a foot-soldier came with a dog and walked the boundaries of the property. The discussion of menus was suspended. They couldn't stretch or clear their throats, but they were confident. If asked, each would have said *he* was the best. That was why they were on the squad, why they had been chosen. The sounds died. The quiet returned. Nothing moved. They waited, watched.

Three cigarettes were smoked, none by him. The filters lay on the paving.

Abruptly, the woman – prospective client – stood up. With the soles of her unmatched shoes, she squashed any life from the butts. The man came out of the pizzeria and looked up and down the street. He was at least fifty paces from where Jago sat but he recognised the man's fear. Then the door slammed after him. They had not reported the incident: had they done so, there would have been a squad car parked nearby. He wondered if the investigator would show, or if the matter was too insignificant. It was at about this time yesterday that the Audi had stopped at the door.

Jago wasn't looking at his 'client'. He was talking mechanically now and she'd have known it. She hadn't given him a card or scribbled a phone number for an appointment, and she was on her way. It was a brush-off but seemed immaterial. He said, from the side of his mouth, his eyes on the door, 'Thank you for your interest. I'll follow it up with my manager.'

Marcantonio left his apartment. He was on his way to collect the first instalment of a *pizzo*, and was confident that what he could extract from the sister and brother at the pizzeria would soon escalate. It was acknowledged in Reggio, Catanzaro and Cosenza that the families knew more about the profit possibilities of a business than its owners. He would advise them, convince them that he was not an enemy – he might even gain their gratitude: a saviour who had, at small cost, kept their premises safe.

He had on a new shirt, not his most recent purchase but from the summer, and his windcheater was hooked on his shoulder. His partner of the night had left already. A pinch of her cheek as she slept, then a smack on her buttocks, and she had got dressed up. None of his women were allowed to stay in the apartment after he had gone out, and none had her own key. A Bulgarian woman came in to clean, but only when he was there and the contents had been sanitised: papers and property brochures were locked in a floor safe.

His boys were waiting with the car. He liked to think of them as his 'boys', though both were older than Marcantonio, because they were more distant than he was from the heart of the family. Their fathers would not have considered making an important decision without referring first to a *padrino*. Nothing would be decided – in Milan, Germany, some Canadian cities or Australia – without sanction from the towns on the Ionian coast or the communities high in the Aspromonte. His boys drove him, watched over him, pimped for him and bolstered his ego.

It might be amusing, a diversion from the tedium of life in the German capital, and a decent parting gift before he flew south that evening. The girl had been feisty and spirited, although the man had been weak.

He expected her to be calm now and rational, and her brother to co-operate. Not immediately, but quickly – it might be necessary to show them the plastic milk bottle, with urine coloured contents and the rag in its neck, and to produce the claw hammer that could splinter the pizzeria's windows. But they wouldn't offer serious opposition. He thought that when he came back to Berlin he would seek out more Italian businesses that didn't yet pay for protection and begin to build a small client list. The car was open-topped. He vaulted into the passenger seat.

One boy drove. The other sat awkwardly behind Marcantonio in the bucket seat. He anticipated feigned anger, then compliance. Who would stand up to Marcantonio? Very few. The car accelerated and the wind whipped his spiked hair and riffled the front of his new shirt. The chain of gold links jumped over the hairs on his chest – so few.

They wove among cars and taxis – a bus had to brake sharply

to give them room. Nobody confronted him. Nobody gave him serious aggravation, nor ever had. He was the grandson of the *padrino*. He had pedigree and authority. At the age of twelve, his grandfather had given him a Kalashnikov assault rifle to hold, then shown him how a magazine was locked on, and pointed down the hill to the village on the last day of the year. His celebration of the end of 2007, and the imminent start of 2008, was to walk through the village at dusk, loosing off shots of high-velocity bullets at chimney stacks, roof tiles and the wheels of the car that belonged to the school teacher who had once tried to detain him for additional study.

There had been no telephone calls to the *carabinieri*, no anonymous complaints posted to their nearest barracks. No one had come up the track to his father's home, or his grandfather's, and denounced him in person. He had understood, with the thudding of the weapon in his shoulder, the power born into him through blood.

And girls. The first – not at the brothel in Locri, an older, experienced woman – had been halfway through his fourteenth year. There had been three more before his fourteenth birthday. He had taken them into the woods in the summer and to goatherds' huts in winter, all willing because of his status in their community. No parent had complained and he could have had as many as he wanted.

Soon after his fifteenth birthday he had been called upon to help his grandfather end a man's life, by manual strangulation, and had not been found wanting. He had seen the approval – near pride – in the old eyes. No patrol car of the *polizia* had come, and no wagon from the *carabinieri*. When his father and uncle had been taken, Marcantonio had been ignored.

He was *intoccabile*, untouchable.

Tomorrow he would bask in the approval of his family, tell stories of deals successfully concluded, and see their love. Of course, there, he would be discreet. *There* was not here.

There was *pizzo* money to be had. He shouldn't have touched such a trivial matter in Berlin, where the business of the families was high finance, but he was addicted to his old life.

He was driven towards the square where the cash would be waiting for him. There was a crisp early-morning chill in the air and the wind blew into their faces. The three voices joined in a song from the Aspromonte they had learned at their mothers' knees.

They hit the square. Marcantonio flipped his legs over the car door and headed for the pizzeria.

Jago Browne watched from the bench. The young man, the leader, strode to the door. Another followed him and the third stayed outside, between the car and the door. His hand was inside his loose coat as if a weapon was hidden beneath it. He watched. What would Jago do? He didn't know and told himself he couldn't make decisions on hypothetical actions. Put it off. The investigator had told him to *get a life and look the other way*, which was not what his mother had done when the issue was the phone she had bought for him.

Jago said, 'I'll see how it pans out. No harm in that.'

Punctual, but without the buzz of enthusiasm that had once been his trademark, Carlo left for work.

His home, rented, was down a lane, a century-old cottage of local brick. That Carlo had three suitcases' worth of clothes inside the house was remarkable, considering the state of his finances. He paid half the rent and Sandy paid the rest. He sent money to Aggie, his first wife, living in Bristol with a near-delinquent son, who might be Carlo's and might not; another slice of his income went to Betty, his second wife, who was in Essex, with squatter's rights on the marital home. He was lucky to have found Sandy. She wasn't at the door, when he set off. Sandy bred Labradors and spaniels, and seemed not to notice whether he was there or not, which suited him. Not many fell on their feet, third time round, but he might have.

It would take him twenty minutes in the rain to get to the parking bay beneath his office. Had Sandy been at the door, with the tribe at her knees, nudging her hands for titbits, she might have asked what time he would be home.

'The usual. Not expecting anything new – not scheduled anyway.'

She might then have suggested a hook-up with some friends of hers for the weekend: a walk on the beaches by Orford – let the pack have a run – then a picnic lunch, rain or shine.

'Can't see why not. No panic that I know of.' He might have added, more grimly, 'And when was there last a panic?' But she had gone for her morning trudge.

Carlo was reputed to smoke and drink heavily. She seemed not to care about that, or about his moustache. She didn't want to hear his stories about the good old days with the Investigation Unit or about his Rome attachment. And Sandy, bless her, never said she knew his favourites by heart – such as the one he claimed had made him an icon at the Custom House: the 'fight' and the 'visit'. They had been the Immortals: they had worked from a big room in the Investigation Unit, which housed two teams. All were perpetually exhausted from the long hours they put in and were watched over by a legion of bureaucrats, who had no comprehension of the traumas of front-line work. A mood had snapped and a fist fight had broken out. Grown men, mostly middle-aged, belting each other when the newly installed director of investigations had walked in. Shock horror. But, as someone had pointed out breathlessly, 'You can't put lions on the street and expect kittens in the office.' He loved that one, told it most weeks. But Carlo was no longer a lion, and no longer on the street. He did kitten work now.

What he would most have liked in his life was the unpredictable: getting up in the morning and not knowing what would have hit him by the evening, the raw excitement and the fear of falling short.

He drove towards Felixstowe Docks – and maybe a seizure, another that was not worth him getting into.

The young man came out, sauntered across the pavement and held up a wad of notes so that the goon who had stayed outside could see that the *pizzo* had been paid. They waited for the other.

Perhaps he'd gone to the toilet. The money had gone into a pocket and the two embraced. The pizzeria man was at the far side of the door and Jago thought he was crying – the back of his hand went twice over his eyes. He didn't know what to do so he did nothing.

'Bent by name and bent by nature.' He rather liked that, thought of it as a compliment because it meant they were talking about him.

He was Bentley Horrocks. In many files of the organisations tasked with combating crime barons, his age was listed as fifty-one. His address was given as a seven-bedroom mansion, south of Meopham in Kent. His wife was down as Angela, but he referred to her as 'Angel', and he had two daughters in private education. A mistress, Tracey, was installed at Canada Wharf. He visited her every Tuesday and on occasional Fridays. The files encompassed his dealings in property development in south-east London, reclamation of wasteground, scrap-metal clearance – also extortion, Class-A importation, money-laundering and other 'interests' in Peckham and Rotherhithe, and Bermondsey, south of the river. He had been subject to four heavyweight investigations and, each time, had seen them off.

He walked in the grounds of his property, circling in the centre of a wide lawn, with Jack – around the same age but not his equal. Both men, on that wet, windy morning, wore anoraks, with scarves covering their lower faces. Bent assumed that he was continuously under police surveillance and even here, with no sign of watchers or cameras, he reckoned they'd want to video the movement of his mouth, then run the tapes for lip-readers to interpret. He had made a science of caution, and was a free man.

'Can't stand still,' was one of Bent's maxims.

Jack usually answered, 'Too right, Bent. Just can't stand still.'

A dilemma faced him. Should he keep climbing the increasingly fragile ladder, or stay at the level he was at? A big force inside the United Kingdom, a man who could 'melt' hard guys with his stare . . .

'It's when you're weak, when you're not moving forward . . .'

'Spot on, Bent. Weak when you're not going forward . . .'

Jack told him about the pattern of flights they would use, what passports through which airport, and when they were due to arrive at their destination. A big step, beyond any comfort zone he was familiar with.

'What sort of place is it?'

Jack answered, obsequious, an accountant who took care of detail and was not consulted on strategy. 'A good place for you, Bent. Not like the shit here, but on a different level. Where you should be, Bent. Where the big money is and the big players, Bent. When you're there, you've left this garbage behind you.'

He paused. He kicked a few of the early leaves that had come down in the night, and the rain dribbled on his face, soaking into his scarf. Jack stayed close to him and would have tried to read his mind. The scumbag made an issue of reading his mind and his mood . . . Heroin was dead, the amphetamine trade was saturated, but the cocaine marketplace had room, in his estimation, for further expansion, which was why he would break a self-imposed rule, and travel far from his own territory. He barely knew where it was.

'We'll enjoy it, won't we? Calabria, where the action is?'

'And do some serious business, Bent.'

Jack had said they were little more than peasants – and Jack would know because he'd been christened Giacomo and was from good Italian stock, immigrants and ice cream, who had settled in Chatham. They'd show Bent proper deference, not like those Russian bastards. Deference always topped the list of Bent's demands. He'd offer big money and make bigger money, times over. A different level, higher up the ladder. He whistled for his dogs, pulled his scarf off his mouth and went back to his house. Angel – if she wasn't still pissed from last night – would have done him breakfast. The forecast said it would rain most of the day – but his iPad said that the sun would be shining on the Calabrian coast. He thought himself beyond the reach of little people, out of their league.

*   *   *

Another scream, a man's voice. At first the cry was of surprise, then of extreme pain. The one who had stayed longer inside came through the door, bent at the stomach, head lowered, his hands over his groin.

Jago was on his feet.

The park was empty – no dog-walkers, no buggy-pushers, no smokers. The traffic flowed on the street and pedestrians were moving briskly past the pizzeria. The citizens of Savignyplatz and Charlottenburg ignored the movements and sounds they skirted. The girl had followed the guy out, defiant.

The young man had twisted to face the action. The one by the car, rooted to the spot, watched his friend staggering towards him. That didn't figure in the equation of a simple cash collection. Behind the girl was the man who would have paid over the *pizzo* that had been waved on the pavement as a symbol of success. She might have barged past him, elbowed him clear, and had kneed or kicked the groin of the guy who had lingered – perhaps gone to the toilet.

Jago watched. The man was not a fighter. He lacked the hand-to-eye co-ordination that was second nature in the Canning Town warrens. The younger man, the leader, flattened him. He was a fighter. The grabbing of a wrist, and the twist of the arm, provoked a squeal of pain, and the man was prone on the pavement. He wore a long waiter's apron, which had been crisp and white and was now dirty. He writhed, helpless and defenceless. The man by the car had a pistol out. The leader had his arm behind him, hand outstretched, waited, then snapped his fingers. The magazine was detached, a bullet prised out. It went into the leader's hand. He held it close to the waiter's face, fingers, then forced it between his teeth as he gasped and retched. An awful croak. Jago heard it, but no one else did.

They laughed. She came past the man. She took their attention.

The man on the ground spat out the bullet, which rolled along the pavement. The faint sunlight caught it, a jewel among the dirt.

Her target was the leader.

To Jago, there was at that moment a trace of confusion on the man's face. His hand went back behind him, reaching for the pistol, which was given to him.

Jago couldn't shout.

A hand reached out – quite delicate fingers, with manicured nails. Every detail was clear to Jago, and he started to run. It had the girl by the throat, and the pistol came slowly from behind. The man held her at arm's length, keeping her clear of him, except for her feet. She hopped from one foot to the other, swinging the free foot at his shins. Her shoes were light, for wearing all day in a pizzeria, not for brawling on the street and disputing extortion money.

Jago ran.

He seemed to see his mother, the pocket-sized Carmel, who had come back into their home, breathing hard, and had tipped his phone onto the table where his homework was unfinished. Then she had enrolled him in the boxing club. Two weeks later he had fought for survival in the ring and stayed on his feet. Four weeks after that, one of the boys who had taken his phone was mismatched with a clever fighter and had had the arrogance punched out of him. Jago had gone to boxing all the time he had been at St Bonaventure's and had never been hurt again. He had been left alone.

He ran out of the park, through the gap in the trimmed privet hedge, and into the street. Two cars blasted their horns at him, and he heard the screech of tyres.

She had not been shot, but the barrel, a dull black, was inches from her forehead.

There were shootings, knifings and kickings in Canning Town, reports of such filling the local paper, but he had never seen one. He didn't know what a shooting would look like.

The pistol was used as a blunt instrument. Jago thought it deliberate, calculated. The barrel went into her face, the tip buried in her cheek. The foresight was jerked up, tearing apart the skin, the muscle and cartilage. He saw the blood.

The fight had gone out of her. The hand came off her throat and she sank to the ground.

Jago was on the pavement. What to do?

The leader showed no pleasure in what he had done, no concern, and acted like it was everyday business. In a sharp movement he wiped the barrel and the bloodied foresight on her jeans and apron. A last glance at the wound and the blood now was flowing freely. She whimpered, beaten. The bullet lay close to her. It was picked up and pocketed.

A life-defining moment. Jago took his last steps across the pavement, readied himself for the impact and flew. It would have been a leg that tripped him. He had no control and his arms couldn't break his fall. The pavement soared at him. He struck it and the breath jerked out of him. He gasped. There was blood on his face. He had no strength. A car pulled away. She cried softly, and he saw the length of the cut on her face, how wide it was. He felt vomit rising into his throat, and felt the depths, too, of his failure.

Bernardo heard the child.

He heard her most clearly, and the clank of the chain, when he had switched off the bunker's internal lights and was on his hands and knees in the tunnel. The concrete was rough against his trousers, his bones ached and he had only a small torch beam to show him how near he was to the outer entrance.

The child had been in a cave, its opening between slabs of granite, half hidden by boulders. First the family had found the cave, then raised the money to buy the child. She came from Firenze, a surgeon's youngest, aged twelve. She had been walking to school when she was taken and had been held for two weeks while her captors looked for a buyer in the Aspromonte. It was the first time that the family had invested in the trade. They had paid the equivalent in lira of a hundred thousand euros. The child had been driven south and the handover had taken place in a disused quarry off the main highway near to Capistrano. There was no sign of illness – only terror.

Bernardo had dragged her into the cave – his brothers had held back – and had fastened the chain to the ring they had concreted in the previous week. There was straw for her, and a bottle of water – it was summer so it would not have been too cold. Bernardo, of course, had never been to Firenze, had never seen the luxurious apartment block where the family of a prominent surgeon might live. He would have understood little of the child's mind, would have thought it similar to his sons' – they were close to that age. But he had barely known them, and had waited impatiently for them to grow up. He had lit her candle for her, then shown her the lavatory bucket, the bucket that held washing water, the water bottles – even some sandwiches that Mamma had made. He had turned his back on the candle and the crying, and had wormed his way out of the narrow exit. All the time he could hear, as he went away, the crying and the rattle of the chain as she tugged at it. He had left her. Thirty-six years ago she had been worth the equivalent of a million American dollars, which would set up the family for their next venture. Today Giulietta would have called it 'seed money' or 'venture capital'.

He had never exchanged a single word with her, had merely gesticulated with his hands. Bernardo, who was a *padrino* within his community, had power over almost everything that affected him, but he could not lose the sound of the child's voice and the choke of the tears.

The door moved and Mamma was in front of him with the bowl in which she had brought the fowls' feed. They were round her ankles, busy pecking. A good day faced him. His grandson would travel that evening.

He straightened, and could no longer hear the child.

Jago crawled towards a rubbish bin, one with different slots for plastic, newspapers and bottles. He reached up and pulled himself first to his knees, then almost upright. He leaned on the top, where people stubbed out their fags. He looked around him.

She wasn't there. A dribble of blood showed where she had been.

He sagged. He saw the shoes, the same mismatch. Small pieces of torn card drifted down. The logo of his bank was visible, then shifted when a dog on a lead walked over it. He looked up: an expensive skirt, a coat that stank of money. She would have been a prime client. He was supposed to care. Corporate discipline demanded he be devastated that he had lost a potential customer because he had brawled in the street, had joined an argument in which he had no stake. She walked away. He used the bin again as a prop and levered himself upright. A sign in the pizzeria's window said the place was shut. The inside lights were off. People watched him. Mothers, teenagers, children, a postman . . .

'Where are they? A man and a woman – she was hurt? Cut in the face. Didn't you see? Was an ambulance called?'

No answer from the teenagers, the kids who were skipping school, the dog-walkers or the postman. A mother told him that the man and the woman with the big facial wound had gone in a taxi to the hospital, the one on Spandauer Damm.

'Has anyone rung the police at Bismarckstrasse?'

He had lost his audience. He could see himself reflected in the glass. There was no blood on his face or his shirt. His hair was dishevelled and his right trouser leg torn. Jago thought he looked drunk rather than injured. He was alive and standing, asking questions, and the entertainment was over: they flowed around him.

Jago Browne went in search of an investigator. Failure loomed large in his mind.

4

'You took your time.'

'It's a busy city.'

'I've been here three-quarters of an hour.' Jago Browne stood up, feet a little apart, hands on hips, chin jutting.

'And in forty-five minutes you had ample opportunity to report a crime at the desk. You didn't use it,' the investigator countered.

He had strode into the reception area of the police station on Bismarckstrasse and given the name of the man he wanted to see, had watched the woman behind the reinforced glass make the first phone call, then another. Nothing had happened. He had been asked if he wanted to see another officer because Seitz was engaged in a meeting. He had declined. Anger had built. Around him things had continued much as on the previous day – the same stereotypical victims and low-life, the same smell of urine, vomit, cleaning fluid and sweat.

The investigator had come out of an inner corridor, joking with a colleague, then had spoken to the woman at the counter. She had gestured with her head towards Jago, and the man had nodded. He had shown no embarrassment at keeping him waiting, no frustration that a bad penny had returned, neither indifference nor pleasure at the renewed contact. Another day at the coal face. He had come out through the security door, and had indicated, with a finger, that they'd talk in the public area.

'I wanted to see you because it's about yesterday but further along than before.'

'As I remember, Mr Browne, you were there then to visit a client. Did your client's needs bring you across the city a second time?'

'Actually, I was there to see whether extortion was alive and well in Savignyplatz, whether street violence could flourish in Charlottenburg. Do you want to know, or do you know already?'

The investigator did not. 'I am not in direct contact with the operations room.'

'I did the good-citizen bit yesterday when I made a report to you.'

'Which provoked an appropriate response.'

'As I remember it, "Go home, forget the world outside, go to a disco, get laid, go to work." Seems close to your response.'

'The incident didn't happen where you live or where you work. What's your interest?'

'I thought it important and . . .'

The investigator peered at him. Perhaps, for close work, he wore spectacles.

'Or was it because you were dumped on your backside yesterday – and apparently on your face this morning? A pity – that looks like an expensive suit and "invisible mending" won't fix the tear in the knee. "Important" has already cost you at least five hundred euros. Now, what can I do for you?'

'You can check with your operations room for a report on a young woman so badly injured by a blow to the face that she'll be scarred for the rest of her life. Try that for a start.'

The investigator swivelled away and spoke into his mobile phone.

For Jago, the girl's face was clear. Blood oozed from the wound and there was shock in her eyes. He saw the man who had been behind her, cringing. He saw the money held out in a wad. It was a game of control.

The phone was snapped off. 'There is no report of any incident in the place you have described, not yesterday and not today.'

He took the policeman's arm. If he'd done that in Canning Town, he'd have had his fingers rapped, hard, with a collapsible baton. Not here. They walked back into the fresh air of the morning. On the way to the square, Jago explained what had happened to the girl, his intervention and failure. The policeman did not interrupt. At the end of his description of the events, he'd stumbled. He couldn't answer the investigator's final question: 'What the hell were you doing there?' Jago thought himself a victim – his chin was grazed, his knee was bruised and his clothes were torn and dirtied.

They were at the square.

Jago led the other man into the small garden with the benches. Across the street, the door to the pizzeria was shut and the closed sign hung at an angle. He could see the pavement – there should be bloodstains on it. He spotted a dark patch on the concrete, with a trickle line to the gutter – it was there that he had been tripped. The woman with the mismatched shoes was there, reading the *Berliner Morgenpost*. Jago had told the investigator about her and her shoes. He pointed her out, then hung back.

The investigator went up to her, bent so that his head was level with hers and spoke to her with what seemed deference and respect. What had she seen? He was answered decisively. She looked up, saw Jago, seemed to peer through him, then turned to the policeman and shook her head decisively. She had seen nothing.

Jago and the investigator walked away, into the heart of Charlottenburg and towards the hospital that had an Accident and Emergency department. Jago had to scurry to keep up with him. Left to himself he might have given up.

Giulietta knelt in front of her father. Bernardo had rolled up his trouser leg and his wife watched as his daughter massaged the knee, more effective than if he took the powerful painkillers their doctor – always discreet, always well rewarded – would have prescribed. When the ache in his knee was relieved, his hip hurt less. He loved Giulietta as if she had been a son.

She talked of her day. She'd left home the previous morning, then driven, with Stefano at the wheel, to the airport. She'd taken the flight north, then the shuttle bus from Milan to Novara. Forty-five minutes with her brother, Domenico, the widower of Annunziata, not a minute more and not a minute less, because the restrictions on visits to prisoners held under Article 41*bis* were sacrosanct. She had spoken to him through a wall of reinforced glass, communicating via microphone and earpiece. His voice, she reported, was metallic and thin. He seemed to have lost his defiance.

Bernardo thought that Giulietta, had she not been his daughter, might have gone to the university across the mountains, at Reggio. She could have become a poet. He couldn't remember when he had last read a book. She had a way with words. There was a statue in Locri, close to the shoreline, dedicated to the memory of Nosside, the girl poet of the Greek settlers in the city, three centuries before the birth of Christ. It would have been pleasing if Giulietta had been able to utilise her talent with words ... His daughter's ability to master the family's investments, though, was more important to him. And she was good at choosing the men who would carry out that work on their behalf. She was indispensable to him.

She told him about her visit to Novara in graphic detail. It was rooted in the old tradition of the 'Ndrangheta: men should serve time in gaol and come out stronger, with greater authority; they should not weaken. It was easier when the gaol was down the road, across the peninsula, to the south of Reggio. In the gaol at San Pietro, a *padrino* could live well. Paulo de Stefano had had the 'suite' there and had lived almost in luxury, until Article 41*bis* had been introduced. The accursed Sicilians, with their campaigns of assassination and bombings, had provoked the state and Article 41*bis* – isolation and slow, rotting decline – had been the response. Giulietta answered the question without him asking it: their son had not asked after him or Mamma. Domenico had spoken of his children and his eyes had filled with tears when he had talked about his dead wife, disappeared. There had been mention of the food and the exercise he was allowed. Giulietta would not have said that her brother had spoken well of them if he had not. She told no lies to please.

He slept most nights in the bunker because of Article 41*bis*. A few, not many, could continue to control their family's affairs from one of the gaols with segregated blocks; they used codes based on books, and the visitors would carry back a message of which book and which page, then describe how the words should be pulled out so that the instructions could be interpreted. Bernardo would have been among the many – as were Domenico, and Rocco. From the bunker, Bernardo could exercise a degree of power, but not from a prison cell. Soon, he would no longer have to sleep in the bunker. He had been told so. Mamma brought him some coffee. The clerk in the Palace of Justice had said that the prosecutor searching for him was under pressure to reduce the resources used in the investigation. Bernardo did not know what resources had been deployed, but it seemed they were nearly exhausted.

He was quiet when Giulietta had finished.

She had returned late from her journey. The round trip would have been in excess of 2,500 kilometres. She went once a month to see both of her brothers. In the summer, when it was warm, she could take Mamma with her, or Teresa. Otherwise she went on her own – it would have been too tiring for Mamma and too tedious for Teresa, who had the two sets of children to care for.

Bernardo imagined himself in a cell: the hours became days, the days weeks, the weeks faded to months, and hope failed . . . It would have been like that for the child in the cave, with the chain on her ankle, in the dark, while they negotiated the ransom.

Mamma was back in the kitchen. He coughed.

Which of them would come to visit him? Each evening Stefano was given a plastic bag with the stubs of the cigars Bernardo had smoked during the day and the ash. He would take them to the incinerator. Windows were always open in the house, and Mamma usually had a cigarette burning in the kitchen. It was the care of small details that kept men free. Who would come?

He clapped his hands, and the sound bounced off the walls. Marcantonio would be home late that night. He cleansed his mind of the image of the cell where Domenico was held, the image of the child and the sound of her frail voice. The picture in his mind of the prosecutor, from the *Cronaca*, had gone. He thought of his grandson and the pleasure the boy had given him.

He might hear that day, or the next, that a turncoat had died from a bullet wound. He felt good, and would feel even better when the family was gathered, the investigation was scaled down and his own bed beckoned. He slapped the table and the coffee cup jumped. A little spilled but he felt safer. He clapped loudly again and the sound bounced off the walls. He was secure.

Most people ignored them. They were on the Via Nazionale Pentimele, the main road cutting through Archi, satellite of Reggio Calabria. Consolata was on the pavement closest to the sea, and Massimo had the side that was near to the main railway line. They might not have been there for all the attention they attracted.

A few took their fliers, glanced at them and discarded them. The majority sidestepped Massimo and Consolata, even crossed the road to avoid them. It was her home but she hated this place.

She made a point of staring into the faces of the men and women, locking eyes and daring them to break the contact. Some, not many, would have benefited from the clans who ran the town, the families who exercised control over life and death – they would have taken a share each month of the profits from drugs trafficking, extortion and corruption of local government.

Abruptly, her face lit.

The man was of the 'grey zone'. She was from the 'white zone' and so, after a fashion, were Massimo, her parents, the magistrates, some of the prosecutors and most, but not all, of the police and *carabinieri*. The 'black zone' was inhabited by the Men of Honour – she shuddered at the irony – from the de Stefano, Condello, Tegano and Imerti families. She despised the grey zone more than the organised-crime groups.

The grey-zone man approaching her had the bearing of one who had sold out, a lawyer, banker or accountant. The criminals flourished through the professional help of such scum. Such a man danced to the families' music, and might not be trusted but received fat fees. He would have a large villa facing the beach and would dread the arrival of the police at dawn or news that the shares bought with laundered money had collapsed. Perhaps, inhabiting the grey zone, they feared less the police coming at first light to arrest them than losing the families' money. Perhaps the greater terror would come from trying to explain that a share price could go down as easily as up, that what had seemed a good investment was based on shifting sand. She watched the man. Tall, heavy, well-dressed in a three-piece suit, a phone at his ear. He had to come close to her because part of the pavement was blocked with uncollected bursting rubbish bags. Other people passed him and ignored her, as she now ignored them, but she could play a little with him.

'Are you prepared to denounce the criminal profiteering of the 'Ndrangheta? Are you prepared to condemn the intimidation practised by the clans? Do you look forward to a day when our local government can be liberated from corruption? If so what are you prepared to do to bring it forward?'

Refuse clearance was at the dictate of the families. It was a matter of control: they decided who worked and when, who had a business and at what profit margin, whose son went to university and won good grades, who had access to corporation housing. He would step around the rubbish, cannon into her and apologise. A flier would be in his hand and her voice would be in his ear. He'd have to step into the filth to get past her.

Consolata did not see the boys. They came up behind the man, elbowed past him, and stood in front of her. They would have owed allegiance to the same family. The feud – the *faida* – that had divided the clans, let blood flow in the gutters, a hundred men dead in this town alone, had been patched up with marriages of convenience.

Their leader stood a half pace in front of them. He was smart, well turned-out, and might have come that morning from a hairdressing salon. The grey-zone man was behind her. The traffic was heavy and it was likely that Massimo was unaware that danger had surfaced. She felt threatened. Did they know her name? Probably not. It was too early in the day, perhaps, for them to be doing the rounds, collecting *pizzo* from shopkeepers and bar managers: they had identified her as potential amusement.

The one at the front was so polite. Could he, please, see a copy of what she was handing out?

She looked into the young face – he might already be a million-aire. If she had been a song bird they might have wanted to slice off her wings while she was alive. She couldn't back away. If she did, she would betray every point she had made in the squat, about picket lines at the residences and confrontations with the principals of the families who controlled Archi. She hoped that her fingers were steady. He smiled at her.

She extracted one of the sheets. She remembered the crap that Piero and the others had cobbled together: she had thought it embarrassing and clichéd, and had said so. She passed it to him. He leaned forward and nodded, glanced at the page, then turned it upside-down, as if he could neither read nor write. Behind him there was laughter and two of his men sniggered.

It was the closest she had been, in all her years of protest, to a major family's heir. He passed the sheet of paper to the kid who stood on his right and murmured to the one on his left. He loosened his belt, took back the sheet and made a play of wiping his arse with it. The one on the left flicked the top two buttons of her blouse, which opened easily. The leader had refastened his belt and was still smiling. He slipped the paper into the gap between her breasts.

Trying to keep her voice steady, Consolata said, 'Go fuck your mother.'

He spat.

Consolata bit her lip. His saliva was on her trainers. For a moment longer they watched her, then were gone. She could barely stand. She felt faint and the paper tickled her skin. She wore no bra, which was supposed to be a statement. What shamed her most was the fear she had felt, and the effort she had had to make to keep it from them.

She pulled out the flier, smoothed it and put it back into the bag. Massimo was at her side. Was she all right? Of course she was. She was very pale, he said. Then he suggested they take a train into Reggio and work there – he needed to reach more people. Was she sure she was all right? She realised he had seen nothing. She buttoned her blouse. They didn't know her name, and she had achieved nothing against them. It would be easier to give out fliers on the streets in Reggio. She strode towards the station, and Massimo followed.

It was not the way of Fred Seitz to justify himself, his time and how he used it. He gave explanations of what he had done, not done or what he intended to do. He went into the hospital on Spandauer Damm and flashed his warrant card. He walked to the head of a queue. A receptionist pointed. He scribbled on a piece of paper. The English boy would stay in his wake.

Down a corridor, past a bank of lifts, up a wide flight of stairs, two at a time. He had not told the boy that he had worked hard the previous evening, on his computer. He had a car registration from CCTV, and a named owner from the licensing authority, with an address and a nationality. He had contacts, former colleagues, from the sunshine days. He had rung the GICO people in the far south of Italy and they had pushed him towards the ROS. There was a family with that name. Friends had done him a favour over the phone. There was no electronic print. To have done it formally, it would been a month before authorisation had come for that information to be released, and old spats between German and Italian law-enforcers would have surfaced. He had pushed aside work that was more pressing. He had reached home late and had packed for the weekend. That afternoon he and his wife would be heading north. He went down another corridor, past the bays of treatment cubicles, then checked a number.

It was empty, the bed crumpled. A nurse passed. Where should he look? She shrugged, offered a possibility. Down another flight of stairs. A pharmacy hatch. A plastic bag was passed across the counter. A man stood beside a girl and reached for it. They turned.

Seitz was an officer of old-school and old-fashioned methods. He thought himself hardened – he could do homicide and not throw up on the carpet. The wound on her face was almost from the ear to the mouth. Her eyes were blank, as if she were past weeping. The wound was dark, impossible to ignore. A little of him winced. He wondered how the kids who worked around him would have responded.

With a hand behind his back, he gestured for the English boy to stand aside. The girl ignored him. The man with her was a brother – his computer had thrown it up. A treasure trove loaned by parents, uncles and cousins would have gone into the rent and fittings of a pizzeria in that district, and they had moved east from Lübeck, which might have been at the extremity of 'Ndrangheta reach in Germany. They might have believed that the crime families didn't operate in the capital. A bad mistake. She would have the scar until the day she died, and she wore no ring. The wound disfigured her.

He had his ID card in his hand, and showed it. He spoke softly and, he hoped, gently. Could he, please, interview her? Could he, please, take a statement from her? Could he, please . . . Her elbow went hard into his chest.

It would have collided with the butt of his PPK, carried in the leather shoulder-holster beneath his jacket. The weapon was a further symbol of his authority. He thought that, behind him, the English boy might have reached out to slow her. She didn't stop. The brother swore at Fred quietly, but the word was clear enough to anyone with a knowledge of the Italian vernacular – similar to what a referee might have been called in the Stadio Olimpico or the Stadio San Paolo where the Naples *tifosi* had earned a reputation for quality abuse. They went past him and disappeared round a corner. A lesson learned, no surprise to him, but he doubted he would gain the thanks of his pupil, Jago Browne, who was an innocent abroad.

He thought of fear as a virus and was grateful that he was rarely exposed to it.

He was a student of military history. The prosecutor, when left at home by his personal protection officers, found relaxation in reading of defeats or hollow victories in the six years of the Second World War. His father had served in North Africa, had gone into the cage, and had always said he thanked God for his capture. Now he was in the courtyard at the *carabinieri* headquarters in the north of the city, an austere building.

To the prosecutor, the fate of the seamen on the USS *Indianapolis* seemed appropriate. He had read of it many times. More than a thousand men had gone into the Pacific from the torpedoed battleship and were not rescued for days. Sharks had circled them, picking the weakest off. Less than a third had survived. It was the circling sharks he thought of, going round and round the diminishing clusters of men who hung on to debris. The image of the sharks was in his mind now. He was at the building for a routine meeting.

A theatrical scene played out as he emerged from his armour-plated Lancia. Photographers were there. Cars and jeeps of the ROS group waited, their exhausts billowing fumes. Had he wished to, he would not have been able to get through the door ahead, which was filled with uniforms. In the pale light of the inner court-yard the camera flashes were bright. Prisoners were escorted forward, pullovers or windcheaters covering their wrists because it would impugn their dignity to be seen handcuffed. Some of the escorts wore paramilitary combat tunics, and others wore gilets with the name of their force emblazoned on them, but their features were guarded from the lenses by balaclavas. A few wore their best uniforms. The images would go into the *Cronaca*, *Messag'ero* in the capital, to *Corriere* in the north, and round the world from ANSA, Reuters and Associated Press. A minister would speak of a 'heavy blow' delivered at the core leadership of the 'Ndrangheta, and dignitaries would stand in front of micro-phones. He hated the spectacle because they were not his captives. It was too long since a minister had pirouetted before the cameras and claimed, because of the prosecutor's diligence, that a 'signifi-cant strike' had been dealt against the tentacles of organised crime. He watched. His protection team would have understood how he felt and hung back. It wasn't their job to bolster his sagging morale.

The vehicles had gone. The sole reason for bringing the pris-oners to the headquarters building was for photographs. It was a competitive world in which the prosecutor existed. Resources were the key: the more resources, the more arrests; the more arrests, the more advancement. Glittering prizes awaited the most successful in their ranks: the rewards could be political sinecures, appointments to Rome and big-budget departments. For those who failed to gather the headlines that ministers craved, the future offered more years at the grindstone of Calabrian law enforcement. They had never won, would never win.

He swore.

The sharks circled. They would be at the meeting. He appreciated that he could justify keeping his surveillance team in place for only a limited period, days not weeks. There was also the amount of time *he* was spending on his investigation into Bernardo Cancello. He would try to defend himself. The men of USS *Indianapolis* had screamed each time the sharks had come under them to snatch at the legs of one of their number. His fight would be conducted with propriety, but the knives would be as sharp as sharks' incisors. He could plead for another week, no longer.

He congratulated the colleague who had brought in the prisoners. It hurt the prosecutor to abandon an investigation, to dump the case notes and the surveillance reports – paper always a useful second behind the electronic library – in the cupboard in his office.

He depended on the surveillance team – he had no other weapon to fight with. He could hope to win another week.

They had talked about socks. Later they would talk about belts. Further down the agenda was the preference for the Beretta 92, fifteen-shot magazine, against the Glock 17, seventeen-shot magazine, which the Gruppo Intervento Speciale favoured. Neither Fabio nor Ciccio had applied to join that section of the *carabinieri*, which was thought to be the best.

In time they could move onto the question of food, what sort of assignment they'd want after this one had run its course, then, as a last resort, their wives. They were almost at the end of the road. Nothing was happening. The daughter, the grandchildren, the daughter-in-law, the matriarch, Stefano, the handyman, the youngster who hung around the back door and the dogs were always on the move, taking grain for the chickens and bringing a bowl of eggs back. They'd have to be desperate to talk about their wives: Fabio's was Chiara, and Ciccio's was Neomi. The women knew and confided in each other. Ciccio knew that Chiara had issued an ultimatum: she would leave him if he didn't cut his hours and was away less often; Fabio knew that Neomi had been diagnosed with a degenerative hip condition. Each had heard about the women the other had been with before his marriage. Pistols were more interesting to talk about than the wives.

Fabio said, 'I can feel it. He's here, Bravo Charlie is. Has to be.'

Good to believe. Shit to do surveillance and not believe.

Ciccio said, 'He has to show himself. We have to see him before the place can be hit. Seen, photographed, identified. We've got none of that. I'm saying this'll be our last shift here.'

'You crying?'

'If he's here, we've missed him. The *capo* will get hurt bad.'

Fabio said, 'I "believe" in *tacchino in gelatina*. Nothing better.'

'I don't want to quit.'

'Shut up.'

'I hate to lose.'

'He's here. I'm certain of it. It's how they are – never far from base. Maybe it's us – wrong location, too far back . . .'

'That's crazy,' Ciccio murmured. 'We looked. We had the aerials. We couldn't be closer or the dogs would have us. Then we'd be off the face of the planet, fed to the pigs or buried at the back of a cave. Take your own advice and shut up.'

The day wore on, and they almost slept until there was a convulsion from Ciccio, and a curse from Fabio: another scorpion fly in the bottle, the perforated cap back on, and the thing was trapped. Another diversion, better than the usual talk. It was good to look at the captured fly with a tail that looked lethal. Interesting to watch it scrabble for freedom, and fail.

There were two hard chairs in the interview room. They had walked back to the police station.

Jago Browne was surprised that the investigator had invited him in. 'It's been a long day and a traumatic one for you. I'd like to offer you coffee and straighten out a couple of points.'

Jago had been left alone. He checked his phone. Four messages from the *FrauBoss*, which displayed her irritation at him taking sick leave, then not answering his landline, emails or her texts. The investigator had come back into the room with two coffees, card-board mugs, on top of his Apple iPad. He passed Jago one of the coffees, switched on the iPad, produced a packet of biscuits and split the wrapper. Jago's anger ebbed over what had been done to the girl, but still burned for what had been done to himself. He sipped the coffee, which was dreadful, and listened, as was expected of him.

'You think me idle, uncaring, and you are entitled to your opinion. I do what I can and don't attempt the impossible because that way my time is wasted and I burn. *They* defeat me. Understand. We are the power house of Europe. It is natural that another colossus, from the top of European criminal activity, should make a second home in Germany. They are not Sicilian or Neapolitan, but 'Ndrangheta from Calabria. They seek to be, as you would say, 'under the radar'. They infiltrate and bring with them their money, huge profits from cocaine–, weapons–, child– and any other trafficking. We are a country and a people burdened by the past. We had a police state. We had draconian laws. Then came 1945 and an Allied military government, the imposition of democ-racy, and a constitution with the purpose of preventing the abuses that a Fascist government had practised. That is very good. The freedom of the individual is guaranteed. The police cannot abuse ordinary people. Much to admire . . . and it is admired hugely by the Calabrian gangster families who come here. They buy a lot and sell a little, and they have created a diaspora inside Germany. They are allowed, almost, to walk free. The young man who sliced a girl's face is Marcantonio. He is twenty. Don't let your coffee get cold.'

He ignored the coffee, and ate another biscuit. Sometimes, as the investigator talked, he hit keys, then turned back to Jago. He seemed sincere, and was probably more than twice Jago's age. At the bank they were lectured on money-laundering and the proce-dures to counter it; the younger personnel were cautioned against the friendship of potential investors with cash, and little rewards that were hardly worth noticing. He pushed away the cup.

'It is possible to intercept his phones, but before I can do that, under German law, I must offer precise evidence in justification. I cannot say that I *believe* or *suspect* criminal involvement. My chiefs are against allowing Italian officers onto our territory. They despise our brothers from the Mediterranean. A man who was a waiter in a Leipzig trattoria, earning a thousand euros a month, suddenly finds the cash to buy a ten-million-euro hotel. I am certain he is a 'place man' but cannot prove it, so I cannot tap into his conversations. They are peasants and without education, my superiors reckon, but they are capable of dealing in huge sums on the Frankfurt bourse. When, finally, we awoke to the situation – and the British are like us, no better, no worse – it was too late. They are embedded. They own significant percentages of our hotels, restaurants, travel agents and prostitutes. I go to my chief, who is many years younger than me and a bureaucrat, and request resources for an investigation. His first question to me is 'Has there been a complaint? Show me.' Now I have to say there has been no complaint lodged by a victim of assault. The end. I urge you to take my advice. Be very careful, Jago Browne, because they're serious people. When they come out from 'under the radar', they're unpleasant. They're cruel and arrogant, which comes from the belief that they are beyond the law. Sometimes they are right. Would you like a fresh coffee? Of course you would.'

His mug was picked up. Across the table from Jago, the wrong way round for him, was the iPad. He saw, inverted, a head-and-shoulders photograph with text alongside it and headings.

'Milk, no sugar, yes?'

The door closed.

There was a coffee machine in the corridor a few metres from the interview room. He might have a minute, perhaps two. Jago scrabbled in his pocket. There was a receipt from a dry cleaner on Lietzenburgerstrasse, near the language school where the bank employees had a discount. He had his pen. He turned the iPad and began to scribble.

He found the address in Berlin of Marcantonio Cancello, then the name of the village on the eastern side of Calabria. He flicked the screen and saw the names of parents and an uncle, who had children but no wife. A little pyramid had been constructed with the names, 'Bernardo' at the top and his date of birth, then Bernardo's wife. He wrote everything he could get onto the small piece of paper and cursed that he had not picked up a notebook at his apartment.

He heard the footfall in the corridor and flipped the iPad back as it had been.

Extraordinary. Bizarre.

He sat back in his chair, played bored, looked at the door as the handle turned.

Fred Seitz, regarded by his colleagues as dull but honest, had satisfied himself that the young man had had time to gut the entry on his iPad.

Kindness? Not really. In respect for a Samaritan who had tried to help? Something like that. In the room, which was often used by the investigator and his colleagues, a camera beamed back to a screen an image of the interview room's interior. He had seen Jago Browne writing frantically. He rarely had an opportunity to move outside the constrictions of his service. He went.

'The machine is broken. We must survive without coffee. Of course, my friend, you should always leave police work to policemen – it's safer. Like you, in spite of the firearm I carry and my warrant card, I feel frustrated at the lack of arrests and my inability to hurt dangerous people. They are conceited. We are the little people and do not matter, and they keep around them only those who are frightened of them. My parents were in Rostock. You know Rostock? The great port city for heavy ship-building in Communist times. Gangsters came there after reunification. A nephew of my cousin was once slapped in the face for not getting off the pavement when a gang leader passed. I'm sorry – I am rambling. The nephew saw the car they had just parked, a BMW, took out his house keys, scratched two lines along the length of the bodywork and ran. If they had caught him, they would have killed him. I told that boy some harsh truths. Gangsters hate violation of their property because that is disrespect, and he should make sure he is fit and can sprint fast. He should also get out of Rostock. I told him I did not condone what he had done and would arrest him without hesitation if he did it again. I don't want to see you again, Jago Browne. You should go back to your bank, and be a success in your chosen industry. Don't look for excitement in any unknown area. I shall be away for a few days, and when I come back I shall do what I can within my schedules and budget, but it will not be much.'

He showed Jago out. He yearned for the freedom of a beach.

Marcantonio swore and dropped his bag onto the pavement. He had forgotten the small porcelain Madonna he was taking to his grandmother – and he was already late for the flight. He turned on his heel, ran up the steps to the front entrance and had to key in the code.

'It's the only Lamezia connection! You'd better hurry,' came the yell. His distant cousin was at the wheel of the car and glanced pointedly at his watch.

A man was approaching the vehicle, but he barely noticed him as the door swung open and he started for the stairs – the lift was too slow. He heard a shout – not pain, but naked fury. What to do? In Marcantonio's life his grandmother was more important than his cousin's shout of protest. He went on up the stairs and had to unlock the mortise, go inside and disable the alarm, then into the bedroom. Where was it? He had forgotten what the wrapping paper looked like. What colour? And the blinds were down so it was dark.

He found it. It went into his pocket. The figure was beautiful in his eyes, and she would like it. He had nothing for the *padrino*, his grandfather, but the old man would be well satisfied.

He came out, did the alarm, then went quickly down the stairs, but had to find the button that unlatched the door. He heard the crescendo of his driver's shouts. He went out, skipped down the steps to the pavement and nearly tripped over his bag. He saw what had been done to the passenger side of the Audi. Two silver lines sliced the paintwork. A young man, back to him, was sauntering down the street, well dressed, in a suit, the glint of keys in his hand.

The car was Marcantonio's pride and joy, and it was ruined. Had it happened at his home, in the foothills of the mountains, a life would have been taken – but he had a flight to catch. Anyone nearby would have heard him as he spat the words but none would have understood the dialect of the eastern side of the Aspromonte mountains. 'I'll have your balls if I ever see you again. You're dead. Dead, do you hear me?' He hadn't seen the vandal's face, but he was tall, erect and walking steadily – then disappeared around the corner.

Jago Browne had never done anything like that before. He could still feel the gentle pressure he'd applied to the key, the ease with which it had floated across the paintwork. It was what kids did, anywhere between the Beckton Arms and the bottom of Freemasons Road, not what young bank executives did when supposedly on sick leave.

There was an alleyway at the side of a building. He ducked into it, went to a recessed doorway and pulled out his phone. Lamezia? The screen told where it was, and which airlines flew there. He began to shiver. It was step towards a different level. Was he a career banker, on the path that would lead him one day to become a successor to the *FrauBoss*? Did he care if clients slept with true 'peace of mind' because *he* watched over their finances? He shut his eyes and saw the scar on the girl's face, the scar on the bodywork of a top-of-the-range car. He walked away, back to the street.

Hilde would drive north from Berlin to the coast and was already at the wheel of the camper.

Fred Seitz carried their bags out of the apartment door. His office computer was switched off, as was his phone. Hilde's was on: if their son or daughter wanted them they would call her. If someone at Bismarckstrasse wanted him, they could wait. He dumped the bags in the boot and got into the passenger seat. Hilde eased the car out into the street. Ahead of them were the high walls of the Moabit gaol, where some of his clients would sleep that night. He would sit quietly, at least for the start of the 220–kilometre drive to the Baltic. They would grab fast food in Rostock, then go west towards Rerik and park among the dunes above their favourite beach. He wanted quiet because of what he had seen that day, what he had said about getting a life and . . . The girl's face, had upset him. Leaving his iPad switched on had been unprofessional and irresponsible. There were moments when his work seemed to constrict him. He needed to be away, to forget.

He was probably making too much of what he had done.

The *FrauBoss* had been surprised to see him, but Jago had explained that the pills must be working because he felt better. He needn't have come in at all, late on a Friday afternoon. He had gone through his emails, which had piled up.

Was he going away for the weekend? Hannelore was taking an evening flight to Stuttgart to see her parents – he was welcome to go with her. Magda was ready for her run but she supposed he wasn't up to joining her. Sigismund and Elke were going to the new DiCaprio, and the *FrauBoss* was without her nanny that evening so she was off home.

They drifted away.

He had gone back to his apartment earlier, put on his other work suit and taken the damaged trousers to the dry cleaner's. They would do what they could with the tear. The previous receipt they had issued him was in his wallet. The woman had been sympathetic about the trousers, and unconcerned about the 'lost' receipt. He had taken home his clean clothes.

The *FrauBoss* and her team had gone; the great clocks that showed the time in other countries had been dimmed. There was a night-duty boy, Boris, but only the crown of his head was visible above the partitions. The TV screen flickered but the sound was off, and he had little interest in how the Dow was performing.

Jago saw the face of the girl, the scar that would never heal, and the face of Marcantonio. He worked at his computer and the emails diminished.

What was he for? He didn't know. When would he find the answer?

Soon, perhaps, because it would be difficult if he did not.

5

The team at the bank was paramount. It had an ethos, a code, a discipline. Jago turned his back on them. A guy at Broadgate, in a bar after dismissal for poor time-keeping, had yelled: 'The best-kept secret in that bloody place? There's life outside.' The bank was supposed to be his life, his horizon, would answer all his needs in exchange for total loyalty. Now he opened the door to another world.

It was the door to his apartment. He was at the top of the building. Below him was a house of several storeys, unoccupied because the family were on sabbatical. He looked back. The bedroom light was off, but the bed was made, his clothing neatly stowed in drawers and the wardrobe. His accommodation was occupied but anonymous. In the kitchen, the shelves were clean, the crockery washed, the tea-towel folded and the cleaning stuff put away. In the living area, the television was unplugged, the chair cushions plumped and the parquet swept. He had made no life-changing decision about not coming back.

He hesitated. The staircase in front of him led downwards. Jago realised what now it would mean to him when he closed the door and took the first step in his descent. A pause . . . He could not justify indecision. He was supposed to have organised his mind during the night when he had lain on his back and stared up at the ceiling, waiting for the alarm to go off. He had seen the slash of the pistol down the girl's cheek, the pride with which she had shouldered aside the investigator in the hospital corridor. He had felt himself on the ground and the humiliation of looking up from the pavement at the amusement he had aroused in passers-by. He sensed again the pleasure of walking past the BMW, holding the key and applying pressure, the thrill of the hearing shouting behind him. It was about more than the girl's face, and more than the investigator's old-world indifference.

The key might have been enough, but was not. He didn't do drugs, but assumed that the first time would be as mind-blowing as running a key down the side of a sixty-thousand-euro car.

He closed the door. It had been a 'defining moment' of the sort that the motivational speakers, beloved by the bank, preached. The *FrauBoss*, the blessed Wilhelmina, was big on motivation, as had been the man who had dragged him into Canary Wharf, giving him a chance. He started down the stairs. His bag was light. No bank uniform. Instead he had with him what he would have worn if he'd gone with Hannelore on a Sunday walk round the lakes at Köpenick and the Langer See. Jeans and trainers, T-shirt, fleece and a light anorak.

He opened the front door, stepped out and looked right, then left on Stresemannstrasse. He wondered if, at the bank, anyone would say as an epitaph that he had been good at his work.

It was hard for Jago to imagine how this street had been before the end of 1989. The Wall had run down the centre and beyond had been the free-fire area, a death zone. Elke was from the old east and had told him over a sandwich in Ernst Thalman Park that the guards, armed with assault rifles, were given cash bonuses if they shot a fugitive. The street was poorly lit now, but then the high lamps would have produced perpetual daylight.

At that time of morning, dawn, only a few people were about, those with pressing business. The first cigarettes were lit and newspaper headlines glanced at. Jago made for the U-bahn station. A street-cleaning cart followed him along the pavement. The girls and boys at the bank would still be in bed. Perhaps contemplating the gym. Jago Browne couldn't imagine what the day would bring him. He pressed on, dropping a letter into a postbox as he passed it. The envelope contained a message to the *FrauBoss*: *Dear Wilhelmina, Apologies for my no-show. I've been called away on personal business. I'll be in touch soon. Regards, Jago*. It would arrive on Monday morning. He doubted any of his colleagues had seen a cheek slashed with a pistol, that they had vandalised a top-range car, argued with a KrimPol investigator or challenged a youthful gang leader. He wanted more.

Much more? Was he ready to burn his boats?

The motivational speakers talked about thinking 'outside the box'. Jago would have said he was 'not quite there' and that his options remained open. His target? It was a 'work in progress', but he was far enough down that road to know that he wanted to stand in front of Marcantonio, showing no fear, and faze the little bastard. If he had to burn his boats, he would, but not yet. He wanted to stand in front of him and see his confusion spread.

His journey had begun. At the station, he bought his train ticket.

Driving fast, in poor visibility, taking a bend on a mountain road, the farmer did not see the animal before he hit it. The vehicle jolted, and the creature flew upside-down past the windscreen to the edge of the road, where the pine trees pressed close. There were dogs of that size but he thought it more likely to have been a rarely seen wolf. A motorbike was speeding towards him, its head-lights dazzling. He could hardly see and had to swerve. He thought the earlier impact would have dented his bumper, but the lights weren't broken. He was fifteen minutes from the outskirts of a village close to Locri, and his bed. He assumed he had killed whatever animal he had hit.

The delays seemed endless, one after another. Stefano was driving Marcantonio home. Now they were in fog. Stefano spoke little: from long association with the *padrino*, he had learned to hold his tongue until he was asked for his opinion. There was no direct flight between Berlin and Lamezia but there were good connections via Budapest and Nice, then on through Milan. If there had been a direct flight, Marcantonio would not have booked it. He was coming home and took precautions. Any direct flight to the far south would be under close scrutiny. It was always necessary to be careful at home.

As they came through the mountains, the light lifted and the dawn mist was visible in the valleys.

Marcantonio had never needed to consider what any item cost before he purchased it. His grandfather was a millionaire many times over, but used this vehicle, the rusty old Fiat City-Van and Marcantonio followed the example he had been set. He had bought a ticket to Budapest on a budget airline, but the flight had been cancelled because the plane had engine trouble. A feeder flight from Budapest to Milan had already left, so he had been stuck in a transit hall for six hours, then bribed his way onto a tourist charter. From Milan, he had been on the red-eye flight down to Lamezia. Stefano had waited for him, with trademark patience, and had not complained. Instead he had kissed Marcantonio's cheeks and settled him into the passenger seat. He had cleared out rubbish and a pair of vegetable crates, than rear-ranged an empty chicken-feed bag so that the rust holes were hidden beneath Marcantonio's feet.

Stefano had to drive slowly, which irritated Marcantonio, who was reminded of the acceleration his Audi was capable of, then of the scar along the bodywork. He was angry: they hadn't followed the bastard who had done it because of the supposed tight flight schedule. They could have chased him, caught him, beaten him into the ground and dumped him in the canal or had a driver take him out to the Grunewald and dig a grave for him – and still have had time to cancel the booking and buy another ticket. He had sent no message ahead. He would not have used a phone to communicate with his family.

They were on the back road, far beyond Taurianova and Cittanova. It was narrow, with sharp bends, and rock faces towered above them. He saw a boy with a herd of goats, a teenager, prob-ably only three or four years younger than himself. The kid would have seen the little vehicle coming towards him and slowing because the road was filled with his animals. The kid went forward with his dog and a stick to move them to give the City-Van free passage. That was when Marcantonio knew he was close to home. The vehicle had been recognised. The kid waved cheerfully as they passed him . . . In time, Marcantonio would rule the village, and his word would be law. He did not know how long it would be.

He saw a church, a small bar where a man was wiping the tables, and the first children were arriving at a school, an old woman walking along the road, bent under a load of wood. All gestured with affection and respect to the little vehicle that Stefano drove.

If there had been watchers, the City-Van would have aroused no suspicion, as a Mercedes or BMW might have done. Such vehicles were suitable for Locri, Siderno and Bovalino, where the tourist hotels were, but in the foothills of the Aspromonte, money was guarded and kept hidden. There was a story Marcantonio loved. An old man, a leader of a *cosca* – a favourite word, the protection of close, tough leaves – had buried eight million euro in banknotes to keep them safe from the *polizia* and *carabinieri*. He had dug a pit, put the cash in plastic bags, then filled in the hole. Later, the bags had been dug up. The notes were sodden, disfigured and useless. Eight million euros! They had been left beside the road.

They were in the village and drove up the one street. There were waves from a woman sweeping her step and a man smoking a cigarette. He felt good, safe, and the frustrations of the journey were behind him.

The family always kept the wooden shutters closed at the front of the house. At the back, in the sweltering heat of high summer, every door and window was wide open. A mother lived there, with her son, the son's partner, and two small children. They would have heard, early in the morning, the chugging engine of the Fiat City-Van. Everyone in the village knew the sound of that engine. It was because of the mother's first-born, the son's elder brother, the wife's brother-in-law and the children's uncle that they lived in a bubble of privacy; the mother wore black, although she wasn't widowed – her husband was employed on building sites in Scandinavia. The son wore black, too, and the daughter-in-law, and the children didn't play in the street. They were isolated, had nowhere to make another home. It was because of the elder son, the elder brother, the uncle. He was a *pentito* – meaning 'penitent', or 'he who repents' – and was long gone. He had last been seen in

Calabria when giving evidence in the *aula bunker*, the underground, bombproof courtroom, against Rocco and Domenico
Cancello, plus nine of their blood relations and associates. He had
been granted immunity from prosecution because his evidence
had resulted in two sentences of Article 41 *bis* and other terms of
imprisonment ranging from nine to fifteen years. He had not
repented, but had faced the prospect of a lengthy stretch for acting
as a courier in bringing forty kilos of unrefined cocaine out of the
Gioia Tauro port complex. He had collaborated with the state,
believing that to be a fair exchange. The remaining members of
that household walked a tightrope close to death because they had
harboured an *infame*, a traitor. They were cousins, with a trace of
blood to Bernardo. They wore black to imitate a state of mourning.
They said, to whoever would listen, 'We are no longer his family,'
and had made a statement to the *Cronaca* declaring, 'He is not and
never has been worthy of belonging to a clean-living, honest
family like ours.'

That had saved them from assassination.

Since the day he had been taken out of the *aula bunker* to the
helicopter pad they had had no contact with him. They didn't
know where he was resettled and what identity had been given
him. They were captives in the village, an example to others of the
danger of harbouring a turncoat, an informer. Now they
denounced him but on the day before he had set off for the docks
to drive away with Class-A drugs he would have been called 'a
wonderful son . . . a beloved brother, an uncle who was a gift from
God'. Always, in that house with the closed shutters, there was
tension when they heard that engine. Their survival rested on the
goodwill of the *padrino*, who held their lives in his hand. After him
it would be his potential successor, the grandson. They lived under
the shadow of fear.

He was alone and lonely.

Loathed by his family, despised by his community and hunted
by his enemies, he trudged along a street. He was at the outer edge
of central Rome, and away to his right was the expanse of the

Borghese Gardens. That was where he would be later. Now he was on his way back from an early visit to the convenience store where he had bought milk, cheese and ham. For four years he hadn't spoken to his mother, his brother or any of the extended family.

He came past the big red-brick church dedicated to St Teresa d'Avila – a sixteenth-century Carmelite nun – and crossed himself. She looked down on him with what he reckoned was love. No one else did, except the dogs. Behind him was the Porta Pia and the Via Venti Settembre. When he was there he liked to stare through the railings at the gracious lawns and fountains of the British embassy, and would stay until the troops on guard waved him away. In front of him was the turning towards the apartment blocks where he worked and existed.

That he survived, he thought, was because St Teresa d'Avila watched over him, but should she be distracted . . . There was rubbish in the doorways – kids came out of school, bought fast food on little polystyrene trays, gobbled it and dropped them. In the days when the security men were still with him, a few weeks after the trial, they had referred to the kids as 'feral vermin' . . . Let them visit Reggio Calabria, then see if they complained of Rome's pavements.

He hurried. The men, and sometimes women, of Public Security, who looked after state witnesses before they gave evidence, then briefly prepared them for an afterlife, had long been withdrawn. One day they were with him – a curt handshake, a telephone call from a magistrate wishing him well and thanking him for what he had done – and the next gone. He was left with an emergency phone number, and had been told that the heavens would have to fall in before he gained any response from the operations room at the end of the line.

He turned into Via Giacomo Puccini, then the gated, sprawling apartment block. He was lucky they'd found him a job, they'd told him. He was in the basement, close to the communal boilers, and had a cramped room near the *portiere*'s small apartment. That man, with a uniform, regarded him with suspicion.

They would find him, one day. He had gambled and lost – was condemned.

The milk, ham and cheese were not for him: the *portiere* would take them to different households in the block above, and would receive a gratuity. He could be grateful for little, that he was still alive, that today he was beyond the reach of Bernardo, the *padrino*, his wife, the sons in the northern gaols and the grandson who, they said, was more brutal than any older member of the family. They had such power that all efforts against them were doomed. He had heard a journalist from Reggio say on television, 'If the 'Ndrangheta target a man he is dead. There would be no escape not even on a Pacific island. When they want to kill him and are ready to do so, they will.' He tapped in the code, let himself through the gates and did not look back. He was the walking dead.

He was in Rome.

The girl on the desk shrugged. Jago's ticket was for Lamezia Terme, not Reggio Calabria's Tito Minniti airport. Anyway, the next two flights to the city were fully booked so he would be on stand-by. Would he get on? Another shrug. And the connection to Lamezia Terme? A flight was due to leave in an hour. There were seats on it, but it was delayed. How long? There was a dispute with baggage handlers at Lamezia Terme. The early-morning flights were not affected because the baggage was handled by night-duty staff. The day shift were taking industrial action.

His certainty had slipped.

Men and women from around the world swept past and around him, anxious to display the urgency of their business. He was told that the industrial action at Lamezia Terme would be settled towards the end of the day shift because they would be paid electronically before the start of the weekend. No one was particularly helpful to him: why should they be?

He was not asked his business in Reggio Calabria, why it was important for him to travel and what priority he might be afforded. Had he been, Jago might have struggled to answer coherently. A Lufthansa flight to Berlin was called.

He could have gone to a desk, made a booking, and been back in his apartment by early evening, or searching out a bar where Elke might be. The final call for the Berlin flight. The bench he sat on was uncomfortable but he endured it. Jago was not quite ready to light the fuse that would burn the boat, but was considering his goal: it was not just to stand in front of the young man and see confusion but to achieve more. How? No idea.

He waited.

Bernardo heard the entry sounds. The outer doorway squeaked when it was opened or closed. Scrapes and scuffles came to him from the tunnel's pipes. A smile lit his face.

In his mind he had been with the child in the cave, on one of those days when he had brought food to her and she lay on her side, convulsed in coughing, no longer crying. By the second week only Bernardo would take food to her – bread, cheese, perhaps an apple, water – and the dogs with him wouldn't come into the cave. They stayed outside, their ears flat to their heads. His torch would find her in the far corner of the cave, beyond the lichen, and she cowered away from him. He never brought his boys, Rocco and Domenico, to the cave because he didn't trust their reaction. The girl had given the family everything. She had been a sound, shrewd investment, and was the basis of the family's success.

He heard the light knock on the outer wall of the container, scrambled across the interior and unfastened the makeshift doorway. Fresh air engulfed him as he held the boy who was his future, the dynasty's.

They hugged, the clasp of two men, one old, one young, who had for each other the love that kept the family alive and was its strength. He remembered when he had struggled with his hands on the man's throat and had called his fifteen-year-old grandson to his side, shown him the grip and had him finish the strangulation. He hadn't seen him for six months. He had missed him. Now his grandson led the way. Bernardo switched off the lights, closed the inner door after him and started the long crawl up the sewer pipe.

Coming into the daylight was like breaking the surface of the sea after a dive – not that Bernardo could swim, but he had seen divers on the films. The chickens were round his feet, and Marcantonio had the bowl for their corn. They took the hidden path, passed Mamma's sheets, then the trellis. He was in the kitchen, and had forgotten the child in the cave. He saw the pure joy on Mamma's face.

A call came to the private-wealth section at the bank. A junior in the analysis unit, on a weekend watch, had had a query from a client in Bad Godesberg. The client, a widow, Frau Niemann, was persistent. She had been talking to her nephew, who was with Deutsche, and needed to know whether her account was listed as medium or low risk. She was an important client because her investment portfolio was worth some ten million euros. The junior was sitting at the end of a long work area, no natural light, and promised the client he would get straight back to her with an answer.

He rang the manager of the sales section, with overall responsibility for the client's account, at home. He reached her as children flooded into her apartment for a birthday party. He heard the din, apologised to Wilhelmina for bothering her and was told to call Jago Browne immediately. Was Jago Browne not listed on the weekend duty sheet as being on stand-by? If he wasn't, he should have been. Jago Browne knew about Frau Niemann's affairs. He had been sick but was in the office the previous evening so had obviously recovered.

The junior found Jago Browne's corporate mobile number, dialled it and let it ring. It went unanswered. The client's enquiry was only about medium or low risk, and could have waited forty-eight hours to be dealt with on Monday morning. He called the number again.

Within a half-hour he had tried it seven times. It was unprofessional for any stand-by executive to be away from their phone for as long as thirty minutes. He rang the client, apologised and grovelled. He would be able to get back to her again within an hour.

*   *   *

He walked along the beach, the soft dry sand trapped between his toes. Fred Seitz felt free. His wife was nearer the sea, paddling and looking for shells. He *almost* felt free.

It was where he was happiest. Almost free, because the beach was almost a naturist venue. Nothing could be quite perfect. His work lingered because the break they had taken was not long enough for him to shrug it off entirely: he dealt with muggings and burglaries – not the small-scale thieves and pickpockets but those in large gangs with serious turn-over – day-to-day, but had responsibility at the station for organised crime with international implications. It could be Russian-originated, Albanian or Lithuanian, or it might have the stamp of the 'Ndrangheta. If it had been a 'listed' beach, Hilde would not have gone there.

It was early autumn and the usual chilly wind came off the sea and from the Scandinavian plains. She was topless but with a thick towel hanging round her shoulders and she wore drill shorts. Fred, in deference to the weather, also wore shorts.

Fred had cooked lunch in the camper and they'd slept after the meal. The sun was slipping now and he thought the day *almost* perfect. He was never away from his job. The kids in the section had lives beyond the police station – they went clubbing, rode mountain bikes in the forests around the capital, joined book groups and socialised with each other. Some studied for university-sponsored e-degrees. The wind tugged at his close-cropped hair and some-times a gust shook him or he shivered. He was dedicated to a job that the kids found obsessive – and tedious. His wife, bless her, knew when to leave him to his thoughts. He nurtured images, couldn't escape them: the scar, the girl pushing past, elbowing him aside.

She hummed softly beside him, and the gulls screamed. One naturist had braved the chill, a woman, and a small dog scurried close to her. It wasn't fair. If the victim made no accusation and no other witness corroborated the Englishman's story, the case would collapse.

Fred walked on. He knew where the boy came from – he had been to San Luca, Plati and the coast at Locri, where the beaches were warm and the *carabinieri* had their barracks.

Did he make a difference? he wondered. The question nagged at him whether he was at work or not. It was hard to imagine that he did, or ever had, and even harder to believe he could in the future.

'The key thing to remember, all of you, whatever your rank, is that you make a difference.'

Carlo sat at the back. The canteen was the usual venue for a talk by an HMRC visitor from London. The woman doing the chat might have been from Human Resources or one of the myriad managers who seemed capable of beating the cull that emasculated uniforms and investigations.

'What we're aiming for is what I call "harm reduction". Cutting down the damage caused to the addicts in our society, and getting a firmer grip on the revenue lost to the Treasury by the smuggling industry. We want a lean, modern organisation to be at the cutting edge of knocking back the power of today's criminal sitting cockily on the international scene.'

He didn't yawn. Some of the younger uniforms seemed impressed that a big player had travelled to see them, and at a weekend. The old sweats – Carlo to the fore – were too canny to show their contempt.

'We know when we're on course because the price of cocaine rises. The higher it goes – through your efforts – tells us we're doing well, seizures are up and the criminals are suffering, losing money. The higher the price, the better we're placed. It's evidence of our success at interception. You are on the front line and you're doing damn well.'

Except that the price was in free-fall. There was a journalist at the back, from a national paper, scribbling energetically. He might even have believed some of the crap that the press office was feeding him. In common with most of the guys who had cut their teeth on Green Lanes, Carlo was underwhelmed by administrators. But he needed his job and kept quiet. He should have been at home, raking leaves or . . . If redundancy beckoned, the future didn't look good.

'We want to improve the statistical rate of seizures, arrests and convictions. They all send a message loud and clear that the United Kingdom has elite security on its borders. We want to see a rise in the confiscation of assets, so that felons cannot live the good life after release from well-deserved custody sentences. Whatever it is – bootleg vodka, cigarettes without duty paid, bogus labels on clothing that comes from cheap sweat-shop labour – we want to demonstrate zero tolerance. You are achieving this, and we're sincerely grateful to you. Thank you.'

No mention of cutbacks or staff lay-offs, nothing about the price of Class-A stuff being at rock bottom because narcotics were swamping the country . . . and nothing about China, the big moneybags who must not be offended: a container load of cheap leather wallets of third-world origin is shipped to a UK dock, then reshipped to Naples on Gioia Tauro, where the fake Gucci labels are added, and sent on, as genuine, to China. The Italians bankroll the operation with British criminal connivance, and the money comes back from China, rinsed and dried, perfectly laundered.

There was faint applause, then a stampede to get back to the duty posts. He would return to the cottage, maybe do some expenses, rake some leaves and dream.

'It's an opportunity. Don't know much about the people or the place . . .'

Bent Horrocks lay on his back and the woman's fingers, not her finest feature but with long nails, played in his chest hairs. By now Angel, his wife, would also be flat on her back, snoring quietly after her lunchtime drink: 'I'm not an alco, love, just like a drop to help my digestion.'

'Can't take you, Trace. Like to, course I would. Hardly fun, but an opportunity.'

The apartment he had bought her was high in the tower. One of the best that had been available in Canada Wharf, it was convenient and discreet. There were lifts, or staircases, if he had the energy. He was not at his best that afternoon. His mind was not on the business of justifying the basic outlay of a thousand a week, which was what it cost to keep the roof over Trace's head, food in her belly, the frequent hair and nail appointments, the holidays with her sister, clothes and pocket money. A grand a week wasn't unreasonable.

It was his fault. She'd tried hard – wasted effort. She was unsettled and it showed. Bent could have said, no fear of contradiction, that he ruled that part of east London – Rotherhithe, Bermondsey, Peckham – where Trace was installed. No one would have denied it, neither the Flying Squad detective who'd checked his file, nor any dealer in the area. He'd dealt with foreigners enough times, of course, and none had considered taking a liberty with him, except one Russian. The man had gone home and would have had a bad flight – difficult to travel by air with a leg in plaster because your kneecap's shattered. Different, what was coming. Off his territory. He'd not met them, didn't speak their language.

Trace said, 'You'll be all right, Bent. It'll be fine, like it always is.'

The room behind the floor-to-ceiling plate-glass window, with a view up the Thames to die for, was immaculate. He liked it that way, ordered. Her clothes were folded in a small pile on a chair, and his hung from hangers. He disliked mess and confusion. He had a phobia about the unknown, but his life was about taking opportunity when it came up. He couldn't back off.

He said, 'Good one, Trace. Fine for me, like it always is.'

The party was finishing. The magician had performed well. The bell was ringing as parents came to collect their children. Wilhelmina was on the phone and the noise swelled around her. The junior in the analysis section was adamant. Jago Browne wasn't answering his landline or returning mobile calls. He hadn't responded to emails or texts.

Wilhelmina spluttered indignation and wiped a child's chocolaty face. There was lemonade on the cheque for the caterers. It was about discipline. She had no quarrel with his work, his attitude towards clients or his behaviour in the office – but he was foreign. Also, he was aloof, and not a team player. With discipline went the requirement that he should be on call one Saturday in three and one Sunday in five. He could be in the middle of an ice-rink, or with a girl in the Tiergarten, playing tennis or at the cinema, but on those few days he was required to answer his phone – and had not.

Peculiar. Three parents waved and left. The birthday party was, for her, a major social opportunity and a chance to identify possible clients. It was more than peculiar. Wilhelmina, annoyed, was unforgiving and formidable.

She said, 'Leave it to me. I'll speak to the client. Thank you. And I'll deal with the young man who is on call.'

'It's a murderous place. They slaughter them and enjoy it. Barbarians . . .'

The man was two rows behind Jago Browne and he spoke with a thick Yorkshire accent. The coach was taking them from Lamezia Terme airport to Reggio, and tempers had frayed. Jago hadn't noticed his fellow travellers in Rome or on the flight.

'They butcher them. It's a mark of manhood, down here, to kill."

There were eight of them and they belonged, he'd gathered, to a conservation group. Their speciality was watching birds' migration routes, and a hot-spot was the straits between Sicily and Calabria, which was less than three miles wide at the narrowest point.

'They're not choosy, a vulture or an eagle, a harrier or a falcon – but they love to massacre the buzzards. It's a sort of choke point for the birds, and the bastards are waiting for them. It must be like flying in a Wellington through concentrated flak, if you're a raptor.'

A woman said, 'For God's sake, Duncan, leave it.'

'Top of the list is the honey buzzard. If any make it over the strait, going south now or north in the spring, it's a miracle. Tells you what the people are like. If your top thrill is bringing down something as beautiful as one of those, it shows what you're made of.'

'People are on holiday, Duncan, looking for a break. They haven't asked for your opinions.'

He'd seen them board the coach, lugging rucksacks and tripods.

Their spotter scopes were in canvas lagging. Jago had never done any birdwatching, but there had been people in Lancashire, at the university, who had gone out onto the sands of Morecambe Bay. He'd never seen the point. But the relevance of the story was forced down his throat.

'Why shed a tear, if you're Calabrian, for a honey buzzard, or a lammergeier, or an imperial eagle? Life's cheap down there. Murders are two a penny. No bigger deal to take a human life than to blast a kite or a sparrow hawk to kingdom come.'

Another voice: 'The killing of raptors at migration is well documented, but we hope to show by the example of our international interest that all wildlife matters. We don't want only to look on the dark side.'

The Doomsday merchant came back strongly: 'And this road we're on. It's wonderful – and so it should be for what it's cost over the last thirty years. It's a Mafia road, courtesy of European taxpayers. Billions paid, and most of it into gangster pockets . . . I bet there's a fair few in the concrete. This lot down here, they make ours look like choristers.'

'Shut up, Duncan.'

Now there was quiet behind him. They went along a wide, fast road, through massive tunnels that lanced big spurs of rock, over steepling viaducts and could see tiny lights, isolated, in the deep gorge valleys below. There were lines of cones and stretches where the work had been left unfinished. It was fifteen hours, close enough, since he had left Berlin.

The talk behind him changed, and the gloom lifted. He wavered. Jago's bag was in the overhead rack. He didn't know whether he would dump it in Reggio later that evening, or in the airport at Lamezia Terme. They compared makes of spotter scopes to the Swarovski range. Jago had no interest in that, but had heard about the killing of people, rip-offs on construction projects and the slaughter of birds. He sat upright, rigid, and could not recapture his earlier certainty.

There were banks of lights ahead, but to his right a dark strip, a gulf, then more streetlights and homes. He checked his phone screen and realised they were close to the strait and Sicily. He sought to grip the talisman images and sounds: a facial scar and twin scratches in metallic paint, a shout of shock and a yell of venom. He had no plan, he was hungry, and someone behind him was snoring softly. He would look into the man's face, into the eyes, see confusion and fear . . . They came into the city, and he was beyond the limits of his experience.

Consolata could have taken his eyes out with her fingers, but kept them clamped tight on her bag. It was the end of their wasted day.

Massimo had said, 'I'm entitled to criticise you. Your bag is almost full and mine is almost empty because I have given out our fliers and you have not. You glare at people and you're rude to them. Your problem is that you don't believe in non-violent action.'

He had gone back to his mother with his empty bag. He would eat with her, then take a bus to Archi. In the squat he would tell them about Consolata's heresies. The air would be thick with cigarette smoke and she would be denounced.

She sat on a bench. Consolata could recall each word that had been said and fancied her link with the group had been cut. 'You seem to threaten people when you want to show an alternative to the aggression of 'Ndrangheta. I wouldn't stop to talk to you. You saw for yourself where your attitude takes you – they hurry past you. They don't want a lecture. Consolata, 'Ndrangheta is a criminal conspiracy that depends upon fear, terror and suspicion. If you hector those you seek to influence, you show no alternative to the gangsters. It's about turning the other cheek and demonstrating the supreme example of non-violence. I don't think you're capable of that. You want to fight, fight, fight.'

He had walked away, tall and haughty. By now he would be regaling his mother with Consolata's shortcomings. He would have rated it a thoroughly satisfactory day, in which he had spread the word of opposition to criminality and corruption. He believed in the group's solidarity and that radical opinions should not be tolerated. No quick fix but the importance of holding the high moral ground.

He had left her on the street in the gathering darkness. The Corso Giuseppe Garibaldi was the nearest Reggio Calabria had to a main shopping street. There were good brand names on display, but many were fakes, and the premier banks that did well out of the region's criminality: the families needed banks, accountants and lawyers, and paid them well.

She had tried. She had stood in the middle of the street, pedestrianised, and had handed out fliers that called for non-payment of the *pizzo*, a boycott of any business that bowed to extortion and contributed. She had been ostracised. She accepted that *perhaps* her voice had become more shrill, as the evening crowds of window-shoppers and promenaders flowed around her. Most had looked at her with contempt. Some had brushed aside her outstretched arm. Others had glanced at what she held, then shaken their heads. The bag had stayed full. Then the shutters had begun to come down, and the lights behind the window displays had gone off, doors were locked and the street was emptied. She had finally turned away when the accordionist ceased playing.

The bench was in a small piazza. There was an obligatory monument to the writer Corrado Alvaro: celebrated, revered and taught in schools. At the bottom end of the piazza was the museum, but she had never been inside it. The foliage on the trees was thick and in daylight threw shade. At night it blocked out the light from the streetlamps. It was, she supposed, a pivotal moment. The wind was gathering off the sea, funnelled up the strait to enter the chokepoints between the buildings, and leaves blustered around her ankles. The bag was on the seat beside her. Her anger soared, its target the group. It wouldn't last – after a couple more years its members would be applying for college places or town-hall jobs – all those places of employment where the introduction of a 'friend' was essential. Perhaps handing out leaflets was a rite of passage for the young before the serious business of adulthood and collaboration or the blind eye. If she dumped them, there would be no turning back, no crawling late at night to the squat in Archi and begging forgiveness: she would get her clothing and be regarded as a leper. To throw the fliers into the overflowing bin would result in an appearance before the Inquisition: no crime could be greater.

But she did it. She didn't know how to escalate to a different level of protest, strike at 'Ndrangheta families, their corruption and complacency. She felt defeated, worthless.

She took the fliers from the bag and flung them in the general direction of the bin. The wind caught them and they scattered across the paving slabs. The wind was brisk enough to carry some to the darker shadows where other benches were. Dropping litter was an offence. She bent, snatched up some fliers and took them to the bin, then went for more.

Jago couldn't read what was printed on the flier. He had stepped off at the small bus station on the sea front and approached some men to ask for a connection to the far side of the Calabria peninsula. They had pulled faces, made gestures of ignorance and turned their backs. He had walked past two four-star hotels and it was after eleven. There was a bench in a park, and the wind was strong but warm, with none of the cutting cold he had experienced in Berlin. He had sat on the bench.

The papers blew towards him and the girl followed them. He watched. He didn't have the language to understand what was printed on them. She scooped them up and flounced to the bin, then went for more. She was, he thought, at the end of her tether.

She reached him – she was slight, muscular, nothing smart about her. A flicker of light showed she wore no makeup. Studs in her ears, nothing else. And there was no scar on her cheek. He'd almost looked for it. The face was the same as the girl's in Berlin, with defiance written on it. He thought she was angry. Now she was on her knees, close to his legs, rooting beside his trainers and under the bench for more of the fliers. She snatched one in his hand.

'What does it say?' He had no Italian so asked in English. She looked up at him. Her eyes pierced him, and her lip curled. Jago persisted, 'Please, would you tell me what it is?'

On the sheet of paper there were close-printed lines of text. In the first two or three, just below the headline, he saw a word he knew – *pizzo*. Then a frown cut her forehead. He thought she had been about to stand, take the last sheet from him and stride towards the bin.

She was someone to talk to – he groped towards the contact. 'What does it say?'

She sucked in a long breath. 'You are English?'

'Yes.'

'You have been many times to Reggio Calabria?'

'It's my first time.'

'You sit on a bench at night, and the city is about to sleep. Why?'

'I have nowhere to go to.'

'There are hotels, plenty, all prices. Why not go to one?'

'Confusion. Lack of certainty.'

'What is confused? What is uncertain?'

It was a staccato interrogation and the frown had deepened. At any meeting with a client, in London or Berlin, he would have covered his true aims and intentions. There was honesty in her face, though, which trapped him. He wouldn't dare lie to her. The night was around him and nothing intruded.

'I'm confused about why I came here and uncertain about what I'll do. What is the flier about?'

'If you haven't been here before, it will mean nothing to you.'

'Try me. I know what *pizzo* is.'

She rapped out the translation. The fight against corruption. The demand for civil courage. The call for honesty in the judiciary and among politicians. The announcement of a march for peace and justice next week. There was no animation in her voice – she might have been a child parroting a Bible text. She finished. 'For what reason have you come to Reggio?'

Jago said, 'Why does an activist take a bag of fliers and dump them? Why aren't they stuck to shop windows, under windscreen wipers?'

She stood up. He caught at her arm. She shrugged him off.

'Because we lose. Too often we lose. More exact, every time we lose. You fight a force that has incredible strength, and you look for reaction and for small victories. I see none. Against 'Ndrangheta we do not win. Today I know it. We have forgotten what is winning.'

She had the empty bag on her shoulder. The last papers were in her hand and she was at the bin. She dumped them, rubbed her hands together and took the first step towards the piazza's exit.

He called into the night, 'I think I know what winning is, against them. I did it yesterday. It was only small but I won.'

She stopped and turned.

6

'What was "winning"?'

She had good, accented English. He had her attention. She was in the heart of the small piazza, and what light there was filtered through the trees, silhouetting her body against the backdrop of a building behind her. He had halted her in mid-stride, hands on hips. In her question he heard a trace of annoyance, as if a foreigner, a stranger, had no right to mock her. But she had given him her attention. Jago named the place. She nodded. She knew of that village.

He kept his voice quiet and conversational and made her strain to hear him. A dog howled and youngsters laughed, all far away and unseen. They had the stage. Jago named the family, the old man who had topped the pyramid on the laptop report in the interview room.

There was no response, except a low hiss. She knew the village and the family. He told her the name of the grandson.

She walked back to him. They made an island in a sea, as if a spotlight were trained on them in the darkness.

'I'm Jago.'

'And I am Consolata. What happened?'

He was a banker, had gone to see a client in Charlottenburg, had time to kill, sat in a park. She flapped a hand at him. He told the story with no more fanfare than if he had been speaking to the *FrauBoss* – the first incident outside the pizzeria, his visit to the police station and what he had been told there. Then the second: a pistol produced, a girl's face slashed, his charge at the young man, the trip and the hospital. She was on the bench beside him. He went on to detail his return to the police station, and the open screen.

Then he told her about the pavement, the keys, the Audi convertible and drawing the tip of the key along the paintwork. She laughed. He told her of how the guy behind the wheel had yelled as he had walked away, then of Marcantonio's fury. She laughed again.

'What's so funny? I won, didn't I?'

He had enjoyed telling the story, and had felt a trace of certainty return to him. But she had laughed. He thought she was ready to push herself up from the bench and leave.

Jago said, 'If you'd heard him you'd have known I won. He was late for his flight and couldn't chase me. He would have tried to kill me – he was that angry. I might as well have pissed in his face. That's winning. I don't believe anything like that had ever happened to him before. Any sort of comfort zone he inhabited, well, I'd bounced him out of it.'

Her hand touched his arm. 'That was Berlin. This is Reggio Calabria. That was day, not night. Why not stay in Germany and continue with vandalism?'

'Because of the girl. I don't know her name, but I came because of her.'

'That is ridiculous.'

'Have you ever done anything that wasn't *sensible*? It seemed a good enough reason.'

'And here?'

'Next week, next month, next year, that girl will live with the ugliness of that scar, deliberately inflicted. I was told by a policeman it was too small a matter for serious investigation. Marcantonio believed himself immune, that he could just walk away. Then I heard his fury. I came here to hear it again. I bought into it and now I want more. Is that a drug? I don't know about narcotics but I want to hear that anger again. More than anything. That would be winning big.'

'You would kill him?' Her lips were close to his ear.

'I don't know. A big step, beyond my pay grade.'

'And you tell a stranger all this.'

'We all make judgements on trust.'

'I said "ridiculous". That was the wrong word. Remarkable. But you will hurt him?'

Jago said, with child's simplicity, 'I will do what I can to make him feel pain. I don't know how yet. Am I boring you?'

His eyes and mouth were close to hers. He reached up with his hand and used a finger to trace a line across her face: from under the lobe of a small ear, across a thin cheek to a point just below her lips. She did not flinch or push away his hand. He had traced where the scar was. His finger dropped. Her eyes had never left his. He supposed she needed a final instalment of explanation.

'I work in a bank. I handle other people's money, their pensions, life savings and inheritances. I'm supposed to be logical, careful and risk averse. Everything I've done in the last twenty-four hours contradicts all of that. That's how it is. It's what I want to do and will do. Time you were getting home. Goodnight.'

She stood, then reached back and took his hand. She yanked him to his feet. He picked up his bag and she led him towards the lights and the sea.

Giulietta had condemned him. Information had reached her. Marcantonio was at home but that did not change its import.

He crawled, alone, the length of the tunnel.

A paid informant at the Palace of Justice had stated that a particular prosecutor had won three more days of resources to target Bernardo. The official did not know what that meant – a phone tap, a surveillance team, aerial plotting of the village by the air force. He had told Giulietta also of tensions inside the Palace, arguments concerning priorities. She had told her father that he must be patient: she had condemned him, as he saw it, to a few more days and nights – the rest of the week – in the bunker. He was grateful for the diligence with which she protected him.

If they came for him, it would be in the small hours. The Squadra Mobile or the *carabinieri* usually swooped between four in the morning and six. They liked to take a man when he was half asleep. Stefano had led him back to the bunker's outer entrance; the dogs had been sent to roam the boundaries of the property before the two men had slipped out of the rear door. Bernardo relied on the dogs for the quality of their noses and sensitivity to sound and movement.

He put on the light, which flooded the inside of the buried container. He hated being alone in the bunker in darkness because then he saw the child in the cave, looking at him. The dogs captured a mood. Many litters back, they had been with him when he had tramped up the hill to the cave with the basic supplies. They would never go inside, but that day they had howled. They had not done so on the day his father or mother had died, and had always been quiet when the *carabinieri* searched the villa. They had never made it before or since.

She had been dead in the cave and the dogs outside had known it. She had been dead and cold.

In the bunker, when the lights were out, he saw her face: It was strip illumination and he kept it on when he tried to sleep.

When he had satisfied himself that the child was dead, he had gone back and told his father. They had found a camera and returned to the cave, bringing Mamma with them, a bucket of hot water and cloths. He hoped, soon, he would be able to sleep in his bed, away from the sight of the child.

He anticipated a good day ahead for the family. Good news, good business, and celebrations for his wife's birthday. He thought his gift to her was appropriate and would be appreciated.

The man sat in the passenger seat of his car. The block with the windows facing out onto the Villa Borghese and its gardens was behind him, and he could see the gate on the far side of the Via Pinciana, that the *infame* would use. He knew the route, but was there at night to cover all opportunities. The route he expected the bastard to take was from the block's gates, between the Harley Davidson showroom and the windows behind which he could see Ferraris and Maseratis. Then he would cross the road and the dogs would drag him towards the grass. Some mornings, the traitor took the dogs into the gardens first, then went to buy milk and pastries near to the Porta Pia. The presence of the British embassy, always guarded, meant there were too many troops and police near to the gates for the man to approach his quarry. The gardens offered a better opportunity. He had killed *pentiti* of the Cosa Nostra groups in Sicily, and from the Camorra in Naples. He had never knifed, strangled or shot one of the 'Ndrangheta: there were so few.

If he had used a phone he would have left a trace, so he sat and made quiet small-talk with his driver, mostly about football, but a little about children and women – not their wives but whores. There was soft music on the radio, which soothed him. The pistol was under his thigh, uncomfortable but convenient. They had water to drink, needed nothing else, and waited. Both men were calm. They watched for him, and thought of home and the mountains, of a celebration for a respected family.

She was first out of the taxi and let Jago follow her.

The moon was up and its light shimmered on the street. She waited. The driver had his hand out of the window. Consolata let Jago pay. He was five or six years younger than her, and she thought he had talked with a teenager's enthusiasm. He passed her the money, and she was left to negotiate and challenge the driver's estimate – he hadn't switched on the meter. She beat the man down, paid him, and, was sworn at. The taxi drove away, but the driver gave her the finger.

They had hardly spoken in the car. She had said she would take him to the village. He had thanked her. Consolata thought him an innocent.

They were outside her home. Since her fifth birthday she hadn't met anyone, male or female, educated or ignorant, young or old, who knew so little about 'Ndrangheta. She had done well at school, had been to college, but had never lived outside Calabria. Everyone knew of the 'Ndrangheta and its ability to destroy. No one she knew was ignorant of it: to explain anything about the 'Ndrangheta, other than at a comic-book level, was beyond her. She reflected. To travel as he had – away from Berlin and from the security of a job he should be returning to the next morning – was the mark of an innocent or a fool. But there had been, she acknowledged, something honest and clean in his ambition. The ambition of an imbecile?

The streetlights were dim. There was a glimmer behind the door, but the upstairs window was dark. She did not plan to give him a tour. The cruise boats came into Catania, across the strait, and Naples. They sailed past Archi through the narrow point where the Scylla and Charybdis myth had originated. Few tourists visited Calabria and needed guiding. She would not have known how to go about it.

If it had not been for the moon she would not have seen the high rubbish pile outside the doorway. Men loitered across the street, which stank: it was now the fourth week that the refuse carts had been on strike in her parents' area. It was ingrained in her: in Archi there were always men on street corners who watched. In daylight and at night, men watched to see who came and went.

She rang the bell. They would be asleep – they had to be up early to get to work, driving the courier van across the strait, in Messina, or cleaning a local hotel. She would not show him either of the de Stefano villas, with the high walls around them, or the modern church where the body of Paolo de Stefano had been greeted by the priests in a way that would have graced a head of state. Thousands had gathered to watch the coffin arrive, drawn by eight coal-black horses; he had been killed – without dignity – in a drive-by shooting. She would not show him the social centre, expensively built and never used: the 'Ndrangheta would not tolerate a government programme that in any way violated their control. They had put horses into the grounds and the buildings stood derelict. She would not show him the prime locations of the *faida*: the street corners where the great feud had claimed the lives of the most powerful families' blood relations. She would not show him the filth and decay, where hope had died – her hope. A window opened above her.

She called up to her father, told him what she wanted. She heard her mother's voice, no warmth in it – they had given her the opportunity and she had not taken it. She was still there, wasted, and even the dream had died. Her father held the key away from the window and dropped it.

Jago caught it.

She called up again. Her father shuffled away and her mother came to the window and hung out a towel, big and pink. The wind whipped it and she let it go. Consolata snatched it before it hit the pavement. The window was closed.

He handed her the key. Consolata thought he would serve a purpose. She knew the village on the far side of the Aspromonte mountains, and the name of the *padrino*. In fact, she knew most of the names in Calabria because a police map had been donated to the anti-racket protesters; it had listed the location of each family with the name of its head. Some were now out of date, but this one was still relevant. The *padrino* was at large, as was his grandson, who would succeed him. She knew from that map where the family's principal villa was, and the homes of their relatives.

They walked to her parents' car. It was the best they could afford, a Fiat 500, nine years old, with many thousands of kilometres on the clock.

She would take him there, but first she would learn more about him. It would be necessary to lose inhibitions. She was confident she knew what was correct, what was needed from him. He had not asked what action she had taken, as a campaigner and voice of protest, to rouse the fury of the gangs. She could only have told him that they did not know her name. The car was at the back of the block.

She would drive. They went north, close to the sea, and soon were on the great highway, which the birdwatcher had described as the milch-cow of the Mafia. Excitement gripped her. She tossed aside inhibition. She would play a part in the creation of chaos. He needed her help. When it was done, whatever it was, it would have her handprint on it. She felt a flush of pride. Of course he was a fool – what else could he be?

She asked him about his past.

Jago did not think she was truly interested, but if they talked about his youth, his studying and his breakthrough job, he would not be able to interrogate her. When he tried, she deflected him.

He spoke of Canning Town, his mother, cul-de-sacs with violent histories – flowers laid on anniversaries – and his school.

'Are we going to the village tonight?'

He spoke of a school that commemorated martyrs, men of faith, the inspiration of a teacher and the influence of a captain of finance.

'Whether it matters or not, Consolata – that's a beautiful name – I don't know what I'm going to do. I'll get there, and hope for an opportunity. What will it be like? I'll find out when I'm there, then work out what's possible. Something to hurt and make them angry . . .'

He talked of university, a useful course, ambition growing, not knowing why the captain of finance had selected him, whether he had salved a fat cat's conscience or encountered a Samaritan.

'Marcantonio was strutting about, arrogant. If I can knock him off balance, he'll be humiliated. Can't ask for more than that. Can I get close to him?'

He talked about his first job, and supposed that work in this part of Italy was baking pizza, sweeping streets, pushing paper in a town hall or serving in a shop. He talked about the City, what he did there and how opportunities came on a conveyor-belt, then about the Berlin transfer because he had been marked out for fast-tracking.

He coughed. 'I know what I want to do – and I'm frightened. Sort of beyond my experience.'

Her hand came off the wheel, and found his. She never looked at him – kept her eyes on the road. When vehicles drove towards them, he saw in the headlights that her face was calm. The hand was there to comfort him, did its job, then went back to the wheel. There was a great lit area to their left and across the bay, endless high lights, and he saw the dark shapes of heavy ships.

'What's that?'

'The port of Gioia Tauro.'

'It's huge.'

'The biggest in the Mediterranean. The life blood of southern Italy.'

'What industry does it support? Is it export primarily?'

Again her laughter, brittle. 'It's for import. It keeps this part of Italy alive. It's the chokepoint for the European cocaine trade. Jago, some 80 per cent of all cocaine in Europe comes through this port. We are talking not in kilos but in tons, not millions of euros but billions. To keep the trade flourishing the 'Ndrangheta must employ many thousands of men. Where you are going there is a small family, not unimportant but of minor influence. Marcantonio is old enough to cut a girl's face but not old enough to be a prominent player. We talk about "winning". A boy, not old enough to shave each day, is angry because a car is damaged. Creating rage – is that "winning"? I repeat what I said to you. They do not know who I am, so I do not criticise you, I help you.'

She turned off the highway. The window was down and he smelt the sea and heard the wind. The little car chugged towards a small town, and the moon made silver lines on the rippling water.

Consolata said, 'I think, Jago, you smell. Do not be frightened. And I also smell. Each time they make you frightened, it is their victory. We cannot smell and go to war.'

Fred stood outside the camper, and smoked his pipe. He could hear his wife's rhythmic breathing. The smoke broke the scent of the sea. He was among the dunes and could feel the wind and see the small navigation lights of a freighter in the Baltic's lanes.

He was in a good place to achieve what all older police officers found necessary: purging his memories. He went through them, analysed them, took the failures and gave himself no credit for successes. The corralling of a group of Albanian cigarette smugglers, operating in Hohenschönhausen . . . The identification of a Ukrainian bank-robbery team, targeting branches in the Treptow area, shots exchanged at the arrests . . . And – more recently – the delicate investigation he had headed in which two local politicians had been on a monthly wage from a Camorra group and peddling the contracts for the building of three new schools in Reinickendorf

. . . Each of those in the last four years had been a success, but he did not consider them while he smoked in the darkness and silence. He was drawn to failure. He was, his wife said, a 'miserable crow of a man'.

Failure haunted him. A four-month-long operation to intercept a shipment of Moldovan children being brought to Berlin for paedophiles: the van was tracked from the Czech border and north through Erfurt and Halle; the operation had been close-guarded by the KrimPol in the capital, and the van had been lost among a confusion of roadworks short of Potsdam. It had disappeared. That had hurt, as had an arrest request from Palermo for a Mafia fugitive holed up in Siemensstadt; the building had been under surveillance and magistrates had queried the warrant the Italians had issued. The Sicilian was required to answer three counts of murder: the wife, father and child of an informer. Would the informer give evidence against a prominent gang leader after three killings in his family? The killer should have rotted in a high-security Italian prison, but the magistrates had rejected the warrant and an opportunity was lost. That was failure.

More recent failure: in the week he had just escaped from a young man had reported extortion. Fred had made a few calls, and put together a little profile. No action had been taken although a girl had been scarred hideously – perhaps because his focus had been on a weekend in Mecklenburg-Vorpommern.

She slept; he watched the shore. A principle: consequences ruled and clocks could not be wound back. He had failed that girl and doubted he could put it right. Leaving open his laptop was poor recompense for failure.

They'd set off for home in the late afternoon. The past gave no second chances. He might take another look at the matter, but doubted it.

Carlo was on a bench behind Sandy's greenhouse, where her tomatoes ripened. A spit of rain was in the air but he wore only pyjamas, with an anorak round his shoulders. He smoked, felt empty. The hope that he could sit in the darkness unnoticed was daft. Any time he tried it, the dogs were roused. Two were with him; others would have woken her.

She came silently. A whispered question: 'Who said and did what? Why?'

He had never had been sure what role he played in Sandy's life: not intellectual, not financial security. He was as useful as an old waxed coat. Carlo said, 'The woman who spoke to us at Dooley gave us the usual pep talk. There'll be no new money, no new people, no new kit, but they're all unimportant because "You make a difference." It's simply untrue. I know it, and if she doesn't she's a fool.'

'Does it matter?'

'I suppose it does – lies count.'

'You have to believe.'

'It was a lie, that we make a difference.'

'Then you're wasting your time. Perhaps it's the moment to step aside. Leave it to others.'

'I can't. Other than you, it's all I have.'

'Carlo, if you, with your savvy, can't keep faith with it, who will?'

'The youngsters treat it like it's a duty, a vocation.'

'You must believe you can make a difference.'

'I have to try.'

She left him, and the dogs followed her. He lit another cigarette. Kind words from her, but he couldn't imagine that an individual might 'make a difference'. That wasn't life as he knew it – as he had seen it. Plenty trying, all failing. As he laughed sharply to himself, he saw steam rising. A man had opened his flies, a battle raging around him, and pissed on the slots into the water-cooling system around the barrel of a Vickers machine-gun. He might have had his pecker shot off, but he was keeping the barrel cool enough for the weapon to go on firing. He loved it – the importance of the little man who had pissed to keep the defensive line intact and wouldn't get a medal or a mention in despatches. Carlo's sort of man. He had been in Rome when a junior Treasury minister had swanned through and asked Carlo whether he felt his work was sufficiently valued. He had probably asked the same question fifty times on that tour. He'd told her about the value of the man who pissed on a machine-gun to keep the barrel cool, then added, 'Everyone has worth, not just the glory boys. He was that sort of man.' The minister, a smart young woman, had blushed and turned on her heel. He'd skipped the ambassador's reception for her that evening – he'd been at his desk, working.

Bent Horrocks was beside the water. She'd wanted to talk; he hadn't. When she wanted to, and he didn't, she'd sulk. Might sulk too much one day. He sat on the cold concrete of a wall that enclosed a small garden feature. It was five hours till Jack would pick him up, but he was wearing his suit. His shirt and tie were impeccable, and he had on the cufflinks Trace had bought him for his birthday, with his money. His shoes were polished. He would travel as an anonymous businessman. He had been to Spain, years before, done cigarettes there, had thought the place 'leaky' and felt his security was compromised. He had not been abroad, looking for contacts, in years. He questioned his position, let it revolve on a flywheel in his head. He could hear distant traffic but the area around the block was pedestrian. The last of the drinkers were going home; an Afro-Caribbean man came past him with a rubbish trolley and a broom, emptied a bin and wished him well. A stranger wishing Bent Horrocks 'well'? That didn't often happen. His photo was never in the papers. He was in a few Flying Squad files but had arrangements in place that would let him know of new investigations.

He was troubled. He didn't share his anxieties with associates, with the lawyer he kept on retainer or his money-man, and certainly not with Jack, who carried his bags and did the administration, Angel or Trace. There was an Irishman in Silvertown, who seemed short of respect for him and had taken two waste-clearance contracts that Bent had regarded as his own. There was an Asian crowd in Peckham, flush with the rewards of a vodka scam – they were bringing in bootleg booze from Naples, sticking on brand labels and selling it on to corner shops. They had two clubs now within spitting distance of premises Bent owned, and were undercutting him. Troubling. . . . But before he went to war, last resort, he'd need to strengthen his powerbase.

The deal abroad would ensure it. But Bent didn't know 'abroad'. He didn't know the people from 'abroad', and didn't speak the language. What he did know was that they had cocaine, top quality, in tons. It would lift him if he did the deal, put him way above the Irish shite and the Asians. He sat on the concrete – troubled, but didn't know another way. Jack was clear on it – Jack, who was Giacomo and whose family were in Chatham, had done the outline fixing. He had said nothing could go wrong – nothing. Bent liked to have control, was nervous when it slipped away.

'Now we go to swim, Jago.'

'Swim? You sure?'

'Of course I am . . . You can swim, Jago?'

'Yes.'

In the moonlight the beach was the colour of silver, clean and without rocks. It was broken only by two open boats, for inshore fishing, that had been pulled high beyond the tide line. Even after midnight, it was the sort of place that featured in holiday brochures. They'd have called it 'quaint', 'old world' and 'unspoiled'. She had left the Fiat in a parking bay overlooking the beach. There was a sharp wind and he'd felt it when he stepped from the car, heaved himself upright and stretched. His back had cracked. She had said, in the car, that the town was Scilla – did he know the myth of Scylla and Charybdis? He didn't. Off the headland of Scilla knife-edge rocks would tear the bottom out of a boat, and Charybdis was the fearsome whirlpool that could suck boats down and swallow them. Odysseus, according to Homer, had come through the strait and had had to decide whether to go near to the whirl-pool or the rocks. He had gone towards Scilla, had thought he might lose a few sailors when tossed among the rocks but that was better than risking the whole crew and the boat in the whirlpool. He'd said, again, that he didn't know the story, but it sounded like out of the frying pan and into the fire.

Jago didn't believe that Consolata did anything by chance. He barely knew her, hadn't seen her face in daylight, had endured long silences beside her, but felt sure of her. The story she had told him was about choices. The chance of him spinning on his heel and taking transport to the north had diminished. In five hours the first of the bank's team would be at their desks, charging up their screens; in six the *FrauBoss* would be in her chair, and his place would be empty. A 'die has been cast' moment. He thought Consolata subtle and softly manipulative. She would use him as a vehicle to go where she hadn't travelled before – it was obvious to him, and he accepted it. For now it was about mutual reliance.

Music wafted to him softly over the sounds of the sea and the whip of the wind in the awnings of the cafés behind them. Jago followed her. She kicked off her shoes. So did he. The sand had a chill and there were islands of smooth shingle that they avoided. Further down the beach, towards a castle built on a rock beyond the stranded boats, a couple lay on a rug or a towel with a radio playing, the source of the music. It didn't break the mood of the beach. She walked him to the edge of the tide line, with its fringe of seaweed.

She said, 'I smell and you smell. It is necessary to be clean.'

He had swilled his face with cold water in the toilets at the airport in Rome, and he had a washbag in his holdall, but that was in the little car. The darkness gave a sort of privacy. He had learned to swim at school, splashing clumsily in a public pool. Twice he had been down to an apartment in a complex between Málaga and Marbella when he was in the City, sharing it with a gang. They'd spent time in the pool, less on the beach.

The moonlight was bright enough to prohibit modesty. She settled on a place where the sand was dry. She pulled off her coat, then her T-shirt, and bra. She undid her belt and took off her jeans and pants, then her wristwatch. The light played on her back and he saw the shape of her pelvis, the narrowness of the waist and the strong muscles at her shoulders. She turned. She had covered nothing and challenged him.

He took off his coat, sweater, shirt, vest, trainers, jeans and socks, then his watch. He hesitated.

She chuckled softly. 'If you wear them, they'll get wet and you will not be able to dry them.'

Jago dropped his pants. There was her untidy pile and his, neatly folded. Between them lay the towel.

She defined the moment, calculated, clever. She didn't run into the water, dive, surface and lie on her back to wait for him. Instead she walked into the water and waded out until the ripples were against her chest. She never looked behind her. He walked where she had, sometimes over shingle or broken shells. He joined her where the water was deeper.

Consolata had begun to wash. Her hands went from her neck, scooping water there, to her armpits and then she dipped her head under. No gasps at the cold water, no squeals. She stood and watched him. He did the same. It was a funny way to come and fight a war. She incubated his certainty and brought it to life. She eyed him, didn't turn away. A little piece of weed had snagged on her breast and she let it lie there. She was no more than a foot and a half from him. In the movie version the gap would have closed. Now she put up her arms, stretched to her full height and water dribbled off her skin. The weed was dislodged by a wave. He did the same. He couldn't read her. So close and their arms high above their heads. He didn't know whether he would make the move – as in the film – or she would. Neither did.

They hadn't touched. He wondered at what stage of the night she had choreographed the situation. It would have been after he had retorted about winning, and before they had taken the taxi to her parents' home. It would have been easy to believe she came here most weeks, with different guys, and skinny-dipped where, legend had it, Greek sailors of centuries before Christ's birth had drowned. He didn't think she had done it before. He reckoned it had been a fast decision, taken on the hoof.

She leaned forward, imperceptibly, then seemed to screw up her nose. The moonlight hit the water on her skin and hair, brighter than diamonds. She sniffed, then nodded as if she were satisfied.

Jago Browne dropped his hands. It would have been so easy to touch her, but he didn't.

'Do you want to swim?'

'I don't think so. It is time to go to work.'

Jago grimaced. She began the tramp back to the beach. It was an idyllic place, and he felt a sense of renewal. He was thought to be bright and intelligent. He was paid to look into people's faces and read their minds, whether or not they had small breasts, fine hips and skin without wrinkles. He thought he had read her now. His shyness was gone, his hesitation past. He had the certainty. It was about winning. Why had she gone to the trouble? She must have thought that the experience would challenge and harden him, take him further from what was familiar. Too bloody right. And that was important because, where he was going, nothing would be familiar.

She started to dry herself. He watched. Then, she threw him the towel and began to dress.

They turned their backs to the sea, the moonlight that dappled it, the castle high on the rock above the bay, the shuttered bars where the canopies flapped, and went to the car. They had not touched. There had been no discussion on why each needed the other in a relationship of convenience. It was recognised. No explanations, none needed. She drove up the hill towards the dark mass of the mountains where, soon, the dawn would come.

The team manager had phoned Magda. She'd left her boyfriend in the club and taken a taxi to Stresemannstrasse.

Wilhelmina knew something of her father's background. The family was prosperous and had settled in west Berlin, with a fine house in the suburbs. The business had thrived, and Magda's father's past occupation had been erased, almost. He had served in the State Security Service, had risen to warrant officer in the political police and headed a small team responsible for the internal security of the Democratic Republic. On a frozen December morning in 1989, he had dumped his uniform, abandoned his flat, crossed the Wall with his family, then taken a train to the Tegel district on the other side of Berlin and had not looked back. Before he had gone into business, he had burgled and bugged his way the length and breadth of the former East Germany. The first time Magda had lost the key to her school locker, she had called home in a panic and been told what to do. Once, when a filing cabinet at the bank jammed, she had shown her talent.

The Englishman, Jago Browne, had long intrigued and attracted her, but he had always declined her invitations. She had sensed crisis in the air, and she was the last resort before the police were called. If a bank employee was 'missing' and worked in a department with knowledge of wealthy investors' affairs, the situation was serious. She'd heard the edge in Wilhelmina's voice: no panic yet, but it wasn't far away. The outer door was a challenge, but she'd managed it. The inner door, leading into the apartment, was easier.

So neat, so tidy, so soulless. The two rooms, the bathroom and kitchen, she thought, had been cleaned specifically, and the occupant would not be back in the morning.

It was child's play to Magda, no need to call her father. A notepad beside the telephone. A clean sheet uppermost.

She did not need to scatter black powder from a printer toner on the top sheet of the pad. She crouched, tilted her head, let her auburn hair flop over her face and read. She phoned, even though it was past three in the morning. 'Wilhelmina? He was in touch with a travel agent by phone, one on Friedrichstrasse. He bought an economy ticket, via Rome, to Lamezia Terme, which is in Calabria, southern Italy. Lamezia is the final destination. It was a one-way ticket. There is no indication of a hotel booking, or that he called ahead to arrange to be met by friends. Didn't he intervene in a fight among Italians? You have enough, Wilhelmina?'

'I think so.'

'May I suggest . . .'

'You may.'

'I apologise, but it is a police matter. The client list, the portfolios, the one-way ticket, the brawl in the street . . . it is for the police.' Magda owed Jago Browne nothing: he had deflected her. He could sink or swim: it wasn't her problem. The bank's client security was paramount.

She drove and she collected. Between stops, where she picked up what she wanted, Consolata talked. She told him the history of the 'Ndrangheta movement – the word came from the old Greek dialect of the peninsula – of the great military drives of the nineteenth century to eradicate the brigands, the ferocity of the Napoleonic generals, the brutality of executions, and the survival of hard, ruthless men in the mountains. She explained it all, Mussolini's failed attempts to combat the threat, then the indifference of the American occupiers. Even Rome had tried at the end of the last century. Too late, and now it was endemic. They climbed high, leaving the coast behind.

A collection of small homes were built into a rock face, and the headlights of the Fiat 500 captured a line of washing, perhaps done that evening. It was a clear night and there would be no frost. He would not have seen the heavy bottle-green trousers pegged to a line in front of one house. She was gone only moments from the car, and whacked them into his lap. After history came geography. The great families of Reggio Calabria, Archi, Gioia Tauro and Rosarno lived on the Tyrrhenian Sea; family groups from San Luca, Plati and Locri were on the Ionian. The Aspromonte mountains – from which the 'second coming' of the 'Ndrangheta had appeared, then the wisdom of investing in the cocaine market – separated them.

Higher, where the air was cold and mist had gathered between the trees, there was a woodman's hut with a decent padlock. She stopped, rummaged under the back seat for a toolbox, took a tyre lever and broke the lock. She found a camouflage coat, a forestry warden's, and a pair of heavy boots.

After geography came economics, the science of money-laundering and clean investment with washed funds, the creation of legitimate business where taxes were paid and respectability purchased.

She drove through the dark and hammered the detail at him.

Politics was about making contact with men of political ambition, national and regional, and insinuation into the secretive world of freemasonry, from which came influence and contracts for infra-structure development. After politics, there was law – or its violation. Discipline was enforced with extreme violence and rumour, which ruined a man's marriage and estranged his children. Then, a sort of anthropology: the development of the family and alliances with relatives. His head reeled, but his certainty was solid.

Silence. There was a camp site. Jago recognised the pennants on poles driven into the ground. The kids would be Scouts. Their fire had almost died, but the ground sheets had been hung on a line to freshen. She took only one.

She didn't smile, didn't seem either to congratulate herself on her acquisitions or feel the need to apologise for her thefts. Jago's English master had read aloud *The Jackdaw of Rheims*, about a bird that had stolen a cleric's ring. There was no traffic, no police or *carabinieri* roadblocks, but once a deer broke cover and bounded across in front of them. He thought she was bored with talking about organised crime.

'Jago, I give you a final opportunity.'

'To do what?'

'I can turn round, leave you at a bus station and in a few hours there will be a connection to Lamezia. No one will know where you have been, what you have walked away from. Where you are going and what you try to do – if you fail, if they catch you . . .'

'Consolata . . .'

'. . . they will kill you, strangle you, bury you. Jago, you under-stand that?'

He nodded. They climbed higher. The moon was behind them and the beach forgotten. He was there because he had stayed to watch a spider trap and kill a fly. He shivered. If he had turned round, been at the bank late but before lunch, he couldn't have lived with himself. A simple question floated in his mind: why had she not taken the lead on the beach? He knew the answer: she was a camp follower. She had never crossed a street to intervene, stumbling, outside a pizzeria. Useful, though? Yes.

7

Dawn broke: a tinge of grey in the skies that hovered over the tips of the pines. They were on steep roads that zigzagged around rock bluffs.

She talked, gave staccato information. There had been small-holdings, in village clusters, behind them. She'd pointed out the olive groves, where the harvest was almost ready, goats grazed, and sheep, cows and pigs were corralled. It was the world of peasants, Jago thought. He had seen nothing like it in England or in the few parts of Germany he knew, or on his brief trips to Spain. Dim lights burned in the houses. The work would have broken backs when the terrace fields were made and the retaining walls built to hold the soil, all done with muscle and sweat.

She wrestled with the wheel of the little car to get round the hairpins, and he reckoned she talked on so that he wouldn't chicken out. It would have been easy to do so – 'Excuse me, thanks for everything but I should be getting to the airport. This seemed a good idea twenty-four hours ago, not now. Somebody told me to get a life, move on and forget an everyday story of pizza-bar folk. You've been good company, but I have to get back to the real world of clients, their portfolios, and my bonus at the end of the year.' She kept talking – her way of focusing him on what lay ahead.

She stopped by a rough concrete shrine two or three feet across and the same in height, with a roof of clay tiles to keep the weather off the interior. There was no figure of the Virgin, but a sealed photograph of a serious young man, called Romeo, who had a sharp haircut and wore a dark jacket, white shirt and neutral tie.

His widow and his family had built the shrine. There were plastic flowers with the picture. It was here that he had been shot dead. She said that he was part of one family and had been killed by 'men of honour' of another family in one of the feuds that had split the 'Ndrangheta. Jago thought Consolata needed him as much as he needed her. She was dedicated to her work behind the combat lines, while he was governed by impulse. He was not allowed to brood or weaken. She spoke good enough English, had a dry sense of humour, and tried to interest him.

The second stop, higher up the road, was at a German-built machine-gun bunker. It had been constructed with expertise, reinforced concrete slit trenches leading down from a command post to the forward position where some poor bastard would have been holed up to await the arrival of UK or Canadian troops. The defenders had withdrawn and gone north. The car strained against the steepness of the road, and the light grew steadily.

One more stop. If he had complained she would have listened. A high plateau, a flattened chain-link fence, a concrete building – the place had been systematically wrecked. There were deep bunkers, concrete foundations and heaps of rubble. It had been a Cold War listening point, she said. There might also have been long-range missiles there, with targets beyond the Iron Curtain; they might have had nuclear warheads. Jago wondered how it would have been for the military there. He didn't know many Americans, but he imagined them marooned in these mountains, with a cinema and a PX shop to keep them sane, the quiet broken by their radios and Elvis Presley belting out over the emptiness. Lonely, maybe nervous, and isolated.

There was a wooden building near the summit; its windows were shuttered and the gravel car park was empty; she said it was for the use of forestry wardens. She told him local people despised them and the restrictions they brought with them. A wolf had been shot and its carcass hung in front of their shed. It was a protected animal, and its killing was a sign of indifference to authority. She spoke of the French general, Charles Antoine Manhès, and the villagers he had hanged in an attempt to subdue the mountain people. He had failed. Later in the morning, she said, the lay-bys along the road would be full as the elderly came with big baskets and searched among the forest trees for mushrooms and other fungus. She showed him a place where a great meeting of the heads of families had been held but the police had scattered them: the work of an informer, a *soffiato*. The word derived from *soffiata*, meaning 'the whisper of the wind'. 'Aspromonte', she said, came either from the Greek, for 'white mountain' or the Latin, which, loosely, meant 'mean, bitter or brutal mountain'. It was there that kidnap victims were brought – taken in the north, sold on, driven ever further south, kept in conditions of appalling barbarity while their freedom was negotiated.' She showed no emotion.

The light grew. There was nothing gentle about her face, nothing sleek about her hair, which was a messy chaos of naturally blonde strands, and nothing insignificant about her sharp-angled nose, her mouth, full lips and teeth. They had peaked a summit and she drove faster down the hill. There was a first glimpse of the sun across the sea and beyond the black outlines, ragged and sharp, of the mountains' lesser peaks. At last, now, she was quiet.

Her phone screen showed the crabbed lines of roads. One went close to a winking red point. A download from the group she was with – confidential to the leader but she'd hacked into it: the locations of the leading families' principal homes. She'd grimaced as she'd told him that Bernardo Cancello was fortunate to have been allocated that status along with the de Stefanos, the Pesches, Condellos, Pelles and Miromallis. What would Jago do? Wait and see, take a look. Enough? Perhaps and perhaps not. He'd do what he could.

She swore. The road was blocked. A boy drove goats. Dogs ran among them and they stampeded. The boy cursed at her for frightening his animals and Jago smelt the acrid scent of the tyres, then the livestock pressed against his door. She went on, bundling the goats aside. Behind him, on the small bucket seat, were the clothing and the ground sheet she had stolen. She would want the cover of darkness and shadows, not the brightness of sunshine. He had nothing sensible to say.

In less than an hour the first of the team would arrive at the bank, where his life had been nailed down. Around him there was only desperate, cruel country, rocks, sharp stones, gorges, tumbled boulders, then lights, far ahead.

Stefano, a shrewd old bird for all his image as a helpless and limited buffoon, had reversed the City-Van to the back door, which led into the kitchen. He had unloaded some baskets, vegetable trays and firewood, then Bernardo had slipped from the cover of the doorway into the back. He had a large foam cushion to sit on. Marcantonio was with him.

Stefano drove. Bernardo reflected on the meeting ahead of him. His grandson yawned. Bernardo did not know which girl's bed the boy had graced, whether he had been into the village or had gone as far as Locri to find company. He wondered where Marcantonio would find a wife. He had discussed it with Mamma – he would not make a decision based on her opinions, but would consider her suggestions as to who would be suitable. Mamma would know which families had a history of fertile women, and which were plagued with miscarriages or deformities through breeding too close to the blood line. His own opinion would be based on matters of finance and power, areas of influence and control of territory. There were families in Locri and Siderno, and one at Brancaleone with daughters, but serious negotiation had not begun. The windows at the back of the City-Van were dusty but Stefano had drawn a small smiley face in one so that Bernardo could see out.

The boy yawned again. God, had he been at it all night? It was a long time since Bernardo had been his age. In his day, a girl would fight tooth and nail to preserve her virginity. Now she would drop her knickers in exchange for a mandarin or a ripe lemon. He strained to see through the window. They passed the house where the shutters were always closed. He kept that traitor's family there as an example. They existed in a living hell, as he intended. He saw them sometimes as they trudged, isolated and ignored, through the village. They had no money, no friends, and even the priest did not visit. Maybe they would watch television that day.

Stefano drove out of the village and pulled into an abandoned quarry.

A kid on a scooter waited there.

The kid knew him, was bright-eyed and eager to please him. He knew Stefano and helped him clean engines, learning how they worked. The boy knew Marcantonio, too, and had joined the school at Locri when Marcantonio was leaving. The kid knew them better than he knew his own father, who was serving the twelfth year of twenty after conviction for murder: Bernardo had ordered the killing. The height of the kid's ambition was to become a *giovane d'onore*, 'honoured youth', rise to *picciotto* and gain the family's trust. He had a Vespa, the Piaggio model, 124cc engine. It was silver, his pride and joy, and had cost more than two thousand euros. The kid waved to them: cheeky, cocky and proud to be close to them. The family's trust showed in the cost of the scooter, paid for by Bernardo, which was the envy of other village boys. He might marry into the fringes of the extended family. The kid was important, and Bernardo, with Stefano driving, went nowhere without him.

Stefano told the kid where they would go, which route they should take. The kid had a mobile phone in his jacket pocket and waved it at them. Then Stefano rifled in a bag at his feet and peered through his spectacles at a dozen different mobile phones, their distinguishing covers, and frowned as he remembered which one he needed. He concentrated, selected and tossed it into Marcantonio's lap. It was switched on. The kid was told that the phone was live.

They went in humble transport to meet a man with whom the final decisions would be taken on the purchase of a half-ton of pure cocaine. They would also discuss the transshipment of Syrian exiles inside the EU. The Arabs would be provided with well-forged documentation. It was good that he had brought his grandson: the boy's presence would show that Bernardo's dynasty had a future. The scooter would travel at a little under forty kilometres an hour, and the gap between them would be two kilometres. The kid's phone was live, the number set. He would have to press a single button to indicate that a *carabinieri* or *polizia* roadblock was in place. They would pass through a remote area of countryside. On some roads there would be interference or a weak signal, but they would avoid them.

He was uncomfortable in the back but accepted the hardship. The road surface was poor and the cushion gave him only limited protection from the ruts. A few more days, and he would be able to ride again in the front. He would know that a special investigation on him was closed, the file consigned to a cupboard, the spotlight moved elsewhere. With Stefano, he would go to the open market in Locri and to Brancaleone. He would sit in the mountains where his father used to go, while Mamma and Stefano searched for mushrooms. He would plan and . . . There was much to look forward to.

In truth, Bernardo wanted little. They had a decent television but not an exceptional one, a decent kitchen, but not from one of the magazines that Annunziata had enjoyed, and a decent bed, old and breathing family history. He had no luxury. Neither did Mamma. They lived without gold taps, jewellery, and servants, yet the family had such wealth that only Giulietta and her calculator could accurately assess it. Great riches meant little to him. The most important matter in his life, which was drifting to a close – not tomorrow but not far away – was that he could pass on what he had achieved to Marcantonio and know his legacy was in safe hands. His grandfather had done that for his father, and his father for him. Marcantonio was a good boy. He could strangle a man and kill a woman. Now he must learn more about the trade of the clans.

The light broke. The sun came low through gaps in the foothills and rose above the sea behind them, throwing long shadows.

They were late. She drove recklessly. The car was not built to negotiate mountain switchback roads and twice she had lost control. The tyres had slid and they'd skidded close to the edge. Both times, there had been a thirty-metre drop. He did not seem to react. Most would have been clinging to the top of the glove box for dear life, white-knuckled. She supposed it was 'the calm before a storm'.

She thought they had met through luck, coincidence and chance. She said to herself silently, 'When was life different?' She thought of the people she knew, who reckoned they had control over their lives. They were fools and failures. He seemed remarkable to her. She swerved to give more room to a tractor pulling a trailer of cattle fodder for the winter and drove a scooter off the road. She was on the wrong side of the road on a bend and had to heave the wheel to miss a Fiat City-Van driven by an old man, with a boy beside him, and . . . The light was coming.

Too much time on the beach at Scilla? If accused of it, she would have answered robustly: he had lost his inhibitions there; with inhibitions, where he was going, he was the walking dead – no use to man, beast or her. Consolata started to talk about covert surveillance in the mountains, relaying all she had been told by the guy in the ROS who did stake-outs. She told Jago about the basics of survival – but he would be without a firearm, a colleague, a radio, and back-up poised for fast intervention. She talked about stiffness, the cold and damp. The guy, Francesco, had not enjoyed being quizzed about intelligence gathering, but they'd had fun in the hills, playing concealment games. She'd hide, and he'd find her, or she'd hide and he'd look for but not locate her. Or he'd be on a hillside and have to move, and she'd be at an observation point and yell when she saw him. When he lost he was pissed off. She remembered everything he'd taught her, and now passed it to the Englishman: he would be going close to the house, near extreme danger, where she would not go. She helped him and he would hurt them. Then she would rejoice . . . and he was nice-looking.

If they found him close to the house then he would have to have shed every inhibition drilled into him at home and work, since he was a child. Any inhibition, failure to fight, and he was dead.

Consolata had been with him for about twelve hours but already she cared. He had not touched her in the sea or on the beach. She had never cared for a man so quickly before.

She told him everything she knew, hammered into him the detail she had learned when she was with that guy. She remembered her parents' shock when the shop and the business were taken from them, their humiliation. They'd had no one to turn to in Archi. No wonder she hated the families.

She drove him to a place that the map on her phone indicated could be a drop-off point. The light rose.

She was a manager.

Wilhelmina, as an employee with status, working for a prestigious bank, could demand attention – and did.

She was put on hold, but only briefly. A middle-ranking official at police headquarters on the Platz der Luftbrücke, where memories of the Berlin airlift were celebrated, had contacted the station on Bismarckstrasse, talked with the KrimPol unit there, ascertained the complaint that Jago Browne had made, concerning assault and extortion, determined who had fielded the complaint and what action had been taken. They had to consider the importance of the known facts when set against the – out of character – disappearance of the individual, and his apparent journey to Calabria. The official pleaded for a few more moments of her time.

'I can refer this to one of my bank's vice presidents, who would expect to speak to an officer of higher rank than yours. Your name would feature in any such conversation.'

That was not necessary, she was assured. It was always a pleasure to co-operate with the banking industry. Her aggression was fuelled by nerves. She knew of the crime networks based in the extreme south of Italy, the corruption, the danger of extreme violence. She did not know what had been downloaded, what confidentiality was compromised. Her fingers drummed on her desk.

An answer. Seitz, an investigator in the KrimPol unit at Bismarckstrasse, had been recalled from his weekend vacation and would visit her by midday. The official hoped that was satisfactory. He was pleased to have been of service. She accepted what she was told. She had set a train in motion, did not know where the journey would end but felt confident that her back was covered.

His empty seat intrigued her. Magda had mentioned how little the apartment had told of its tenant. Wilhelmina had left her children with her neighbour because her husband was abroad. She wasn't thinking of the kids, or the chaos at home after the birthday party, or the state of her marriage, but was gazing at Jago Browne's seat. Where was he? And why was he there? She gripped a pencil between her fingers, bank issue, twisted – and broke it.

A phone call. Confidences.

Magda said, 'It's a police matter now. He's fucked.'

Elke said, 'Finished, so I'll never know.'

'You didn't go out with him?'

'Not for want of trying.'

'Nor me. I put a Post-it on his screen. Nothing happened.'

'We weren't grand enough.'

'I think he would have done well with Wilhelmina. I reckon she was ready for him.'

'Bastard. He'll go through the mill now.'

'We never knew him.'

'Right. Never did – he wouldn't let us.'

It was their sacred home. His grandmother, had she been there, and his mother, would have bent the knee, kissed crucifixes and muttered prayers. They had come down the steep road, leaving the hillsides of rock and scrub high above them, and were beside a dry stream. The scooter was parked and the kid drank fruit juice.

The sacred home of the 'Ndrangheta, certainly for the clans on the eastern coast, was the shrine at Polsi, dedicated to the Madonna of the Mountains. It was regarded as holy and valued. Marcantonio had just travelled from Berlin, where there was no rubbish, no filth, no litter. This was a precious site. He saw the weeds between the cobbles, the carpet of cigarette ends, the fast-food wrappers and the booths where souvenirs were sold. Mass would be said in the morning at the church, but his grandfather and Stefano would duck their heads in sham respect at the outer door and not enter. They sidled into the shadows thrown by the early sunlight. He followed. He had been away for six months but took no liberties with his grandfather. He hung back and would come forward when called.

A guide was leading the first pilgrims of the day on a tour and told them that initial Christian recognition of Polsi's significance had come from Roger II of Sicily, in the twelfth century: he'd had three wives, ten children by them, five more from his mistresses, and had begun the veneration of the Madonna here. The guide added that there had been pagan ceremonies on the site linked to the goddess Persephone and fertility, but it was too early for the pilgrims to chuckle.

Marcantonio had been brought here a month before the killing of Annunziata, and his grandfather had taken him to a ramshackle café above the church. They had had a lunch, cooked in primitive conditions, and planned how he would deal with his aunt, then go to Germany. Nowhere in Germany, in any Italian restaurant, had he eaten such superb goat's cheese, neck of pig and stomach wall, or strawberry grapes. The woman who had cooked for them had looked hard at him, then said, 'I hope the Madonna will help you. If you touch her heart, you will come back.' That day they were not in Polsi to linger.

It was important to be there, to be seen. In days past, the principals of all the families had met at Polsi to share business, examine procedures and settle disputes. Men came from Australia, Canada, Germany, Holland and northern Italy, and followed the instructions of the elders. Years later, when he was in his early teens, men had been photographed by an undercover *carabinieri* officer, with a camera strapped to his belt and a lens hard against a fake button in his coat. The big groups no longer came. Because of undercover efforts, many had gone to gaol, but Polsi was good for small meetings.

His grandfather met two men in shadows against a wall. He gestured Marcantonio forward. Two cold faces, two forced smiles, two iron handshakes. He was looked over as if he were an unbroken horse – perhaps promising, perhaps not, perhaps good for a marriage, perhaps not. He was waved away. If his grandfather felt disappointed or annoyed at his dismissal, he did not show it. For fuck's sake, he had been up early, left the girl, had dressed and shaved, then sat in the car. Had he come all this way to be ignored? He bowed and moved back graciously, giving no hint of his irritation. Marcantonio understood the powers that existed in the mountains and did not challenge them. His time would come. His grandfather was frail, heavy on his feet, and breathed hard when climbing steps. His time would come soon.

The man had dozed and dawn rose over the gates of the city's premier public gardens.

The movement of their car alerted him. The engine was switched on and the lights of the dashboard brightened. A high performance vehicle.

He glanced into the rear-view mirror. They had seen him enough times not to need a photograph. He eased his buttocks across the seat and freed the pistol, then reached inside the compartment above his knees, with a gloved hand, for the silencer. He screwed it on fast, and cocked the weapon. Better to arm it inside the car and have the scrape suppressed by the closed windows.

The target, to the man with the pistol, seemed pathetic. He had four dogs with him, two big and two small. All had been washed and clipped. They dragged on their leashes, ran excitedly around his legs and had him tangled and stumbling. He had once been, the gunman knew, a player with a certain respect, a second cousin of the inner family, close to the *cosca* but not quite part of it. Useful but not essential. Well paid but not wealthy . . . Capable of saving himself from long imprisonment with information that had put the two brothers into the *aula bunker*, then into the isolation cells. The gunman did not reckon that the *pentito* had understood, when he had begun the 'collaboration', that funds would dry up and he would be cut adrift. He tripped over the leashes. An owner, high in the block, wouldn't tolerate him jerking the leash and wrenching the dog's neck. He was attempting to free himself. He looked as if he had slept poorly. They crossed the road, the dogs dragging him excitedly. The gloved hand reached for the car's door handle.

The dogs might be his best friends, his only friends. The gunman had no pets. The dogs he had known were those that patrolled the perimeters of the various gaols where he'd been held. These animals were pampered and exclusive. He would have liked to take their lives as well as his target's. The *pentito* was dragged into the gardens, through wide gates and down the hill. There were joggers about at this hour, cyclists and more dog people. He drew down the balaclava, eased out of the car, then reached back. His clenched fist touched the driver's. He had the weapon hidden under his coat, held tightly to it. Another *pentito*, a Sicilian, had been about to give evidence in Palermo, then had retracted. He had been debriefed by interested individuals: he had been taken to the Borghese Gardens, in Rome, by his protection team for exercise; they had seemed over familiar with the paths cutting through it, and had been on good terms with the owner of a mobile bar who served coffee and brandy in winter, ice cream in summer. A watch had been kept. This *pentito* had been spotted three days before the withdrawal of the security men. An entrepreneur had circulated the picture of the potential target. No takers in Palermo, or in Naples, but identified in Reggio Calabria from a performance on the witness stand at the *aula bunker*. Money had been paid, a date named.

The gunman let the car door swing shut, but not fasten. The dogs rambled at the extent of their retractable leads and were in the grass near to the statue of King Umberto I. The gunman had little idea of the historic significance of the king, but had noted that the target used the same bench each day. He could have been shot many times over, but this was the given date. He came from behind. For the first time he reached to his belt and checked the knife. His instructions were specific, the reward was considerable.

He was close.

A dog growled. The other three edged back, their leads tightening as the man sat on the bench and smoked. When the dogs showed fear, he would have known. The gunman thought he would have expected him and was unlikely to bolt. The target did not move. The gunman fired into the back of the head and blood spurted. There was an explosion of skin, bone and matter from the exit hole. The target toppled. His hand let go of the leashes and the dogs scampered away. A cyclist watched but was fifty metres away, and two joggers seemed to stop in mid-stride, but they were more than a hundred metres from him. The target lay on his side across the bench.

He came to the front of the bench, slid the pistol into his pocket and released the knife from his belt. He crouched over the man, groped below the belt and found the zip. His movement was clumsy because of the gloves. He undid the trousers, reached inside and exposed the man. He used the knife. Firm incisions, no hesitation. The mouth was conveniently open. He tilted the head a little, then forced penis and testicles into the mouth, hard enough for them to lodge in the throat. Sometimes banknotes were used, but he thought this sent a better message – and it was better paid.

He did not run. At the gate, he pushed up the balaclava. He heard no shouts behind him. The chance of intervention by a member of the public was small. He did not look back, did not need to. His driver would have taken him well clear of the Borghese by the time the sirens blared. He had done as he had been told.

She'd spun the wheel, let the tyres skid, then stamped on the brake. There was an old shed, stone walls and a sagging roof, space for her to inch into, but no door. It was near to the road, fifteen paces along a track with old wheel indents and grass growing. She would be there just moments – for the last two kilometres she'd had a hand locked on her phone and the map. Sometimes Jago's hand had been steering, and she was then using her free one to flick around the gears.

'It's the best I can do.'

He took a deep breath. Consolata reached behind him and grabbed the kit. He already had the boots on, not a bad fit. She had the ground sheet and the coat, then scampered to the back, opened the boot and rooted in a toolbox. She brought out a penknife, a three-foot-long tyre iron, a small first-aid kit, a water bottle and a pocket torch, then slammed the lid. There was chocolate in her pocket, a fancy bar – Jago thought it might have been her dinner.

He clenched his fist. She looked into his face. He reckoned he saw happiness. Her fist smacked into his. They crossed the road. She glanced at the phone screen, seemed to line herself up, then plunged down a slope.

It was almost a helter-skelter. She was lighter than him, bounced on rocks and evaded the tree trunks he careered into. It might have been a goat trail, but the marks and indentations were clear to follow. They would be overlooking the top end of the village. Consolata stopped. He cannoned into her. Jago wasn't sure if he could see, far below, the colours of clay roof tiles. She pointed, jabbed her finger. Funny old life – different worries now from what he usually had on board: the *FrauBoss*, whether a potential client would switch to them if the portfolio value might increase by 7.5 per cent, the bonus and the holidays chart. He didn't want her to leave him.

She caught his arm. 'This is the place,' she whispered.

'Yes.'

'Where I'll come in forty-eight hours, twenty-four if it is possible, so you can eat and drink.'

'Yes.'

'Food, water, or to take you out.'

'Of course.'

'Hurt them.'

'That's what I came for. It was good that we met.'

She pointed down the slope. He could barely see a way, at best a scramble, at worst a fall, with rocks to block him. But he heard, very faintly, dogs barking. A kiss? No. A handshake? No. He had the ground sheet, the coat, the water bottle, and her chocolate was in his pocket, the tyre iron in his belt. He looked down to see where his first step should be, then back to make sure he remembered the place, and she was gone. He heard a twig break and a rustle of leaves, then nothing. He had made a bed and had better now think of lying on it. He would have liked to touch her face, run his finger again where a scar might have been. Jago bit his lip. The quiet settled about him, and the aloneness. He took the first step, then another, clung to a small birch and allowed it to sag while he slid over a vertical rock face. He let it spring back, and found another to latch to.

He went on down, and the barking of the dogs was sharper.

'What was that?'

'What? Where?'

Fabio had been dozing, and Ciccio shook him. The night's cold was in their bones and they were hungry. Ciccio gripped Fabio's shoulder. He peered forward, and the wall of quiet bounced back at him.

Fabio said, 'We have twenty-two scorpion flies in the jar, all dead. Twenty-two is enough. Did you see another?'

'Fuck you.'

'What's for breakfast?'

'Are you dead? Didn't you see?'

'I'd like the fruit candy and the bread. I want to piss and—'

Ciccio hit him on the back of the head, hard.

'What did you see?'

'A man passed us. Went on down towards the Bravo Charlie house.'

'Description?'

'I think camouflage clothing. I saw him for two, three seconds, then he was gone. What does that tell us?'

Fabio didn't answer. Both men were alert, gazing down at what little of the house they could see. Nothing was different. They heard only the barking of the dogs, then the chugging of the City-Van, which backed close to the kitchen door. Marcantonio was there, and Stefano had driven.

'They can't link it, can they?' Fabio said. 'The wife is screwing the boyfriend because Article 41*bis* has left her short. The boyfriend is dead. The woman has disappeared, but it will be *lupara bianca*, of course. What else? Her husband is in gaol. Her father-in-law is too old. The boy is capable. But the prosecutor has no evidence against him, and we can't identify the presence of the old man. What does it add up to?'

'That we go somewhere else next week to look for scorpion flies.'

'I need a piss.'

Ciccio murmured. 'Go ahead, and don't spill it. I don't know what I saw. No weapon.'

He had been up from before first light. The prosecutor lived in a respected quarter of Reggio, in a house that was like most others in the street – four bedrooms, two bathrooms, an office downstairs, a front garden laid out as a labour-saving patio, another patio at the back, with an unsatisfactory view of distant hills and the start of the Aspromonte range. His home was different from the others around it because of an ugly concrete wall, crudely rendered, that surrounded it. The gates at the front were higher than an eyeline.

A peculiar life. When he went to work he was low in the back of the armoured car, his escort tailing him. If he took the kids to school, it was the same escort and protection. If his wife did it, she went alone. Always, when he was at home, the car was outside and two of the guards were in it. Always, the rest of the team were in the wooden hut at the back. He lived with them, as did his wife and children.

For what? For the future of Scorpion Fly. From dawn, he had sat at his desk. He had rung three colleagues, two men and the third was the new female star at the Palace of Justice.

Poison had dripped into his ear.

One of the men had refused to speak on his behalf about surveillance resources and deployment extension, had described his efforts as feeble and said a conclusion was overdue in the investigation into that 'minor' family. The second man had seemed to wring his hands at the injustice of such a situation, then countered: 'The rest of us are worthless. We acknowledge the importance of what you're doing, my friend, but we would be grateful for the return of the resources when you have no further need of them.'

The woman had talked to him, at length, about investigations she was carrying out into the activities of the Strangio, Nirta, Pelle and Votari families, all of San Luca. Would he care to send her a paper in which he explained why the disappearance and probable murder of the wife of a comparatively insignificant criminal from a family of secondary importance should outweigh her efforts in bringing charges against the leading clans in the hierarchy of the 'Ndrangheta? She asked if he had managed to catch her TV appearance on Rai Uno the previous week, and her emphasis on the bringing to justice of those whose arrests 'mattered' in the war.

A *carabinieri* colonel had told him, 'My hands are tied. It isn't my decision.' A Squadra Mobile officer had seemed to shrug helplessly and had confessed, 'If I had men, Dottore, with the necessary skills, I would task them for you. I don't so. I can't help.'

Each looked to their own future. His was bleak.

It was stubbornness that had caused him to fight his corner, push harder than he might otherwise have done, and he had thought this a soft target after the evidence laid by a turncoat. The opportunity to bring down an entire family was appealing, not merely to lop the branches of the tree but to fell the whole thing. He gazed out of his window, through the bulletproof glass. Two of his escort lounged on plastic chairs and smoked. Sometimes they played basketball with his kids or chatted to his wife. If he capitulated, as his country had done in 1943 with the landing of the Allies in the south, his bodyguards would be reassigned. They would have other children to play with, other wives to talk to, other bulletproof cars to drive.

It hung by a thread, which might hold for a few more days or might not. He relied on the abilities, and dedication, of the boys on the mountain, hidden and watching. Without a sighting the poison of colleagues would kill him. An irony, a harsh one, was that the scorpion fly only simulated a killer. His phone rang.

He snatched it up, a drowning man gripping a straw. He was told of a killing in Rome, in the Borghese Gardens, of a *pentito*, a man who had been isolated and abandoned. He listened, replaced the phone, and sat at his desk with his head lowered. He believed the family of Bernardo, *padrino*, were mocking him.

*   *   *

The family was gathered. Bernardo sat beside her. No general gifts were permitted, but the porcelain Madonna stood in front of her, and Marcantonio sat opposite. Giulietta was there and Teresa, and the smaller grandchildren, who had no mother.

Stefano did not sit with them but played a small accordion, the old music, songs of the 'Ndrangheta and the mountains. Mamma had cooked and Giulietta had helped. Teresa had fussed around them, but it was Mamma's day and she had called the shots. A small, discreet, careful celebration. One outsider only was invited to share the meal with the family: the priest. Father Demetrio sat on the far side of Bernardo, near to Giulietta, and already their heads were close. Bernardo assumed they were not discussing the Rosary, any order of service or the latest pronouncement from the Holy See: Father Demetrio had a good head for figures, had baptised all the grandchildren and had married Rocco and Domenico. Bernardo would talk to him, but later.

There was a little wine, watered for the children. Pasta with seafood was served first, then beef, chewy and on the bone, but Mamma had good teeth. She might be enjoying it, Bernardo thought, but didn't show it. When had she ever shown pleasure? When had she ever shown tenderness or grief? She was as hard as the rock of the cliffs behind the house and he doubted that she missed him when he slept in his buried bunker . . . but she was a good wife. She had never criticised him, never complained about his behaviour, especially in the days when he had made many afternoon visits to Brancaleone, and she kept a good home for him.

The mood of the gathering was triumphant. As it should have been.

And Giulietta, his conduit of news, had met a courier from the city across the mountains. She had been handed a message written with a fine nib on a single cigarette paper, which told of bitterness and division at the Palace of Justice, the weakening of a certain prosecutor's influence, and confirmed what he had heard earlier: that an investigation had run its course and had failed.

There were toasts, which Mamma acknowledged, and more toasts to the absent ones, Rocco and Domenico. The Priest's face had been suitably impassive. He had not glanced at the small children, Nando and Salvo, when their father's name was spoken.

Marcantonio praised his grandmother and received the dismissive wave of a gnarled fist. Bernardo thought the family at peace.

After the beef there was cake, a *crochette* of dried figs. Giulietta had slipped away to the first floor where she had an office – nothing kept in it was incriminating, but she dealt there with legal matters. Bernardo heard the printer. He used a BlackBerry occasionally, not since word of the investigation had been passed to him, but never a computer. He left no footprint: his daughter was his link with sophisticated modern life.

He waited for her return. Without his sons and his grandson, he had depended on her. There were cousins and nephews on the fringe of the family who fulfilled functions and had responsibilities, but if they observed him to be weakening they would close in on him. There was no place among the families for an enfeebled *padrino*. And good times lay ahead: soon Marcantonio would be at home, playing his part. There were no gifts that day, but he had prepared a small offering for Mamma that he believed she would like. By now, the family who lived behind shuttered front windows would have seen the young Indian-born deacon who assisted Father Demetrio. They would know, but would make no public sign of grief – they wouldn't dare.

Giulietta brought in the tureen of white china, not used by Mamma for years. A little frown knitted Mamma's forehead – she hadn't planned this. A sharp look at Giulietta. The lid was whipped away. Mamma peered at the photograph inside the tureen, and understood. Bernardo would have sworn that his wife *almost* smiled. It was the ANSA agency photograph, posted on the internet. The man was on the bench, slumped sideways. Blood obscured much of his face, but his mouth bulged, as if something filled it. The crotch of his trousers was dark-stained. She lifted out the photograph and took a sip of water, as if that were enough celebration for the killing of an *infame* who had damaged her family. Teresa saw it and nodded; Father Demetrio was impassive. The children were not shown it, but Marcantonio grinned. Bernardo heard him murmur to Giulietta that he felt jealous of the man who had done it.

Mamma cackled, a crow's call, as she realised what was filling the dead man's mouth. The music was louder, perfect for the day, and power had been asserted.

'I wouldn't question your ability to handle banking matters so please don't question my professionalism as a police officer.'

She was talking to him as if he were a hotel porter. What had Fred Seitz done? What had he not done? How would Jago Browne, on a year's exchange from London, know that a brawl in the street, and the subsequent disfiguring attack on a young woman, involved crime families in the Italian region of Calabria? She might have sensed weakness in his posture, detected bluster and evasion, but could not have proved it. His temper had risen because his job hung on a laptop left open when he had gone for coffee. If that were discovered, he would be out of KrimPol by the end of the weekend. His temper was exacerbated by her haughty superiority and his own vulnerability.

'You did nothing.'

'I will not answer to a civilian for my actions. More important, what has he taken?'

He was angry, too, because his weekend was wrecked. A call from a senior for him to hit the road, so he had . . . hit the road. They would already have gone through his calls on the desk phone and been into his laptop. They would have traced messages to and from *carabinieri* records, a family named and biographies passed, all done through an old network and not submitted for approval. He liked his job, and it was falling apart in his hands. There was sand in his shoes and he was dressed for the weekend. The bitch across the table was in her finery.

'Perhaps he took nothing.'

'He met you. Did you brief him on Calabria?'

An old lesson, long learned. If you're telling a lie, tell it decisively. 'I did not. That is a disgraceful, slanderous suggestion – and we're wasting time. Describe him to me.'

'He was not one of us. He's different.'

'In what way?' He thought it important that he regained partial control.

'I was uncertain of his enthusiasm for our work culture.'

'He's a bank employee. Must he live, breathe, sleep the bank?'

'You don't understand. He works for our much-admired bank. Young men and women go to great lengths to be allowed through our doors. For him, it was a privilege. Young people come as interns, *unpaid*, and are grateful for the opportunity. We safeguard our clients' money. We protect them from the turbulence of the modern financial world. It should be everything in his life and I don't think it was.'

'Please explain.'

'I can't. I find it incomprehensible that anyone should need anything away from the bank.'

He thanked her brusquely and was on his way. He did not give her a chance to regain the high ground and probe with more questions. He understood the business perfectly – he came across them; middle-class kids, comfortable, destroyed by the boredom of safety. They could have been flogging narcotics, eking out the dream of Baader-Meinhof and looking to be a 'white skin' for a Middle Eastern group. They might have been buying a handgun and holding up immigrant cafés – or have gone to kick shite out of an 'Ndrangheta family's star kid, which would be exciting – and lunacy. Much of his own life was dull, which he could handle. Responsibility for his actions weighed on him, almost crushed him. Fred Seitz was on a plane in the morning.

A call came, on a weekend afternoon.

'Yes?'

'Carlo? That my old mate?'

'Yes.' A familiar voice.

'Bagsy here.'

'What the hell do you want?' He knew Bagsy well enough, had

been on the team in Green Lanes with him. Bagsy had been promoted over him, and now ran the unit that controlled the liaison officers abroad, had looked after him during the Rome years and had signed off his expenses.

'Actually, I want you in London.'

He knew his diary, didn't need to flip it up on his phone. 'Next week I can make Wednesday – leaving drinks? Would Wednesday suit?'

'Last time I did the drive from where you are up to Custom House it took a bit over two hours. Let's say three. Custom House in three. That's today, Carlo, three from now. Bring a bag of warm-weather stuff and your passport. Cheers, Carlo.'

He was still shaking.

It was not what he had seen ahead and below that had caused a wave of near panic to engulf him. Jago couldn't hold his hands steady, and he had been in the place a few minutes more than six hours. It was a good place, the best he had seen. He had slid down a short rock face and had found it at the base. Two boulders had lodged against each other, leaving a space into which he had wriggled. He assumed that the boulders were securely together and would stand firm.

He had a view of the house. He could see, about a hundred yards away, the area for cars to turn in front of it, and one side of it, and the kitchen door. There was a vine trellis, washing hanging on the line, limp sheets, and a stone shed – he could see half of a wall, its roof and where chickens scratched. It was what he had seen on his way to this place under the twin boulders that had caused him, almost, to yell. He had seen the matriarch, the daughter who had been on the police file, the small children and their mother, the other two, who were orphaned. And, as he had known he would, he had seen Marcantonio, who sauntered in the sunshine in front of the house, smoked, scratched an armpit and smoothed his hair. Jago remembered the anger he had caused, the adrenalin rush it had given him – but he couldn't stop shaking because of the cave he had stumbled on. As if it haunted him.

8

He supposed it a house like any other, that of a peasant who had done well. How well? He couldn't tell.

He could see a building of perhaps a half-dozen bedrooms, and a patio at the front with plant pots, but they were empty. There was a portico over the front door that looked like a recent addition, and an extension to the side facing him. The portico's pillars were fresh and clean, but the side wall was still concrete blocks, short of the rendering needed to finish it. Cement was visible in the gaps round the windows on the ground floor and upstairs. Outside the kitchen door there was a row of boots and a heap of chopped wood, but his view was broken by the thickness of the vine stems on the trellis. He thought a path went up from the backyard, beyond the trellis and the washing line, but then there was a wall, solid bushes, perhaps laurel, and the shed.

Jago could see little behind him, and the views to either side of his position were restricted by rock outcrops and the trees that sprouted from sheer rock slopes. Music drifted up to him, and a murmur of voices. Marcantonio was playing football with the children at the front – it was landscaped and had been grassed but not watered so the 'pitch' was a dull ochre. There was no big car, just a Fiat van and Fiat saloon, the priest's. The daughter and daughter-in-law were at the back – they might have been taking a break from washing the dishes after the Sunday meal. The daughter-in-law was a smart, stylish woman, but the daughter was drab. He saw the matriarch again, and a handyman who carried out a bucket of vegetable peelings for the chickens.

The shake in his hands was dying.

Watching the family after their Sunday meal calmed him. Little actions that reeked of the ordinary, the occasional shouts from the football game. He had noted that Marcantonio was never successfully tackled, never lost the ball, never missed a shot on the goal. The others had sight of it only when he decided they would. The boy never looked up. His gaze never raked the rock faces behind the house.

He thought the shaking would be back during the night. What he had seen in the cave would touch him. He had found it soon after she had left him. A few steps, a scramble, a roll across a bank of moss, then the old path, grass growing on it – he thought he was the first to use it for years – and the entrance to a cave. There was a patch in front of it where there was only dried mud and worn stone. He had hesitated and considered. He could hear sounds from below him, a radio, voices and a vehicle. Was there any virtue in exploring the cleft in the rock? It might have potential as a sort of refuge. He had switched on his small torch and crawled inside.

The beam had picked up one of those small orange boxes that used to hold Kodak film. He'd lifted it up and the date was stamped on it – 1987. He had gone further in. His feet had snagged on cloth, and the torch had shown him a child's dress and small shoes with tarnished buckles, scuffed at the toe. There were blankets and two buckets, a plastic plate, several plastic cups and a candle-holder. In a recess he found a rotting mattress. He'd seen a chain – it had fine links but was strong enough to withstand the efforts of a kid to break it, and ended with an iron collar where a padlock was still fastened. The far end disappeared under the mattress. He was driven by a compulsion to know where the chain led. He pulled back the mattress and mice scampered out. He saw the staple buried in the stone – it would have been driven home with a sledgehammer. There were small socks, skimpy underwear and a pullover of fine-quality wool. He was in a den where a child, aged ten or twelve, had been chained.

He had gone back out into the light, which seemed heaven-sent after the depths of the cave. He imagined the child held there, wondered how long she had been there and how it had ended.

Jago watched the house, and the shaking ebbed. Impossible, but he tried to square a circle: a home where a sort of normality seemed unthreatening, and a cave where a child had been chained in darkness, with rats and mice, mosquitoes, cold – and fear.

He caught the movement. It was in the corner of his eye. He focused. A boy, seventeen or eighteen, slender, sallow-skinned, dark curly hair, walked along a track above and to the right of where Jago was, with three dogs. It was not a Sunday-afternoon stroll. The dogs were doing a job, scampering around him, over rocks and among trees. Often enough Jago lost them. Consolata had taken him into the water and made him wash off the smell of sweat. The dogs were thin. Their ribs and teeth showed. The boy controlled them with a thin whistle and shrill commands. He would have been a hundred feet above Jago and there were cliffs between them . . .

There was a shout from far below. A hoarse old voice. The boy called the dogs to him and started to retrace his steps, the dogs bustling around his legs. Jago reckoned that if the kid had kept going, and continued around the hillside he would have crossed, with his dogs, the line of his own descent.

He breathed hard and forgot the cave. He had a good view of the house. Jago felt calm, as if his earlier confusions were settled, as if he had signed a last will and testament. Why was he there? He knew the answer to that. What would he do? Take time to learn. He would not stampede down the hill. They would know he had been there, he promised them that. Specific action? He needed time to decide and would not be hustled: that preconceived ideas were usually rubbish was a lesson he had learned at the Bank. Learn and assimilate, they preached. Then act.

The dogs milled around the back door, and the old man who had called was gunning his van. Marcantonio's football game was over and he had slipped into the passenger seat. The boy with the dogs, recognisable by his shirt, had a crash helmet on his head now, the visor over his face. He drove away on a scooter, the van following.

Jago lay on his stomach. The shadows were longer, and the day died.

*   *   *

The investigator called from his apartment in the Moabit district and spoke to a friend who was also at home, an apartment overlooking the Ionian Sea, at the Catanzaro marina. From his time with the ROS, the GICO and the Squadra Mobile, Fred Seitz had learned that bureaucratic labyrinths were best avoided by personal and discreet contacts. He did not explain why he needed help, and would return the favour in the future. He was told the implications of a failed inquiry.

'This is the situation, Fred. For this prosecutor much rests on it, not least his prestige. The operation is called Scorpion Fly and the target is Bernardo Cancello, from the hills above Locri. He's not in the first flight but is still considered a high-value target. His two sons are in gaol – they'll be old men when they're freed. He has a grandson, Marcantonio, who will succeed him. The aim of the investigation was to arrest the target – Bravo Charlie to us – and cut down the family. I don't know how much evidence can be laid against him, but the immediate problem is that the old man has gone to ground so cannot be arrested. Normally, Fred, as you know, we rely on phone intercepts for nailing locations. This family doesn't use electronic communication so we have to deploy human surveillance. I can get the air force up, with heat-seeking gadgets, more easily than a skilled surveillance team. The prosecutor's running out of time – he has only a few days left. Anything that interferes with his remaining time would be a serious blow to him. The competition among the prosecutors and magistrates for surveillance teams is intense. No result, the team is withdrawn. I think this investigation is floundering. That's a black mark against the prosecutor. These people fight like feral cats. Sometimes I watch those wildlife films from the Serengeti. There's an old wildebeest, legs going, unable to graze because its teeth are rotten, can't keep up with the herd. High in the sky, there's a speck. The old wildebeest knows it's there, and that there'll be another, and another. Vultures sense weakness. They'll drop, circle and land. Whether the animal is dead or still alive, they'll start to feast. Understand what I'm saying, Fred?'

He went back to his packing.

*   *   *

'What does he think it'll be like, going after those people? Does he think it's some sort of squirrel shoot – out with an air rifle? Is he dumb, ignorant or both?'

Bagsy said, 'Not too sure, Carlo. But the people down in Reggio are going to blow a gasket when they hear a freelancer, our national, is plodding about close to a prime investigation target.'

'Why me?'

'Good question, Carlo.'

The building had the echoing quiet of any government institution at a weekend. A file had been flipped in Carlo's direction: Jago Browne, copies of a confirmed air ticket, a decent-quality picture of him going onto a pier at Rome. All that was in the file would be backed up on the phone, and there was a contact address. Carlo could play gruff but in fact he appreciated being dragged out of his home, and had driven fast to get there. Bagsy would have skipped a pub session to field him. They went back a long way.

'I tried your successor out there. Can't do much arm-twisting at a range of fifteen hundred miles. He refused – pretty much made an issue of it. He wasn't going to traipse down to Calabria and tell them that a loose-cannon Brit was about to screw them up big-time – and I don't blame him. He has to work there. It's liaison, as you know, and that's a two-way trade. He's better off out of the bad-news zone. You speak the language.'

'What's our line?'

'Grovel?'

'And I'm with a Hun?'

'Organised-crime officer in Berlin, did an exchange after Duisburg. They're shitting themselves that this boy is about to trample over a sensitive investigation at a critical time. I'm not briefed up on the connection between the policeman and our banker boy but it exists. You suggested, Carlo, that the boy is either dumb, ignorant or both. Could be both. What's his motive? Fuck knows. Maybe *he* doesn't know. It used to be your territory – and it's not a nice place. Right?'

'You could say that.'

Bernardo had regarded Father Demetrio as a friend, for many years.

Friendship could be temporary or everlasting.

Two old men, in the twilight of their working lives, sipping brandy with water: the friendship was sealed because each knew enough of the other for a prison sentence stretching to a distant future, a bullet and a body in a ditch, or a disappearance.

The priest had a history of collaboration and association with Bernardo's family. Bernardo had committed the grievous crime of child murder and the priest had played a peripheral part in the disposal of a body. Neither was free of the other. Priests had been shot dead, had found severed pigs' heads on the sacristy steps, had been denounced for the abuse of children to the bishop and forced into premature retirement and poverty. Bernardo worried about his friend Father Demetrio.

It was in Bernardo's nature to identify a cause of worry and take action to staunch it.

They talked about men they had known who had died in their beds, women who were eccentric, younger men who languished in the prisons of the north, the weather forecast for the coming month, and the quality that year – good – of the projected olive harvest. They smoked and talked of plans for a new football pitch in the village that would need heavy plant to level a playing area, a project likely to warrant plaudits to the priest from his bishop, and credit to Bernardo, who would bankroll it. It would bring enhanced respectability to both men. They discussed the price of diesel – and, briefly, the increasingly intrusive investigations by the *carabinieri* and the Squadra Mobile. They did not mention the death of an informer, or a family in the village who now mourned a murdered but disowned man.

Bernardo's anxieties stemmed from being alone in the bunker, from hearing and seeing the child. Her open eyes had caught the light of the flash and the newspaper had been laid on her chest. The photograph had told the lie. His age and his loneliness in the bunker made him think most nights of the cave and their prisoner. Mamma had insisted that Father Demetrio should come to the place in the woods. In the years of his married life, Bernardo had listened to her only rarely on a matter of conscience or tactics. He had then.

He let the priest shuffle the deck. They would play cards for an hour and talk a little more, though silences between them were not awkward. There was an old cellar underneath the kitchen of the presbytery where the priest lived. Once, both of Bernardo's sons had hidden there when the *carabinieri* had come for them – the steps down were well disguised in a pantry cupboard. The church roof had been a good enough reward, new timbers and tiles; the school had needed new toilets and the bureaucracy in Reggio had backed away at the cost.

The cards were dealt. Father Demetrio's hands were unlike Bernardo's: no callouses, few wrinkles and no old blisters from hard work with tools. They were smooth-skinned and narrow, the nails clipped like a woman's. There might have been truth in the rumours of where those hands had strayed but Bernardo had scotched them. He lifted his cards and scanned them.

It was about his age, the faint weakening of his resolve, and his inability to wipe away the image of the child. He worried that Father Demetrio might harbour similar feelings. The papers had said police were searching for a child, and later reported that a photograph of her, living, had been sent to her family, then that a ransom had been paid, but the parents had not been reunited with their child. That money, a million American dollars, had paid for the first investment, a deal done in Medellin in distant Colombia. The priest had been called and escorted to the place. He had knelt on a plastic bag beside the grave, a mound of earth. He would have realised a child lay in it, from its length, and had said a prayer.

He was ageing now. He would want to go to his Maker having made a clean breast of it. Presumably the priest believed in his Maker. Increasingly Bernardo worried that Father Demetrio might visit a senior figure in the archdiocese and confess his part in the matter.

It was a day of celebration, Mamma's sixty-third birthday. Their grandson was at home with them. A ship was approaching the docks at Gioia Tauro, and a foreigner was coming in the hope of doing business – Giulietta had slid him a slip of paper with nine figures in a row on it, then had burned it and kissed him. He studied his cards.

Anxiety and worry were to be avoided at his age. He did not tolerate either. Neither would he accept a possible threat to his security. The priest might wish to purge old guilt. Bernardo's security depended on constant vigilance and confronting danger.

Bernardo smiled – a decision taken – and topped up Father Demetrio's glass. He played a card. All danger should be confronted.

Consolata was on the beach.

A fisherman was repairing a small net to her right, and a couple lay a hundred yards from her, towards the castle high on the rock, and music came from the café behind. Later she would return her parents' car and borrow it again the night after next to go back to the place she had named. Tomorrow she would have a radio on, tuned to the local Radio Gamma NonStop. She would hear if he had done anything and thought he would. Consolata had a psychologist's mind: she could predict men's actions. She was on her back, soaking up the last of the sun, stretched across the still-damp pink towel.

She thought she had helped him towards a goal. She had provided support and steeled him. She didn't understand him – couldn't comprehend why he had travelled so far and on such vague terms, but that didn't matter: he was there, in place.

She didn't know what he would do, or the likely consequences of any action he took. A broken window, a vandalised car, paint daubed on a wall in the village – even a fire started. Any of those she could have justified. Her part in them would have been worthwhile – more so than handing out leaflets. If he did something more dramatic she would know of it from the radio – and would know also if the family caught him.

If he was caught he might be hurt. Consolata did not regard that as her responsibility. She had only aided him on his way. If he suffered, it wouldn't be down to her, whatever the radio said . . . but he was attractive.

Her skin was warm. She had watched him scrub himself clean, washing away his inhibitions. A smile wreathed her face.

The prosecutor's protection team would have caught his mood.

The shift had changed.

He had seen the little huddles form as they exchanged gossip.

His wife had gone to her mother, the children with her.

He sat in the garden as the light faded. He was low in the easy chair but could see the top of the nearest hills, the depth of the range behind them, and each flaw in the brickwork of the wall that surrounded him. He had dreamed a little. How things would have been if . . . Other prosecutors would be hovering in the courtyard, clutching files, hemmed in by their guards and jostled by photographers. His prisoner would be led past the flash bulbs. A tray of coffee would be brought from the café nearest the barracks, and he would see Bernardo. They would greet each other, a moment of respect. They were such vain men, the high-value targets, and expected to be treated with dignity, the handcuffs hidden from the lenses. It was usual for these 'great men' to congratulate the prosecutor responsible for their arrest, as if only a man of immense talent could have achieved it. He had been asked once by a foreign journalist whether he would sidle close to his prisoner while the shock of arrest was still at its height and suggest he might 'turn', become a *pentito*. He had been amazed. Such an idea would offend the prisoner: he would be insulted. The prisoner must initiate such a move. The journalist hadn't understood. Would the prosecutor see the day when Bernardo was brought by *carabinieri* helicopter to Reggio?

There were two men on the hillside above the house. The forecast was poor, but he depended on them.

*   *   *

They didn't talk about kit or food. It was all about what Ciccio had seen and Fabio's insistence that he describe the man again and again. There was nothing about scorpion flies. They discussed the pistol that Ciccio had drawn and the pepper spray that Fabio had pulled out of his rucksack. Nothing moved on the slope between them and the house. A boy had been out with dogs well below them. They knew his route and had based their hide well clear of him – they were up an escarpment from the track he took and thought themselves far enough away for the dogs not to pick up their scent.

A decision had to be taken: what should they report? They were professionals, well versed in the ways of their world. Communicate to back-up and have those guys at an additional state of alert. They were now on Black. 'An unknown in camouflage going past, close, then disappearing' would trigger Amber. Back-up would report to ROS HQ. The weekend-duty officer, bored out of his mind, would log it, then refer it higher. A honcho would be called from his barbecue to receive a garbled message and they would be ordered back. That was the way it went when small stuff was passed up the command chain. If they were recalled, they would never return.

Ciccio didn't know what he had seen. Fabio had seen nothing.

'If we've shown, and they're flushing us out, we'd have a problem. But I reckon we'd see signs of it at the house. At least, that's what I'd like to think.'

The hide was one of the best, in that cleft, that Ciccio and Fabio had found. As good as any they had used before. The guy coming past? Might have been a hitman from another family, but he'd had no rifle or rucksack of explosives. Perhaps he was with the Agenzia Informazioni e Sicurezza Interna. If so, he might be working alongside the 'Ndrangheta families or against them. But his approach down the slope had not been that of a trained man or of a covert source.

'Call in and it's panic.'

'Their health and our safety. They wouldn't take a chance, just bring us out.'

'We wouldn't be coming back.'

'Don't know what we'd hit on the way out.'

'But we wouldn't be back.'

Ciccio said, 'I couldn't face our prosecutor, poor bastard. I'd swim the Strait to avoid him questioning me.'

Fabio said, 'We've given our prosecutor precious little. We've not found what he wants. We'll stay as long as we can – but it'll be a bitter pill for him to swallow when we pull out.

Ciccio, bemused: 'Who could it have been, coming past us – and why?'

They were motionless, breathing suppressed to basic need, coughs and sneezes stifled. There was a wonderful moment – they knew it well – when their information nailed a prized target to the boards, and a bleak period after a mission had failed.

Ciccio said, 'He didn't get as far down as the house, but I'd swear he's in front of us. He's hidden. Why?'

'He's too close because of the dogs.'

He soaked up information.

The cold was in his bones and his skin itched. It was almost a first for Jago Browne. There had been a long-ago camping trip down to the West Country, a few nights under canvas on Dartmoor – a Duke of Edinburgh Award venture – his only previous experience of roughing it – but he had never had to lie still like this, not coughing or fidgeting.

He wasn't close enough to watch the daily life of the house. At school it had been thought that the trip to the great outdoors was 'character building'. He'd loathed it: the chill, the damp, the barely cooked sausages, the communality of the tent where others were close to him, could tease, ignore or hurt, and his aloneness was challenged. The men at the banks who had given him the chance to shine had been impressed by his enhanced description of the experience. For that they would have thought of him as a good team player, a man unlikely to hide behind a curtain of comfort. He had not disabused them. But he could cope – he had to.

He had eaten only half of the chocolate. At any other time, in any other place, if he had bought chocolate he would have ripped off the wrapper and wolfed the contents. He had created a regime of rationing. There had been nowhere en route to buy food. He would survive, though, he didn't doubt it.

He saw the old woman. He had a fine memory, as his employers recognised. When a query was thrown up at a meeting, he seldom needed to go to his screen and hunt for an answer: if he had read it once, it was stored in his head. On the file, she was Bernardo's wife, and he could have listed the names of her three children. Jago understood the scale of the family's wealth. He was on the periphery of the team that handled the accounts of clients who were valued in excess of ten million euros. One young woman was handled exclusively by the *FrauBoss*. She was an heiress of divorced parents, living on the lake of Geneva, and came to Berlin four times a year to meet her asset handlers, accountants and lawyers. She was worth close to fifty million euros. He had met her. She had not shaken his hand but had acknowledged him. He had carried Wilhelmina's laptop bag and a file, had sat at the side and not spoken. He thought that the people whose accounts he had monitored in London and Berlin were almost paupers in comparison to the family whose home he watched, if he could believe what Consolata had told him, and he had no reason not to.

The old woman moved awkwardly, as if her hips hurt. The day was nudging on but she was hanging sheets and towels on a line. Jago studied her. She had plastic clothes pegs between her teeth, and more in a bag that hung from her shoulder. No servant did that job – she did it. When she had finished she stood to admire it. He thought she took great care over hanging several double sheets and large towels.

In her face he saw neither happiness nor misery, and thought her a woman without emotion. She did not pause to watch the chickens at her feet, or to gaze at the grapes hanging from the vine or entwined in the trellis. He considered the sheets. There was no breeze and the sun would soon dip behind the trees' foliage. He watched her move away. Despite her hip problem, she betrayed no pain, and he thought her eyes were hard.

He was proud that he had eaten only half of his chocolate, and drunk less than half of the water.

Jago couldn't read the old woman: he didn't know whether she had enjoyed the time with her grandchildren or whether she had felt loved. He hadn't seen, at her throat or on her fingers, any of the diamonds that would be commensurate with her wealth. When he strained he could just see a slender gold ring on the wedding finger. He had noticed the handyman leave a plastic bowl of vegetable peelings where the chickens were, and that the path the man took was behind the sheets.

The priest left.

The children were taken home.

He saw Marcantonio.

He saw the daughter, Giulietta – she had a bent nose. It would have been broken many years before and not set correctly. Her chin jutted out too far and her teeth overlapped. She wore no jewellery. Jago knew who she was from her photograph in the file, and that she was in her early thirties. She had glasses perched on the end of her nose.

Jago watched, the plan not yet firm in his mind. He remembered the pizzeria girl's face, the impact with which he had hit the ground, the blows thrown at him. He remembered the anger of the shouts as he had pocketed his keys. He had started to know them all – except the head of the family.

'It should have been me.'

'Our father never thought it would be you.'

Marcantonio pirouetted on his heel. 'Because of where my father and my uncle are, I should have done the bastard.'

His aunt, Giulietta, countered, 'It was never going to be you. Our father always had it done by those not associated with us. It's a mechanical process.'

'I wanted to hurt him – I wanted to look into his face and see the fear, hear him beg. Then I wanted to finish him.'

'What you did with the whore was different. It was personal to all of us. Marcantonio, you're the future.'

'I would have done it. I'd *like* to have done it.'

'You're in Berlin to learn a new life – to learn about investment and opportunity. Marcantonio, your father and your uncle are in gaol. The family needs your vitality, your youth and strength, if it's to survive.'

She stroked his arm. He recognised the moment. Down the

road, in the village, there were cats. Sometimes they were shot to keep down the numbers. Often, a litter was put in a sack and taken to the stream, usually by boys, then thrown in to drown. The boys did it so that they could kill if they had to. Sometimes the female cat was old but would nuzzle the youngest male. He lifted the hand. It was large, pudgy, sinewy and strong. It could have strangled as well as his could. He kissed the back. And did it again. And laughed. Marcantonio had had girls in Berlin and in the village. Giulietta did not have boys – Stefano had told him so. He allowed his lips to linger on her skin and she did not snatch away her hand.

They were in the open, as far as possible from any hidden microphone, and switched to the dialect they had been taught as children. Business talk – what would happen, the successes were close at hand.

'It's a dump.'

'Right, Bent.'

'Why'd they put us here?'

'It'll be because they own it.'

'It's crap . . .' He saw Jack's face screw up. 'I'd thought they'd do better for us.'

'As you say, Bent. They might have done better for us. But . . .'

They were in Brancaleone, which barely figured in the guide-books. The hotel was on the hill behind it. An English guy lived up the coast – Humphrey. He'd met the flight and driven them down in an old Jaguar, almost a museum piece. He'd checked them in but hadn't come upstairs with them: the lifts were 'resting'. Humphrey had been, long ago, a sharp junior who had traded at Woolwich Crown Court on the defence side, taken early retirement to Torquay, needing a quick change of location, then made another move. He 'fixed' for trusted people, and was now in a development seven klicks towards Reggio. Humphrey had seen that there was no need for passports to be shown at the desk – good ones or otherwise – no signatures or addresses required. Now he had gone, and had been vague about the schedule. It had been a long day, and Bent had spent half the night sitting out at

Canada Wharf. He felt nervous, and his temper was short. They were on the second floor. The room was for tourists and the signs were in German. Jack was pointing, jabbing with his finger.

It took Bent a moment to read him. The finger went from the ceiling light to the television, from the floor switch to the air-conditioner, then to the telephone.

Bent said, 'Will we get a steak here?'

Jack answered him, 'More likely pasta, then fish.'

'And a mouthful of bones.'

'What you say, Bent.'

The sliding door squealed and he went out onto the balcony. From the keys hanging on hooks at Reception, Bent Horrocks had reckoned they had about 15 per cent occupancy, but it might have been less. It would have throbbed in high season – maybe half of Hamburg or the Ruhr would have been there. There was a ribbon road below them with shops and small businesses, nothing much that caught his eye, a few villas and some two-storey apartment blocks – the latter confused him, half built, floors, roof and supports but no walls – then the beach. Not pretty, like the Algarve or anywhere Trace would have liked. The sand was dun-coloured, like the biscuits his mother always had in the tin when he went to Margate. He had sharp eyes, and even at that distance, it was obvious that the rubbish had not been cleared from round the bins. Jack had joined him, cigarettes out. They lit up.

Side of mouth: 'We likely to be bugged?'

'My advice, Bent, say nothing except when you're wanting a piss, unless Humphrey's with us. He'll know. If it's you and me it's down on the beach. It's a serious place, Bent, with serious people, and big rewards for getting it right.'

'I hear you. Why are all those blocks unfinished? Seems a waste to . . .'

'What you say, Bent, a waste. Could have been a laundering job, but the law landed on them and confiscated the property. They do that, take the assets.'

'We right to come here?'

'It's the big league, Bent. Where you should be.'

'Where I want to be.'

'And ought to be.'

'I'll not take shit from them. Never have and never will.'

'It'll be good, Bent. Big league.'

It looked a pretty ordinary place. Quiet. It looked as if not much happened at Brancaleone. He liked the thought of 'big league'.

'If he's in difficulties, he'll get no sympathy.' Carlo had taken a train.

'Too grand for us. We're not up to his standards.' He'd walked from the station.

'Forgot about us and where he came from.' There were little side roads off the main streets, and cul-de-sacs. The light was going and TV sets flickered. The kids were out on the corners, hoods up and forward, scarves looped across their faces. Too late for children to be playing outside. The fast-food outlets were slack. He'd been past the pub, had known of it from his days working in London, and Freemasons Road. He found the turning he wanted. The kids would have reckoned him a policeman because of his walk and posture. They'd have known about policemen, every last one of them.

'Don't they call it the throw-away society? If you're last year's big thing, you don't take kindly to being trashed.' He'd rung the bell. A girl had answered it, nice nails and hair. She'd have been the sister listed in the file. Behind her was the brother, different father. Carlo had introduced himself. He could do the look well when he needed help. He'd been gestured in, had wiped his shoes carefully, shown respect. It was a decent home, clean and warm. Comfortable, but the value of money counted. There were neat front doors and handkerchief gardens in the street, all filled with refuse bins. The mother was washing her hair but came down, with a towel as a turban. She sat on the sofa, her daughter and son behind her, as if she needed their protection.

'We did all that we could for him, and got nothing back.' She was slight, her face worn and tired. She might have been attractive once, a long time ago. Still, she had managed to attract three different blokes – nothing to do with Carlo. He had to build a profile and start to understand the man who had gone bare-arsed to Calabria, planning to start a commotion. He might get his head blown off or his face rearranged to the extent that he was unrecognisable when he lay in intensive care. Bizarre. Carlo had come to Canning Town expecting to hear about a good guy who helped old ladies across busy roads, did meals on wheels at weekends, but his own mother had bad-mouthed him.

'He went to the best school round here. Uniform was dear. Billy and Georgina went short because of him. He had the chance to break free . . . I'm not saying we wanted to cling to his coat tails and have him pull us up, not saying that, but Jago hasn't been to see us for two years, not even at Christmas. You want to know about him? He needs to win. Going to university was winning. Getting into a bank was winning. You say he's on an exchange in Germany. He'd count that as winning. He'd see us as losers, wouldn't want to know. Where he's gone, what he's going to do there – what's brought you here on a Sunday afternoon – it'll be about winning. You say it started with a girl getting her face slashed. It'll be about excitement. Excitement is winning. From you being here, I suppose it's a bad place to go for excitement and a hard place for winning. Don't answer that. It was good of you to call, but you needn't come back. A text will do if you've something to say.'

He let himself out.

There was a guesthouse by the airport where they'd booked him in, convenient for early-morning flights. Nothing was as it seemed – the spice of life. It never was, in Carlo's experience. He'd have agreed with what she'd said. *A hard place for winning.* That hit the nail on the head. He walked fast towards the station. There'd be tears at the end of it. There usually were when amateurs got involved.

The beast was hurt. It was separated from the pack, frightened, and flies clustered over the wound. It was hungry, isolated and lost. The clouds had built. Evening seemed to come fast and the light failed.

* * *

A big clap of thunder.

Jago was on his stomach. He had not decided what he would do. He was uncertain about his target. He had a degree of security when he was wedged into the space under the two great boulders but had not yet summoned the strength of purpose – guts or commitment – to wriggle out of his hide, go down the slope and do something.

He was on the groundsheet, wrapped in the coat. Wind blustered through the trees, scattering leaves. The sheets behind the house had begun to flap where previously they had been limp.

The first drops fell. He was watching the back door, wondering which of them would run out to snatch the laundry off the line, throw them into a basket and rush back inside. He waited and watched and no one came.

Lights went on inside, and he saw two windows closed. Big drops of rain hit the leaves above and the stones in front of him. The first little river had begun to flow. There was more thunder, and sheet lightning. He wondered whether a shower or a storm was coming.

The rain pattered hard and Jago had nowhere to shelter.

9

When he moved, a lake of trapped water lapped round him. There was no light, only a lessening of the total blackness.

It was not the best place to be. Jago had thought himself blessed when he had found the gap under the two great stones. It gave him a matchless vantage point where he was protected and hidden. Now, the rain made rivers on the hillside. One tumbled under the twin boulders and flowed over the slab where he lay, dammed by his body. Its depth built up under his armpits and against his crotch. His clothing was inadequate and the ground sheet useless.

It had seemed to Jago that the village marked the epicentre of the storm. Thunder had crashed and flashes of lightning had lit the roof of the house . . . The cockerel had woken him, crowing for attention. There were no cockerels in Canning Town or Stresemannstrasse.

Rainwater cascaded down the slopes of the boulders to fall on his shoulders and the back of his head. It was down his neck and had puddled under his chest and waist. It dribbled across his fore-head into his eyes and mouth.

The cockerel had given up. Other than the rain, Jago heard nothing. He had begun to take pride in his disciplines. He didn't cough or sneeze, and stayed where he was – he didn't know where the dogs slept. There was a covered box near the back door and they had hung around it during daylight, but whether they were there now asleep or awake and alert, he had no idea.

He had put off a big moment. When to eat the second half of the chocolate. Now resolve fled. Jago fished it out of his pocket. It was soaked and the chocolate was sticky as he peeled off the wrapper. There were no lights in the upper windows of the house. There was nothing there on which he should concentrate. He ate the chocolate in three mouthfuls. It was not how they ate at the bank, either in the coffee shop before the day started or when the trolley came round mid-morning. Some would already have been to the gym, then showered and headed for coffee and a biscuit – they would have taken tiny bites and made it last. When the trolley came there were fat-free meals – salads, fruit and fish. It would have been noticed halfway across Sales if he had gobbled half a bar of a chocolate in three bites.

The lake he was lying in had become a fast-flowing stream. He wanted to pee. Should he manoeuvre onto his side, put his weight on his hip, then try to direct the urine into the rainwater coming past him? The alternative was to crawl forward, drag himself upright and hope his hands weren't too frozen to fumble with his zip. Important to check the wind direction. It would be futile to attempt to determine the value of being where he was. Better to worry about relieving himself and at what speed to eat chocolate.

A man sneezed.

There was the noise of water flowing, of the wind catching high branches, and the crisp, clear sound of a sneeze, then a choke, which was a second stifled. It had come from behind and above him. He couldn't have estimated how close it had been because the wind was blowing from that direction. Twenty yards or fifty.

Jago lay on his stomach. He didn't pee, just strained to hear better. The second sneeze had been fainter, more muffled. He froze, as still as stone.

Ciccio thought it a noise to raise the dead. Fabio was humiliated.

Ciccio couldn't believe that his friend, colleague and surveillance partner would sneeze so loudly. Fabio gripped the sleeve of Ciccio's jacket: his gesture of apology. The moment passed.

They were dry. Their gear was waterproof and they could shelter in the recess. That bloody bird had woken Ciccio while Fabio was on watch. There were no lights in the house that they could see. Fabio murmured another apology, and Ciccio punched him.

The rain was brutal. Neither man nor beast would be out in it.

Ciccio murmured, mouth to ear, 'Your sneeze makes no difference in the grand scheme of things. Nobody heard you because nobody's around. We're alone. You could take off your clothes, stand in the open, wash yourself in the rain and sing an aria without being seen or heard. I have a problem. Will the scorpion flies in the jar deteriorate in the damp? Will they be useless for my friend's research? Should we ditch them and catch some more when this fucking rain stops?'

Fabio told him he was more interested in discussing breakfast: should they have the fruit candy from the pre-packaged meals today or tomorrow?

Were they wasting their time? Neither, Ciccio knew, could doubt the purpose of the mission. They could harbour doubt but not share it. The cloud was solid and the wind moaned above them. Both men would now have started to count the hours that remained for them to endure on the hillside. They would be thinking of their women, hot showers, proper sleep and beer. It was necessary for both Ciccio and Fabio to remember the good days when they had watched from an eyrie as a storm squad of *cacciatore* troops exploded into a building with stun grenades and went for an arrest based on information provided by the guys in the covert OP. It was always good then, the insect bites and constipation. But they had seen no trace of the target.

Fabio whispered, 'It's under control. It won't happen again.'

'Who was there to hear you? Only that fucking bird.'

The sand was in her hair and on the back of her legs. The tide had reached its high point and waves frothed over her toes. Consolata thought she was in the right place.

The rain had started on the far side of the Aspromonte and would have beaten in off the Ionian Sea, then lingered at the mountain barrier before edging to the Tyrrhenian Sea and the beach. The couple had gone, and so had the man repairing nets. His boat was only a few metres from the incoming tide. She was alone.

She thought of the boy, neither with fondness nor a suggestion of guilt. The water curled between her toes, but fell hard from the sky, soaking her clothes, which stuck to her skin and outlined her body. She pictured the boy: water streaming down his face, hair and clothing drenched, but he would be there. He might have found cover, and might not. He would be close to the house, and might already have cobbled together an idea. He would do something. She herself had crossed a frontier, had aided and abetted illegality, and rejoiced. Nothing would be the same again. She remembered humiliations, inflicted pain, a small shop window where paint tins had been on display. She might have felt gratitude to Jago Browne for changing her.

She was on the beach in the rain, soaked to the skin, and she had shared in his experience. He had seen her in the sea and that would have been enough to send him forward. Of course he would go forward. She couldn't imagine what he would do when he'd cornered Marcantonio. Perhaps nothing. Perhaps he would crumble under a counter-attack. She had played her part and was satisfied.

Close to three millennia before, the boats would have tried to navigate the strait, with the whirlpool of Charybdis or the razor rocks of Scylla. Only the bravest and most skilled were able, in grim weather, to navigate the gap. Consolata was confused. She had happened on him, had heard a gabbled story, had stiffened his resolve, had helped him. She had made retreat difficult. She didn't know whether he was brave and skilful or a lonely fool.

The rain and the wind lashed her.

Carlo had been given the number. He rang it from the airport concourse.

About fifty paces away, a man waved: tall, angular, unshaven, pale. In appearance he was all that Carlo was not. It had been a bumpy flight – cross winds had flung them around on their final descent – and Carlo thought the next hop would be worse. The rain was heavy and there was standing water on the apron.

They met. Carlo had been told that the German, from a

KrimPol unit, had been in Italy, on a steep learning curve, after the Duisburg massacre in 2007: a quiet industrial town in the west of Germany had played host to a big-time 'Ndrangheta *faida* – six dead. The country had woken up to news of a large-scale Calabrian infiltration to their society, and what happened when a feud erupted. It had been going on for sixteen years, had started with offence given when a visiting circus had performed in San Luca; insults were exchanged between two families. Killings punctuated the feud, tit for tat, but the big hit had been in Germany where the families had their major money-spinning interests. The word for Carlo was that the German had been sent to the south of Italy and told not to come back until he understood the organised-crime culture of the area. He had managed to extend his stay – and extend it again. Three days before, he had met the missing Briton. It was a start.

A firm shake of his hand. 'I'm Fred.'

'How did you come by that?'

'From Manfred. But always I have been "Fred". You have a problem with it?'

'No problem. I'm Carlo.'

'Are you Italian background?'

'No.'

It was just the name that he'd attracted while doing his four years as a Liaison Officer of HMRC and attached to the embassy . . . not that he had seen anything of his old stomping ground from the aircraft as it had come in. Dense cloud and the Eternal City was blanketed and they hadn't broken through till almost on the tarmac.

Carlo said, 'Did anyone see you off this morning?'

'When I left Tempelhof? No.'

'No big boss there?'

'No.'

'Did you get a speech – stirring stuff, motivation?'

'Last night they talked about damage limitation.'

Carlo said, 'They wouldn't have wanted guilt by association. I fancy a coffee. I'm to emphasise that we "care passionately about the furtherance of good relations" and also that we "take very seriously an unwarranted intervention" by this crackpot kid. I'm not a senior man, so they sent me.'

'Coffee would be good. I think they scraped the bottom of a sewer to find me. It is not a job for a man of ambition.'

'Plumbed the depths in my case. Can I say something?'

There was a shrug.

'We may not agree on much, but we have a saying – 'We must all hang together or we'll hang separately.' You understand that?'

'Benjamin Franklin, American . . . You want *cappuccino* or a latte, yes? We do a job . . . I do not expect to be loved here, or welcomed.'

'My people say you're at the heart of this, fielding blame.'

A wintry grin. 'My people say the same. If my bosses were here, most of them half my age, not yet out of kindergarten, they would be concerned as to who had seniority on the jaunt. It would be important. Who is Alpha and who is Bravo?'

'But our bosses are not here.'

'So we are felons freed on a day-release scheme. We achieve a little here and there. We are too lowly to harbour ambitions.'

'But expert in screwing up the best-laid plans of mice and men.'

'Approved – which?'

'*Cappuccino*, thanks.'

They were at the bar. A fast transfer, then the next leg. Life would get harder – guaranteed.

It was his favourite film. In his opinion, it was the best movie ever made. Marcantonio was watching Al Pacino as the Cuban kid who made the big-time. He had the DVD back at his apartment in Berlin and saw *Scarface* once a week; he had left his first copy at home when he had gone to Germany. Not that it would have been watched while he was away – his grandmother liked romance, Teresa the programmes on new kitchens. Giulietta had the set tuned to financial news channels. His grandfather, in the bunker, watched crime series. The man Pacino played was a hero to Marcantonio.

It never failed him.

He could recite all of the lines spoken by the star, and the end always excited him. A downfall, a table of scattered coke, then the shoot-out: no pain, a grand death, a man who would never grow old. Marcantonio had little time for the world of business and investment, the milking of public contracts and alliances with other families. To Marcantonio, what mattered was creating fear, winning admiration, being able to walk tall on the street, men bobbing their heads to him and girls edging forward to make the offer. And to kill. He had never fired a machine pistol in the way Al Pacino did, but he had strangled, he had put a live woman into acid and he had shot one round into the back of the head of the man who'd cheated his grandfather. He watched the film: it was near to the shoot-out.

The rain hammered on the windows. He had business later in the day – some shit from abroad. He didn't do drugs – his grand-father would turn him out of the house if he did. There was another family, further north in the mountains, whose eldest son had been identified, by a Squadra Mobile bug in a car, as a rampant homo-sexual. The information had been leaked, and the kid was disowned – as was the kid of another family who dressed as a woman. His grandfather would have thrown him out if he believed that Marcantonio did drugs. It was bad to use them, but good to deal in them. A wide grin played on his face, and the movie came to its conclusion.

His grandmother was in the kitchen and seemed not to notice the amplified soundtrack. She never criticised him, whatever he did. The rain was incessant. He had a man to meet, would weigh and evaluate him, then tell his grandfather what he thought. Marcantonio was trusted, the favourite . . .

Not many stood their ground when Bentley Horrocks's temper flared. 'What are we supposed to do in this fucking place?'

Jack understood the need to bend with the wind and had made it an art form. 'Good shout, Bent. What are we supposed to do?'

'Leaving me hanging about!'

'Wrong, that.'

'And where's the fucking eagle? I pay him enough. He leaves me here, in this dump, and the rain's pissing down. Does he think he has free rein to let me hang about? Nowhere to go, nothing to do. He'll hear my tongue – and so will the local man. He's a big man, the eagle said. He'd better be – and he'd better be ready to crack a good deal, after keeping me cooling my heels. Who do they think they are – and who do they fucking think I am? You tell me.'

It was all said in a whisper, close to Jack's ear, while a game show played on the TV. The eagle was Humphrey. Between them, a legal man – solicitor or barrister – was always an eagle. Humphrey had said that the family would visit later in the day. They could barely see the beach. The cloud was almost flush with it: grey skies, grey beach, grey shoreline. The street running through the strip development of Brancaleone was nearly a river, and the traffic threw up water in waves. The sliding doors leaked at the base and the rain was pooling there. Jack knew enough of his man to sense insecurity. He did the massage of the ego bit, which kept him in his place at Bent's side and good money in his pocket. There had been people before Jack who had thought themselves close to Bent, and hadn't been . . . That had made for a bad future.

'And they deserve it, Bent, your tongue. No call to be leaving you cooling your heels. Who do they think they are? That's what I'm wondering, Bent.'

They were trapped in the room. The smoke alarm in the ceiling was disconnected, the battery removed, and Bent went steadily through his cigarettes. No one had come up from Reception to challenge it – and where else was there to smoke? If you opened the balcony door, the rain came in at an angle, blown on a gale. Bent was a big man at home and owned Crime Squad detectives. He lived well, but always needed to push on. He couldn't stand still and was no good at treading water. Too many little bastards circling, watching, hoping to sniff weakness. He needed a big move forward, which the journey would bring – but insecurity gnawed at him. He had no language and was off his territory.

'Best we can hope for, Bent, is that it lifts and we can take a turn outside.'

'Are you some sort of fucking moron? You see a hole in that lot? I don't. It's solid. I tell you, when this old bastard turns up he'll be in no doubt what I'm thinking, left in this hole. He may be the top man but he'll need some answers before I've finished with him.'

'It's what you deserve, Bent, answers from the top man . . .'

The bunker leaked.

He had the lights full on. Water came out from under the unit on which the microwave was placed and lay on the vinyl there, glistening from the bulbs above. More water had gathered on the carpet towards the chemical toilet. Only in exceptional rain did the container fail to repel the damp.

He had the television on.

The aerial cable went up from the container roof and used the same cavity that brought reasonably fresh air down the pipe – its outlet was in the hollowed-out trunk of the long dead tree above. A little more water dribbled down the pipe, enough to dampen the air inside. The heating created a sweat effect, and twice in the last ten minutes he'd had to wipe the TV screen, which left it smeared. He'd watched the news and the weather forecast. The news had shown flooding of roads on the Ionian side of the Aspromonte and some landslips, and the weather forecaster had said there would be no break in the rain before the end of the afternoon. When it rained incessantly and was damp in the container, Bernardo always kept the lights on.

It had been wet that year. The clouds had been low and heavy day after day, night after night, when the child had been brought down from the north and sold to the family. Bernardo remembered taking the short, steep goats' trail up the slopes behind the house to where they had chained her. So dark in the cave and the torch he had brought with him barely penetrated its depths. It dripped when there was rain and the beam showed the water that fell onto the lower rock surfaces. He had found her dead. Enough water had fallen on the candle to put out the flame. She would have died in darkness. It cost them serious money to buy her, and represented a greater loss to the family than any capsizing at sea of a fast launch bringing in cigarette cartons from north Africa. Financially, it could have proved difficult. Too much money to lose – but negotiations were proceeding. The camera had been brought, and a newspaper.

The child had been propped up and her clothing straightened. It had been Mamma's idea but she had not come to the cave. He had arranged the newspaper, that day's *Corriere della Calabria*, and had used a finger to wipe water from a bucket in a trail down the child's cheeks, having prised back her eyelids: she would appear to be weeping. That would accentuate the misery of her condition and speed the negotiations for the ransom. At the time he had thought nothing of it, and the word from the far north was that the intermediaries believed a deal was possible – probable, in fact. Recently, since he had been sleeping in his bunker, he had remembered – been unable to forget – the damp, cold and darkness in which the child had died. He had every light on, and the heater turned high.

Bernardo was in the container, left to himself, because Giulietta thought – as the hours ticked away and the prosecutor's resources approached their limit – that a raid might be made. Especially in that weather. Better to stay where he was. Neither Marcantonio nor Stefano had visited him. He existed, wiled away time, had no interest in the television ... He thought of the pigs at the farm high in the foothills, and what instruction he must give: it was because he had remembered the child, resurrected her memory, that he must give an order about the pigs. As long as the lights were on, and the heater, he felt secure, safe.

The rain sheeted and water sluiced around him. Jago watched and learned.

In the ferocity of the wind, the handyman held an umbrella. It was one of those issued by construction companies or possibly by a bank after a session for investors. The man by the main door into the house, with the City-Van parked close to the step, clung to it in the gale. It was what a driver did – a lesser person: the vehicle was brought to the front door, a man shivered and got soaked but held an umbrella ready and no one came. Maybe he or she had gone for a last pee, to change a shirt or put on eyeliner. It was an ordinary house, not a palace. But the girl, Consolata, had told him in broad brushstrokes what the family was worth. They could have afforded a gated place, behind high walls and a barricaded entrance, like the ones in west Berlin, where the fat cats lived. The man tried to light a cigarette. Not easy: he had the wind and rain to fight while one fist clung to the umbrella handle and the other had the lighter – the cigarette would be wet so maybe the flame wouldn't take, despite the efforts he was making to shelter it. Smoke billowed.

Jago learned about power. He had ceased to care about the cold, the wet and his hunger. He had no plan, and that nagged. The lesson continued. A master class in power: a man stood in the rain with an umbrella that the storm tossed aside.

Marcantonio came out.

The family had begun to take shape. The mother, the daughter-in-law, the grandchildren, the daughter and Marcantonio. Jago assumed he had had his own car when he lived here, but this was a brief visit. He was to be driven. The hair was spiky. The boy wore a scarlet shirt, a leather black jacket and jeans. From that distance, they looked stylish and expensive. He nodded to the guy with the umbrella. The guy let the rain cascade on his own head and reached forward to open the passenger door – not the Audi that had tramlines etched onto the paintwork, which would be hard to fix. Marcantonio slid inside. Jago waited for a nod of gratitude. None came. The guy went round the van, tossed the sopping umbrella into the back and shook water off an old, weathered face. His coat was dark with damp.

The engine started. The City-Van was driven away.

He had watched the coming power of the family. The destination, Jago reckoned, would be a bar where other local bucks gathered. What story might he tell an audience? About a girl, may be, or a young man who had intervened, an arsehole, or about blood and a kicking. It wouldn't be about damage done to a car. He saw the City-Van disappear, a shield of spray chasing it. That was the vehicle the big man, unseen, had chosen; the house was unattractive, unfinished; the clothes of the women were unre-markable; the family reeked of money. They had the cash to own a football club or racehorses, to live in a spread with a view of the sea and a private beach, and did not. It was a lesson of critical importance Jago reckoned: money was secondary, and power supreme.

He did not yet know what he could do, what would jolt the power.

In Canning Town Jago had not known power other than in the boxing ring. In the City he had not known power, except on hearing one girl say to another, 'He just walked in here, a chance many would kill for, on the say-so of a chap wanting to salve his conscience.' In Berlin, at the bank, he had known power when he had cleared his desk, wiped his computer and gone out through the door without a backward glance. Here, on the hillside, he felt a degree of power because he could watch them.

The message came up on the prosecutor's screen.

He read it, a cigarette in his hand.

A young man from Berlin . . . British nationality . . . witness to an assault outside a pizzeria . . . protection and extortion . . . a subsequent, more serious assault, the girl scarred for life . . . two interventions by the Briton, beaten up both times, no hospitalisa-tion . . . a one-way ticket to Reggio Calabria . . . an idiot who targeted Marcantonio, grandson of Bernardo, and . . .

He stubbed out the cigarette. It was a good ashtray, heavy, cut-glass, a present to his father a half-century before.

Men were coming from Berlin and London to liaise, and it was hoped that the unfortunate presence of Jago Browne, merchant banker, would not jeopardise his investigations into that particular family. Two words lingered: *unfortunate* and *jeopardise*. He had the ashtray in his hand and hurled it at the window. It hit bulletproof glass and shattered. A column of ash and embers made a glowing cloud around the impact point. It would have sounded like a pistol shot. Two of his men were in the room, weapons drawn.

He held his head in his hands, then loosed one to wave them away. He had once been told by an old fighter against an earlier generation of the 'Ndrangheta that it was always necessary to employ extreme care: 'A small mistake in any investigation can cause infinite damage'. An amateur, on a crusade, was blundering towards a target and would – as night follows day – alert him or her. The clock moved towards countdown, and the hours still available to him were fucked. Months of work, in their final hours, were jeopardised, which was unfortunate. Had there been another ashtray on his desk he would have thrown that after the first.

'You want a confession?'

'Always good for the guts.'

The only movements they made were to tilt their heads fractionally when they spoke so that a mouth was against an ear, then to reverse the movement.

'The sneeze,' Fabio whispered. 'My sneeze.'

'Does a priest need to hear about a sneeze?' Ciccio asked.

'What did we say about my sneeze?'

'That didn't matter, the noise, because no one would be out in the storm.'

They lay close for warmth. They often had long conversations to pass the time. They were there as a last resort. There was no bug in the house, or hidden outside the back door, and most mornings the old man, Stefano, swept the vehicle for a tracker. They did not use mobile phones or computers for deals or planning, but relied on written text and couriers. The daughter organised communications. The last resort was having two men in a cleft, almost a cave, and hoping they had the staying power to notice any small but important 'mistake'. The families always made a 'mistake', but it had to be seen, noted and evaluated. They were looking for the old man but hadn't found him.

'What does a priest need to hear?'

'We didn't flag a message through. A man came past us. We couldn't identify or place him. Where's he gone?' Ciccio's voice was lower than the moan of the wind. 'No name, no description,

no reason for him to be on the slope. The significance of this? He
didn't emerge.'

'Shit.'

'We haven't seen him come out at the bottom – and his route
would have taken him below the track where they come with the
dogs. He hasn't shown himself.'

'Shit again.' Fabio's teeth ground. It was the work of survivors
not intellectuals, for those without imagination but strong on
discipline and able to analyse what they saw.

'He's still there.'

'And any man on the slope would have heard that sneeze. We've
shown out.'

'First time ever.' Ciccio gave a little sigh.

'Who should know?'

'Nobody.'

'That's the greater sin, worse than showing out.'

'I can live with it,' Ciccio told him.

'Because the mission and the investigation are fucked. We're in
the final hours.' Fabio gave a minute shrug. 'Not worth confessing.
Think . . . No winners.'

'Wrong. The winner is the entomologist. He has our collection
of carcasses and will make a unique study of the scorpion fly. Be
positive.'

'Our friend is still out there, so we're sharing our space with
him. I say he's no threat to us. Why should he be? Relax, enjoy
your work. If they lay hands on him they'll take the skin off his
back before they kill him. Tonight, we'll be eating *tacchino in
gelatina* . . . We have a grandstand seat – no priests, no confessions.
I didn't sneeze. And, I tell you, *he* is there, the target. He's there.'

His voice trailed away. They watched the rain fall and heard the
wind.

Fred said, 'Here, my friend, a mouse doesn't break wind unless it
has permission.'

Carlo looked around. They had no umbrella between them but
had hired a car at Lamezia, bickered as to whether KrimPol or

HMRC should pay. The Solomon solution was that they would split general costs and HMRC would do meals. On the drive south they had barely talked because the wipers had trouble clearing the windscreen and the lorries threw up spray. Fred drove. Now he'd come off the big highway and driven into the town of Rosarno. He had parked and they had both climbed out. Why? Carlo was unsure.

They stood in the centre of the Piazza Duomo. It was wide and open, and the rain lashed them. Why? Carlo had known of Rosarno but had never investigated the resident families. On one side of the square he could see the Speedy Market Alimentari and opposite, the magnificent church dedicated to San Giovanni Battista. He had read the carving over the main doorway: 'Come, King of Peace, end hatred and turn it to love, revenge into forgiveness.' A tall order.

The town was closed. The doors of the restaurants and bars were shut and the lights off. The parked cars were Mercedes, Audis and BMWs, and the streets were clean – well-paid discipline ruled. On the Via Roma, coming up the hill and into the square, there had been decent small houses, the window boxes alive with geraniums. It was Pesche country. The family had an overview of the docks at Gioia Tauro, with control of the workforce and the routes away from the wharves and containers. Fred had talked about a leader who had buried himself in a bunker but had needed a woman. There was a mistress under surveillance, who came to the safe house close to the bunker and brought her toy dog. She was his weakness and the opportunity for the *cacciatore*. Fred and Carlo were drenched.

'I was there when he was taken,' Fred said. 'It was a mark of the trust they had in me that I was allowed to witness a significant arrest. He had assets in Germany, which was why I was permitted access. He lived in a hole in the ground, but he had champagne and caviar. It was an important arrest but nothing changed. He was in a cell, but the power of the family was as great as before. In the town there are good churches, and there was affluence, but no one seemed to have a job and there was no industry, except the port. I found it depressing – beautiful but an example of a broken state. And this is Europe. It makes me sad if I think too hard about it. I reckon I understand your English boy.'

'Tell me.'

'I think he was disrespected. He is a banker, has a good job, is a subject of envy and would regard himself as a member of an elite. He is different from many other young men. An incident plays out in front of him, and he responds, expecting the bad boys to back off. He is dumped on the pavement. I think he yearns for respect and needs to earn it. He's no Knight Templar riding to the rescue of holy sites in Jerusalem, but an arrogant boy whose pride was hurt.'

They started to walk back towards the car. The rain was irrelevant. Carlo thought the assessment sounded fair. They would not hurry to fulfil the purpose of the journey – to make their apologies at the Palace of Justice. He thought two old men had been dragged from the comfort of their jobs because they were pawns of diminished status, suitable for work that no ambitious officer would want.

'Where to?' Fred asked.

Carlo told him.

The rainwater pooled in their seats and under their feet. They drove towards Reggio and the skies stayed ashen.

It was a little lighter over the sea. Giulietta was at her computer; the screen showed the returns on investments in hotel resorts on the Brazilian coast, made comparisons with Florida, and threw up launch costs and profit margins. She shut it down. Nothing illegal there. Nothing that could justify a charge of 'Mafia association' if the house was raided and the hard drive taken. She shrugged on a coat, went out into the rain and lit a cigarillo, stronger than a cigarette. It was her problem that she had not been born a boy. What power she had would soon be stripped away from her when Marcantonio came home for good.

She felt contempt for her nephew. Had she been born a boy she would by now have been undisputed head of the family and her father would have been an old man with memories and little else. He had left her with a twisted nose: when she was fourteen months old, he had dropped her on a stone floor. Her nose had been broken and allowed to knit by itself. She had no lover because of her status. A young man in the village could not have considered walking out with her. A young man from another family, equal in importance to her own, would have raged if his father had told him that Giulietta Cancello was his chosen bride. She had no girl-friends with whom she could go to a disco at a hotel in Locri, Brancaleone or Siderno. Love was beyond her reach.

Teresa, her sister-in-law, had once bought her some clothes from the new boutique in the mall outside Locri but she didn't wear them – her mother would cluck with disapproval if she did. Annunziata had treated her as if she were an imbecile. Giulietta had denounced Annunziata, condemning her.

She threw away the cigarillo. Marcantonio would go back to Berlin. Word would seep from the Palace of Justice that a prosecutor's investigation had run its course. They owned enough men in the Palace for the information to be reliable. Her father would emerge from his bunker, and Marcantonio would return from Germany. She would spend more time at the computer, offering advice, seeing it ignored, as age chased her.

A shipment was coming into Gioia Tauro in the rudder trunk of a cargo ship from Venezuela. An Englishman was installed at Brancaleone and would stay there until the family was prepared to meet him, hear his proposition and determine whether or not he was safe as a commercial partner. Her nephew would be in a bar and other boys would be around him, hanging on his stories. At the tables, girls hoped to be noticed and that a finger would beckon them over. Stefano would be by the door, in the City-Van, the rainwater sloshing dirt off the bodywork. No one called for Giulietta, or waited for her, or hoped she would notice them. She kicked a pebble, which ricocheted into the bushes. She had seen how her mother smiled only when Marcantonio was near her, and that the porcelain Madonna was positioned prominently on the window ledge. It was quiet and the dogs were alert. She would have sworn that nothing moved near the house, that no one was close, that there was no threat. She went inside.

Nine calls had been received at a bed-and-breakfast on the north side of the city. The same answer was given each time: the guests had not yet arrived. No message was left. The rain made a river of the street, and the hills – usually a fine sight – were buried in cloud.

Carlo said, 'I wasn't on the street here. I would have liked to be around when they took him. He was one of the men who controlled the whole of Reggio, and blood would have been dripping off his fingers. I saw him when the *carabinieri* took him past the cameras. I was there for a meeting, about stuff going into London. Anyway, they lifted the guy on this street.'

It was the Via Pio. Rain came off the roofs, and gutters overflowed. No point in wearing their coats.

While the man had been in hiding he had needed someone he trusted to be his courier. His son-in-law was among thirty who ran messages, brought food and set up meetings. He had been using eleven different safe houses. All thirty had to be located, bugged and tracked, but the son-in-law – the most trusted – was the bad link in the chain and blew him out. It had taken four years to pinpoint where the guy was. He was armed when they went in, but didn't try to use his weapon, went quietly. Four years for one man, with scores of people working on the case. Carlo told the story. It was important to him – the only time he had been there when the cameras flashed. The guy would have been worth hundreds of millions of euros. To go after a target for four years and believe that the investigation would be successful was dedication.

They were two old men, who stood on a pavement, had no protection against the rain and seemed not to notice. A German and a Briton . . . They might have been veterans of Cassino on the road to Rome, in opposite slit trenches, now meeting in a graveyard, or at Juno Beach and falling on each other's necks, but instead, they had war stories of Rosarno and the Via Pio. It was important to demonstrate that they knew what the game was about.

Carlo said, 'If, towards the end of that stake-out, a fly-by-night had screwed up what they had, the anger would have been indescribable. We're not going to be anyone's favourite visitors. We put all the money towards anti-terrorism now, but the real threat to our society is the corruption and criminality of the gangs. It's a cancer. Does a young banker go to war in a grey suit with a neutral tie? I don't know. I do know that he's gone into acute personal danger. Do we cheer him on or call him fucking stupid?'

'If only it were that simple. . .'

Carlo said, 'You told me his boss spoke poorly of him. I can cap that. His own mother bad-mouthed him. A confusing picture. I believe you win some and lose some. Nothing's personal. How do you see your future?'

The walls of the gaol were behind them and a little queue of women, black clothes and inadequate umbrellas, were waiting for visiting time.

'I hope Carlo, to be on a naturist beach and feel freshness on my skin.'

'I rate the boy. Are you going to strip off? I've never been driven by a bare-arsed chauffeur. It was good to come here, see the place.'

Fred said, 'Nobody I've spoken to has had a good word for him. He has no friends, no champions. It makes him more interesting and less predictable. Do I sound like a profiler? I hate them. He's independent – and not liked.'

'Irrelevant. Who said, 'The enemy of my enemy is my friend'? If he bloodies a nose or kicks a shin, that's good enough. I don't have to like him. You met him. How will he strike me?'

The pipe was out. Fred shielded the bowl as he tried to relight it. A cascade of failed matches fell to the pavement. 'He is a banker, investment and sales. They are not impetuous. He will wait. It will be similar to the market performing as he wishes it. He will be patient. It will be in his time of choosing. I think he will be out there, in this weather, and it will not concern him. I think he has the talent to surprise us. Time to go.'

'It can't be put off.'

'We face the music, and it'll be an orchestra, full blown.'

They went to the car.

Jago set himself puzzles. They had started as mental arithmetic on the portfolios at the bank. The light dipped fast, and it was almost the time that the majority of the team would be leaving the building, heading for the bars or coffee shops, the gymnasium along the street and the launderette. None of that had any relevance to where he was and what he was doing.

He had found a good teaser. It had legs and ran.

The sheets on the line attracted him.

The rain fell on them and, though sodden and heavy, they flapped in the wind. Some of the pegs had been dislodged, but as day disappeared and grey dusk settled, those remaining seemed to do a job. They were good sheets, for king-sized beds, a rich blue that was similar to the sea. Four sheets, and they obscured a stretch of the route between the trellis and the wall short of the dilapidated shed. Trees blocked his view of most of the building, but the sheets . . . He turned the matter in his mind.

And remembered.

A shower in Canning Town, washing out on the lines in the little back gardens or slung along the balconies of the blocks, and the women were straight out quick with white plastic baskets to scoop the clothes and bedding off the lines. They did it at speed. Nobody in Canning Town left the washing on the line when it rained. The mother could have taken it in, or the daughter, or even the driver while he waited for Marcantonio, slasher of a girl's face, to come out. Even Marcantonio might have done it. But the bedding had been abandoned on the line through a storm, as dusk merged with night.

The rain had eased but not stopped. The skies melded with the ground and distant lights brightened. Through the kitchen window he saw the mother and thought she was preparing vegetables. The cold had set in. Had it not been for the teaser – why was the washing still on the line? – he might have frozen solid. He had to keep on his clothing because to take it off would expose him to the water and the wind.

He knew that behind him, higher, there was another vantage point, and at least one more watcher. The kid came up the track to the house and Jago saw a torch shone in his face and the outlines of two men, broader and taller than the kid. Cigarettes were exchanged, a lighter flashed, and he heard a low cackle.

The kid went to the back door, knocked and waited. When it was opened, the dogs bounded out. Jago realised they had been brought in during the storm, but not the washing. The kid left and the door was closed after him. He used no torch. Jago assumed he knew each stone, each trail; none was visible now.

The kid had gone up the slope behind the derelict shed, climbed higher than where Jago was hidden, then looped behind him. Jago's scent had been washed away by the sea, and now the route he had taken through the trees and over the rocks that had been cleansed by the rain, all trace of him gone. The dogs moved behind and above him. He wondered how close they were to the point where a man had sneezed twice.

They would kill him if they found him. Well, he knew that.

He had never been so cold. He had never before lost the free movement of his limbs. He had never been so hungry.

He heard the dogs and the whistled commands. They said, at the money-laundering lectures he had attended, that the art of investigation was 'follow the cash'. Jago had survived the storm and clung to a talisman. Follow the sheets. The dogs had gone, the wind was dropping and the rain had turned to drizzle. He could hear, if he strained to listen, the flap of the sheets as the pegs loosened.

He had endured, which might have been a triumph but was not: he had done nothing. The night closed in and an owl screamed. The washing line was locked in his mind.

10

The rain had stopped but the wind was stronger. Jago saw home: his mother, brother and sister, Christmas, a few presents under a plastic tree. He had not wanted to play the games she'd bought after they'd had the turkey and hadn't wanted to wear a paper hat. He saw the big office in the big building and the man who had greeted him as if he was going to be a satisfying 'work in progress'. A girl in Lancaster had laughed in his face when he'd suggested they go out to the pub, and so had another, who had been with him on the dunes near to Carnforth – they'd watched the cockle pickers far out on the sands.

The people in adjacent seats to his in the City were around him, as were those who sat near him in the Berlin office. He came back to the girl on the beach, to being in the sea and looking across the Strait. All was calm and peaceful – but those people were edging away from him now, and he wanted to call them back.

Eventually he saw the monochrome face – as from a photograph – of Bernardo in the old picture, which showed a man of middle age, smiling and confident . . . and, last, there was another girl, the wound on her face open and oozing.

Each time the madness unhinged him and the shout welled in his throat, he put his clenched fist into his mouth and clamped down his teeth until the blood ran. The pain brought respite from the dreams, but then he would slide back. When he was capable of rational thought he assumed he was subject to delirium, brought on by cold, hunger and lack of movement.

First he saw stars. Then he saw the edge of a cloud wall. At its rim, it glowed silver.

The daughter had come out to smoke again. Men had had

torches and shown their faces when cigarettes were lit on the track.

The kid had been out again with the dogs, no light, and had gone behind Jago, then joined the men on the track to the house. The wind was fiercer and branches cracked. Water tumbled to his right. The cloud was pushed on fast.

The moon broke free of the cloud. The puddles under his body seeped away each time he wriggled. Jago thought, with the moon's appearance, that the delirium might wane. The blood on his hand had dried. There were lights on in the house, more down the track, and a concentration of them in two towns, then the darkness of the sea. He thought he knew the family now and was almost a part of them. He knew the girl who smoked and the mother who ruled the kitchen. He knew the old man, the head of the family, whom he had never seen, and the handyman who drove the car. He knew Marcantonio.

He crawled from the hole in which he had been hidden, and the madness left him. He pushed himself up into a crouch, then stretched. The bones in his back cracked as he straightened. The wind blew against him. He picked up the groundsheet and shook off the water. He laid it in front of him, then started to strip.

He took off each garment, wrung it out and found a little point of rock where he could lodge it. He had satisfied himself that it could not be seen, that the undergrowth and the sight line hid it. The overhang behind him would prevent it being visible to the upper point from which he estimated the sneeze had come. He guessed the man who had sneezed was on surveillance and would have the best gear. He would be dry and snug. The wind swirled around him, and he held his arms across the front of his body. He tipped the water out of his trainers. His body was dry now, but the wind was cold.

A matter of time: how long before the clothes dried in the wind? Another matter: how long before he froze to death, naked? And another: how long before the moon had climbed high enough to light the ledge where he stood? He didn't think he could be seen from behind, where the sneezes had come from, or by the men down the track or the kid with the dogs.

His vest went.

It was white, had been washed at the laundry off Stresemann-strasse. Something, a twig or a leaf, had caught between the toes of his left foot. He had kicked out and the movement had dislodged the vest. It had been laid neatly. The wind had lifted it as if it was a crisps packet at a school gate. He lurched to catch it.

And failed.

He trod on sharp rock and recoiled.

But for that pain, Jago might have caught his vest. It floated, and the wind took it across to where the hillside fell away. It cleared some scrub and snagged on a branch, waving like a flag.

Jago sagged. He could have cried. He was no longer a part of that family.

They were in a bed-and-breakfast because the German embassy in Rome had not thought it appropriate to book them into a hotel. The place was three streets back from the Corso Vittorio Emanuele, no view from either room, but the showers were hot.

They had come back to the address and checked in. They had left a trail of rivulets from the front door to the reception table, made lakes under their feet while they checked in, then splashed towards the stairs. That had been where Carlo had declared himself. He'd said, 'Fred, I want you to know I'm a low achiever, a plodder. That's the nature of my working life.'

The German had answered, 'I am no different. Our word is *Arbeitstier*. I do what I can, give my best, but have not yet changed the world. My best is probably poor. I am beyond middle age, almost a veteran, and I am not considered suitable for promotion.'

A sodden hug at the top of the stairs and they had gone to their rooms. Carlo assumed that a pile of clothing lay abandoned on Fred's floor. The shower warmed him – gave him hope for the future. But the knock on the door was peremptory, the sort that cops or Customs delivered. He'd done it himself. There was a towel round his waist when he opened the door, and he'd dripped more water across the floor from the bathroom.

Carlo had said, 'A "plodder" is an honourable rank, but seldom wins a medal. I think we oil the cogs.'

Fred had replied, 'The crowds don't cheer when an *Arbeitstier* goes by, but we have a part to play.'

Three *carabinieri* stood in the doorway: impeccable uniforms, laundered white shirts, neatly knotted ties. One's fists were clenched, all had set jaws, and no respect in their eyes. Carlo was not sure whether the tuck he'd done with the towel would hold, and whether he'd suffer worse embarrassment. The next door was open too: Fred's head poked out. There was a face at the back, the last of the three. He might have been an older man, with three-day designer stubble. The uniform looked inappropriate on him. His face lightened. The grin cracked it open. Laughter rang out. 'Hey, it's Carlo!'

'Fuck me, Tano! Top man.'

The guy's arms wrapped around him. The towel might have slipped but it didn't seem to matter. The *carabinieri* hadn't been given their names, but knew where they were staying. They had come to deliver an ultimatum from the prosecutor: the Palace of Justice at eight in the morning. An old association was rekindled, and kisses were exchanged. Then Fred was pulled in, and the other two in their uniforms. Fred said whom he had worked with after Duisburg. No one talked shop, and nothing was said about the missing Jago Browne. There was chatter about promotion and retirement, marriages and mistresses, who had moved away, who was disgraced, and a time was fixed for a meeting in the Ciroma Bar when the uniforms would have been ditched for jeans and T-shirts.

A grimace, and Tano, the *maresciallo* with the build of a veteran boxer said, 'But I could weep for the circumstances that bring you back to us, Carlo. Your fugitive may speed the professional death of a valued law enforcer – but that's for tomorrow. Tonight is old times.'

They were gone. He clutched the towel and felt a little better.

Fred smiled, wintry. 'Friendship is good but never helped put on handcuffs. A girl's face was cut, there was extortion. I was as unprofessional as I've ever been. I, too, want to hurt that family. We are not here for a vacation, a circus or nostalgia.'

'A few beers, and whatever we can manage, that's all we can hope for. Why they sent us.'

'We are here to cringe, Carlo, because of Jago Browne. They will piss on the *Arbeitstier* and the plodder.'

They closed their doors, went to dress.

The bet had been on two safe certainties. Marcantonio had watched the transfer from the fishing boat in the port of Villa San Giovanni.

It wasn't unusual for the boat to have been out in poor weather because swordfish was a delicacy and paid better in the market than anything else dragged out of the strait. Also, the fishermen were exceptional sailors – and these were difficult financial times: work must be done. The boat had brought in two fifty-kilo packs of the highest quality cocaine, the purest – the profit margin for the family would be at least ten times what they had paid for it. It had been hidden in the space above the rudder-shaft housing before the container vessel had left Venezuelan waters. North of the strait, a crew member had checked the flotation belts and that the electronics on the packages were armed, then tipped them into the sea at a point registered by his GPS gear. The fishermen had caught no swordfish but the cargo they brought back was worth infinitely more.

Marcantonio had been at the back of the quay when the two parcels were lifted ashore, Stefano alongside him. Rigging rattled sharply around them. It would have been a hard night at sea – the gusts were fierce, channelled up the strait. Neither the fishermen nor the men who had met them spoke to him. They were free-lancers, available for hire. His own family took charge of moving the cocaine, wrapped in protective canvas, with water-resistant paper underneath. Heavy adhesive strips held the packages together. It was good that he should be seen, but he would not interfere: he had to keep a firewall, if possible, between himself and those who handled the product. That he was there showed he would soon be a major player. The craft bounced against the quay, its rigging rattling. There would have been officials on duty in the port offices but they were looked after when a consignment came ashore.

They had driven north.

Now they were stopped on a side-road, south of Rosarno, due east of Gioia Tauro and a kilometre beyond the few lights of Rizziconi. The road ran straight and headlights could be seen from hundreds of metres in either direction. Two Ford vans waited and men talked quietly, smoking hard. There was occasional muffled laughter.

When the first lights appeared there was a simultaneous radio message, a number of bleeps. The backs of the vans were opened, and the drivers readied the engines. There would be two more packages, each weighing in at fifty kilos. They had been among the container ship's cargo when it docked that evening. The men who controlled the docks could decide in which order containers were taken off by the cranes. Others, who had duplicate seals for the container locks, could open them and put the bags holding the product inside a 'clean' container then replace the seal. The main exporter did not know that they were being used as a mule. Dock workers at the supposedly secure complex at Gioia Tauro, could break the duplicate seal, take out the bags and replace the seal with another. A Customs check would show an unbroken seal and they would have no interest in searching the container, a slow, laborious, man-intensive job, even with dogs. The bags would have gone into the boot of a worker's car and be driven out when he came off shift. Now that car arrived, scraped and muddy after the storm. As was usual, the affluence was hidden.

A man came up to Marcantonio and shook his hand, kissed his cheeks, then ducked his head in respect. The packages were stowed, and the vans' doors closed. The car left, the vans followed. More switches would follow north of Naples, and then beyond Milan. The family had facilitated a sale to a dealer in Hamburg, another in Cologne, and a third package would be split for cutting and degrading, for sale on the streets of Scandinavian cities. The

fourth would be shipped across southern France to northern
Spain, then onwards to markets in Barcelona, Santander and
Bilbao. Marcantonio did not have to be there, but it was further
indication that he would soon be a true Man of Honour. He had
felt the excitement and the tension on the quay and at the road-
side. He felt fulfilled. Berlin was so dull.

He knew the market held up well in difficult times. It was not so
true of Berlin but he had read there of an analysis of sewage in
Milan, Naples and Rome: cocaine sold well and the profits they
enjoyed now seemed guaranteed for the future.

Stefano would drive him home in the City-Van.

Consolata made a list: apples, milk, water, ham, bread, cheese and
energy bars. That was the first. The second should have contained
items such as trainers and waterproofs – but she hadn't enough
money. She was loath to borrow or steal from her mother, and
wasn't prepared to go back to the squat and demand a float from
expenses, so, it remained empty. She could afford to buy some of
the food but she'd get the rest from her mother.

She was at her parents' home. They had gone to bed, and their
car was in the lock-up at the back. She had the foldaway bed in the
room that had once been hers and was now her mother's work-
room – she should not have had to take in sewing. A guest at the
hotel had a jacket that had shed a button: Consolata's mother
would take it home, return it the next day, and a little more cash
would slip into her purse. If the business had not been stolen she
would have worked in the shop, and Consolata's father would not
have had to drive a delivery truck in Sicily.

She had thought of Jago during the night. He was rarely out of
her mind. He would have been cold and drenched. The certainty
would have oozed out of him. She would go back. It was important that she kept her word. The radio news said nothing about
'Ndrangheta but was filled with stories of floods, landslips, closed
roads and power cuts. He might be on the road. She had imagined
him struggling along, shoes waterlogged, no cars stopping on
such a night. She had no idea whether her journey, after daybreak,

would be wasted. She might see him at the rendezvous or on the road, if his resolve had cracked – perhaps even where she was now: Consolata had his rucksack. She did not know how he would have survived the storm.

Consolata had thought she understood the naïve Englishman who had come to Reggio and whom she had accosted. She had searched his rucksack, expecting to learn more about him. He had not touched her on the beach and had not looked back when they'd arrived at the drop-off point, just stared through her. The rucksack had told her nothing. It held the bare necessities – no book, pictures or music. Spare underwear, socks, another shirt, and a pair of trousers. Consolata could not have said what she'd hoped to find in the bag, but she had looked for a degree of meaning and found nothing.

She was annoyed that he confused her. But what he achieved would be on the radio, and she would feel a private pride. She wouldn't share it.

'I sit around all day, half the night, watch the rain falling . . . and wait. What sort of message am I supposed to get from that?'

'Different people from us, Bent, without our sense of time-keeping,' the lawyer, Humphrey, soothed him. 'Not an easy place to do business, but the rewards . . .'

'Do they know who I am? Answer me.'

'I've learned – the hard way – that it's best to relax and go with the flow. Always best, Bent, to keep calm.'

'I might as well go home.'

Jack had been down to Torbay, in south Devon, when Humphrey had last slipped over for a few days with his elderly father, using the Brittany Ferries route from Spain to Plymouth. Humphrey had not enthused at the prospect of Bentley Horrocks making the journey. Jack had insisted. 'He's a big man who's getting bigger.'

Humphrey had grimaced. 'They're picky about who they do business with. They're not just thugs, Jack. They're thugs *and* businessmen.'

They had been in a working men's club and Humphrey had

been moaning about the absence in Calabria of English beer, as they'd talked in a corner – no way Crime Squad detectives would have had a wire in there.

Jack had said, 'He's got young dogs snapping at his heels, and he's static at the moment, needs to move into a bigger league. Big fish in a puddle. You can fix it.' Most of that day, Jack had wished that the old solicitor – good at what he did and always close to the wind – had turned him down. He hadn't. Now they were in the crap hotel in Brancaleone and a whole day had gone by with barely a view of the beach. He had tried to set some ground rules and top of the list was keeping the mobiles switched off, all six that they had brought with them.

'Sorry and all that, Bent, but walking out won't help. Cutting off your nose to spite your face. I can't—'

'Tell me what you *can* do.'

'—hurry these people up. They're the major players in the world. They have people knocking on the door most days. You have to be patient.'

Another shrug. Jack wondered what they could do to kill time. The food here wasn't great, there was a noisy party going on in the dining room and the pool had been drained. The shops were long closed, and they couldn't even use the phones. There was no Scrabble and he doubted Bent could play chess. Jack thought it interesting that Humphrey, who'd licked arses in London till his tongue was raw, had tried to pacify Bent, stop him pacing and jabbing his finger. He'd stood up for himself. Jack understood: Humphrey now ran with serious players and did little jobs for them. He fed off the crumbs from their table – while Bentley Horrocks was at the level of 'Take it or leave it'.

'What are you saying?'

'I'm saying they know you're here, and they'll come when they're ready.'

'But do they know who I am – who Bentley Horrocks is?'

Jack knew the answer might have been: 'Absolutely, Bent. That's why they're in no hurry to meet you.' If Humphrey had said that the furniture might have started flying. He didn't.

Humphrey said, 'It's nothing personal, Bent. When the top man sees you it'll be worthwhile. That's a promise.'

'Believe me, esteemed colleague, if I could help you I would.'

'But you cannot or will not.'

The prosecutor walked along the wide pavement. To his left was the Via Vittorio Emanuele where the great magnolia trees shook off the last of the rain. To his right was the sea and the far-off lights of Messina, across the strait. The man he was with had hooked a hand into the angle of his arm.

'I cannot – I'm not involved in the investigations into people you've named.'

'There are few friends I can turn to.'

'Forgive me – I have the greatest admiration for your work but you shouldn't attempt to drag me into it.'

The prosecutor was with a middle-ranking officer of the Agency for Information and Security (Internal). The Secret Service played a role in anti-'Ndrangheta operations, but an ill-defined one. It was accepted that their equipment was far superior to that used by the Squadra Mobile and the *carabinieri*. The prosecutor thought that AISI officers had informal links with the gangsters of Calabria, and that the relationships went back to the days when it was convenient for the state to utilise the Mafia groups against Italian Communism.

'I didn't know where else to turn.'

'My apologies. It's always a pleasure to see you, but there are many more fish in the sea. Good night.'

His arm was loosed, and the figure beside him drifted away. The prosecutor was alone for a few seconds, then the escort closed around him. They had given him space while he was with the intelligence officer, but now the cars were brought level with the little group. He was isolated, and knew it. He did not have to say so to his protection detail: they would have observed and recognised the signs of rejection. Time slipped through his fingers.

The City-Van drove through the village, where men watched and noted it, waved to Stefano and showed respect to the *padrino*'s grandson. Lights lit the front of the house and the trees to the side and behind. Marcantonio thought a white plastic bag was flapping in a tree a little up the hill. He ignored it. He went through the front door, and Stefano used the back, where the dogs were. The wind was bad – there had been branches down over the road. The dogs wouldn't go far tonight because they were valuable and it would be dangerous for them if a tree split or fell.

Every light was on in his bunker. Bernardo lay on his back. He had changed into flannelette pyjamas, but had kept on his vest and socks. The air was damp, and he could hear the TV programme but hardly see it because condensation blurred the screen.

He knew that Marcantonio had been taken to witness the landing and distribution of the latest shipment. It was a step forward in his grandson's advancement to be seen by the foot-soldiers. It would give him authority. That had been how his own father had brought Bernardo forward, and how, twenty years ago, he had introduced Rocco and Domenico to other families. His father was buried in the village cemetery, killed in a knife attack in Siderno. His sons were in gaol. The future of the *cosca* depended on the boy.

That worried him. At least, it was among the worries that burdened him, but they were linked. The light dazzled him, but that was as nothing against his growing horror of the darkness.

The priest, Father Demetrio, was prominent in his mind.

There had been no explanations, but the old fool would have understood. A stumbling progress up the hill to a small flat area, where there had been sufficient earth to dig the hole with a spade and pickaxe. A crude mound where the soil had not yet sunk over the small, near-emaciated corpse. Some gabbled prayers. The photograph of the child with the newspaper would, the day after, have been delivered to the parents. It was rare for Bernardo to listen to Mamma's blunt demand: a prayer had to be said over a grave. She could not do it. Since that day, neither he nor Father Demetrio had mentioned the grave or whose body lay within it. But Bernardo no longer trusted his old friend to keep silent – and had condemned him.

How to kill a priest? The question exercised him.

One had been shot dead while he was putting on his vestments, but that was twenty years ago, near Naples. Another had been shot outside his church but that was even longer ago, in Sicily. Among the Aspromonte villages one had had a pistol fired at him, unsuccessfully, four years previously. A severed pig's head had been left on the doorstep of Father Stamile's home further up the coast from Locri. It was a big decision for Bernardo, but he had taken it. The priest would be silenced. It was about the child, the grave he had never revisited, the money paid by the duped parents that had set the family on the road to huge wealth. Other families, after this child's death and the ransom payment, had given up taking the children of rich northerners and bringing them south: they had claimed that the cases attracted too much attention from the *carabinieri* and Squadra Mobile. The families had met, head man with head man, on the hills – where they could pose to the inquisitive as mushroom pickers – and the practice had been ended. The investment in the child had enabled Bernardo's first purchase of uncut cocaine, and he had not looked back until now.

More than two hundred kidnappings had been controlled from the villages close to where Bernardo lived, many millions of dollars paid in ransom. One man had escaped from the prison where his captors had held him, reached a house and begged the occupants to call the *carabinieri*. He was given coffee and bread and sat in the warmth until men arrived, but not from the barracks. The man of the house had returned the escaper to his gaolers. What else would he have done? Another had freed himself, blundered into the forest and come across women searching for *porcini*. They had overpowered him, brought him back to the village and passed him to their men. Best of all, in Bovalino, down the coast from Locri, there was a part of the town that local people called Polghettopoli after the billionaire's grandson, Paul Getty, for whom more than three million dollars were paid. They had sliced off a part of the kid's ear and posted it to the *Messaggero* newspaper in Rome, with the demand that the family speed up the negotiation. They had not realised that the postal workers were on strike so it had taken three weeks to reach the capital. Another captive had managed to flee, had been hunted down, shot dead, then kept in a bar's freezer so he could be regularly lifted out, propped up and photographed to encourage the closing of a final deal. Good stories. They roved in his mind but came back, always, to Father Demetrio and the danger to the family's future. And with Father Demetrio was the image of the child . . .

An accident, perhaps . . . Bernardo considered the options.

Soon, he would try to sleep. The light would stay on.

Jago might have slept. The moon was bright and there were stars high above, but dawn was not far off. He was so cold, so cramped and so hungry.

His clothing was laid out around him – why? He remembered. The moonlight showed Jago his trainers, trousers, coat, pants and socks. His vest had floated away on the wind.

He looked for it.

Anxiety gripped him. As he recalled it, the vest had caught on a tree that was level with the near end of the house. He could see the tree, and the spread of its branches, but not his vest. The wind was still strong so the vest should have been flying, like a windsock at an airfield, stretched horizontally. He couldn't see it. He had been wondering how he'd get up a tree and crawl along a branch . . .

Then he saw his vest. It was crumpled on the ground. It had to be retrieved or . . . He could turn his back, put on his clothing and forget the vest. He could get to the road, hitch a ride, find a bus or walk to whatever degree of civilisation existed in this neck of the woods, and put himself clear. He might be at the bank by lunchtime.

The *FrauBoss*: 'Where have you been, Jago? We were worried, and you've missed several meetings.'

Jago Browne: 'Something that seemed a good idea at the time. Apologies, Wilhelmina. It won't happen again.' At school they'd had lectures on responsibility and consequences – *For want of a battle the kingdom was lost, And all for the want of a horseshoe nail.* The nail this time was an old vest from Marks & Spencer.

It lay close to the City-Van, within five metres of the front door. He could get it or he could turn back.

Jago started to dress, his clothes still very damp. The cockerel crowed. He could retrieve his vest or abandon it and be gone before daylight. A choice.

Fabio and Ciccio watched.

They had night-vision optics and binoculars but they hardly needed the enhancing gear as the scene was played out in front of them. Ciccio had been sleeping when he'd started awake, Fabio's hand across his mouth. A little stab of his partner's finger had told Ciccio where to look.

'There's clothing by the vehicle.'

'I don't believe this.'

'It'll be what flew past – belongs to whoever's further down. He'll be wet through with no proper kit, trying to dry it and himself. The wind took his vest. And that's where it landed.'

'Look how he's moving – doesn't know where any trail is. Where are the dogs? What do we do?'

'I don't know! He's on borrowed time.'

They watched.

A shadowy figure came out of the thin line of trees at the base of the hill. It crouched, took stock, then went forward, bent double. The wind pitched him forward and he lost his balance, then regained it. There was a light inside the house, on the main landing at the top of the stairs.

A dog barked.

The man went forward, a sort of crabbing movement, towards the vest. He dropped down beside it, picked it up and thrust it into a pocket. He was wearing a camouflage jacket, jeans and trainers. His shirt clung to his body and his jacket flapped open. He seemed to hesitate.

Fabio said, 'The dogs are shut inside. If they'd been loose . . . What's so important about a vest?'

'Thank him,' Ciccio muttered. 'If they'd found it there would be a search – and we're where they'd look.'

A dog barked, woke the pack. A cacophony of noise came from the house towards them . . .

They did surveillance: they were there to observe and the unforgivable crime was to blow a position. It was the ultimate sin. They could use force only if their lives were endangered. They could do nothing but watch. The man seemed to grope in his trousers and was beside the City-Van.

'Fuck me! Did you see that?'

He thought the man, from the glint of poor light on chrome, had keys out of his pocket and was beside the City-Van. Incomprehensible.

He held the keys hard against the bodywork of the vehicle, took a deep breath and walked.

He did it steadily, as if he had time to kill.

A few metres away the dogs pounded against the door.

He had a job to do. He would do it in his own time as best he could.

The line was cut into the paintwork as he went from rear to front. Jago pressed hard with the short blade of the penknife Consolata has given him. Above the front wheel, he turned and started back. He did it methodically. It seemed important to use the blade.

He heard a shout from inside the house and lights were coming on upstairs. His clothing chilled him, and the light-headed recklessness he felt was close to the delirium he had experienced at the height of the storm . . .

There were cats in Canning Town, around their building, and many were strays. Some were put out at night and allowed in only to be fed; others were pampered, their owner's best or only friend. It didn't matter whether the cat was an outsider or on the inside track if it was male: they sprayed their territory so that every other cat knew they had been there. They made their mark. Jago left the scratch, tramlines, the best he could manage.

If he'd had petrol and matches he could have sloshed it over the vehicle and set fire to it. If he'd had some dry paper and a functioning fag-lighter he could have made a spill and flung it down the fuel pipe. He had the penknife. He bent one last time and stabbed, with all his strength, at the rear passenger-side tyre. He felt the rubber give under the pressure and the blade slipped in. He tugged it back, folded and pocketed it . . .

There had been a teacher at his school who was ex-military, a disciplinarian, and never took shite from the kids. That teacher never hurried. When there was a fight in the playground, he never sprinted to break it up. Never broke sweat. Jago turned away.

A light on now downstairs and shouts from far away on the track. Jago slipped back towards the cover of the trees.

He didn't know whether what he had done was puerile or something to be proud of. Would he, one day, be sitting in a comfortable swing chair in a glass-sided office and considering with satisfaction what he had done against the might of 'Ndrangheta, organised-crime barons, annual turnover approximately forty-five billion euros? He climbed. He had little light to guide him, using his fingers to haul himself up the wet rock faces.

The dogs were out. The men who came up the track shouted and waved torches. The daughter, Giulietta, was outside – he could hear her voice and the orders she gave.

The dogs quartered the ground, scattering gravel, bursting through the lower scrub, but the wind would have screwed up their sense of smell. He noted a thinner voice then, and thought the boy who patrolled with the dogs was there, and the man who drove the car. They were all milling around, confused.

Would he go back to Lamezia, ferried there by Consolata, and tell her he had done well? That he had confronted the family, taken a step against them? What had he done? she might ask, as she drove towards the airport. He had put the penknife she'd given him to good use. How good? He had scratched the side of a vehicle. A Maserati, a Ferrari, a top-of-the-range Porsche? No. A City-Van fit for the scrapyard. And he had punctured one of its tyres. He might give her back her penknife or keep it as a souvenir. Her head would shake and any admiration in her eyes would vanish.

He could return to Berlin, take the S-bahn across the city, go to the square and sit on a bench, then wait to see if the girl came out of the pizzeria. If she did, he could go to her, tell her that he had been to Calabria, had hidden above the home of her attacker and scratched the paintwork of a car. He might even show her the penknife. She would look at him with contempt.

Jago climbed on. The last of the moonlight guided him. He heard Marcantonio's voice. He found the two boulders, twisted round and slid backwards inside.

Giulietta had a dressing-gown on, was bare-legged – she seemed to have lost interest. Marcantonio was beside the City-Van, Stefano showing him the scratches. Jago was just near enough to see his astonishment. Marcantonio wore boxer shorts, flip-flops and a T-shirt, his carefully spiked hair a wild mess. Only Marcantonio understood.

Jago lay very still. He saw that Marcantonio had a torch, a spotlight type, with a long, powerful beam. It was aimed up the slope, showing branches, tree trunks, and bounced off rock faces. Because of the torch he could no longer see Marcantonio's face but imagined it creased with fury. It was still dark, but dawn was on the horizon. It would not be bright for hours. Marcantonio had time to brood on the City-Van's scratches.

It was personal, between himself and the grandson of the family, who could strut about and not be confronted. Jago wondered how it would be to have come from a family of huge wealth and power, and be destined for vast authority. The torch beam played on the trees and found nothing. The others would have wondered when the vehicle had been damaged by vandals, wherever it had been. Not Marcantonio.

The torch was killed. The dogs were quiet. Marcantonio and Giulietta headed for the house, as did the driver. The kid, half dressed, called the dogs. The men went away down the track, and silence fell, but for the wind in the trees.

He thought he had done well. The rain had passed. Jago imagined the anger he had provoked. He wanted to see more. Today would be bright and hot. He hadn't done enough but it was a start.

I I

He had not seen it before the sun had risen high enough to clear the trees. An emptiness. There were heavy shadows behind the back door of the house, and beyond the line of the overgrown vine on the trellis, then darkness.

When the sun cleared the roof tiles, the warmth fell not only on Jago but also onto the washing line. The light was brilliant so he had a clear view of the path and the low retaining wall behind it. He could follow the broken stone paving to a halfway point where the slabs had slipped. The ground under them had slid down and the path went on to the pole from which the line was slung, then another wall and the roof of the derelict shed. Without the sun, Jago would not have registered the path and its emptiness.

The wind had dropped: the gale was now a blustery breeze. He studied the track, and the taut line.

The sheets had been a casualty. They were in the mud at the side of the path, trapped against the stones of the retaining wall. They were of good quality, he thought, better than those he had had in the attic studio on Stresemannstrasse, but had been left out to take their chance when the storm had hit. They lay in crumpled heaps. The emptiness was where they had been. Now they would need a double wash, with plenty of detergent – they were covered with mud.

Jago studied them. He was supposed to be capable of making good judgements. The bank paid him to be sharp.

Between the third and fourth sheets, where they had been dumped by the wind the path was deeper in the centre and shallower at the edges. The slip ran for some three metres, more than a third of the distance between the trellis and the wall that blocked the view of the near-ruined shed.

A cable . . .

. . . He could see a join in the centre of a length of cable – electrician's tape had been used to join two lengths, then wrapped in transparent plastic. The cable had been buried along the part of the path that was hidden by the sheets. Not now.

At Canary Wharf, they'd rated him as intelligent. They'd thought the same of him at the university, where he'd done a business course, and in the City, where he had been recruited by the bank and reckoned worthy of the transfer to Berlin. They had rated him sharp and bright enough to go after prospective clients and meet those who had already signed up. The sun was on the cable. In Jago's estimation, it had been laid recently – the plastic coating was not yet stained with damp or deterioration. It ran from the back of the house, below the path and towards the derelict shed. Then it continued alongside the building to a slope where rubble and earth were heaped high. Thorn and broom bushes grew there, but no trees.

It was as if his lottery numbers had come up. A special moment. A new challenge screamed at him that good times lay ahead. Jago was always at his best when he was challenged – and that was why he hadn't run when he'd done the car.

The back door opened.

He felt elation. It wasn't a moment for punching the air – as some in the City did when news of bonuses came through – but more as if he'd sipped a good whisky in front of a blazing log fire. He felt contented, as he had that Christmas when he he'd stayed in the country-house hotel. Answers tumbled towards him.

The old woman came out of the back door, the dogs close to her, and saw her sheets on the ground. In her black cardigan and skirt, black socks and black shoes, with the black scarf knotted over her head, it was clear she had no truck with sunshine. She would despise 'luxury', he thought. No silk underwear for her, no stylists queuing to do her hair. A stupid thought: he'd bet what little money he had in his wallet that she'd have cooked him an amazing pasta dish, and would have dried his clothes, then ironed them expertly. Nothing about her was attractive. Her photograph had been on the policeman's file in the station on Bismarckstrasse so she had flitted into Berlin and was linked, therefore, to a slashed face. He was there, in part, because of her and what she would have taught her grandson.

A second stupid thought: she would fight to her last breath to protect her family.

She smacked her hands together, then spread her feet so that she could bend down to collect the sheets. She moved along the path and stopped short of where the ground had slipped. The hole was in front of her and one more sheet lay on the far side. She whistled, a note he recognised: it was the one the kid used when he had the dogs on the hills. The dog closest to her knee was brindled, a crossbreed. The command – from between her teeth – was faint but clear. It bounded forward, reached the last sheet, scratched it into a tighter ball, then clamped its jaws on it and dragged it to the woman. Jago looked for a sign of appreciation shared between the dog and its mistress. He saw no love, no gratitude. She looked towards the end of the path, stared at the honeysuckle that grew up the building's wall, still in flower. Her mouth twitched. Then she wiped the back of her hand across her nose and went back to the house.

The sun rose. The cable was now in dense shadow.

Jago understood. What to do with his knowledge would exercise him. What to do that was more than scratching vehicles. He thought her magnificent, uncompromising.

Jago checked his watch, worked out when he could make the rendezvous with Consolata and have water, food and clothing. He wondered briefly what she would bring, but was more concerned with the exposed cable.

'What could you see?'

Fabio answered, 'I can't see from here where the sheets were – that rock blocks it – but she's picked them up, the four sheets.'

Ciccio tapped the newest message into the keypad.

'And what do they make of what happened last night?'

'Not my problem.'

They lapsed into silence and the message was sent. Ciccio had one certainty: it was someone else's problem. He didn't know who that someone was, had seen only a shadow moving, and the image-intensifier glasses had not shown him a face. The shadow had crawled out of the night and attacked the home of a noted player, the head of a medium-ranking family. He had not dynamited the place or splashed petrol on the door and tossed a match or sprayed the upper windows with automatic fire from an AK. He had scratched a car. Why? And the consequences?

That was easier to answer. Ciccio had seen the results of 'Ndrangheta killings, those who had been strangled, starved to death in makeshift gaols and shot in the street. Once, part of a corpse had not quite dissolved because the acid in the vat had been used too often. As a consequence there would be a body. They had done their job, had observed and reported, and it was for others to pick over the information they had provided. It seemed to have no relevance to the Scorpion Fly surveillance operation. The clock ticked, and time slipped by.

'Can I tell you something?'

'What?'

'The scorpion flies we collected are dead and useless. We tried. Is that good enough?'

'Always. We tried and there's a reward.'

It diverted them to talk about the insect that looked like a killer and was harmless. The fate of the scorpion fly collection mattered almost as much as sighting the target. The wretched little creatures gave them a degree of sanity. They treated themselves to a dawn lunch, *wurstel* and a can of fruit cocktail. The combination would play havoc with their digestion, but they reckoned they deserved it. To Ciccio, the consequence for the shadowy figure was inevitable – as night follows day.

'You've been here before?' Carlo snapped, from the side of his mouth.

They were escorted up wide stairs – it hadn't seemed worth waiting for the lift. A uniformed man was ahead. They had been through a metal detector – they had dumped their change and phones in a tray for X-ray, and their ID cards and passports had been photocopied. 'Yes. Nothing's different,' Fred answered him.

'We have an agenda?'

'Bend the knee, apologise, be helpful. Say as little as possible.'

It was a best-clothing occasion, trousers, jackets, ties. The walls had been recently painted but institutional grime seemed to cling to them. There were no works of art, and the paintwork was a dull cream. On the landing there were ranks of closed doors, numbered, the occupants' names not displayed. They walked the length of a corridor. Ahead they could see an open lobby area.

Men pushed up from the sofas and hard chairs where they smoked, read magazines or watched their phones' screens. They were not those who had entertained them in the Ciroma bar the previous night. Carlo had drunk too much and Fred had matched him beer for beer. It was the story of his life that, too often, he was half-cut when he needed to be stone-cold sober, his antennae alert. He felt flushed and sweaty. The German looked better, which was a bitter pill for Carlo to swallow: Fred could hold his beer better than himself.

The men were the protection team. Some carped that they were superfluous, and, he'd heard, when he'd done the liaison from Rome, that they provided a visual symbol of ego. He knew enough of the differing Mafia groups to believe they sensed weakness and exploited it. They would kill their enemies, if it suited them.

He had been told a story about the killing of Paolo Borsellino, in Palermo, when that prosecutor had been a 'walking cadaver' and it was known he had been condemned. He'd had a team of five guards, always with him, in as much danger as he was. It was said that Borsellino used to evade the team and go out, when he needed cigarettes, that he hoped he would be shot then, alone, so that their lives would be spared. They had all died with him, four policemen and a policewoman.

These men would be the prosecutor's family. Their anoraks and denim jackets were on the arms of the sofa and they wore their shoulder holsters. They would know that their man was facing ever-increasing isolation, and that an investigation was close to failure

– all in the 'briefing' at the bar. He and Fred added to the burden on
the man's shoulders. The Mafia sent out their gunmen and their
bombmakers when a target was isolated. Now he and Fred faced
cold stares. He would have expected nothing else. One checked
their names, their ID, went to an unmarked door and spoke into a
microphone. They were waved inside. He doubted a single prosecutor in London or Berlin grasped this man's lifestyle.

A cigarette burned in a cheap tourist ashtray, already half filled
with butts, and the day had barely started. He wore braces, his shirt
was unbuttoned low on his chest – a crucifix hung from a chain
round his neck – and his fingers were stained mahogany with nicotine. The shirt cuffs were open, the links undone. He had three or
four days' stubble on his cheeks and his spectacles were balanced
high on the crown of his head. The wall, predictably, was covered
with the shields of other forces: German, French, the FBI, the Drug
Enforcement Administration, Spain, Greece and an elaborate one
from Colombia. A *carabinieri* cap lay on a shelf, with a child's model
of a helicopter in *carabinieri* livery. In Carlo's experience, some men
carried the burden of their work easily and could muster a smile of
welcome. In a few, hope had died. The other shelves groaned under
the weight of the files stacked on them.

Nothing had changed. It was as Carlo remembered it. They
dealt in paper, made mountains of it, and the burden grew. In
London, in Green Lanes, Peckham, Deptford or out on the Essex
fringes, there might be a celebration in a bar if a big player was
brought in. There was nothing as crude here as a rogues' gallery
of wanted men: there wasn't room – it would have covered all of
the walls and maybe the ceiling.

The prosecutor sat down. They were not offered chairs.

'You came to tell me . . .'.

The German spoke up. He was good at taking blame and
accepting shit. He talked about a bank worker and a pizzeria in
Berlin's smart Charlottenburg, the young man's intervention, a
girl's face disfigured and . . .

'Would you get to the point?'

Fred spoke good enough Italian. He told the prosecutor of an error made, a file left visible on a computer screen, a message calling him from the room. The bank worker's disappearance, a vandalised car . . .

'The car was the property of the grandson of Bernardo Cancello? And the vandalism was the act of a Briton, Jago Browne?' The prosecutor spoke reasonable English. 'What was the act of vandalism?'

Fred told him. A uniformed policeman from Bismarckstrasse had checked Marcantonio's address. The vehicle had been parked outside and two parallel lines had been scraped on the bodywork: expensive to repair.

'He's there. Your man, Browne, has reached us. Last night, officers on surveillance duty witnessed an unidentified man scratch the sides of a City-Van outside the home of that *padrino*. The vehicle is an artisan's transport, old and worthless. He is there for what purpose other than to scratch cars?'

Fred said he didn't know what the Englishman, who had no military training, no police experience, no law-enforcement knowledge, intended. He was in the sales division of a bank specialising in attracting investors. It was unlikely he had either accomplices or a lethal weapon.

Carlo did not intervene. They had come to help in any way possible, to be present, demonstrate solidarity and liaise. He saw the cigarette ground out and another lit. He reckoned Fred had done well in the circumstances.

'He is now in hiding. I think that soon they will find him. If they do, they will kill him. To me that is irrelevant. I am looking for Bernardo Cancello. I am coming towards the end of a lengthy investigation that depends on his capture. With a stranger close to him, he will have gone even further into those goddamn mountains where an army can disappear. Will I try to save him and thereby wreck the last hours of my mission? Or do I leave him to his fate? I don't doubt its certainty. At the end of the week I lose my assets, my eyes on the ground, and start on another case. I shall have failed. Where I work there is danger in failure. Each time *I* fail, or *we* fail, *they* have won. They exploit all victories. Your man is helping me to fail. Have you anything else to say?'

Fred nodded in agreement with all that had been said – no medals in confrontation – and said that their bosses expected them to remain in Calabria until the bank worker could be located and brought home: repatriated, alive or dead. The prosecutor scribbled a name on a sheet of paper and a phone number in the *carabinieri* building on Via Aschenez. A file was opened and a meeting ended.

A final word: 'And stay the fuck out of my way.'

They were outside.

'You did well,' Carlo told him.

Fred clasped the scrap of paper with the name and number. They'd get some paperwork done.

'Just have to look on the bright side,' Carlo said. 'Achieve what's possible . . . It's what we do every day.'

Fred said, 'Yes.'

'Can't do any more. Won't be anything new.'

'Because we're just the little people. I said it's "unlikely" that he had accomplices. But he can't have got himself this far without help.'

'In the time he had available, it would have been impossible.'

'Don't sell him short,' Fred said. 'I did – I won't again.'

The sun shone as they emerged from the building.

'Is this any business of ours?'

'We should make it our business.'

Carlo paused on the pavement. 'Tell me, he has no experience of the military, no training in covert warfare, has never fought hand to hand, except perhaps as a kid. Is he better off for knowing nothing? Or is he a lamb to the slaughter? I don't know.'

Fred frowned. 'Might be better off. He's not dependent on support, back-up, no rule book in his pocket, no commander bleating in his ear. And he's a true volunteer. I think he's better off. But he is not quite alone because he has a helper. God, what do I know?'

She had done her shopping early at the mini-mart, put fuel in her parents' car and was on the road. Nothing on the radio that involved her, except reports of flooding in the north and landslips on a railtrack south of Naples, the usual shit about a month's rain falling in a day. Consolata had gone through his rucksack again and taken out dry clothing.

She drove north of Archi, then turned off the main road at Gallico towards the mountains and began the climb. Had anyone been with her, she would have said that you left civilisation at Santo Stefano in Aspromonte. There were few road signs but she was comfortable enough with the route. Boys herding goats, women collecting mushrooms, hikers in columns, cars travelling fast and lorries hugging cliff edges. The sun was higher and the road gleamed in her face. She had the window down and let the wind ripple the skin of her arms and throat. She was east of Varapodio, making good time, while the radio played soft music between news bulletins and weather reports and— She hit the brake.

The tyres screamed, burned. If she hadn't stamped on the pedal, she would have hit the car in front of her. In front of it, a tractor was towing a trailer and in front of the tractor there was a roadblock.

She didn't know what had happened on the hill above the house. Didn't know what he had done. Didn't know if they had her name. Didn't know whether he was alive, dead or hunted. She had food for him. His rucksack was in the back of her car, with travel documents in his name; she had fuel for the vehicle in a plastic litre bottle. The roadblock was mounted by *carabinieri*, but not the ones with the fancy uniforms. These men wore military combat clothing, with sub-machine guns. Their protective vests were weighed down with reserve ammunition magazines and they carried gas, pistols and handcuffs on their belts. She thought she was about five kilometres from the point above the village where she had parked and left him.

What to do? The tractor driver was being interrogated. He was not handed back his papers and waved through. This was planned and thorough. If they had his and her names, she would go into a cage.

Consolata swung the wheel – she did the equivalent of tiptoeing away. A discreet three-point turn, and then she hit the zigzags. So, he had no food, no water and wet clothing – if he was still there. She shrugged. She'd come back when the roadblock had gone. She didn't know him and the radio had said nothing about him. She retraced her route. She barely understood him and he hadn't helped. She resented that – she wanted to know him . . .

He watched Giulietta.

The confirmations came in a line . . .

Jago knew the bus route to school that went along Barking Road. The shelter was inadequate if it rained, but he'd have to wait ages – then three would come at once. Old rule. Predictable. Three confirmations in a line, like London buses.

There was Giulietta and the washing for the line. The handyman was following with a spade. The chickens and the dogs were with them.

He could see enough.

Giulietta would have been barely older than the girls at the bank, but Renate, Elke and Hannelore wouldn't have been seen dead in clothing like hers or have left their hair to its own devices, as Giulietta did. She had a plastic basket tucked under one arm, which she put on the ground. She shook out the folded sheets, then started to peg them to the line. Each time a sheet was placed in position, it denied Jago a view of that section of the path. The sheets made a screen. To a casual observer, they were there to dry. The second fell off at one end and she had to go back to refasten it.

The handyman was in front of her with the spade and dug a trench, then toed the cable into it and patted the earth back into place, stamped on the loose soil, and manoeuvred the slabs so that the walkway was smoother. He worked where earth had subsided and Jago had seen the join in the cable. Giulietta jabbed her finger at him, issued instructions and flounced about in annoyance at the time he took. The chickens squawked and bustled at her feet. Twice she aimed a kick at them. When all the sheets were hung, and the path had been levelled, Jago could no longer see the cable.

The join in it had been a yard left of where the third and fourth sheets overlapped. Jago took two small twigs, fallen in the night and scratched a line with his penknife on a rock; beyond it he worked the twigs into the ground. He had a pointer to the overlap of the sheets and the join in the cable.

There was a whistle and a shout. Marcantonio was at the back door, dressed. The sunlight caught the muscles in his arms and his hair. The dogs came to the whistle, and the kid to the shout.

Jago couldn't see either Giulietta or the handyman on the path because they were on the far side of the sheets. He breathed an oath. The young man, Marcantonio, had called the dogs and the kid, then had gone back into the kitchen and retrieved a shotgun. The barrels were sawn off a little more than halfway down.

Jago had time now to break and run.

Marcantonio gazed up and around, his eyes raking across the trees, slopes and sheer rock faces, as if he knew. It stood to reason: a man who had scratched his car in Berlin wouldn't come all this way to do the same to another a vehicle then quit. The scratches symbolised a challenge to fight. Had Jago meant that? His difficulty now was to get clear. He had to come out of the hole under the two boulders, then scramble up a rock face where he would be silhouetted against light grey rock and soft lichen. He didn't know if he was within range of the shotgun, but the dogs would have him. He lay still, barely breathing, head down. In his mind he saw Marcantonio's face: cold, brutal and angry – the latter a victory of sorts.

He heard whistles and shouts. He thought Marcantonio and the kid had taken different routes but the dogs ran between them. How would it be if feet or paws appeared before his eyes? The penknife was in his hand, the short blade exposed.

'What did the woman do, Fabio?'

'Hung out the washing, of course.'

'I saw that – but what did he do with the spade?'

'I don't know. But the grandson's out with a firearm and the fucking dogs.'

'What's the engagement regulation again?'

'You know that as well as I do, Fabio. If our lives are threatened we can shoot.'

'Ciccio, if we shoot, we can't expect support in high places. But those bastards won't take me . . . Do we just get the hell out?'

There was no answer. Both men had eased their Berettas clear of the holsters, armed them and checked the safety. Both hardly dared to breathe. It was the body smells they feared, the food wrappers in their bag, the excrement in the tinfoil . . . Fabio watched as Ciccio sent a message of the danger closing in on them. They heard whistles, shouts and dogs barking.

The boy went directly behind the house and climbed a scree slope. Marcantonio was to his left, and the dogs roved between them.

Below, Stefano had the City-Van jacked up and the spare wheel ready on the ground.

Marcantonio came warily. He had explained little to the kid of why they were searching the wooded, rocky slope or what they expected to find. The kid was the son of a cousin and would never be within the family's inner loop. He would be a foot-soldier, a *picciotto*, and would grow old in a junior rank. He might go to gaol for years, and would never be able to break free of the family's control. Now, and in the future, the kid would do as he was told, and receive explanations only if it suited. He didn't know where the City-Van had been when scratched, or when the tyre had been cut.

Marcantonio couldn't control the dogs the way the kid did – the kid guided them with shrill whistles, but Marcantonio had to shout at them. He stumbled twice. His trainers had lightly ribbed soles, good for walking in Locri or Siderno, but not suitable for the hills. He had been a child when his father was taken, but his father had rarely been in the valleys or on the mountains. He had spent time in Reggio and Milan. Marcantonio wasn't used to covering almost vertical ground where the rock could be razor sharp or slid away under his weight. The kid was like a goat, and climbed fast. The dogs wanted to be with him, not with Marcantonio.

It was years since he had fired a shotgun, and then it had been at a cardboard box, at a range of twenty metres. The spread would have brought down a running man or crippled a deer, but that was the limit. He was poor with a pistol, had seldom been out with other teenagers to fire at cans – for fear of failing. It was not in the nature of the 'Ndrangheta to kill at random. His grandfather had always said that killing was done to exert extreme pressure on enemies and remove obstacles to a quiet life. He had enough reason to carry the shotgun, which was loaded, and it would have been the work of three or four seconds to lock it, draw back the hammer, squeeze and fire.

Two lines had been scratched on the body of the car – done with a knife or keys. The second stumble had pitched him onto his knee and ripped his jeans – Ralph Lauren, bought on the Ku'damm, when he had put them on he hadn't realised how difficult it would be to scramble around the rocks with the dogs. His knee was bleeding. As he went higher, Capo, the alpha dog, was close to him. There were moments when it seemed to go after a scent, but there would have been rabbits here, and small deer or a boar or— He slipped again, went down several metres on his backside. He couldn't use his hands to steady himself because they were on the shotgun. Eventually a bush broke the fall, but his pride was dented. He heard the kid whistling for his dogs, then Capo above him, and Stefano banging the new wheel into position. He was high above the bunker. It was sad that his grandfather had to live in that hole . . . He thought of how it would be when he headed the family and the old man was buried in the cemetery at the bottom of the village. Marcantonio would be a man of status, his name displayed in the files of the *carabinieri* and the Squadra Mobile. There would be meetings in the Palace of Justice to discuss evidence that could be brought against him.

It was a diversion. He was on a hillside, being teased and laughed at. The old City-Van had had twin lines drawn on it and Marcantonio alone knew why. He barely remembered the girl's face. A man had come to taunt him.

His knee hurt.

He sat down. He had not been with a woman since he'd got home. He had listened as his grandmother had talked interminably about the priest, the Madonna of the Mountains and the small children, Annunziata's. His mother, Teresa, had watched him with suspicion: Berlin might have alienated him from his home and if he became part of a city's life the family would fail. His grandfather was old and whined . . . and above him, some way distant, he heard a dog growl.

It had come upon them. Fabio had the Beretta pistol, cocked. Ciccio had the Sabre Red, law-enforcement strength, CS tear gas/ red pepper canister.

Fabio had not spent a day on the range for eight months. Ciccio had seen a demonstration of the spray's effect two years before.

Their bodies were fused, Siamese style, thigh to thigh, hip to hip, shoulder to shoulder, the canister and the pistol pointed at the dog's head. It snarled, showing its teeth. Some were missing or broken, but Ciccio reckoned there were enough in place to do serious damage. The dog had its front feet forward and was ready to spring. There were more dogs to their right, but this was the one that mattered. The brute had almost passed them, had been at the edge of the little parapet in front of their hole. They had lain stock still and stifled their breathing. It had stopped, sat on its arse, and scratched, then faced them. Ciccio knew it was his call, and that Fabio would not shoot. He sensed that sound welled deep in the dog's throat. It would bark, high-pitched, urgent, and the kid would come with others. Marcantonio was carrying a sawn-off shotgun. They couldn't run and abandon their gear. They knew why the hillside was being searched. They'd had a message: a man was on the hill, had scraped a car of Marcantonio's in Berlin, had travelled to Calabria and scratched the car here. Dry mouths, hearts pounding, slow breathing – and fear. Ciccio thought it not a dog to be bought off with a biscuit.

He used the spray, his target the centre of the dog's face, at less than two metres range. On the canister the instructions gave four metres as the maximum effective distance. Two fast squirts – not enough to blind, but enough to irritate.

The dog backed away, blinked and whined. Its tail was locked under its legs.

It came down, reached Marcantonio and moaned. It was bouncing off the bushes, trying to rub its nose with a front paw. Marcantonio did not know why dogs had facial irritations. He looked for the kid and saw him high on a crest, above the back of the house. He had business to do and time was running out. It was possible he had been mistaken: perhaps the City-Van had been out of sight when they were at the docks, close to Villa San Giovanni. He waved, caught the kid's attention, pointed back down. The boy started his descent. In front of the house the wheel was on and Stefano had gone. In his opinion, Stefano was arrogant, too much listened to. He would be cut down to size when Marcantonio took control of the family's affairs.

'I want my breakfast,' Bernardo had shouted.

He had been told to wait. Either Mamma or Stefano, sometimes Giulietta, gave him the all-clear to leave the bunker.

'Wait,' had been Stefano's surly response.

'I want my breakfast in the kitchen, not in this hole.'

'You must wait.'

Bernardo had waited. When he was about to emerge from the bunker, the walls seemed to press harder against him and the container to have shrunk. He was carried back to the cave – and the child. He would not emerge unless his wife, daughter or Stefano sanctioned it. Stefano was a rogue and took liberties with him, but Bernardo would have trusted him with his life.

'How long must I wait?' he had called up the tunnel.

The delay with the ransom had not resulted from the parents' suspicions that their daughter was already dead. They had had to persuade cousins, uncles and close friends to help because their own resources did not match the demand.

The family, in Calabria, had manipulated the situation well. Two lawyers, with roots in the region, had been appointed as go-betweens. One had taken the role of 'friend' and had seemed to wring his hands at the pain the parents suffered and work tirelessly for the child's freedom. The second had played the part of the enemy, bullying them with demands for speedy payment or their child would die. The parents had regarded the friend as a sympathiser, and the enemy as scum. But the money had been paid over, in a rucksack that had been left beside the bronze statue of Christ above the town of Plati. It was extraordinary: at that time in that area seven kidnapped children were held, awaiting ransom, all giving employment because each needed at least ten men to guard them and look out for the *carabinieri*. The money had been brought to a house in the village, where many had had to be paid for their work during the long wait. He remembered it all . . . and that in her life with them, the child had never been given clean clothing. On her back had come Bernardo's family's advancement, wealth and power. Of course she was not forgotten.

He called again: 'What's the delay?'

'Your grandson.'

'Why?' Bernardo knew that Stefano had little affection for his grandson, that he did not value Marcantonio's talents, which might – one day, after Bernardo's passing – kill him.

'He's searching the hill above us with the dogs.'

'What for?'

'I didn't ask but, you should. And ask him what happened in the night to my vehicle.'

The kid didn't know what had happened to Capo's eyes. He might have been stung by a wasp. He sat on a low wall beyond the trellis and bathed the dog's eyes in warm water that Mamma had brought. The wind had dropped and the sun was high and warm, all trace of the storm gone, but for a scattering of leaves on the slabs by the door.

*　　　*　　　*

Jago saw Marcantonio – only a snip of him after he came out of the back door, then went behind the trellis, but his spiked hair stuck up above the hanging sheets.

It would have been further confirmation, if Jago had needed it, but he didn't. The sun's warmth bounced from the stone in front of him into the recess under the boulders. He didn't know what had happened with the search and the dogs, but thought himself lucky. The penknife was close to his hand.

The family had learned a lesson. Any of them could live a lie, but if that lie challenged Bernardo's authority only an imbecile would fail to confess it to him. The same lesson was taught in every family, each *cosca*, in the mountain communities. Marcantonio might have lied to his sister-in-law, might even have been flexible with the truth to his grandmother, and would have lied relentlessly if questioned by a prosecutor, but he would not lie to his grandfather.

He talked of the boredom in Berlin. He hung his head. The old man horsewhipped him with words: he was a fool.

He talked of a new pizzeria in a good inner suburb of the city, Italians managing it and money from a Baltic town. Had he been greedy and reckless? He didn't deny it.

He talked of going to collect the first *pizzo*, a fiery girl, making a point to her that she had ignored, a pistol-whipping. Had he not been told to learn the arts of finance and to cause no trouble?

He had accepted the blame – and told his grandfather about a man who had intervened and been put down, and should then have backed off. As he talked he saw the old man's frown slip away and the fist unclench. He was asked how it had ended. The old man's hand was on his and they shared the tunnel.

He talked of the scrape on his car and seeing a man walk away, but he was late for his flight to come home for Mamma's birthday, the street was one-way and they couldn't drive after him, so the act had gone unanswered. And last night, the rear tyre of the City-Van had been slashed and there were scratches on the side. He had searched the slope and found nothing. Was Marcantonio saying that a man had come here from Berlin – because he had been knocked down and kicked? To do what? To scratch Stefano's vehicle? His grandfather's face creased in puzzlement.

He couldn't answer Bernardo's questions. No boy of Marcantonio's own age had ever stood up to him in the village or at school. None had tried to face him down. He had the authority of his blood, his face and name were known and what he said went unchallenged. If he wanted a girl, a father didn't dispute it. If he wanted a *pizzo*, a shopkeeper or bar owner would hand it over. When he was about to drown Annunziata in acid she had looked at him with loathing, but had not fought him. He couldn't say why that young man had joined in with an argument that was none of his business. He shrugged. To his grandfather he had shown humility and honesty, and Bernardo kissed his cheeks.

The old man said, 'I have a problem with the priest, Father Demetrio. Mamma doesn't know. For him, an accident – very soon, before you go back. Dear boy, I trust you.'

They crawled along the tunnel together, threw the switches and opened the outer door. Marcantonio went first into the sunlight, his grandfather following. They shut the door behind them, and stayed close to the sheets as they scurried towards the back door. The City-Van was backed up there and masked the entrance. Soon Marcantonio would go to do business, and after he returned he would talk to his grandfather about the priest, the man who had baptised him and heard his confession – all shit – and consider how best to cause an accident.

The sun's warmth swamped him.

Bent walked on the beach. Jack stayed behind him, giving him space.

There were clusters of pebbles and broken shells on the sand, but near to the tideline so Bent could go barefoot. Jack knew when to ingratiate himself and when to back off, which was now. The beach was littered with the sea's debris. Jack had little trouble with dropping a fag packet, an apple core or a fast-food carton, but the rubbish thrown up by the storms' winds was exceptional. He saw plastic bottles, fuel cans, rope, oil slicks and birds that had been swamped. Heavy industrial trays and a couple of wood pallets. The chance of the rubbish being picked up, from what Jack knew of his parents' former homeland, was remote, at least before next spring and the arrival of the German hordes. In these parts there was little interest in the cleanliness of the environment. It wasn't Jack's concern, but he knew that the water tables in Campania, inland from Naples – the source of the prized mozzarella cheese from the buffalo herds – were contaminated. Toxic waste was dumped there: Mafiosi scams brought the industrial filth down from the north and the cancer rates soared. He knew also that a *pentito* from Calabria, one of the few, had alleged that waste was brought by lorry to Ionian sea ports and loaded onto old cargo ships, which were taken out to sea and scuttled. It was said that waste seeped from the hulls into the Mediterranean and poisoned it. Calabria cared little about the environment. Jack had seen uncollected rubbish mountains in Reggio when they had driven through.

Bent would have been suffering worse withdrawal symptoms than an addict short of smack at being unable to use his phone, deprived of deals to close. Sensible of Jack to hold back.

Carrying his shoes and socks, his jeans rolled above his ankles, Bent was paddling, and the sun made a narrow shadow of him as he tripped through the wavelets. Some, it was said, in south London regarded Bentley Horrocks as an ogre, but here he was like any other end-of-season tourist. The storm was past and – pray God – the big man of the family would attend to them that day.

Jack knew how to deflect attention and keep himself clear of responsibility. There was a saying of the Cosa Nostra in Sicily: 'When the wind blows, become a reed.' That was Jack's way. His own parents, good people, working all the hours the Lord sent and ignoring retirement age, would likely have died convulsed with shame if they'd known what their beloved son did for a living and who he associated with. When Jack went to see them in Chatham he took a small car from one of Bent's scrapyards, leaving his own pricey wheels behind.

When the big man came, Jack would have lectured Bent on the etiquette of respect. He would translate for them, and a deal could be done. Bent needed to close a deal because of the little fuckers that were snapping at his heels.

The cramps had got him again. Sometimes Jago writhed in agony, kicking into the back of the hole behind him. Then there were the stabbing pains in his skull, his clothing was still damp and he was close to fainting from lack of food. He had been back up the hill and had found the place they had agreed on. He had waited there for fifteen minutes.

She should have been there, sitting under a tree or on a rock. At worst she should have left a bag of food, water and dry clothing, then drifted away. She was not there. Neither was a bag. He had two options: he could head for the road or return to the small open space, hedged by beech and birch trees, the next day.

He had gone back to his hide. He had thought he might have passed close to where the sneeze he'd heard had come from, but had gone on and felt a sort of comfort when he got back to his familiar spot. The only place in Calabria he knew: a sodden bed of stone, grass, moss and a groundsheet under two boulders. The hunger hurt.

He wondered how many more chances he would ignore. It would have been acceptable to give up when the girl had not been there – as it would have been when his vest had taken flight, when he had flopped down on the bench in the park or had been naked on the beach. He had rejected each opportunity. Enough of that. She had come out.

He watched Giulietta. The sun caught the side of the big Zippo lighter, the flame flashed and smoke blew away from her face. She paced away from him. He thought her handsome. Wilhelmina was handsome. He thought her five or six years older than himself.

Stefano came back with the City-Van and brought it to the front door. She did not get out of his way but made him wait until she had walked across the space where he'd park. She did not acknowledge him but smoked and looked up at the slope. She had her hand to her forehead to shield her eyes from the sun. She studied the slope, as the driver did. The last time that the mother had appeared she had done the same. When the kid was there, he gazed at the hillside, as the dogs did. He thought them uncertain that danger lurked there. He had seen the path and the cable, which played in his mind.

He watched her. She tossed away the filter. He knew their names, what they wore, knew their posture and gait – all except those of the family's leader. Marcantonio was out of the front door now and he, too, studied the hill, the dense trees, their heavy foliage and the bleak rocks. Then, he walked to the vehicle. The driver was already inside and it started to move before the passenger had closed his door.

It might be the next day that it finished, or longer. Should Consolata not come, it couldn't be more than two days. He cursed to himself. A broken promise. He felt himself drift, and sleep culled him.

12

The whiskers woke him.

He had been asleep, flat out, dead to the world, and his trainers were off, drying hopefully. The soft brush of whiskers nuzzled his ankles. Jago blinked to work focus back into his eyes. The shadows had lengthened but the sun was still above the trees to his right. It was the most delicate movement, little sweeps of the whiskers where his shin ended at the ankle. He didn't dare to twist round and peer back into the gap where he had made his refuge. He heard sniffing and sensed that a snout was almost on his ankle. He lay motionless.

The smell of the creature's breath alerted him. It was feral. Less penetrating was the odour of the body, which was damp and unclean. He could see down in front of him to the shallow ledge, then a cliff and the confusion of trees rooted in crevices, the roof of the derelict shed, the walls and the washing. He could also see the dogs. The biggest was the brindle cross, which lay in a shady corner, avoiding the sunlight. Every few seconds it would scrape at the fur under its eyes. He counted the dogs: all present. The mother was outside the kitchen door, flapping a floor mat, and the dogs watched her.

There was a snort. He couldn't see the beast but his hearing was acute and he realised that the nostrils were inside his trainers. He heard one shoe lifted, then dropped. Next, the bottom of his left trouser leg was tugged, then dropped. The whiskers were off his skin. He heard a sharp scraping sound: strong claws getting a grip on the back of the big boulders under which he lay. The sounds came from above him, where the boulders lodged together. The animal skidded – the claws had no traction. It came down clumsily.

The wolf eyed him. It was bigger than any of the dogs that

milled around the family's back door. It had a thick grey coat, and vertical russet lines on its legs. It was thin and the ribs showed. Its head was a foot from Jago's face. His own eyes would have been wide, and his breathing harsh. Jago didn't know much about dogs. His mother had never had one. There were strays on the streets in Canning Town, and there were dealers on the far side of Freemasons Road with bull terriers that lunged at pedestrians. Some of the girls in the City banks had stuck photos of Labradors or spaniels around their work spaces. Beyond the physical similarity, nothing about this creature was domestic.

The eyes were yellow and brown, the iris was solid and the gaze never shifted, were riveted on him. There was life in them, not the dead and the cold that Jago thought would have been obvious if the creature was about to savage him. He took it from the eyes that the threat was not imminent, but what did he know? Sod all. Jago Browne had no knowledge of a wild creature's mood swings.

He thought his breath would have been in the wolf's nostrils. They twitched, seemed to take in the scents that came from his mouth. The lower part of the snout, where the hair was short, was scarred. At least three lines were etched there and all had healed. Below the nostrils was the mouth: a long tongue, reddish interior with pink streaks, ranks of teeth. Jago concentrated on the teeth: bright, clean, sharp. Behind them were the shoulders that would give the jaw the purchase it needed to tear him apart.

The wound gaped in front of him. It was behind the right shoulder, low on the flank and near to immature nipples, long, deep and nearly clean, but flies buzzed around it. He thought the animal young, hungry and separated, at the peak of the storm, from its pack. It would be frightened, hurt, lost. It was a bad wound—

It was gone. The wolf went over the rim of the platform in front of him. He heard it land, not a controlled fall but a stumble. A branch snapped and smaller stones tumbled further down. Then silence. The dogs at the kitchen door were aware of the movement and had their ears back, but didn't bark.

How long? Jago thought he had shared space with the wolf for not quite a minute. He felt good.

*   *   *

'Can you see it?' Ciccio asked.

'Yes.'

'Where?'

'On a rock.'

'I saw it move once, then lost it.' Ciccio grimaced.

'It's on a rock and I can see its haunches.' It was licking itself, working solidly on one place.

'First time I've seen one.'

'There are just two or three packs in the entire Aspromonte. It's incredibly rare.'

'It was injured.'

'A cut, a lateral one. It couldn't move properly.'

'It's young. The family will kill it.'

'They'll shoot it or the dogs'll get it,' Fabio muttered.

'Not our problem.' Ciccio usually led their conversations. A listener could have been less than five metres from them and heard nothing. Often Ciccio talked while Fabio slept – it comforted him. 'We might get a city stake-out after this, with rats. I'd rather have a wolf at a distance than rats.'

Fabio understood the need to talk, and the crisis in Ciccio's life, with Neomi's degenerative condition. 'Makes no difference to me. We'll have some beer, a shower and sleep, then go on to the next job. I don't care who the target is. More important, if the dogs come again, will the spray keep them off? You saw Mamma then and Giulietta, both looking up here – because he scratched the car. Why the fuck did he do that? Makes it more difficult for us – even worse for that young wolf. What are you thinking?'

'That he's in front of us.'

'Close to the wolf?'

'Just a feeling,' Ciccio muttered.

'And he didn't spook it?' Fabio could see the wolf's tail and part of its rear. If he strained to his left he could watch the animal working to clean the wound – it had to or gangrene would set in. He had heard they killed the wolves not to protect the goats and sheep but for sport and because the government had issued a protection order for them. 'I don't know. We're on the final countdown. Maybe we'll have a chance tomorrow, if it's warm, to get some more scorpion flies . . . I'm exhausted and I need some sleep – but I can't. When I get home I'll watch crap TV and hit the gym. Last time I went round rubbish bins looking for cast-off clothes to use on street surveillance, or I hiked in the mountains. Where *is* the target?'

Ciccio didn't answer. He couldn't have said anything sensible. Fabio was tempted to slide forward on his belly and find the man who was sharing the hillside with them. Why was he there?

It wasn't the wolf that was a problem but the dogs. If the dogs came for the intruder, what would they do? Not their job to do anything. He wondered if the man had a courier, but there had been no indication of back-up. He and Ciccio watched, as they were paid to. Two little cogs in the slow engine that confronted the 'Ndrangheta machine, which was sleek, oiled, expensively maintained. He watched the wolf, too, and bonded with it a little. He had come to care about the wound. It was a quiet late afternoon, with sunshine, the damp steaming off the rocks and from the ground at the base of the trees. He waited.

As she came into the room she was watched. There was no welcome for her. Only Piero did not look up. Instead he studied, pointedly, the laptop that lay on his knees. A meeting was in progress and she had intruded. She had rung the bell. They would have known who was at the door because there was a camera above it and the picture would have been beamed inside. They had made her wait until Piero had finished speaking. He and six others were there, the hard-core, the believers. Consolata smiled, ducked her head to them and put her bag on the floor.

An explanation was demanded of her, she felt, and gave it.

She regretted her actions in moving out of Headquarters, and apologised for her rant about direct action. She had been away from them long enough to reassess the virtues of non-violent confrontation. She wanted, she told them, more leaflets to hand out in central Reggio. She had reflected sufficiently to realise the errors in her attitude.

Why? She was hungry. Why again? She craved to belong. And why once more? Because being with them purged her guilt at having broken her end of a bargain: a rendezvous.

She was accepted without enthusiasm. Her room in the squat had been assigned to a new volunteer, but she could have a camp bed in the store room in the basement. She went down, set up the bed, found a sleeping bag stuffed into a corner and put on her radio. Consolata needed company and to be busy. She didn't like the thought of another night on the beach at Scilla or in her parents' small apartment – they would question her incessantly on her plans for the future, when would she work, why had she no man . . .

The radio was on an orange box that would be her bedside table. Nothing about him. Instead she heard a litany of stories on the aftermath of the storm, and that arrests had been made in Rosarno for 'Mafia association'; a trial dragged on in the *aula bunker* and the financial crisis was rampant.

She had no plans for her future. She would work as an unpaid volunteer, would beg and borrow from her mother and father. She had a man: slim body, pale skin, flat belly, thin legs and arms, bright eyes and a dream. She had guided him to a hillside on the far slopes of the Aspromonte, and could tell no one what she had done. She could not be alone, not while he was . . .

Consolata went upstairs. 'What can I do?' she asked cheerfully. 'How can I help?'

She would do leaflets, then try to get across country and close to him. The guilt was crushing: she was warm, dry and fed. She had failed to make a rendezvous.

'I have roadblocks in place.' The colonel sipped coffee. It had not been brought in from a bar but made in the Palace of Justice and tasted disgusting. He was in the building because a meeting was due to start in a few minutes. A major investigation, centred on the town of Taurianova, was to be planned. It had priority.

The prosecutor answered, 'I'm exceptionally grateful for the allocation of resources.'

'Only the main roads. I can't seal off the village.'

'A show. Sometimes all we can do is make gestures.' The prosecutor's tiredness was poorly hidden. That morning, his wife had suggested forcefully that he call in sick, rest and try to clear his mind. He had ridiculed the idea.

'A display of force for two more days.'

'Would there be . . . I wondered if . . .' The prosecutor hesitated. An indication of a failing cause was the inability to make specific demands. 'If it were possible to . . .'

He was helped. He enjoyed the company of the colonel. The senior officer had done time in Iraq and that other 'bad land', the flat plain inland from Naples where the Camorra families ruled. He was straight-speaking and thinking. He seemed sympathetic. 'What do you want?'

'I want the property of Bernardo Cancello searched by an experienced team. He's there, I'm sure of it. Months of work committed, resources I've fought for. It's all slipping away from me. Please. I need a cordon set up close to the house and a quality team.'

The answer came fast – it might have been rehearsed. 'I can't authorise that. Too many men, too many hours, too much preparation, and no prior intelligence. Get me the man's location and I'll be there. No location, no search.'

'He's there. *La presenza e potenza*. He *has* to be there.' But he'd said the obvious, which wouldn't change the colonel's mind. All of those who worked from the Palace took as a maxim for any *padrino* who had dropped out of sight that 'presence is power': they must be close to their contacts, dominate their heartland, be known to have control. He had aerial photographs of the house where the wife lived, with the daughter, and where the grandson was staying at the moment. When he gazed at the roof, the small backyard, the washing lines, the shed, and the old car at the front, he could also see caves, gullies, rock clefts and herdsmen's tracks, a landscape that could swallow an army.

'If you find intelligence, you'll have support.'

He had no intelligence, and had the added complication of the man who had hidden near to the house. They shook hands and he let the *carabinieri* officer go to his meeting.

The door closed. He was alone – and had been for several days – and would soon be even more isolated. In the corridors people would whisper to each other behind their hands, and voices would drop when he passed.

They stood, facing the door.

The lawyer had warned them that the family's arrival was imminent, then had hurried to the car park to greet them.

Bentley Horrocks was a half-pace ahead of Jack and stood with his arms folded and feet a little apart. He was working at the look he would give the man when he pitched up. Bent had enjoyed his walk in the sunshine, but now he had changed into an expensive shirt and trousers: Jack had polished his shoes. In his head he had the figure he would pay, and he knew the profit margins. Nervous? A little. Far from home and what he knew? A long way. He thought Humphrey, the lawyer, was a smarmy little bastard. He had been good in the old days when he'd practised close to the Central Criminal Court, and at Snaresbrook and Southwark, but had gone downhill since he'd moved to the sunshine and new avenues.

He broke his silence. 'Getting near the big-time, Jack.'

'Too right, Bent. The big-time, nearly there.'

'I've come a long way for this.'

'You have, Bent. A proper long way.'

'And I'll not be fucked about.'

'Wouldn't be clever, Bent, to fuck you about. They won't, though. You're meeting a main man, not just a gofer. Know what I mean?'

'Someone at my level. Yes.'

He heard the sharp intake of Jack's breath and a little involuntary whistle. It was a noise similar to the one Trace made when he shagged her. He missed Trace – missed everything he'd left behind in London or at the big house in the Kent countryside. Might even miss his wife.

'Can I say something, Bent?'

It wasn't often that Jack struck up a conversation. Far down the corridor, he heard a fire door slam. He nodded, waited to hear the footsteps. It was about status and prestige, him being accepted as a major player, meeting a leader of equal importance – not of greater importance – and doing business with a man such as himself who had clawed his way up the ladder to the heights. A man such as himself would value meeting Bentley Horrocks, who ran an area of south-east London, a man who stayed free and was, at a cost, untouchable. He had bought enough police to fill a section house, he liked to joke to himself, when he walked in his garden with the dogs for company.

'Bent . . .'

Now he heard the footsteps. 'Shoot.'

A touch of a stammer: 'Give them respect, Bent. My advice is—'

'I don't beg, Jack. You learned nothing?'

'You don't have to beg, Bent. Just give them respect. It matters to them. Do it like you've never had to before. Please, Bent, respect.'

Of course he would. It would be an old man, a veteran of survival, like himself. There was a light tap on the door. He said, 'Enter.' First through was the lawyer, who stepped aside. Bent's jaw sagged. It was a fucking kid. The lawyer was gabbling a name, but Bent didn't take it in. His fists clenched. A fucking kid. Anywhere on his territory, south of the river, a kid of that age would reckon himself honoured to be tossed Bent's car keys and told to park the motor. It would make his evening if he were given a few notes and told to fetch Trace and him a takeaway.

A hand was offered. He took it. The handshake was indifferent. He thought the kid reckoned it a chore to have to shake his hand, like he was doing Bent a favour. The kid looked into his face, seemed to evaluate him and showed no indication of being impressed. He sat down in the chair that Bent would have taken, and Humphrey lowered himself towards the carpet – he needed help to get down, then produced a notepad and pencil. That was how they would do business: with a notepad.

Jack whispered in his ear, 'Steady, Bent. Outline agreed now, then a handshake, and no going back. The detail tomorrow, or the day after. The handshake is final, Bent. It's the big man's grandson. Bent, please, smile at him. They'll want to know how much weight, cost per kilo and shipment, which is extra.'

The kid lounged in the chair, then swung his feet onto the low table, scattering the magazines and brochures. His eyes went to the TV and lit up – girls were dancing on the screen. The kid had good hands, solid, chunky fingers. No acne, only a small scar. Humphrey reached to Bent, tugged at his trouser leg, pointed to a hard chair and started to write.

Bent brought the chair forward. The kid ignored him. The lawyer had written on three lines: *Weight. Price. Delivery.* No hassle, no barter, no bargain – he could have been in a fucking pound shop down the Elephant and Castle. He bit his tongue, held tight to the pencil, and considered what he would do to Jack when he was shot of the business. He considered what weight he'd buy, how much he would pay, and where he would want delivery. But the kid turned away from the TV screen. Humphrey muttered in his ear, then wrote down the figure for the weight they would sell, the price per kilo and where they would deliver to. The pad was passed back to Bent. No negotiation, no respect. He seethed.

He moved, not with a plan but from desperation.

Jago was in poorer shape than the wolf. Hard to see the beast but it lay on its side on a slab of rock, the wound open to the air. Since it had found the slab, it hadn't moved.

Only God knew how many hours earlier he had heard the sneeze – too long now to be clear in his mind. He came out of the gap where the two boulders bedded and turned away from the wolf, from the kid who was feeding the dogs from a washing-up bowl, from the old woman, who had brought out Marcantonio's shirts and hung them from hooks behind the trellis – there was no room for them on the line with the bed linen – and away from Giulietta, who paced and smoked and quartered the front area. It was obvious to Jago that Bernardo's shirts would be washed, dried and ironed inside, then taken to the cellar or the excavated hole or the cave to which the cable ran.

He went up the hill, with only the memory of the sneeze to guide him. He had known, through the late afternoon and into the early evening, with the light failing, that he must find food. Two choices: he could go down, bang on the door, appear, like a vagabond in the kitchen and ask to be fed or go up the hill, in the direction of the sneeze, and try to locate whoever was there. Jago was close to collapse. Delirium lapped in his mind, threatening to drown him. He had to eat. He didn't know whom he would find, whether he would be welcomed or attacked. Uppermost in his mind was the certainty that he could not see through another night without food. It was a steep climb.

If he came to the place where a man had sneezed, it would be by an animal's instinct: he had no other guide.

He reckoned himself close to the end of the road. Last time he'd been there? Maybe when his phone had been taken and Billy had saved him. He should have collected water during the storm and hadn't. The hunger-strikers in Ireland had used water to prolong their fast. He hadn't eaten or drunk any water and the weakness ran through him. Each movement seemed to weaken him further. He went on. He tried to be quiet but sometimes a twig cracked beneath his feet and song birds careered away from him. He went on, and his mind rambled . . . dishes his mother cooked, the stuff that came round on the trolley in the City, the health fascists' favourites in Berlin, a spider's meal and . . . He was on his knees and his hands. It was aimed at the centre of his forehead.

He saw the darkened recess. He saw two faces and camouflage clothing.

Closest to him was the barrel of the pistol, and the foresight; its paintwork was chipped. The pistol had the look of a world-weary object, but one that was kept in good enough order to work. The hand holding it was steady. Jago had found the man who had sneezed.

He stood. He was confused and it was an effort to get upright, but the elementary truth was that they wouldn't shoot because of the noise. He saw another hand, which clutched a canister. He remembered, hazily, the dog with impaired eyesight. Jago stood upright. He spoke no Italian and imagined that the men were unlikely to speak English. He had no wish to debate. The pistol barrel followed him. He put his fingers to his mouth and made a chewing motion. Simple enough. Then he gave them a profile, raised his hands and cupped them at his mouth, as if he was about to shout. Clear enough. The final signal: his hands – with two thumbs and eight fingers he seemed to start a countdown. The pistol was loosed and laid in front of them.

Food materialised in small sealed packs and juice sachets. Not much, sufficient. Nothing was said. He was crouched and stumbling, grabbing at the pieces and stuffing them into pockets. A hand that held a phone or transmitter snaked to him, holding a lit screen. It was for him to look at. Jago saw himself. He wore a suit, a decent shirt and a quiet, conservative tie, as the bank required. He smiled, in the picture, self-deprecating, not arrogant, as Wilhelmina would have wished. He didn't know what to say.

One grinned, then gave him the universal sign, the middle finger, and waved him away. One called after him, with a hint of humour, '*Vaffanculo, amico.*'

Jago was gone. He thought he understood what they had told him, grimaced, and went down.

Bernardo ate an early dinner with Mamma.

She served pasta with tomato sauce, then pork. Later she would bring cheese. Bernardo consumed his food at a steady pace, but his plate was overloaded. Age and lack of exercise had curbed his appetite. He had downed only half of the pasta, and now he struggled with the pork. She ate little, had never eaten much, and had never cooked well. She was unimaginative with what she prepared, which was the prime reason why Giulietta joined them infrequently at the table. She often had meals at Teresa's, or went to Siderno where there was a lawyer with whom she did business. She'd eat with him twice a week, or take a sandwich to her office. He didn't need to eat out of politeness for his wife's efforts. If he didn't like what she had made, he would push it away. He didn't eat that late afternoon because a new worry had begun to nag at him.

As Giulietta had worked on her computer, two development possibilities had caught her attention – apartments and a club-house on the extreme southern sliver of land where Croatia met Serbia, and a similar site on the Bulgarian coast north-east of Varna, near to the border with Romania. He might need to invest up to five million euros, and couldn't make such a decision without her advice. It would be good when Marcantonio came back to live with them. Then he could rest, knowing his back was protected.

The nagging worry was about protection. The decision on the priest, his long-time friend Father Demetrio, had been taken. When his mind was made up on such a matter, he did not change it. It was as if a door had closed. The method of the accident would be resolved. After the priest, who posed the next threat? Who, outside the close blood links of the family, could wound him?

He had known Stefano since his driver was a baby and he himself was ten. Stefano had been at his side as punch-bag, servant, driver and keeper of secrets. Stefano had carried the child, dead, cold and stiff, head lolling – out of the cave, into the daylight and up the hill. He had searched out a place for the grave and dug it. He had wrapped a towel around the body, than had covered it with the soil. Bernardo had been unable to watch – too difficult. The worst part was when the priest had said the prayers two days later, and they had scrambled down the hill afterwards without a backward glance. He had studied Stefano's face, expecting to see moisture in the eyes – nothing. Months later, the money had come. It had been on the old oak table in the kitchen and it had taken most of an afternoon to count it. It had stayed that night in the bag under the big bed. The family had not looked back from the day it had been invested and the first shipment had come through.

He wondered now from which man came the greater threat: from the priest or his driver, who brought food to the house, cleared the fires, was always at the kitchen door and knew the entry mechanism for the bunker. Bernardo had killed men and had brought into Europe vast quantities of narcotics. He had bought and sold firearms, and had traded in juveniles, who went to the brothels of northern Europe or Spain. He had cheated the government, and the taxpayers of the European Union. All of this, yet it was only the child that lingered with him.

Now he considered Stefano to be a threat. Headlights flared through the front windows, pierced an open door and briefly lit the table. He heard the chugging engine of the City-Van. Bernardo could not live beside a threat.

Doors slammed. The dogs bounded to the back of the kitchen, the utility area where they slept, and scratched at the outer door. His grandson had returned. Marcantonio nodded to him, kissed his grandmother, then went to the fridge for a beer. Stefano was in the doorway, calm and impassive. He might be a threat. Bernardo was alone. He doubted he had a friend in the world.

It had been a huge decision. Father Demetrio rarely shocked himself, but had done so that afternoon. He was at the funeral.

He had not been in church but was at the cemetery. For many years in the village, he had been pliant. His mind was almost made up. A road stretched ahead of him, and it was not yet too late for him to reverse back the way he had come. He stood among tall gravestones, apart from the small group of mourners. None of the dead man's family was present. They would have stayed in the village and might have worn bright clothing to demonstrate that nothing deserved any show of grief. A son had died, a brother and husband, but not a tear would be shed in that home, and no word of covert sadness would reach the *padrino*, whose home was high on the hill. Father Demetrio had barely known the *pentito*, had baptised and christened him, had rarely heard his confession, had kept away from the man's home when Rocco and Domenico Cancello had been convicted on his sworn evidence.

The low light threw long shadows and made the stones huge

and grotesque. The cemetery was outside the town of Melito di Porto Salvo, north of the E90 highway, and the throb of lorries' engines drowned the words that were spoken. It was a little less than an hour's drive from the village. The man had been brought back to Calabria, but was distanced from his bloodline. Father Demetrio tested himself by his presence – he was not a fool. A retired schoolmaster was there and would have taught the turn-coat, a *carabinieri* officer, who might have watched over him before he had given his testimony, two young women, who wore the T-shirts of the Addio Pizzo movement, a gravedigger and a junior priest, who had gabbled the prayers. Father Demetrio thought the priest would have experienced real fear if a camera was present to record him officiating: few volunteered to stand against the current's flow. The mayor was present.

Father Demetrio understood. Something about the way the *padrino* had eyed him at the old woman's lunch. Something about the old City-Van that had followed him for a time that morning, or the scooter that had trailed him the previous evening. He knew so much. It was often done in the aftermath of a substantial meal. A man slipped unseen behind the victim's chair and hands gripped the throat. Death by strangulation: said to take four or five minutes. He suspected it. It had been a gesture of defiance to come to the cemetery; he had challenged his conscience, his courage – and his cowardice. The grave was in a corner of the cemetery, with only one bouquet. He mouthed the prayers, wished he had had the nerve to take the service himself. Father Demetrio harboured ever-present shame for having said similar obsequies over a mound in the hills.

He toyed with the decision, as yet unmade.

'Rubbish': that was what he called the Englishman he had met.

The Englishman was 'useless', 'boastful' and 'boring'. He snapped through the figures. The *cosca* of Bernardo bought fifty kilos of 80 per cent pure, and paid twelve hundred dollars per kilo to the agents at the Latin-American end of the supply route. It arrived in Europe and the family must pay transportation costs before selling on to an agent in northern Italy, who paid forty-five thousand dollars per kilo for 50 per cent purity. When the cocaine was offered for sale in London, a kilo, further diluted with baking powder, would bring in ninety-five thousand dollars. The man hadn't known where he wanted to buy: he could buy in Calabria and be responsible for all shipments onwards, or he could buy in Rotterdam, Felixstowe or Hamburg. Alternatively, he could take his chance in the port cities of Venezuela, the jungle of northern Peru or in Medellín with the cartels. He said that tomorrow Giulietta could visit the hotel in Brancaleone to find out what the man would pay and under what terms, but the money should be up front. 'Perhaps he should stick to cigarettes,' Marcantonio had told his grandfather. He knew the figures and the profit margins, and thought the Englishman incapable of getting his mind around the monies involved. He had come on the scene too late in life. The newspapers in Germany had recently focused on an Italian academic study. In the city of Brescia, population 200,000, it was estimated that $750,000 was spent on cocaine every day – *every day*. He had escorted his grandfather back to the bunker, had crawled after him down the concrete piping and smelt the damp.

The lights were on. His grandfather sat in his chair.

Marcantonio thought the old man might be better off in a cell at Novara or Ascoli, where his father and uncle were. *Scarface* had ended in the shoot-out because Al Pacino would not be taken. He said he would be outside for hours that evening with a shotgun and the dogs. He would be careful, he promised. He was told that a road accident would be arranged for the priest. He accepted that, but asked, 'Why not send him away with money, *padrino*?'

Because Father Demetrio was an old man and had no use for it.

'But you can buy anyone – a judge, a clerk, a colonel, a mayor.'

He wouldn't want money, only to cleanse his soul.

'Grandfather, is your own soul in need of washing?'

The boy laughed. He did not see the flash in his grandfather's eyes, when he repeated that it would be a road accident, on a bend where there was a cliff. Marcantonio left, and the quiet closed round him. He scrabbled to find the television zapper – he needed company. He wondered who was watching his home and what they had learned . . .

Fabio said, 'Should we have done that? Given him food?'

'I didn't see anyone give him anything,' Ciccio murmured.

The screen was on. Fabio used his hand to shade the picture. He flipped between the two images. He wondered why a young man would give up life in a suit and tie and a job with a hefty salary to become what they had seen. He wondered, too, how far it would take him. The light was falling. He liked it when dusk came because then they had the chance to crawl out of the hole among the rocks, merge with the trees and stretch, drop their trousers, squat and hold the tinfoil in position. He didn't see how they could have helped him more, other than by pressing grenades into his hand. He felt inadequate, and reckoned Ciccio did too. He seemed to see the gaunt, stubbled face, the mud on the skin and in the hair, the depth of the eyes beyond anything he could read, and the pain. For what? He cut the picture. The log on the screen showed that Marcantonio – Mike/Alpha Bravo – had returned in the vehicle driven by Stefano, Sierra Bravo, and that the message had been sent. It did not refer to the stranger who shared the hillside with them, whom they had fed and in whose interests they had jeopardised their careers. Funny old world . . . A convulsion would happen soon. Couldn't say when or what it would be, but blood would be drawn.

'You all right?' Fabio asked.

'Sure. Better than rotting in a jar.'

They had had lunch. They had been to the *carabinieri* headquarters, on Via Aschenez, had proffered the piece of paper and met those they had been drinking with the previous night. They had been rewarded with a temporary ID slip, which requested that they be granted reasonable co-operation, then had arranged to meet again.

They had seen the gaol in the rain, and the *aula bunker* where the 'Ndrangheta accused stood before judges in an escape-proof, bombproof underground courtroom so they went for a walk, in sunshine, along the sea front.

It was better, Fred had said, than coming away from Bismarck-strasse in rush-hour. He'd been told that the Dooley Terminal, HMRC section, was a living death.

In 1908, Calabria had suffered an earthquake, thirty thousand killed, and another forty thousand in Messina across the Strait. No historic buildings had survived. They watched men fishing with rods from the base of the monument to Victor Emmanuel III, had seen nothing caught, but it had been worth lingering because the views across to Sicily and smoking Etna were good.

They had visited the Roman baths, part excavated, and looked down on the uncovered Greek walls of the city, dating back eight centuries *avanti Christi*. Fred had talked of Barbary pirates raiding the city centuries later and taking men to slavery in Tunisia. The money for more digging seemed to have run out. Fred confessed that, already, he was bored with his mission, and that knee-bending rarely suited him. They should get the hell out of this city and head for where any action might be.

Fred said, matter of fact, 'We said nobody liked him, our boy from the bank.'

Carlo said, 'And we reckoned that didn't matter.'

'We might get to like him.'

'How come?'

'He's out there, sitting, watching and absorbing. Everything is swimming in his mind. When he moves, he'll make chaos.'

'He'll shake the tree violently, which spells . . .?'

'Mistakes. Bad boys making 'mistakes'.

'I'm getting to like your drift, Fred . . . might be entertaining. Mistakes, yes, and they add to vulnerability. Not often that we get a show put on for us.'

'It would place the boredom, Carlo, on the back burner . . .'

The oleander was in flower, the rubbish bins overflowing. The great magnolia trees gave shade and they sat under one. Fred took a penknife from his pocket, passed it to Carlo and let him perform the first act of vandalism. He gouged the shape of a heart, put an arrow through it, then cut the initials and handed back the knife. Fred scratched 'KrimPol' beside the arrow's head and 'HMRC' by its feathers. A gesture of affection between two old stagers in the law-enforcement gig.

'How old?' Fred asked.

Carlo looked down the line of trees, which dwarfed a memorial to the fallen soldiers of an Italian war he knew nothing about. 'Could be fifty years, could be a hundred. They look healthy – probably see us out.'

They reached a compromise, which neither was used to. They would go at dawn. Now they would make time for Fred to buy swimming trunks and a beach towel, and, by way of exchange, they would walk up to the Castello Aragonese, gaze at the great twin towers, and bemoan the lack of activity in restoring the rest, which had toppled in the earthquake. The Corso Giuseppe Garibaldi crossed their route. When Fred went into a shop for his swimming kit, Carlo waited outside. A girl approached him – quite pretty. She wore the usual uniform of jeans and trainers but her T-shirt bore the logo of Reggio Libera, and she thrust a leaflet into his hands. She seemed to challenge him as he glanced at it. He said, in Italian, with a grin, 'I congratulate you, signorina, for taking on the challenge of a Sisyphean labour, fighting organised crime in its best backyard. From my experience, you're pushing a rock up a steep hill. As soon as you get it to the top it'll roll back down again. Good luck.'

'What would you know?'

He chuckled. 'Not much. Only that it's hard to change the world.'

'Somebody has to try. With the restrictions of non-violence, it's difficult, but must be attempted.' She spoke without enthusiasm or sincerity.

'Accepted – but it's a road of hard knocks, cuts and bruises.'

'And you're a policeman?'

'Is it that obvious?'

Fred had come to his side with a plastic shopping bag.

'And my friend is from Berlin, hoping to swim in the warm sea and—'

'You are English and travel with a colleague who is from Berlin, yes?'

There was something droll in her eyes: a hint of the magic moment when all the boxes were ticked. A half-smile played at her mouth. Not a girl he would have followed to the gates of Hell and beyond, but he would have gone pretty close to the entrance. Too many women had flitted into and out of Carlo's life, and most had led him a dance. Few had been as attractive as this one. But he was too bloody old for her now. She had turned away from them to give out another of her leaflets. A woman looked at it and dropped it. Carlo was paid to have a nose, to make deductions. Seemed pretty bloody obvious to him.

He crouched, picked it up for the girl and said quietly in her ear, 'We wondered how he got there, who guided him. Did you twist his mind? He's an innocent. He shouldn't be there, and anyone with influence over him should get him out. It's a bad place at a bad time. Anything you'd like to tell me?'

She gazed into his eyes, seemed to regard him as a lesser species, and ran down the street into an ice-cream parlour. A hundred metres back a young man was wearing the same T-shirt. Carlo was at his side, and asked his name – Massimo. Then he asked for his colleague's name, and a phone number for their principled campaign. She was Consolata. He could have made a call, given a name, a location and a contact, and she'd have been in the cells within a half-hour.

Carlo said to Fred, 'Tilting at windmills, or slaying dragons? I'm no good at it.'

'My ambition is to hold the line. When I quit, I want to be able to say that things were no worse under my watch. That's about all. You going to turn her in?'

Carlo said softly, 'I'm going to look at the castle, and then we're going to have a beer. Not because we don't care.'

'Maybe we care too much.'

Birds were gathering in the trees above him.

Jago had no idea why they had selected those trees, oaks and high birches. The crows had come first, then pigeons. The food had filled his stomach but had had little effect on his thinking, which was still rambling, confused. He had scrambled to collect the wrappings before they blew away and had wedged them under the boulder at his right hip. He was waiting for darkness.

The wolf on the rock slab was just visible if he screwed his eyes tight and blinked hard – it was a darker shade on an indistinct ledge. The crows disputed perches on the upper branches, and scores had come.

He had learned a new lesson: that darkness was a friend. There'd have been kids out that night, in the back alleys off Freemasons Road and behind Silvertown Way, who'd have treasured the safety of darkness. He watched the sun, fiercely red, dropping below the trees. His target was the cable.

His stomach rumbled. He had attempted to eat slowly but had failed. Pain stabbed in his upper belly: he had been given *tortellini*, *wurstel*, a can of condensed milk, and a toothbrush impregnated with powder. They could have shot him, but Jago believed they had decided to trust him not to betray their position. He had a mission, and it would not be shoved into the sidings. Compatible? Perhaps – perhaps not. He was flattered that they'd had his photograph but he could have told them it was an image of a man who no longer existed. He was reborn, proud of it, and thought himself free. Confused . . .

The pigeons were quieter than the crows but in greater numbers. They thrashed for space and bickered, but were quicker than the crows to settle. He believed he could see the wolf but his eyes might have tricked him.

He had never seen the old man and wanted to trap him – a rat in a cage. He had seen him only from a monochrome image that had been up on a screen for a few seconds. He knew that Bernardo Cancello exercised power and had wealth beyond imagination, that he was inside the 'Ndrangheta syndicate, which turned over more in a year than Microsoft or Apple. A coarse face in the photograph, a stubby nose, and unforgiving eyes that had not been cowed when he had posed, many years ago, for the police photographer. And the old man took precedence over the grandson who had split open the girl's face.

He knew where the cable was. He would find the place where he had seen it, now screened by a sheet and ... He thought he heard a faint whimper, a small child's cry or that of an animal in pain.

He watched and waited for the darkness to be total, the light in the house bright. Then he would hurt them.

13

Jago had pushed himself out of the cleft under the two great boulders, and had tied the laces of his trainers tightly. He had flexed his hands, then shoved them into the pockets of the coat, where they'd clasped the tyre wrench and the penknife. Then he stood up and rocked backwards and forwards, toe to heel. It was time to do it or to crawl away.

A couple of months back one of the German girls in the bank had talked – over a sandwich and some juice – about her first ski jump: Innsbrück or somewhere. She'd described, with a giggle, being at the top of the ramp and hesitating, looking for an excuse, but knowing it was too late for a bullshit cop-out. She'd taken a great gulp of the winter air, someone might have given her a shove. She'd stopped rocking back and forth, gone down, then been airborne. The elation, after she'd landed that first time, had been – said with a droll German grimace – better than sex. There had been a guy in the City office, a couple of years ago, who'd signed up, in support of a worthy cause, for a virgin parachute jump. Everyone at work had been so awestruck that they'd dug deep and the charity had gained more than five thousand pounds. He'd said that if, getting to the aircraft, he'd been told it was too windy, too cloudy, too any-bloody-thing, he would have screamed for joy. He'd rocked those last few seconds, forward and back, then had the heave and gone.

No one there could give Jago a shove or a heave.

He didn't know the route he would take. The way down to the sheets that camouflaged the path and the disturbed soil had been hidden from him by foliage. He might find an animal track or a cliff face that fell away. He would go near to the wolf – if it was still there. He thought he had heard it a half-hour before, but it might have been the leaves or branches rubbing. He thought he had heard a light cry of suffering.

He rocked again. He believed there was a cellar or an excavated hole under the derelict building. If he cut the power, if he created a panic the like of which the man had never known, if he had him shrieking in pitch darkness, all his wealth, power and authority would be meaningless. That was Jago's aim. He would have bet his life on it: a man could kill, could order others to kill, could inflict misery and pain, but trapped without power in darkness he would crumple in terror. He supposed, at the heart of it, he felt a sort of jealousy at what the old man had achieved: if the *padrino* glanced at others, they would feel fear rising at the nape of the neck; if he smiled, he would leave others brimming with happiness because he approved of them. In Jago's terms, the old man had bypassed the grandson.

He was exposed on his ledge and it was totally dark. He had no excuse. He reached forward and felt for a hazel sapling, let his fingers run down it, then broke it off and stripped away the lesser branches. It was now a blind man's stick and he would feel his way with it.

Lights were on throughout the house. There were more lights down the track that went to the village. Short of the house he saw cigarettes glowing, smoked by the men who watched, night and day. The mother had been out of the kitchen door and had adjusted a rug at the trellis. The daughter had been on the gravel at the front, smoking and pacing. Later she had been at her bedroom window and had not drawn the curtains or lowered a blind. The driver had spent some time with the City-Van, its bonnet open – he might have been checking the oil, but had now gone inside. Jago had to factor in the dogs, but they were quiet. Enough light came from the kitchen for him to see that the kid was tickling their throats, relaxing them.

The kitchen door opened and Marcantonio stepped out. He carried a big flashlight in his left hand, and the sawn-off shotgun in his right. He gazed around him, stood tall, then went behind the draped rug and the trellis. A little of his shadow showed between the vine leaves. The air was clean, cool and quiet, and Jago believed he heard the scrape of metal on concrete – he took it to be a chair's legs grating on a paving stone. He had confirmation of sorts when a cigarette lighter flared.

Time for calculations. Marcantonio had settled near to the point where the join in the cable had been excavated during the storm. The dogs had disappeared from the yard, and he imagined them now close to Marcantonio. It was quiet. The birds in the oaks and birches were calmer – they cackled and flapped but were undisturbed. He didn't know what to do.

Minutes passed. Jago wondered how comfortable Marcantonio was on a hard chair, how long it would be before he was bored and went inside. He heard another cry, the gentlest whimper: the wound must be deeper in the animal's flank than he'd thought. He was surprised that it had stayed on the rock slab. He would have expected it to search for a refuge in which it could curl up and die. He thought for a long time about the wolf and its injury. A clock chimed far down the valley. Some lights had gone off in the house – in the kitchen and in Giulietta's bedroom – but the flash of the lighter warned him that Marcantonio was still keeping watch.

Jago cursed his stupidity. If he hadn't scratched the side of the City-Van, the chair, the flashlight and the shotgun would not be there. He waited. He didn't dare to step back and burrow into his hiding place under the boulders. If he turned, he would keep walking, might see the guys in the sniper suits and say to them, in English: *Sorry, guys, didn't work out so I'm quitting. Thanks for the rations. I'm an idiot for getting involved and should have stayed at my desk.* He knew he would not turn.

Above him the birds had settled. Below, there were the shotgun and the dogs. Jago watched and waited. He thought of the wolf and its pain. He could only watch, wait and hope.

* * *

He had the dogs around him.

The pack leader, still troubled by its watering eyes, was curled across Marcantonio's feet. The shotgun, loaded, was on his lap, the flashlight balanced beside the barrels. When he drew on the cigarette, he cupped his hand over the glowing end to shield it. The chair was hard, the evening air chilly, and the wind blew in the upper trees . . . He could picture the man.

A few years older than himself, a little taller but less muscular at the shoulders, his face far paler, northern European, a straight back, big eyes that widened in astonishment and lips that thinned in anger. He remembered how the man had surged from the park and across the road, how they had felled him – it had been the second time – and remembered the girl's face, the cut and the spilling blood. For Christ's sake, he hadn't intended to split her cheek and if the bitch hadn't . . . It was an 'incident' in his life.

Marcantonio had shot a man for his grandfather and that had, too, been an incident; he had strangled a man for his grandfather, another incident; for his grandfather he had put his aunt into a tank of acid, yet another 'incident'. Incidents littered the life of Marcantonio, aged twenty, and there would be many more. The face of the girl in Charlottenburg was a small incident, trivial.

The chair was hard and his legs cramped. The dogs breathed in a regular rhythm.

He had shot a man. Marcantonio could recall with great clarity how it had felt to arm the pistol, aim at the man's temple, see the flinch in the eyes, the opening of the mouth and the failed scream, the body frozen with fear, unable to escape the car seat, the squeeze on the trigger, and the spatter that had exploded on the inside of the windscreen. And the pressure required to close the windpipe inside a flabby throat – there had been a jowl to push up and out of the way with his thumbs – and the long ache in the muscles he'd used. No problem in recalling the tipping of Annunziata, bound and gagged, into the shimmering darkness of the acid tank. He saw again her eyes, the hatred, the despising, her lover already dead. The last he could barely remember – the girl's face, the pistol raised as a bludgeon, never about to fire it, then the impact and the cutting edge that was the foresight. An incident, but not meaningful.

It was the only one of his 'incidents' that had kicked back. He sat on the chair. It was beyond his capacity to understand: why?

The man might have worked in a tower block of offices – an accountant, a lawyer, a banker or – any of the professions that the family employed to ease the acquisition and multiplication of their wealth. He had twice crossed the road to intervene, then had found Marcantonio's Berlin address and had scraped the side of his pride and joy, the car that was his statement of who he was. Unimportant, even the car. What was bigger than anything else that had intruded into Marcantonio's life was that the man had come in the night to the family's house and used a key, a coin or a knife to leave a mark on the old City-Van. He had pissed on Marcantonio. No one, before, had done that. He sat examinations at school and always passed, well. He wanted a girl, and she was available. He laughed and all those with him laughed. He showed anger and anyone near him looked away. That was the circle enclosing him. He sat on the chair, watched, waited and listened.

When he strained to hear, sometimes, there was a light moan – almost a trick in his ears – and the dogs would stiffen. He could, of course, have called out the village, brought together all the men and had them form scrambling lines to track across the rocks and ravines, poke in the caves and clefts. He could, of course, have told them that in the German capital he had played a second-rate gangster, raising *pizzo* payments, and had been faced down by a guy off the streets. He would not. It was close to night, and the moon was high, throwing rinsed light on the high hillside.

Minutes passed, then hours.

He stood, his back resting against the cleft in the boulders.

There was light from the moon so he could see the outline of the sheets and the dark shape of the trellis but it might have been an hour since he'd last seen the lighter flame's flash. Questions exercised him. From where he was, could he have seen Marcantonio go back to the kitchen? No light had come on in there. It was probable that Marcantonio was still keeping vigil with the dogs and the shotgun.

Jago had never known a soldier. They were of a world divorced from his. Neither had he known a policeman. A man had come from the Serious and Organised Crime Agency to lecture the City bankers and had talked about money-laundering. Jago was ignorant about how covert forces operated – he supposed that the men further up the hill, hidden among the rocks, would be endowed with patience, which Jago was short of. He heard nothing but the wind, the trees rubbing, and the sharper sounds of the wolf's pain. He saw nothing because the moon was still low. Would he take the chance and go down? Would he wait – and for how long?

In the bank, the traders were the elite – aloof young men and women who accepted risk. Supposedly Jago belonged among the teams known for circumspection and calm evaluation, those who were *sensible*. Uncharted waters, new ground . . . The time would come when he went down, did the 'hell or high water' bit.

He thought the wolf's pain was worse. He couldn't help it – he could barely help himself. When he had tried to help a young woman in Charlottenburg he had made a poor fist of it . . . It had gone beyond her, and beyond the girl who had swum with him on the beach. Now it was about himself.

But not yet. He would go later.

He had never killed a priest – he didn't know anyone who had. He hadn't heard of a priest being killed in the Aspromonte.

Marcantonio knew every corner, every bend in the road out of the village and up into the heights of the Aspromonte. It was to be an accident. Along the routes towards the summits, the church of the Madonna and the great bronze cross of Christ, there were stretches where the safety barriers had never been installed and cliffs plummeted towards old mountain streams. It could be done in daylight or darkness. There was never much traffic. He would use a HiLux, one from the village, and would easily tip aside Father Demetrio's small car. He could not refuse.

His throat was dry and he had brought no water. Sometimes the dogs would slip away from him to drink from the bowl in the yard, then return and slobber on his trousers. He loved the dogs, believed they loved him. His grandfather had told him to do it, and Marcantonio could not refuse or argue. He was dead himself if he did so. Any number of men would come up from the village and hold him. Likely it would be Stefano's hands on his throat. A killing such as this was always arranged with deceit. A phone call to the priest's house. Someone was sick and slipping, or bedridden and needing confession; an address would be given for a location in the mountains, only reached on a particular road, and the rider would be that the *padrino* himself had said that Father Demetrio should be called, not his curate. Simple to execute.

Marcantonio had never had any quarrel with Father Demetrio. His grandmother almost worshipped the ground on which Father Demetrio walked.

He would gain nothing from the killing, but his grandfather believed it necessary for his own safety. It tossed in his mind and his concentration on the noises of the night slackened. He barely noticed that the dogs were restless, or cold. Instead he saw the smile on the priest's face, the steepest cliff on a bend in the road towards the village of Molochio, beyond Plati. He saw the car bounce and jump, roll and disintegrate. It was impossible to refuse, and the burden of it distracted him.

*   *   *

'It's not worth what you're doing to yourself,' his wife said, and sat up on her side of the bed.

The prosecutor was late home again. He slumped on to the bed and bent to take off his shoes. He had explained little to her but she was familiar with the script. She had been asleep, had woken up and now vented her feelings.

'You put your work before yourself, your health and me. You ignore the children. The job is a monster.'

He stood up. He put the shoes neatly into the bottom of the wardrobe. He didn't look at her. He slipped off his trousers and put them on a hanger. He padded towards the bathroom. He had come quietly into the house but the slamming of the car doors might have woken her. Usually she suppressed her feelings – not that night.

'The work is killing you. You get no thanks – and you can't win. God knows, we try to support you, but there's a limit.'

She had left a plate for him on the kitchen table – cheese, an apple and some ham under cling-film. He had said to his escort that he had no appetite.

'If we have any life at all it's like a stray dog's – shunned, fearful, desperate for love and not finding it.'

In the bathroom he dumped his underwear in the laundry basket, then brushed his teeth hard. He saw himself in the mirror, bags below his eyes, which had the haunted dullness of failure. He couldn't have argued with a word she had said. What hurt most was that the boys in the escort would have heard it all. Normally he and his wife made a pretence of harmony. He and his team had come from an expensive restaurant, above the city. A dinner had been in progress, a family party to celebrate a birthday, and an officer of the Squadra Mobile had been a principal guest. He had sat in the back of the car, smoked half a packet of cigarettes, drunk two bottles of water, gone behind flowering oleanders to relieve himself and waited for the policeman to come and speak to him. The delay might have been because the officer had received a call from a *carabinieri* colonel.

The two men had paced in the car park. His own people had carried their machine pistols openly and had sanitised the perimeter. He was not refused help from the Squadra Mobile – a blunt denial would have been unthinkable. Anyone who dealt with the Palace of Justice had the attuned antennae that enabled them to recognise whose star climbed and whose was barely seen. Of course he could count on co-operation, but . . . The sort of mission that required a substantial search team, and another deployed for cordon security, couldn't be plucked from the skies. The prosecutor had been promised that a planning team would be put together when the necessary officers were available. They would be tasked to draw up a comprehensive plan for the containment of, and hunt for, a fugitive. It would be – why not? – a priority. Music had spilled out through the restaurant doors. He had thanked the man brusquely and walked back towards his car. He had muttered, and his guards would have heard him, 'A priority – for when? Christmas?' The clock was ticking and time was running out. They had come home.

'Why are you spending so much time on this case? Can't you make a start on another? Is it the only fish in the sea? Calabria is awash with corrupt, evil men.'

She was crying. He was in his pyjamas. He crawled into bed and switched off the light. She shivered. He thought they shared the pain. He was loath to move on and let the investigation slide. He would suffer if he did, and no colleague would share the pain. And there was the Englishman . . . A pleasant-looking lad, from the employee identification-card picture . . . No, he was irrelevant, as were the men who had come to apologise. He might sleep, might not.

'Would you work here? If you had the choice, would you want to transfer to Calabria? Tell me, Carlo.' Old friends and new had gathered. They drank Dutch beer. It was a back bar, far up the Via del Torrione, distant enough from the barracks and their senior officers. They'd eaten but the business of the evening was in the bar. There were old friends for Carlo and new friends for Fred. 'I ask you, Fred, are we all crazy to stay in this city in a shit region?'

There was no need to answer. They could have talked about the Turks of Green Lanes in Haringey, or opened a second front on the Albanian quarter of Berlin, or the Russians, who had a presence in Hamburg, or the Vietnamese . . . It was best just to fight a fast path to the bar and put beers on the tables. There was gossip: who was sailing well, who was shipping water, who was holed in the hull and sinking. There was talk, some proud, of successes, and of the women who had been in the squads in Carlo's time, who they had been with then and who partnered them now. They had the slip of paper that would smooth introductions. Over on the east coast there would be *carabinieri* Fred knew from his time there after the Duisburg massacre. Each had sent a message to his office, in London and Berlin, that they could be useful for another forty-eight hours, and had added that the apology to the prosecutor might require reaffirmation. They had moved on to a vexed subject: the merits of the Glock, the qualities of the PPK, the superiority of the Beretta, and—

A voice behind Carlo: 'Carlo, do you know anything about a man named Horrocks?'

He turned expansively. 'Horrocks? Bent by name and bent by nature. Bentley Horrocks. That who you mean?'

'You know him?' The questioner was young, fresh-faced and pale enough to work in a communications room. He had no beer gut and was ornamented with big spectacles. Probably from the computer world, in which Carlo had few skills and enough sense to offer respect.

'I know of him but he won't have heard of me. He's a bad bastard, south London. Make my day, tell me he's fallen under a bus.'

'A big man, Carlo?'

Serious questions. The young officer, already with the rank of *maresciallo*, had sought him out. That was clear. He would have heard which bar the Englishman from Customs, trusted by colleagues, had decamped to. He would have come off duty at ten that evening and walked up. He was nursing an orange juice in a fragile fist. The questions were serious enough for Carlo to sober up fast.

'He's about as much of a big man as we have in London.'

'His speciality is what?'

'This is a long way ahead of what I do. He's a principal target, a major player. Sorry, I must correct myself. He *should* be a principal target – what we call a high-value target – but he's protected. He has a reputation as an 'untouchable'. We're too yellow bellied to admit it. At my level that's what he is because otherwise he'd be banged up for twenty-five years in high security. What's he into? Extortion, protection, corruption of officials, smuggling Class-A drugs, fags and kids. Or that's what the gossip says.'

'What is "untouchable"?'

'He has police on his payroll, those in the specialist agencies that are supposed to hunt him down, but they take his money, screw up investigations and tell him where potential witnesses are holed up so he can beat hell out of them and they don't testify. It's about buying some people and intimidating others. Why?'

'I was merely clarifying who Horrocks is.'

Carlo gazed at him. 'You'll have to do better than that. Why's he on your radar?'

'Because of where he is.' The officer grinned, as if he was trailing a plastic mouse, on a length of string, in front of a lively kitten.

'Which is where?'

The officer named a hotel, its ownership and location, then offered a confession. The usual – it might have been in English, German, French or Italian: lack of resources; a difficult week. Perhaps the following week would be easier for resources, but there might not be a target to direct them against. A shrug. The *maresciallo* was on the move. He went to another table where others greeted him. Always cocky, the guys who trawled the computers in the warm and dry, had good meal breaks and delivered gold dust.

Carlo said to Fred, 'Did you get that?'

'I think so.'

'Do you have a word for men like Horrocks?'

'It is *Unbestechlicher*, but we do not use it for a gangster. In Hamburg it would be employed for a big businessman living in the "bacon belt" and using bribery to get contracts. In Frankfurt, it would be used for a senior banker who is corrupt, fraudulent and evades tax but is too powerful to bring down, and protected. It's not only Italy.'

'Makes me want to throw up,' Carlo spat. 'Little bastards like me get nowhere because they block us, the detectives and investigators.'

'What might you do, Carlo, while we take our vacation? I have an opportunity, I believe, to assuage my sense of responsibility for this entire affair – for what I did.'

'Not called for.'

'And it would be good to create some collateral. Satisfying.'

'If we get on the road early, we might screw him up.'

They made their excuses. They were the first to leave the party, and their departure was barely noticed. The source had his back to them and was on a second orange juice. They went out into the night.

Fred said, 'I would like to wreck him – far from home and regulation. It would be good to wreck your Bentley Horrocks. I am in that mood.'

It was an hour before dawn. Marcantonio had come inside to make coffee. He might have slept for a while in the chair. The dogs would have growled if they'd been disturbed, but they hadn't.

He put the shotgun on the table. Tiredness wracked him, but it would be simple to have the call made to the priest, then to estimate when Father Demetrio would be on the road. Marcantonio would use the heavy vehicle with the bars on the front. Easy for him, and he didn't need to have slept for that. There was a coffee machine in the kitchen. His grandmother detested it, but it was used. It was the sole relic of Annunziata in the house. Giulietta liked it, and Marcantonio didn't mind it. Four months before she had gone into the acid, Annunziata had bought it for them on a trip to see her husband in gaol in the north. His grandmother hated what was new and mechanical, but there was another in the bunker where his grandfather slept.

The light blazed over him. He heard the door handle turning, then saw Giulietta. No love was lost between nephew and aunt. She gave him a withering glance and her lip curled: her eyes had settled on the shotgun. He had not broken it so she did. She was dressed formally in a dark trouser suit and white blouse. Her hair was pulled up into a ponytail. She wore no jewellery or makeup. He glanced at her nose – twisted from the break. That morning she would play the professional, who could put together an agreement, carrying detail in her head – all that he did not. She would tie together the ends left loose from his meeting with the Englishman, an arrogant shit, and she would do it over breakfast, as if she were a Berlin businesswoman. She looked at him as she peeled a banana, then started to eat it.

She spoke through a mouthful: 'I hear that my father met other men recently to discuss whom you should marry – what alliances we can make with you. A piece of horsemeat for trading.'

Marcantonio couldn't tell her – *yet* – to go shag herself. One day, not far away, she could go out through the door with her bag and the family would belong to him. His word would rule. Soon. Not *yet*.

'When, Aunt, will you consider marriage?' It was said with exaggerated politeness that would not have fooled her.

'When I find the right man, and he will be my choice, not *arranged* as a matter of political gain.' The banana was finished, the skin thrown into the bin. She drank from a water bottle, then rounded on him. 'Is he there, the man who followed you from Germany? You brought this down on us. You sit all night with a gun on your knee because you need to make a few euros. You are responsible for this inconvenience to us. Are you stupid?'

He went out into the night with his gun and the dogs, slipped back across the yard, then behind the trellis, and went to his chair.

He had seen the light come on in the kitchen.

He heard the wind, soft, and the hushed whimpers of the wolf. Jago thought it near the time. He would linger a little longer, to be certain, then move. He thought it enough that the leader of the family should be trapped in his bunker in darkness, panic surging. Then he could climb back up the hillside, find the guys in the camouflage suits, wish them well and thank them for their kindness. He thought again of the huge wealth of the old man in the bunker, the power he wielded over life and death, saw him groping for a hand torch or a candle and matches, the air around him getting damper and colder. He would wait a few more minutes, then move. He was calm and the birds above him were still and quiet. He shared the night with the wolf but could do nothing to salve its wound.

'What do you want?' she demanded.

It had been Fred's idea. He had taken the lead and rung a bell, then beaten his fist on the door. The camera above had swivelled to gain better focus on them. Three hours' sleep. Through the wall Fred had heard Carlo snoring. The door opened and he'd asked for her.

When they had driven into Archi, a sprawled suburb to the

north of Reggio, Carlo had told Fred that he'd have preferred to be snug in the belly of a main battle tank, not in the small airport hire car. It was still night-time and there were watchers on the street: men leaning against lampposts and smoking, men with skinny dogs on leashes, men sitting on benches . . . No one seemed to have anything to do – they weren't hurrying to work or sweeping a pavement before opening a business. They were just watching and keeping track of visitors. Fred had said it was the 'alternative state', demonstrating that strangers were logged in, monitored. He thought it important to be there.

She was smaller than when he'd met her on the street. Then she had been dressed warmly for the late evening: now she had on just a thin cotton nightdress. 'What do you want? Why have you come here?'

She was in the doorway, a man in a dressing-gown hovering behind her.

Fred said, 'It's about Jago Browne, where you took him and—'

'What do you know of him? And what do you know about Calabria and survival in this city?'

Fred stayed calm. The police in Berlin did courses on anger management, how to confront verbal assault. He was the voice of reason. 'He should not be here. Certain matters should be left to law-enforcement officers to deal with.'

'You know nothing.'

'What I do know is that if he is taken he will be cut into small pieces. Without mercy.'

'He's too old to need a nanny.'

Carlo spoke, 'What part of yourself did you wave at him?'

She flared, 'Were you ever on your knees fighting because you believed in something? I think you just took the work benefits and the overtime payments.'

They turned away. Fred thought it a 'clusterfuck' moment. The door slammed behind them.

Fred said, through gritted teeth, 'I don't know why we bother.'

He sensed Carlo's grin. 'Because we get better pensions.'

'God protect us from crusaders, bigots, her and her crowd. You know what we had in Germany in the Middle Ages? We had feudal warrior barons, each with a fortress, and they ran their territories ruthlessly. Their word was law. Nothing changed. It just transferred here from Saxony, Thuringia and Mecklenburg. The Englishman came here with stupidity. She waved God knows what at him . . . She laughs at us because we are the little people.'

'If I was asked, "What did you do, Dad, in the great war against organised crime?" I'd say I ticked off the days till my ID was shredded, put in the expenses, then enjoyed the pension scheme. Anything else?'

Fred felt Carlo's heavy hand settle on his shoulder. Good expenses? Yes, why not? Knowing their place? Absolutely . . . But every once in a while, the 'little people' – he and Carlo – had a special moment: the dawn raid, the ram hitting the door at first light, the dog inside barking, the woman at the top of the stairs with her dressing-gown not properly fastened, the kids howling, and the 'fat cat' stumbling from his bed, muttering to his wife about calling the lawyer, dressing at gunpoint and the cuffs going on. Might be worth ten million or a hundred million. The shock on their faces, and the sense of outrage at an invasion of their world. It happened once in a while.

They would screw Bentley Horrocks in a good cause because he was staying at a hotel that intelligence stated was part of the investment portfolio of Bernardo Cancello and his family. Also, Fred knew Brancaleone and fancied he might get to swim there. He and Carlo were growing closer, near enough now to josh with each other, but Fred could show fierce determination, and he was confident that Carlo would match him.

'I want to say my piece about her. In a theatre she has only a walk-on part. Our dear Consolata is not the lead in the performance. She thinks she is, but she isn't. She's a convenience. Am I right? Time will tell. I'll drive.'

Carlo took the wheel.

It was the hour before dawn, the time when men died in their beds, the lucky and the few. The time when the storm squads of the *cacciatore* would break into a bunker or flood a safe house, throw a flash-and-bang grenade and take a prisoner. It was the time when a man eased from a woman's bed because soon a cuck-olded husband would be back from a night's thieving, the time when dogs slept and owls were quiet. Very soon the cockerel would crow, not that Bernardo would hear it. He tossed in his bed.

The light was on. He heard the whine of the air-conditioner, the hum of the refrigerator and the regular drip of condensation. It would soon be the start of an important day for him, for Giulietta, for Marcantonio. A grim smile. In vest and underpants, he padded towards the basin where his toothbrush was and his shaver. He would not go back to sleep. He would watch something on televi-sion. It would be an important day for his daughter, his grandson and for Father Demetrio, who had been his friend. He took no pleasure from what would happen that day to the priest, nor any sadness. After Giulietta had been to Brancaleone she would go for her weekly rendezvous with the clerk from the Palace of Justice in Reggio. She would meet him near the uppermost peaks of Montalto, and he would tell her the latest developments. Bernardo's privation in the bunker was nearing its end and she would bring confirmation of it. But first she would go to Brancaleone.

He used to go to Brancaleone every Thursday afternoon. He smiled to himself. Peering into the mirror he saw his ravaged old face crack in the lines of his smile. It was a private moment. Sometimes – not often – he went on a Tuesday afternoon as well. A fine woman. She had made him laugh, and almost made him fall in love. A woman who had lived for three and a half years in Brancaleone in an apartment that he had paid for in cash and overlooked the beach. She had summoned the courage to deliver an ultimatum. She had called a halt to their relationship because he would not divorce his wife. To separate legally from Mamma, to marry again, was impossible. It would have broken a relation-ship of convenience with a family from Locri, and he did good business with that family. It was an alliance of substance. That woman now lived in Sicily. It had happened a long time ago, when Giulietta was a child.

He had not flaunted her, had maintained the greatest discretion, had never embarrassed Mamma, had never told anyone: a lawyer from Milan had handled the purchase of the apartment. When he went, less often now, to Brancaleone he always looked for the apartment and the balcony, expecting to see her . . .

A busy day ahead. Excitement still stirred in him at the thought of a killing done in his name.

Stefano had been out for a half-hour and had used his time well. He had polished the interior of the City-Van, using a spray on the plastic, then working at it with a cloth, and had brought out a stiff brush to clean the seat on which she would sit. He loved Giulietta alone among the family.

She came out of the house wearing a smart suit and carrying a lightweight briefcase, which would be for effect only and was probably empty. He heard the drone of the scooter and the kid's lights powered up the track. He might have been her father. For that he would have been killed – not pleasantly. But the risk had fuelled the thrill.

It had not happened often, in days long past, often when the heat was suffocating and the *padrino* was away for a day's discussion with allies. There would have been lemonade on the kitchen table. Mamma had begun it. He would not have dared to. Surprisingly, she was tender. Stefano would sit on a hard chair and she would pour the lemonade, then crouch over him, unbutton his fly, and put the rubber on him. Then she would hitch up her skirt and lower herself onto him. If the *padrino* had known, Stefano's death would have been nightmarish, and his corpse would never have been found. Would Mamma have survived? He had seen the family's reaction when the scandal of Annunziata's affairs became known – and she had refused to follow the constraints of the *vedova bianca*. Slow, exquisite lovemaking. She'd had a sensitivity that he doubted she ever offered to her husband. A hot day, no wind, sweating from outside work, and the supply of condoms had run short. They had done it, and that night, after his return, she had given herself eagerly, as she told it, to her husband and had not made him withdraw. The dates matched. There was a chance that Giulietta was Stefano's, and a chance that she was not. It was many years since he had been with Mamma, on the chair by the kitchen table, and now she touched him only rarely with a little gesture of shared intimacy.

He spoke briefly to the kid, and they checked their phones. The scooter went and its lights caught the men who were down the lane, watching – close enough, if called.

He opened the door for Giulietta. He had used a scent spray in the car so that she would not be put off by the smell of old oil and accumulated sweat. He thought it good that she was going to meet the Englishman early: she would catch him when his concentration was lowest and do the best deal. It was unusual, in an 'Ndrangheta family, for a woman to play such a part. He thought she did it well – better than the little shit, Marcantonio. She might have been his daughter but Stefano was not over-familiar with her. She sat on the cleaned seat, thanked him absently, and he closed the door for her. His phone did not trill so the road ahead would be clear.

He pulled away. He heard the cockerel crowing and wondered how much longer Marcantonio would sit in the yard with the shotgun, and what legacy the little shit had left them. He wondered how the day would eke out – and why a man would come so far and risk so much to end up with parallel scratched lines on a worthless vehicle. He assumed that by now he would have gone back to where he had come from.

He set off for Brancaleone, the coast and saw, in the distance, the first smear of dawn.

They had done it and could not undo it – neither would accept the burden of individual blame. They had not considered the consequences. Lunacy . . .

He had come, taken their food and disappeared back down the slope. There had been neither sight nor sound of him since. They had good night-vision equipment, the same as the regular military used and the secret service, and they knew that Marcantonio was on the seat at the end of the trellis, with the dogs. They had seen Giulietta leave with the driver, the cockerel had crowed, and the day would soon start. Mamma always came out of the kitchen door early with food for the chickens. They could follow her part of the way if they used the 'heat-seeker', but the batteries were damp so it was useless now.

They didn't know where he was. They had not transmitted the picture they had taken of him when they had given him the food. Fabio and Ciccio had acknowledged that there were moments in even the most illustrious careers when information was suppressed, for reasons that were not easily explained. Why was he there? All they had was a meaningless statement concerning a woman's face. They had absorbed the panorama below them without difficulty. They knew the ritual timelines of the family and its protectors, who were down the track, and had observed their routines. They knew, too, that the *padrino* was close by, but he was careful and had outwitted them.

Ciccio had said quietly, 'If we get the old goat, we get him. If we don't then I won't cry myself to sleep. I'll forget him and move on.'

The quiet lulled them. If nothing developed there would be just one more day. Their rubbish, kit and bedding would come out with them, and it would be as if they hadn't lived in the cave. The rats would have free rein. Both were awake, but not alert.

The empty jar was close to Fabio's hand, with the screw-on lid perforated for air circulation. When morning came, and the sun settled on the stone ledge in front of them, there was a good chance that a scorpion fly would materialise, a beautiful creature that Fabio had come to respect. Its forward feelers were as long as its body, and its legs were thin as hair; the wings were long and tucked back when it alighted, and at the base of the body the tail was honey-coloured and pointed at the tip from which its name came. Sad to see it trapped in the jar.

They were a peculiar breed, those who mounted watch on others, observing a target's movements, and likely to be damned. He didn't know if they had the stomach to catch more insects before time was called on Operation Scorpion Fly.

When the light came it was Ciccio's turn to do breakfast. There was stillness in front of them, quiet, a sort of peace.

The slight tide of the Mediterranean pulled back. Bentley Horrocks walked on wet sand. The wind whipped his face. He felt cleansed. There was enough light for him to see the ripples, the water was cold on his feet and the sand clung to his skin. He didn't do holidays. He'd send Trace and her sister away together, and Angel could take warm-weather breaks with the kids – they did the South of France or yacht cruises among the Croatian islands. He'd go to Margate to see his mother, no further, and he'd work, the phone – a different one every other day – latched to his ear, deals done, scores settled.

He felt good, and confident enough to let his anger surge.

They had sent a boy, showing no respect for Bent Horrocks. It would be different today, later this morning, Humphrey, the lawyer, had promised. The big man, the boss. He rehearsed them, the lines in his head. Peasants, weren't they? They had the trade stitched up, the stuff coming on the long sea route from South America, but they were still peasants. He'd take no shit from them. He'd have guarantees of supply dates, and there'd be no payment until delivery reached him. He could have talked through the tactics with Jack, but he was half Italian – might have gone native and forgotten where his lifestyle came from. The lawyer had definitely gone native, and was in their pockets. He had not sought advice, didn't need it. He was content . . .

God, Mum, in the apartment he had bought her at Margate, looking out on Marine Terrace and the beach, would have cackled if she'd seen him with his trousers rolled to the knee and walking in the darkness in the sea. She would have howled with laughter.

The stress of London, of running territory in Peckham, Rotherhithe and Deptford, keeping back the shites who snapped at his ankles, was behind him. He'd walk a bit further before he turned back.

He'd seen the driver leave, with Giulietta, and the kid depart on his scooter. He'd heard the cockerel crow. He hadn't seen the dogs, or Marcantonio, while the kitchen light had been on. It still lit the yard.

He made a mental checklist. Normally he would have made sure his shoes were clean, his tie straight, his jacket not too creased, that his laptop and BlackBerry were charged and the work for his next appointment was loaded, then glanced through his schedule.

Today the checklist was short: a tyre iron, a penknife, the stick and the pocket torch, which he could use only on the track and behind the sheets. He did not know if, from the hiding place, he would hear cries for help when the cable was cut. He didn't know where the air vent was, but there had to be one. There was so much he didn't know.

A last pause and a last listen. He heard the wind in the leaves, and the wolf below him. He had kept vigil with the animal through the night. Together they had endured.

Jago stepped forward, committed. His legs were stiff and his movements clumsy. The night was hard around him. The men behind and above might have seen him from their eyrie. He knelt, swung his legs into the void and scrabbled for a grip. His lead foot found a secure stone, and he was away from the security of the cleft between two great boulders.

He went down. Ledges and cracks in stone to hold his weight, the stick in his hand to guide him. He could make out the sheets that hung on the line, screening the path – he needed the place where the third sheet was against the fourth. He would have been close to the wolf but didn't hear it. He went lower. He saw a film in his head, the one that had been screened every Christmas when he was a kid, and heard the great lines. A man jumped off a ten-storey building, and as he'd gone down on each floor people had heard him say, 'So far so good. So far, so good.' About right. Another line, same movie: a man had stripped off and jumped into a mass of cacti and was asked why he'd done it. 'It seemed a good idea at the time.' A stone slid from under him, bounced, rolled away. Then was still.

The eruption was total. The crows and the pigeons thrashed at leaves and branches and rose, screaming, into the darkness.

The torch came on – but the boy had been in the kitchen. The torch had a strong narrow beam and raked over the hillside. Jago went down on his knees, then his stomach, and tried to burrow but was on unforgiving rock.

14

Every bird rose in flight. The noise split the darkness. If there had been earth under him, Jago would have scraped at it with his fingernails. Impossible. He tried to snuggle lower, but had to see what happened in front of him. The torch was powerful, had a sharp-edged beam.

It would be Marcantonio with the torch. Jago realised he'd been duped. He had thought himself intelligent, street-wise and had believed that the boy's patience was exhausted. Wrong. At the bank, if he had made a mistake, he would expect to be hauled before a mini Star Chamber – Wilhelmina and two grey-faced men – and made to understand that the bank had to put right the loss to a client. A million, a thousand or a hundred euros, whatever the sum the gravity of the error was emphasised. No one was here to watch over him. He thought the men in the camouflage suits, above and behind him – who had his photograph – would be cursing him, with good reason: the torch beam threatened them, as well as Jago.

It had started high in the trees where the crows and pigeons had been, but now raked over the leaves, branches and rock faces. It seemed to pry into the little crannies where there was shadow and wipe away darkness. It moved steadily, avoided nothing, paused where something was unclear, then moved again.

The dogs screamed. Jago had had his head down and dared to lift his face fractionally to peer below him. The scream became a howl. The torch beam would have found the wolf, enough to make the eyes light up, two spots of gold. The dogs were barking, furious but not yet brave enough to scamper from the safety of Marcantonio. The light came back.

He thought the wolf did not have the strength to leap off the rock where it had been through the night. It would stay and fight for the final moments of its life. The beam, on full power, was locked on it. Jago could see part of its head – he thought its mouth was open, teeth showing. It was crouched. If it had not been for the injury, Jago thought, the wolf would have turned tail, slipped from rock to stone, jumped and manoeuvred, scurried, found cover and been gone in the darkness. But it was injured.

The beam lit it.

Then the light shook, was readjusted. The three dogs were flooded with light and danced at Marcantonio's feet, rearing on their back legs and howling. If the wolf responded with growls or snarls, it did so too softly for Jago to hear. He saw why the beam meandered. It was full on Marcantonio's face, then on his arm, which held the shotgun. The boy aimed the weapon, the short-ened barrels were resting on his left arm. His left hand held the torch, which wobbled and wavered, searching for the wolf. Jago almost shouted, but the words stuck in his throat, a jumble about the beast getting clear, using these moments to find a refuge. He held his silence because that was survival.

It was found.

The wolf had risen half up and Jago saw the wound, dark-rimmed, pink at the heart.

The barrel was up. The light was steady. The shadow thrown by the wolf's head was still. First, the flash. Then the puff of the fumes from the barrel, and the crash of the shot. It toppled.

The range was too great. Not a killing shot. The wolf would have been hit by a spray of pellets. The beam leaped off the animal, climbed and seemed to wash the rim of the rock that was in front of Jago's head. He might have been seen and might not and— The beam found the beast.

Jago thought the second shot, from the other barrel, was about to be fired. He was in darkness again. He supposed it would be like the death of a friend. He had no friends who had died. His mother was estranged from her parents, and he didn't know if they were alive or dead. The wife of a director in the City had died in hospital. No one had met her, but her husband received notes of sympathy from his colleagues. He felt for the wolf, and tears welled. He had the tyre wrench in his fist, tightly held. The wolf was upright. There was blood on its face and chest. Jago thought the animal was blinded. It seemed not to know what to do, where to go. It went forward, seemed to grope with its front paws, and fell. Jago heard stones and rocks spiral down with it.

It came to rest.

Still the dogs lacked courage. It was a dozen paces in front of them. They circled it. It seemed barely to have the strength to turn its head to face them. They barked at it. Marcantonio came close, the shotgun aimed, wary . . .

An English class: a young teacher, fresh from training college, had made them read from Tennyson, 'The Revenge'. An Elizabethan galleon had happened across a Spanish fleet, had been overwhelmed by cannon fire and was surrounded, gunpowder exhausted, most of the crew dead or maimed. Jago remembered a line of a survivor, who sees the Spanish circling them: 'But they dared not touch us again, for they feared we still could sting.' Neither the dogs nor Marcantonio went close to the wolf. Jago stood up to his full height.

He had enough blow-back from the torch to see Marcantonio.

It was a target. At the school, discuses had been thrown, hammers and javelins lobbed. He had thrown stones on the beach when his mother had taken him to Southend or Clacton. Now he hurled the tyre iron. It would have been the moment at which Marcantonio's finger left the trigger guard for a close-range shot.

He saw it arc away, watched its flight and saw it strike.

There was an explosion. The light failed. The dogs stopped barking. The tyre iron had hit the boy, who had dropped the torch and pressed on the trigger. The second barrel had fired.

A light went on inside the ground floor.

Then another, brighter. The kitchen door opened. Enough light now spilled out for Jago to see what he had done. He gaped. Marcantonio was on his side, blood pooling from the upper part of his body – his head or his throat. The shotgun was still in his hand.

Jago stood to his full height, and the first warmth of the new day was on his face.

'Mamma's within five metres of him – barefoot and in her dressing-gown,' Fabio murmured.

Ciccio pressed the keys and they had a live connection. The night intensifier had burned out. Sufficient light from the house came through the window and the kitchen door. They had hesitated for a moment, then snatched a link to an operations room in the basement of a barracks on the outskirts of Reggio Calabria. There was never pandemonium when a link came into a communications area, which was as quiet and unemotional as air-traffic control, but a senior man would now be reading over a shoulder. He'd have a phone at his ear and would be warning his own superiors.

'The indications are that Marcantonio, grandson, has a self-inflicted wound, seemingly fatal. A confused run-up. He'd sat out through most of the night, semi-concealed with a sawn-off shotgun. A disturbance on the hill between his position and ours alerted him. Birds taking off. A flashlight identified a wolf – correct, a wolf. He fired one barrel at it, at maximum range. The wolf went down, fell, landed by Marcantonio – sorry, that's Mike/Alpha Charlie, and—'

'I already have that.'

'It's getting complicated. Just listen. Don't send yet. Something hit him. He dropped the flashlight and the weapon fired. I don't know what hit him, but there's an object near to his left foot – a spanner, wrench, iron bar. How did that get to hit him? You hearing me?'

'Sure.'

'It isn't the beach at Tropea here and it isn't Sunday afternoon. Few people could have thrown a piece of metal at him. Only one person I know of.'

'Just one.'

'I don't send that?'

'If you do, you'll open the can, shake out the worms and they'll crawl every-fucking-where. Keep going.'

Fabio did so. 'Mamma reacts – that is, Mike/Charlie reacts. She kneels. It's like the old movies, the Mafia woman, the street, the corpse, the blood. You didn't send that?'

'I already did.'

'They'll eat my balls . . . No, she's up. I tell you the wolf moved. She goes to it – fucking hell! She's kicked its head. Barefoot. That was one hell of a kick, maybe broke its neck. She's set the dogs on it – God, I could throw up. She's gone inside. The dogs are fighting over it. She's back, carrying a chair. Now she's sitting beside the body of her grandson. What can I say?'

'Not much. How about "You reap what you sow"?'

'Or "He that kills with the sword must die by the sword" Book of Revelation . . . The dogs have ripped that fucking wolf apart. It's not pretty. Will the old man show himself?'

Jago backed away. He had killed a man. He supposed he should have been shaking, and turned away to shut out the sight. He was quite calm, but deep in his guts adrenalin pumped.

A tableau laid out below him.

The grandmother was keeping vigil. He'd heard the word, seen TV documentaries on tribal life in Africa: there had been a particular sound that women made, a high-pitched wail. He heard it now, as would the men above him . . . and others.

Villagers came up the track, the thin and fit leading the rest, who were obese or old and struggling. Some had clubs, two carried handguns and one had an assault rifle – Jago thought he had been delayed by the need to go to a hiding place and collect it. It would have been a prime killing machine and marked him out as trusted. They ignored the woman, let her sit and cry while they worked quickly around her. It would have been their evaluation. Some crouched and others stood. They formed a ring around the body, the blood and the old woman's chair. The evidence was noted. The dogs had abandoned the wolf and were now beside and under the old woman's chair. The weapon was close to Marcantonio's right hand and one man lifted it, broke it, ejected the cartridge cases and passed it to the rifleman. Jago saw all of that, the shrugs, the feeble shows of sympathy, and reckoned that the investigation was almost concluded, with a verdict of 'accidental death'. He saw that the tyre iron was between the feet of a big man, one of those who had watched the end of the lane, one of the last to get there, who had taken off his cap and was holding it in respect with both hands.

Jago felt neither guilt nor elation.

Teresa appeared. He knew her from the photographs on the laptop. A good-looking woman, she had thrown on some clothes and a pair of sandals. Jago had seen her several times, at the front door, but the old woman had never come out to see her off: no kissing, no hugs. She crouched over her son's head. It was inevitable that blood from the wound would soak into her blouse. She had done what was asked of her and produced the heir – Jago assumed that Marcantonio had had a destiny in the pyramid structure of the family, had been destined for the top. She had reason to hug the broken head, near to unrecognisable after the pellet blast. Jago fancied he had had an insight into the family's workings. It was an interesting spectacle. He thought himself a changed man.

The man with the cap in his hand caught at the sleeve of the one with the assault rifle, and seemed nervous. He pointed at the tyre iron.

'Just a diversion.'

'Light relief.'

'Go and hack it,' Carlo prompted.

He was a long way from home, the manuals of procedure locked in his floor safe. Being involved in a bit of unauthorised detail gave him acute pleasure – as it had when he had left the fired-up laptop open on the desk.

Fred said, 'Good, isn't it, what we do? Just nudging things along.'

Carlo said, 'We *might* use short-cuts and go up no-entries. Cut corners.'

'Like a couple of puppies off the leash.'

'Cause some havoc . . .'

First light, and the greyness matched the lobby's interior. Fred had left Carlo sitting on the bonnet of the small hire car. He went through the swing doors. A girl was doing her makeup behind the reception desk, and an older woman was manoeuvring a floor polisher. Fred, if pressed, could manage charm and a conspiratorial way that usually saw him home. He had a talent for being believed. He was at the desk, smiled and lowered his head to speak softly to her. She looked up from her mirror.

'You have a gentleman here, a Mr Horrocks, staying with you. I want to surprise him. Which room, please?'

He was told that the gentleman had gone out.

'Already? Extraordinary.'

He was walking on the beach. His friend was still in his room on the second floor. Did the gentleman wish . . .?

'No, thank you. He'll come back through this door, yes? He'll be so pleased to see me.'

The smile, a little wink. He went back out through the swing doors and was crossing the car park when he had to skip out of the way of a Mercedes coupé, driven by a man with a flushed face and sparse silver hair. When he reached Carlo, he told him what had happened.

Carlo said, 'That old guy who almost ran you over – he's Humphrey somebody. Used to work at the Old Bailey, hot-shot lawyer, more twisted than a corkscrew. Interesting if he's meeting Horrocks. I'll get the coffee ordered.'

It looked to be the start of a fine day, and the wind was pleasant. They had a good view of the sea and the narrow beach, and of a man who walked alone. Fred didn't know where the day would lead him.

Quiet and composed, Giulietta ran through the figures in her head.

Stefano drove in a respectful silence. Shipment charges varied if the cargo was sold at the exit point of the Gioia Tauro docks, at a service station south of Salerno on the A3, in Milan, Rotterdam, Felixstowe, Tilbury or the Port of Dublin. No other family on the eastern slopes of the Aspromonte permitted a woman such access to the inner workings of its business. Her own *cosca* would revert to type once her nephew returned permanently from Berlin. Within the next two days he would be on a flight back to the German capital then would be away for, perhaps, another three months. After that he would be at home, calling the shots and . . . She detested him.

The kid on the scooter had long left them. He had been their escort as far as Gabella, almost into Locri, then had gone into the town to hang out with kids he knew. She and Stefano would pick him up on their way home. It was a laborious procedure but she knew the value of care. If caution seemed too great a burden, she would think of her elder brothers in gaol in the far north, the aching boredom of the Article 41*bis* regime. Teresa had said they were weakening. No phone was switched on in the car. Most men who endured the longest sentences could turn their minds back to a call made when it should not have been. There was, she knew it, a building on the south side of Reggio, sandwiched between the railtrack and the beach, close to the prison of San Pietro, where a small army employed by the Direzione Investigativa Anti-Mafia were huddled in half-light over their keyboards, earphones clamped to their heads, and hacked into phone links and internet connections, but the mobile phone was the easiest for them. They were alone in the car, silent – the radio would have disturbed her concentration. Not yet, but soon, they would no longer need the City-Van's headlights.

She had the figures in her head. She would not have to use a calculator. She would dominate the Englishman.

Stefano brought her into the outskirts of Brancaleone, as the town woke.

Bent had come off the beach. They'd seen him there, ambling along, then lost him – and found him again.

The coffee had been on a tray, proof of Fred's expertise with the girl inside. They drained the cups and Carlo took the tray to the hotel's steps. A few moments to wait . . .

'Hello, Bent. How's it going?'

A choice moment for Carlo. He enjoyed it. Not quite as good as those involving the ram on a locked door, but it came close. He'd spoken in his best estuary accent, the one most favoured by detectives from the Flying Squad, the organised-crime teams or the people on the Customs units who dealt with major importers. 'Nice to see you, Bent. Hotel up to scratch?'

Bentley Horrocks – credit to him – didn't duck, skip or scoot. He took his time, stopped, probably set his face in the scowl that did the business as a frightener to most who were stupid enough to pull his pecker. Carlo might just get to dine out on this story, and it wouldn't need embellishment. The man turned, and surprise spread across his face. Carlo could understand that, because he and Bentley Horrocks had never met or spoken. Horrocks would know the senior figures, and those who were on his payroll, but had no idea who this intruder was. His expression was supposed to intimidate – it might have done so on home territory, but not here. A first ray of sunlight came through the hotel garden's trees.

'Always difficult to know, Bent, how a hotel's going to shape up. I'd be careful at this one – just a friendly warning. Keep your wallet on you and your valuables in sight. It's the ownership you want to worry about. One of those 'Ndrangheta clans, via front companies, is the stake-holder. Criminals, Bent – best avoided . . . Nice for you to be getting a bit of sunshine. Weather was awful, wasn't it, back in London? Anyway, good to see you.'

It was, thought Carlo, worth a whole lifetime of freezing stake-outs at dawn when the ice was on the roads and pavements. Nobody spoke in that tone of impertinent familiarity to Bentley Horrocks and the man quite obviously didn't know how to react. It was worth all those years of carbo-excess from fast-food outlets, the cock-ups when they'd shown out or when the Crown Prosecution Service said the evidence wasn't tight enough to warrant charges. And Bentley Horrocks was in the process of walking out on him. He clearly couldn't place either of them and Fred was grinning, like a fool.

Carlo said, as if he was a friend, 'You're wondering who I am.

Fair enough. Haven't the boys you pay all that cash to told you about us? Not sure it's money well spent, Bent. I'm Customs and Excise, and my colleague here is from the German Federal Police, the KrimPol crowd who do stuff in the brackets of Serious and Organised. Anyway, we're just keeping an eye on you, making sure you don't fall foul of some serious people. A pleasure to have met you, Bent. Have a prosperous day – if you're going to have lunch here, the squid is usually good. So, have a good day – and be careful. You've left a trail that my old granny could have followed.'

The lawyer, Humphrey Somebody, was in the lobby, visible through the swing doors. Bent headed through them. Carlo couldn't see his face but had an idea it would have been creased in fury. Time to get the hell out – they might have overstayed their welcome. Fred was still grinning ear to ear.

They hadn't noticed a City-Van, a little Fiat, which looked as though it did runs for a smallholding or a tradesman. It had waited for them because they'd blocked its way into the car park. Both nodded to the driver in apology. Time for coffee and cake, then to head on into downtown Brancaleone.

Funny thing, the City-Van came past them – an old guy driving and a young woman beside him. It kept going, went straight out of the far side of the car park and turned as if to go back onto the main road. Odd.

To Stefano it was obvious.

To Giulietta there was no doubt.

He swore, waited for a lorry to clear the way in front of him and swung onto the coast road. He drove away from the hotel, past the trattoria that would soon be opening for the day. He turned off abruptly, without indicating, and went up a side-street, then accelerated into another that ran parallel to the main drag. He took another turning and parked where he had a good view of the vehicles on the main coast road. She sat boot-faced. She had clamped her arms tight across her chest and bit her lip.

Stefano said to Giulietta, 'The one who was talking with him, the fat one, he was police.'

She said, 'The one who stayed by the car, a hire car from Lamezia, was another policeman.'

'He walked away, smiling, like he'd met a contact. We were early.'

'Looked well pleased with himself. Thank God we were early.'

He said, 'That man, Horrocks, is a danger to the family.'

She said, 'And a danger is never ignored, always faced.'

They saw the hire car, black, go by. Stefano edged the City-Van forward and came to the junction. It was being parked opposite a limp flag, green, white and red. A sign designated the building as the Brancaleone barracks of the *carabinieri*. The jacaranda flowers were still bright purple and overhung the pavement against which the hire car was being manoeuvred. The two men got out of it, crossed the street and went into the building.

Where did she want to go?

Home. The sun was fierce through the windscreen so she peeled off her jacket and tossed it behind her. She was livid.

The old woman screamed. She lifted her head every ten minutes and howled as Jago watched.

Much to observe. The fate of the tyre iron held his attention. The one with the automatic rifle had given it to another to take away.

The old woman threw her head back and vented her grief. Then she sagged on the hard chair. Jago thought her wailing biblical. He assumed that she had accepted her grandson was dead. She would never have chastised him for his criminal actions. She would not have wanted him to train as a teacher or an accountant, and move to the centre or north of the country, divorcing himself from the risk of a prison sentence. The men gave her respectful space. They were joined now by a knot of women, young and old. Then the priest arrived. The body had not been moved and the head was now hidden by a tea-towel someone had brought from the kitchen.

The priest was elderly, overweight but not obese. Jago remembered him from before the storm. He was deferential and talked quietly to the mother. He stood close to her but did not touch her.

He carried a small leather bag with him and now took from it one of his vestments – Jago recognised it from his schooldays. He hung it around his neck and knelt. After the prayer, and the gesture of the cross over the chest, the priest reached behind him and was given a hand to steady him as he stood up. Then he brushed the dirt off the knees of his trousers. Jago had thought the priest would make more of a show, and was puzzled by the lack of ceremony.

Then Teresa was back, the children in her wake. She came running. Jago couldn't understand why she wore smart clothes but lived in an out-of-the-way village. She might have had no life other than the visits he had seen her make to the house. But what did he know? The priest had backed away. Teresa was on the ground, holding her boy's head and the world could hear her sobbing. Jago was a new man, unrecognisable to himself.

He did not regret having hurled the tyre iron. Neither was he triumphant. Other kids from school had supported West Ham, and in the City several of his colleagues had raved about Chelsea, Tottenham Hotspur or Arsenal. When there was a 'result' the excitement was electric. It seemed to Jago that the death of a juvenile crime boss, groomed for high levels of violence, corruption and extortion, should have stacked higher than a goal scored on a September afternoon. He had felt no need to clench his fist and celebrate the moment. He felt very little. He had presided over a killing and now considered that what he had done was nothing special. That was why he was new and unrecognisable to himself.

He often walked from Stresemannstrasse towards the old Gestapo house, then along Niederkirchner-strasse. The pavement ran beside a wall behind which there had been the holding cells from which men and women were taken for interrogation or execution. He imagined that the men who inflicted pain or killed others would have gone home at the end of a day's work and played with the kids, had a beer or shagged the wife. Similar men had tortured, then killed the remembered martyrs of St Bonaventure's heritage – the Blessed Henry Heath, Arthur Bell and John Forest. He felt neither better nor worse for it.

Now Giulietta appeared, the handyman behind her. He took

off his flat cap. She stood back and did not howl like the old woman's or the boy's mother. She stood tall and said a prayer – Jago saw her lips move – then crossed herself. He thought she wouldn't have wanted to hold the shattered head under the tea-towel for fear it would stain her blouse.

Would the grandfather come, the old man? Had he been told? Plenty to watch, much to wait for.

The phone rang beside his bed. He reached for it, knocking away his spectacles. When he was younger there might have been a Beretta automatic pistol there, but his career had supposedly prospered and now he warranted a security detail. He had no personal firearm within arm's reach.

The prosecutor answered it, and listened. He was told what was known.

The call came from the barracks at Locri. The duty officer had first referred the news of the death by gunshot – as relayed by a parish priest – to the operations centre in the region's capital city, Reggio Calabria, but had been directed to call the prosecutor in person. He sat in his pyjamas on the side of the bed, his paunch hanging over the cord. His top was open and his wife massaged the knot of muscle at the back of his neck as he was briefed on what little information was available. Was an ambulance present, with paramedics? They had been refused entry by men blocking the track to the family's residence, but the priest had confirmed death. No pulse, and half of the skull had been removed.

Were investigators present and had there yet been qualified examination of the location? Not yet. The priest had been told that the discharge of the shotgun was 'accidental'. He considered, but took little time over it. A little sunlight came into the bedroom to play on the sheets and his wife's hair. One of the children was at the door, woken by the phone, and he heard his car start outside, as his boys always did when there was a dawn call and they might be leaving in a hurry. He remembered the faces, expressions, sneers, of the families when a man was taken, the lingering hostility he could feel in the glares from the gallery when he appeared in court and worked towards a conviction. He recalled the arrogance of the men, who were punctilious in their politeness, and would have ordered his killing if it had suited them. And the loathing of the women, whose faces contorted with hatred for him.

'Get there. Put a team in,' he rasped into the phone. 'Turn the place over. Look for the old man, any sign of him. It's a gift from Heaven. Don't waste it.' The caller from Locri put in another request for guidance. The prosecutor barely considered the answer, agreed to it – an irrelevance.

There were men and women at the Brancaleone barracks whom Fred knew, and more at Locri. Old friendships did not easily die. They had driven between the two at fearsome speed, with a squad car clearing the way, blue light spinning and siren wailing. There were police from European forces who came to southern Italy and never seemed able to lose the appearance of contempt for their 'colleagues' wrestling with the differing brands of the Mafia, Italy's ever-present, crushing cross. Not Fred. He had spoken his mind quietly when the law-and-order people of Calabria had eaten, drunk and swum with him. He had listened and had been accepted. A bigger point, which weighed well: Fred carried the most recent CCTV pictures of the grandson, Marcantonio, which offered the best hope of a formal identification that did not rely on the family and their associates. He was a friend and beside him was Carlo, who had a magic slip of paper, authorisation, in the breast pocket of his shirt. Things happened in times of confusion; doors were left ajar. Men like himself and Carlo were skilled at getting a foot into the gap and exploiting it. When chaos flooded in so did advantage. It was a rare chance to be marginally useful, and to be closer to where the banker boy was.

The radio played. Consolata stirred on the camp bed in the store-room. She caught a news flash. The station had the name, the village in east Calabria, and the reporter said 'First reports state that the shooting was accidental.' She almost gasped. *Accidental?* She was surrounded by crude shelves on which were stacked packets of paper, pens, pencils, pamphlets, and booklets issued by the government that listed successes in the war against the 'Ndrangheta. Cardboard files held indexed newspaper cuttings going back to the founding of the group's campaign. Her clothes were folded on a wooden chair. She knew . . . *Accidental* . . . She understood.

Consolata had slept poorly, but for some of the night she had dreamed of him. The openness of his face, the flatness of his belly, his quiet when the stress had built as they had approached the village, the way he had left her, not turning for a last glance. She had thought of him, and the dream had carried her towards a time when the winding road on the Aspromonte was behind them, the sunlit beach stretched away, and the castle at Scilla watched over them. She had played her part, and he would have known it. There was chemistry between them, no doubt about it. They would walk on the beach, arm in arm, hip to hip, and elsewhere – far away. Consolata was sure of it. She was off the bed and dressed hurriedly.

It was done, finished. She would extract him.

She slipped out of sight.

It was cold, calculating, and was done. In her room, Giulietta shrugged off her suit, then put on old jeans and a lightweight cardigan. She transferred her cigarillos to her hip pocket.

It was easy for her to go from the kitchen door, unseen, and bypass the gathering on the patio where the corpse still lay: her mother remained in her chair, her sister-in-law was still on her knees, and Annunziata's children hugged the legs of a village woman, a cousin. The men talked quietly, and the priest was on his phone, calling the undertaker in Locri. She went behind them. The wolf's carcass had been kicked aside, and she had to step over it. She had heard already that an ambulance crew was blocked further down the road, near to Teresa's villa, but she assumed the *carabinieri* would soon be there, would demand access, which could not be refused.

She went behind the trellis where the ripe grapes brushed against her hair, and past a child's plastic pedal car. There were small beds where tomatoes grew well, and also chillis. She was behind the sheets. Her head was down so she would not be seen.

To Giulietta, it was a disgrace that her father – past the average age of death in the Aspromonte communities – had to live out his last years in such degrading conditions: a hole in the ground.

There was a switch behind a stone in a wall. The stone was always removed carefully – lichen grew around it and it was kept sprinkled with soil. She pressed it, then replaced the stone. She rarely went into her father's bunker – she detested it. More of the stones were mounted on a vertical slab, concreted and pinned to it; they slid away to expose the tunnel. Stefano oiled the mechanism. She took a deep breath and crawled inside. A concrete sewer pipe stretched ahead of her with low lights to guide her. She pressed another switch and the outer door was sealed. She crawled forward on her hands and her knees. There was another door ahead. Among the families there were many such bunkers. The most significant and luxurious belonged to the Plati clan, but the Pesche clan in Rosarno was similar. Both had refinements that her father had not wanted, that of champagne in the fridge, the internet and . . . She went on down the tunnel, scuffing her jeans. When she reached the door, she paused to collect herself. Was she stricken with grief? Hardly. She had had no love for her nephew, little respect. Was she angry? Consumed by it. More important to her than making an exhibition of grief beside the body was the image in her mind of a foreign client, coming to do business with her, staying at a hotel the family owned and being seen in the car park with two men who were quite obviously from European police agencies. She had seen them only because it was her practice to attend meetings early, scout and watch.

She went inside.

'What in God's name has happened this morning? Where's Stefano? Have you brought my breakfast?'

She brushed the dust from her clothing. Sharply, she told her father to sit down. He did so.

*   *   *

They were given the white paper suits, over-boots and face masks. They were told not to speak. They sat in the back of an armoured jeep.

Carlo said, 'We've fallen on our feet, mate. This beats sitting in an office.'

Fred was grinning. 'We have been lucky, but I like to think that luck only goes to those who deserve it.'

The seats in front of them filled. Some of the men and women wore camouflage gear and others were kitted as they were. They lurched away, heading towards the narrow roads that led into the mountain foothills.

Bernardo listened.

He knew it was said of him, in the village and by other clans, that he had never shed a tear in his life. She spoke briskly, telling him what she knew, the facts. She omitted speculation. He had not wept when his mother had died, when he heard that his father had been killed by people from Siderno, or when his elder brother had died by the knife in a Roman gaol, or when his younger brother had been taken, trussed then thrown to his death in a gorge close to Plati. There had been no tears when news was brought from the *aula bunker* in Reggio that, on the word of a *pentito*, his two sons had been sentenced to the living death of Article 41*bis*. He heard what she said, and reflected. He was told it had been an accident, that a tyre iron, unexplained, had been near the body. She mentioned the wolf and its injury before Marcantonio had shot it at maximum range. He remembered what his grandson had told him – casual, expecting forgiveness, unrepentant – about a girl in a northern sector of inner Berlin who had an injured face, and a young man who had confronted him twice. About a *pizzo* . . . And he remembered what he had been told about an Audi sports car scratched in Berlin along its side, and back again, and the scrape on the City-Van, done during the night. He kept his counsel. If Marcantonio had had half of his aunt's brains, if Giulietta had been a man . . . He could think it but not say it.

She said nothing that indicated any sorrow. He admired her honesty.

She made him coffee. She began to wash up the plates from his dinner. She allowed him to reflect. She went behind him and made the bed. He thought her nose, still bent from when he had dropped her, wrinkled as if the air in the bunker smelt stale. If he had not let her fall, she would have been a fine-looking woman, but he had, and she was not.

She told him about the Englishman.

Bernardo let rip his feelings. He swore, flooding the small area with obscenities. Her eyes seemed to say that he belittled himself. The man, meeting overseas policemen in the place where she had been to visit him, had insulted him grievously. He had never met him, had never seen a photograph of him. He had only the recommendation of an English lawyer living in a housing development up the coast from Brancaleone. He condemned the man. It was to pass sentence on an individual he didn't know. She told him that the matter was safe in her hands. He raised the question of the priest. She would think about it. He sensed the passing of power: the shift from nephew to aunt. All his life he had never been dependent on any one person, not his father, his uncles, his brothers or Mamma. She should think urgently about the priest. And how much longer was he to be shut away under the earth, recycled air to breathe, a proper wash every two days? How much longer? She told him what the clerk had said. Another twenty-four hours maximum, and the pressure of close investigation would be lifted, resources moved and he would have something of his freedom. He asked her opinion: had Marcantonio brought the possibility of ruin on them, the scratched vehicles, or was it his imagination? Was there danger? Were they threatened, or safe?

She told him she didn't know. Then she was gone and he was alone again. He sat, his head in his hands, but his eyes were dry.

There had been negotiations, which Jago had witnessed.

A uniformed *carabinieri* officer had come forward. The man who had held the assault rifle – it had gone – spoke for the family. Jago assumed that 'respect' was called for. The old woman remained in her chair and refused to meet the officer's eyes, and

Teresa was still on her knees. Her children had been escorted away. The men kept a perimeter around the body.

Jago wondered how the officer felt to find himself in the den of an organised-crime family, studying the body of a juvenile criminal whose offences went beyond delinquency. Other movements had attracted Jago's eye. 'Follow the money' was the diktat of the fraud investigators: his was 'Follow Giulietta, the daughter.' He had seen the direction she had gone, past where the cable had been exposed. He thought himself clever. He would wait for an opportunity.

The negotiations were over.

The officer had departed. An ambulance was now coming up the track from the village. In its wake were two all-terrain long-wheel-base vehicles in *carabinieri* colours. Teresa was eased aside by other women. The principal mourner was helped up from her chair. The women, family and spectators, backed towards the kitchen door. A man and a woman crew, neither looking comfortable, came towards the body from the ambulance. They were ringed by the village men, and the handyman was there but stayed back. Jago saw, too, the kid who drove the scooter and handled the dogs. The tea-towel was lifted away. The woman paramedic gulped and sat back on her haunches. Her colleague felt at the neck for a pulse, then shook his head. They had a collapsible stretcher, but were waved away: the scene-of-crime team, after a fashion, took over. The shotgun was bagged in a plastic sack. The tea-towel was removed and they took photographs. The uniforms kept back, leaving the area around the body to the forensics team. They were dressed in brilliant white coveralls, their faces hidden, and Jago wondered how their breath might contaminate the yard. They seemed to take few samples. They were not given the tyre iron.

The wolf carcass was dragged out and examined. It was noted that there was already a considerable wound behind the creature's right shoulder and pellets in the chest and face. They spent time examining the eyes.

Jago noted that two of the uniforms wore protective vests and sub-machine guns slung from straps. They seemed nervous. They would have been looking for the wolf's position, where it might have been when Marcantonio had shot it.

Not the men in uniforms. Not the men crouched over the body and making that examination. There had been a moment, as the cloth was lifted and the face exposed, when the most senior officer had looked behind him, met the glance of one of those men, and there had been a slight nod: that moment in TV cop drama when identification is made in a mortuary chapel, confirmation. Jago focused on the two who seemed to have no role to play. They looked for the ledge on which the wolf had been. The shorter one was slight and his suit too large. The other was heavier, taller and had a beer belly. They looked at the escarpment above the yard. Why were they interested in where the wolf had been? Their noses and mouths were covered with the face masks, but he could see their eyes. Not casual. Both men were gazing across the rocks and trees for a reason. They exchanged comments in whispers, mouth to ear, beyond the hearing of the uniforms, forensic team and village men. Abruptly, both seemed satisfied. It was natural when something of significance had been noted to take a last look, but they did not.

The stretcher was unfolded. The body was lifted, then a blanket pulled over it. The handles were taken but not by the two other men. They left, and the body was loaded into the ambulance.

The handyman brought out a bucket and a yard brush, then washed away the blood, scrubbing hard, then left it to dry. He went to the wolf carcass and lifted it by the tail. Jago saw him take it to the front and down the track, the dogs following hopefully, but he kept them back. Perhaps he threw the wolf into a riverbed in a deep gully. When he came back he filled another bucket, and scrubbed some more. Jago knew what else he should do, but not when.

Soon he would go to look for the girl.

15

Jago wriggled from his belly to his knees and elbows.

The dogs were asleep by the door, and the area where the blood had been swilled away was now drying. The whole yard had been swept and the handyman had gone inside. He had seen no one else. The daughter-in-law and the children had gone, the village men were back down the track. He could smell food cooking. A death in the family but the living needed to eat. And must have needed clean bedding: a half-hour ago the old woman had emerged and hung out double sheets, pillow cases and towels. He'd looked for extra washing – the clothing of the hidden man, the *padrino* – but Marcantonio's shirts, boxers, vests and socks were hanging with the rest. Not dead five hours and his gear was already on the line. No one had come to the house to share with them their grief.

Had the living not liked the boy? Did they find him an arrogant waste of space? Did they exist in a climate of death and judge it an unremarkable event? Jago didn't know. No one was in the yard and the dogs were asleep. The kid wasn't there to take them to work the hillside, and he didn't know how suspicious they were about the tyre iron, but he moved with extreme caution. He thought he had learned fast the ways of the Aspromonte.

He kept his body low, hugging the ground, and went in a sort of spider crawl. In a few yards he was among the trees and the foliage would close behind him so he could straighten. But he didn't hurry. He reckoned himself a good student. He watched for dried leaves and twigs and seemed to remember the route he had taken before. With each hour that had passed, he had become more familiar with the family and was – almost – a part of it, but the old man, the missing piece of the puzzle, was still just a photographic image in monochrome. In it he was young, with a good head of hair and smooth skin. Now the eyes might have dimmed.

He was glad to have moved and not fallen victim to the scent of the cooking coming through the kitchen door. He remembered the wolf, and the feel of its whiskers at his ankles, its gentle tugging with its fangs at the hems of his jeans. He remembered it in the moments before its death: defiant, caught in the beam, too weak to find cover, a proud animal. Best, he remembered how it had not cringed when the dogs had been close and when the barrels were aimed at it.

Many memories . . . A pretty face. A spider that lured a fly into a web. A woman who wore odd shoes, both from expensive pairs. A well-appointed apartment and a client who needed the reassurance that millions of euros were in good hands. A trip on a kerbstone as a hero went forward – no dog in that fight. A cut across a face that was no longer pretty.

He went on up the hill, threading between rocks, and took care that his feet fell mostly often on rock, not on any small pads of bare earth where he might leave prints.

Jago was almost on them before he was aware of it – they wore camouflage, with dark cream or mud on their hands. A fine net of russet material mixed with natural colours – black, olive green, sweeps of brown brushstrokes – but the lens behind it caught the light. He paused for a few seconds, then went past them.

They exchanged no words. It never crossed Jago's mind to offer gratitude for the food they had given him, ask about the weather forecast or the weekend's Serie A games. He could not have said whether they would, from that vantage point, have seen him take aim, then hurl the tyre iron at Marcantonio as he levelled the shotgun on the crippled wolf – Jago's friend. There was only one similarity between him and them. He was quiet, light on his feet, and thought he could compete with them in skills that would be second nature to them and new to himself. The similarity? He knew the family, was growing closer to it, and they, too, would be familiar with its members, their vagaries and habits. A second similarity: they would be waiting for a sighting of the old man and they, too, would have just the black-and-white photograph, decades old, for identification. He and they shared ignorance. Both waited.

Higher up was the open space where trees and foliage pressed close around what a poet might have called a glade. There was grass and soft moss, and the sun filtered through the leaves. In the books his mother read it was the sort of place where a boy might take a girl. It was hidden, and the house was not visible. He sat, checked his watch and determined how long he would wait. He might have slept. If he had slept and dreamed, he might have seen the man he had never met.

Giulietta walked with her father. They were there to be seen. It was a way of answering those who might have whispered the poison of doubt. He had gone past the war memorial of Locri and by the statue in the small square that commemorated Padre Pio. They had had coffee in a bar on a side-street, the Via Piave, had sauntered along Via Giacomo Matteotti, and now he was at the fruit and vegetable market. He would have brought tomatoes and olives here most weeks recently, had he not been incarcerated in the bunker. It was important that day that men should note he was free, not crushed by the death of his grandson. It was on the radio – and would have been the subject of vivid gossip. The corpse was now in the Ospedale Civile, and the rumour mill would be spinning that the death was 'mysterious'. It would have been known that he was in hiding, that a magistrate in Reggio was conducting an investigation into his affairs. It was important to be seen – and to be seen with his daughter. Word would pass to those of influence in the community.

The town of Locri housed a *carabinieri* unit and a team from the Squadra Mobile. The Guardia di Finanze was also present. It was possible, in this town, that a rival might pick up a firearm, hurry to where he was in the marketplace, and blow the back off his head, probably dropping his daughter at the same moment. It was not possible that any man who had seen him on the street, or had taken coffee with him, or now discussed the quality of the fruit and vegetables on sale, the effect of the recent storm on the crops in the poly-tunnels would reach for a mobile phone. Of that he was certain. No one would dial the numbers of any of the three police units in the town. None would be told that a wanted man, gone to ground, was close to them and vulnerable.

He had good conversations in the market, and seemed not to hurry, but Giulietta watched his back and carried in her handbag an Italian-made Beretta 84F.380 Auto calibre, deluxe, with gold inlay. She could use it – probably shot better than his grandson had. Men would murmur about her behind their hands, about her nose, but not to his face. Men talked about the produce, about the weather, and when Marcantonio was mentioned it was with sympathy. It was not Bernardo's prime territory but he was accepted there. He had a financial interest in some bars, a restaurant and two of the new apartment blocks along the Siderno road. It was good to have Giulietta with him, but it hurt that she had no man to look after her and that now no one other than his daughter could take over the family business. Would a woman be tolerated as an equal? He couldn't say. He shrugged off commiseration about his grandson.

He had been seen.

Later, at home, the major personalities from Locri and the foot-hills where his village was would come to pay their respects to him and Mamma. He had no friends in whom he confided, to whom he let slip his worries or to whom he crowed about successes. He had allies and associates, but no friends. That morning he had used, at Giulietta's prompting, a new method of leaving home.

Giulietta had walked down the track to Teresa's villa and borrowed her car. Beppe, once a postman in the village and semi-retired, still wore his old uniform each day and always brought the mail – usually tax demands – on foot to the house. Beppe sat in the kitchen and Mamma give him lunch, breakfast or coffee. Bernardo put on the postal uniform, pulled the cap well down on his forehead, took the sack and swung it over his shoulder, then walked back down the track, where Giulietta picked him up. A change of clothes behind a cow byre – another of Giulietta's ideas.

The sun beat down on him as he left the market.

She said, 'Not long now, Papa. What else do you want to do?'

'We shouldn't waste time, but I'd like to see the sea, be close to it.'

'Have you any idea what we're here for now?' They were on the beach.

The excitement of the early morning had dissipated. Carlo thought he had seen a lens flash in the sun's brightness, and Fred thought it odd that the washing had been left out overnight – 'No one with a cadaver in the backyard is going to go out at first light with a mouthful of pegs.' Fred reckoned his colleague had an itch that needed scratching. He carried his trunks and his towel, rolled together. He couldn't even begin to estimate what sort of payback might be called in at some time in the future for the help given them. He had sensed a failure in morale, a cliff-edge drop in confidence, among the men he had been alongside when he had made two visits to Calabria and been embedded. He thought the mood worse now than when he had first come nine years ago, and when he had been back three and a half years previously.

He didn't answer – Fred was rarely short of words. Which was why Carlo's itch needed scratching. He wanted a response to 'Why?' It was the fourth time he had asked the question which had gone unanswered. It was not a pretty beach and now contained too much debris from the storm. It was unlikely that it would be cleaned before the following spring when the tourists came back. The water would be too cold to swim, but better than the Baltic. The banker boy was up on that slope. Where the lens might have flashed but there would have been a covert team in position there, with a chance to scoot out, but the backup would have been closer. Did he feel responsible for the girl who had been scarred for life? That was what happened, and the boy who had done it had lost his life that morning: was that a fair return? Fred was unsettled because answers should have come easily, and it annoyed him that they didn't. Why were they there?

Carlo said, 'I suppose I want – not that I'd admit it anywhere close to where I work – to help. I'd like to support the people, at the end of the chain, shield them against what's around them. That's narcotics, kids being trafficked, extortion, so that the little money they have is bled out of them, the corruption that means they have to pay a *pizzo*, a bribe. Anything I can do that puts some or all of that family into gaol, I'm in support of it. A guy turns up and isn't governed by endless regulations, well, I can criticise him to my superiors. Out of earshot, I'll cheer him on. If I said as much, and was heard, I'd be sacked. My feet wouldn't touch the ground – I'd be down the stairs on my backside. Why am I here? Because I'm rooting for that young man. He's a fool, and should be well clear of there by now, on the road and into the airport soonest . . . I have a bad feeling, Fred, and there's not much I can do about it. I reckon he'll want to hang around, think himself invincible. I'm saying we do what we can. We don't get in line and wait for citations to be read out, but we contribute if possible, then head off back to our tidy little desks. No one, thank the Lord, knows our names. How's that?'

'Have you finished?'

'Maybe I shouldn't have started. I'm trying to say that he's gone rogue in a hostile environment.'

'Difficult world out there . . .'

'Sorry to have spoiled the walk.'

Fred let his hand rest on Carlo's arm. They had nothing in common except the confused feeling about what was 'right' and what was 'wrong'. It was as if they were bumping around in a darkened room, a brotherhood. He thought of where they were, of the great history of the beach and the town that flanked it, the marvel of the Greek civilisation that had been there millennia before, the artefacts that remained, their writings and sophistication, then of the people who cared nothing for that heritage, polluted it with toxins and ran the cocaine trade. He kicked at the sand. He was only an investigator.

An old man was watching them from close to a statue, a younger woman beside him. When he looked again, they had gone.

It would be good to swim.

It was natural that Father Demetrio, as the hours passed that day, should go to the shrine of the Madonna. He found it a consoling place.

He parked. The church and the dormitories around it, where pilgrims could lodge, were in a steep-sided valley. The sun had still not penetrated and the air was cold. He went towards the church door. The women in the village regarded the shrine as especially important in their lives. The men he baptised, married and buried thought Polsi a useful place of business while their women were at mass when they would huddle in the shadows. Deals were closed, shipments bought and sold, and the problem of those who tried to break away from the authority of the family was settled: strangulation, disappearance or the bullet. The women believed passionately what he told them of the Madonna of the Mountains and of the shrine's value to them as a protector. Prominent men believed they owned the church, its rituals, the priests, and used it as a comforter, in the way that a child would cling to a favourite toy. The holy epicentre of many lives was filthy, with litter and cigarette ends clogging the cobbles. He walked to the church door.

It could be read in the eyes.

Often enough, Father Demetrio had seen in the faces of the prominent men he met the knowledge that they were condemned and that nowhere remained to them as a refuge. He supposed, had he lingered in front of the mirror as he'd shaved and stared hard into his own eyes, that he might recognise his fate. He might have laughed at the irony of it, but it was likely that no attempt would be made on his life until he had conducted the funeral of the loathsome wretch who had been Bernardo's grandson. He would settle his mind. Inside the church there was evidence of artistry, a decorative ceiling by skilled workmen, tasteful flower arrangements, and an altar where dignity and tradition reigned. He knelt, bowed his head. He would be put to death – probably painfully – after Marcantonio was buried.

A big step, perhaps none bigger, confronted him.

The lawyer who had quit London, then fled the south-west coast of England and was now resident on the outskirts of Brancaleone took a mobile call. He had not known the caller's number, nor was he given a name. The information passed to him referred to radio reports that a young man – identity given – was dead from a gunshot wound at his home. Now he had to pacify his client.

Humphrey said, 'It's one of those things, Bent. Nothing can be done. You know the old saying "out of a clear blue sky", well, that's what happened. The guy shot himself, something about a wolf near the chickens and he was outside with a weapon and must have tripped. Dead as mutton. That's why you were stood up. Nothing about disrespect. They take death very seriously in these parts – and so they should. They live close enough to it. Before the funeral, I'm told, which is a reflection of the respect for you, Bent, within twenty-four hours, there'll a meeting with the man himself – not Jack, not me, just you. They'll have their own interpreter. These boys, Bent, don't allow a death in the family to get in the way of a deal. You'll be sorted out and on your way by the end of tomorrow. They know who you are, Bent, the extent of your contacts, your reputation and influence. You'll get what you came for. The kid's dead and that was why they skipped today . . . I saw you talking outside, Bent. Did you meet up with some tourists? A bit off-season but there's always visitors coming here for the sun and the peace.'

'Something like that. Pity about the kid, not that I liked him. Maybe we should have some flowers for them. Pity that. An accident out of a clear blue sky, yes.'

Jack said, 'As you say, Bent, an accident and a clear blue sky. Spot on, Bent.'

'I meant to be here earlier – had to come the back way,' she blurted. Jago sat on the grass, leaning against a mature birch. The sunlight cut through the branches and its warmth played on him.

'I'd have been earlier but for roadblocks. Yesterday I had to turn back. There just wasn't a way through.'

A second excuse. He thought Consolata was flustered.

'They moved the blocks overnight and I was able to go round them. I brought some food and clothes.' She put two plastic bags close to his feet. Then she was on her knees, rummaging in them – food and water from one, socks, underwear and a shirt from the other. It didn't worry Jago that she had been through his rucksack, taken stuff out of it. There was nothing in it of himself. He thought she was anxious.

'God, it's been so long since you've had anything to eat. Was the storm awful? There were floods and landslides, the worst in years. You should eat now – please. Or do you want to change first?' Consolata brought out the wrapped food and the water, then put the clothes near to him. 'It was on the radio. I've been listening to it ever since I dropped you. They said it was an accident but I didn't believe that.'

Jago thought she was desperate to please – she was talking too much. All the time he had been burrowed under the two boulders he hadn't spoken. He remembered how she had been on the beach at Scilla, under the moonlight, it shimmering on her skin. She had been quiet then. And in the car, when they had systematically stolen from washing lines and had talked of concealment, she had been factual and economic. She would have thought a lunatic had wandered across her path, been captivated, and set on a course of action that she had dictated – she might or might not come back with food, water, clean clothes. He started to unbutton his shirt.

'I had the radio on all night – I hardly slept. It was on the earliest news broadcast. Just the first report, but he was dead – confirmed. I had it on in the car and that's when they said about a shotgun. I can't believe it was an accident. You did it. You struck a real blow against the family. I'm proud to have helped. I've done more than I've achieved in years. And we're a team.'

Jago slipped off the shirt and the vest under it. He ignored the food and the water. It was good to get his clothes off. They were drier, but still clung to him. He would have liked to eat, but not yet. The Arena was across the river from Canning Town, one stop on the train, and he'd been there with his sister, when a big boy-band was playing. He'd seen the adoration on her face and those of the other kids, in awe – like the nuns when the Holy Father went walk-about from St Peter's. They'd shown it on TV when he was at the Catholic school. He wouldn't have said her gaze was reaching adoration or awe, but saw admiration and astonishment that he had done what she gave him credit for. She had been aloof and distant on the beach.

'You've really damaged them. It's what a few of us were screaming for. The best I could offer my group was to stand outside the principal home of a Pesche or a di Stefano, give out leaflets and probably get beaten. What you did is incredible. Find a wasps' nest and poke a stick into it, destroy their home and infuriate them. That's direct action. We had urban guerrillas in Italy forty years ago, the Brigate Rosse. They killed people for direct action, and I understand now, for the first time, the value . . .'

He untied his laces and pushed off his trainers and socks. Then he took off his trousers and pants. He felt the sun on him. He saw Marcantonio's face – what had remained of it. He thought of the wolf and where it had spent the long night before its death, and the boy who had kept vigil, as he had. The boy, Jago and the wolf had been together for hours before the first hint of dawn. It was not her business.

'I brought what I thought you might like. It's not as fresh as if I'd bought it today, but I couldn't make it yesterday and started too early today. I'm sorry.'

Jago could have slept in the sun. She wore an anorak, jeans, boots and a couple of T-shirts. She was a few feet from him and was unwrapping the food, then opened a bottle. She was turning herself into a café waitress. He didn't know her. She passed him a sandwich and he saw her face screw up because the bread had curled at the edges. He took it and their fingers touched momentarily. He ate the sandwich, which tasted good but he didn't thank her. Then she held up a water bottle. He took it, tilted it and drank.

He screwed the top back on and let the bottle drop onto the grass. She told him what time the plane was.

'Just after six this evening. Out of Lamezia to Milan. There's a connection about nine for Berlin. When I heard the radio I checked the flights. It'll be late but you'll be back in your own bed tonight. It's incredible, what you've done. I've never managed anything like it. None of the people in my group have. We all talk about it but don't do it. You hurt them, Jago.'

He thought her unsure. It had been easy enough for her to strip when they were on the beach at Scilla, the lights of the town behind them, the waves rippling on the sand, the moon high and heat of the day ebbing off them. Now she started with her anorak, then the outer T-shirt. She moved closer to him so that he could help or take over.

'I've enough to buy a ticket ... Are you understanding me, Jago? I can buy a ticket at Lamezia. I've my passport with me. There's nothing for me here. You've done what you came for. I don't have to stay. Can I be with you?'

Her shoes and socks were off, and her fingers went to her belt, unclasped it, then lowered the zip on her jeans. She reached forward and touched his arms, perhaps to guide them to the waist of her jeans or under the second T-shirt. He pushed her hands back so that they dropped down onto her thighs.

'You've finished here – you've done what you came for. What's the matter, Jago?'

He could have told her what he had finished and what he had yet to do. He could have spoken of the freshly washed sheets, which had been left on the line during the storm, and how a new cable ran in a shallow trench from the back of the house to a building that was semi-derelict. He could have told her about the death of a wolf – could have sat her down beside him and talked for an hour. He had seen so much, and there was still much to do. He supposed he should have thanked her for driving across the Aspromonte, but he said nothing.

'You have finished, haven't you? What else?'

He ate another sandwich and finished the water in the bottle.

He started to dress. Clean underwear, fresh socks and a shirt, then eased back into his jeans and pulled the laces tight on the trainers. A light fleece over his body, then the camouflage coat. He collected up the sandwich wrappings, and the empty bottle, then bagged them with the food he hadn't eaten. His dirty clothes went into the second bag, he gestured for her to dump them. It would have been the same if she had asked about his rucksack – it was of no further use to him. She dressed, clumsily, her eyes blazing but moist. He had needed the dry clothing and the sandwiches, which would last him for the time remaining: not long, two nights under the great boulders where he looked down on the sheets and knew where the join was in the freshly buried cable. A brief smile. It was the smile that a man might give a woman he had sat beside on a bus from Clerkenwell to the City. Uninvolved, strangers passing. No kiss, no handshake, but he let her look into his eyes for whatever she might find. She stared at him, still half dressed.

Jago slipped away, watching the ground where his feet would land. He didn't turn or wave.

Bernardo held court.

It was a continuation of his promenade around the fruit and vegetable market, but now he was at home, and the postman's uniform had been returned to its owner. In his kitchen, the blinds lowered, old men had gathered around the table. Some were more important, more influential than him, and others ran lesser clans.

Their presence showed respect for him.

Outside the front door there was a line of cars, models from the Fiat, Lancia and Alfa production lines that were now discontinued. The men were all of an earlier generation. Their own sons had demanded greater affluence, flaunted wealth, and were either in maximum-security prisons, dead or in hiding abroad. Their grandsons either wore fashionable clothes, drove fast cars and behaved with a stereotypical recklessness or had enrolled on a business-studies course. The men who had come to visit Bernardo had one thing in common: they were as much at ease in dealing with a consignment valued at a hundred million American dollars as they were in resolving a dispute in the village where they lived. An altercation might involve a perceived verbal slight, the location of a market stall or the breaking off of an engagement between a foot-soldier and a man of honour's daughter. A peasant who worked in the olive groves might have an old pushbike stolen: he would expect his *padrino* to identify the thief, retrieve the bicycle and punish. The power of the leader was total. They did not like, individually or collectively, to hand down a sentence of death and order its execution, which attracted unwelcome attention, but would do so if challenged or betrayed.

Now they drank sparingly, wine, coffee, locally made brandy and water, and did not press Bernardo on his future or quiz him on the role his daughter would play. Long silences featured. The language was the dialect of those mountain slopes: something of the ancient Greek settlers and something of old links with Albanian seafarers. A *carabinieri* officer from Rome or Milan – headphones clamped tight on his ears – would understand no more than one word in ten.

Stefano would be outside, and would have brought out jugs of lemonade and plastic cups for the drivers and bodyguards. All of the old men headed families, and the extent of their power, if based on terms of commercial turnover, would have exceeded a billion American dollars each year, if their interests in the region, in Italy and across Europe were put together. Their politeness was marked, but they watched him.

They studied his posture and attempted to evaluate his state of mind. Some would have been present just a few days earlier when, in the shadow of the church at the shrine, he had introduced his grandson, returning from Berlin for the celebration of Mamma's birthday. Would he continue to lead? Had he still the stomach for it?

When his daughter came into the kitchen, she refilled the glasses and prepared more coffee. She was smart and aloof, her own person, but she did not talk or bow to them. Soon, Marcantonio's body would return, and they would escort it into the house. Then the visitors would leave. Bernardo thought the occasion had gone well, that judgements on his ability to continue had been suspended. He could not have hoped for more. He ached at the loss, but the boy had been a fool.

The matter of what Giulietta had seen early that morning, in the car park of a hotel in Brancaleone, clouded his mind. It remained an issue to be dealt with – and those she had seen in Locri, on the beach below the statue to the poet.

Carlo stood on the beach, the ripples of the wavelets against the toes of his shoes. Beside him was a carefully folded pile of clothes and the towel.

Flight out the next evening. Apologies had been made, but they would wait until after the funeral, then quit. Their achievement had been minimal.

Ten metres out, the water above his hips and below his armpits, Fred stood and shivered, then dived and swam powerfully.

Carlo was on his country's business, as was the German. No gold commander waited in a dim-lit bunker for his report, no high-ranking civil servant pondered on the correctness of sending him into a dangerous area. No newspaper executives would be briefed after the mission was wound down. Put simply, in the corridors of Whitehall and the inner sanctums of government, nobody gave a flying fuck. Counter-terrorism would bring out the Parachute Regiment, the Apache gunships and limitless resources but the counter-narcotics programme languished.

What had he achieved so far? How were the chips stacked? Could have been worse. Bentley Horrocks would be wondering why the army of corrupt detectives, safeguarding him, had not given fair warning that he was under surveillance. Good enough to carry on with – and the chance of more to follow. They'd see the boy out, make sure he went clear.

Carlo was facing the sea. Fred had told him about the artefacts from here, how a scuba diver had come across the great bronzes that were now in a museum and internationally famous. He had seen an arm raised out of the sand on the seabed, and thought it was a dead human, but he was wrong. Instead he had happened across a miracle of history. Perhaps old Fred would surface clutching a pottery jar that had been down there for three thousand years.

He didn't see them until they were almost on him. They had come so quietly. Five or six of them. He became aware of them when he smelt stale cigarettes and chilli on the breath. He had half turned. Hands reached up to push him. He stumbled forward.

'For fuck's sake, who the hell do you—?'

He nearly went down but didn't. He careered away, trying to regain his balance, but hands were on his back and his head, and propelling him into the water. Young guys, with spiky hair, bright T-shirts and jeans, Nikes on their feet. There was sand, pebbles and driftwood. He went clumsily over the last of the beach and into the water. They followed him – nothing said, not a word. He didn't see a knife or a cosh, and none of them had a ligature cord or a firearm. He was kicked in the backside and fell forward. Thrashed, swallowed, only a foot and a half deep but he'd gone into it and under. He came up heaving, coughing. Fred stood and watched. Sensible – not much else he could do. They came in after him and took hold of him. He saw Fred's clothes thrown into the sea, his wallet and his trousers. They didn't check what was inside the wallet or look at the ID. They knew whom they had. Some of the clothing floated and the rest sank. Carlo went under. Hands held his head, shoulders and arms, a leg in place to trip him. He flailed and fought but the kids were young – not middle-aged with beer guts and short of breath. He was under and the panic escalated.

He was drowning. Carlo thought Fred had come close to him, tried to free him and failed. He was terrified – Carlo, long-term Customs man and liaison officer, skilled in surveillance, had never known such fear. Under the water, blurred vision, the legs pressing tight on him, his lungs about to burst, he knew he was finished when he blew out the air. He felt the fight in him failing. He was beaten – get it over.

He was let go.

He didn't know whether he was floating, or had gone back under. Fred had him. They were gone.

Fred held Carlo tight, bent him over and slapped his back, making him cough, retch. The water came out in reluctant spurts. He had to blink half a dozen times to clear his vision, then saw them. No jeering, no shouting, no cat-calls or abuse. They just walked back towards the road. Job done.

He was helped back to the beach.

'You all right?'

'Yes,' Carlo said, then coughed and heaved.

'You hurt?'

'I'll live.'

Not a mark on his body. And all because he'd played the clever beggar. Stood to reason. He'd tossed a bit of fun at Bentley Horrocks in a public place and been paid back. And had screwed up his friend. He reached the shore, stood, dripped and thought himself pathetic. And he remembered something that had been said.

Carlo had pontificated to Bagsy: *What does he think it will be like, going after those people? Does he think it's some sort of squirrel shoot – out with an air rifle? Is he dumb or ignorant or both?* He seemed to hear his own voice.

It must have been the time of day in central Locri for the schools to come out. Kids were watching them as if they were aliens. Fred went back into the water to collect his clothing, and fished out all that had been on the beach. He looked into Carlo's face when he had the armful of his clothes and shoes.

'They weren't going to harm us, just frighten us.'

'They did a good job.'

Fred said, 'It's a small insight into the terror they create. To live here and stand against them, you have to be brave, a hero. We are not brave and not heroes.'

'We have been taught a lesson we won't forget.' They hugged.

Consolata sat under the tree where he had been. She felt violated. Her legs were tight together, her arms across her chest and her fingers entwined. She was fully dressed. If a boy from the squat, or one of the older men – Pietro or even Massimo – had treated her in that way, she would have gone at him with fists and teeth. But *he* had gone untouched.

She sat in the quiet.

She had brought her passport with her. No reason why she needed it. She was not going to be a nanny in Madrid, or start a PhD in Paris, or fly to Berlin to sit moonstruck in front of Jago Browne in his apartment and go job hunting with no language. She had a passport because her parents had considered, a few months before their business had been taken from them, a trip for themselves and their teenage daughter to a Tunisian resort, a taste of Africa. It had never been used. She had brought it and wished she had not humiliated herself by saying it was in her bag. She ate some of what she had brought, and drank some water.

She decided she would stay. She couldn't imagine why he had turned away from her. Any other boy would have been pulling her clothes off. She had the picture again in her mind of the men she had met on Corso Giuseppe Garibaldi, and of the night-time visit to the squat, the warnings given her and their belief she was responsible. She would stay. The day wore on. Two mice came close to her. If they had been in her bedroom she would have cringed away from them. Now she threw them crumbs.

He had used her as little more than a driver, and she knew nothing about him – or what he would do next. Knees together, arms tight, she gazed at the density of the foliage, felt the sun and heard the birds. She knew nothing.

The prosecutor agreed. He accepted defeat.

They did not come as a deputation from the *carabinieri*, the Squadra Mobile or the Guardia di Finanze to the Palace of Justice. The messenger was a clerk. The information could have been sent to his screen but was not. Instead there was a single sheet of foolscap. There was no evidence. The surveillance team had failed to locate the fugitive Bravo Charlie. Roadblocks in the area of that village were a drain on manpower and had not trapped the suspect. The assets would be withdrawn under cover of darkness the following evening. The funeral of Golf/Alpha Charlie would be monitored: if Bravo Charlie was seen he would face arrest if the prosecutor supplied evidence for a minimum charge of Mafia association. There were two wardrobe-sized cupboards in the prosecutor's office. The one nearest the window that looked out onto the stairwell contained files on cases that awaited his urgent attention. The cupboard nearest to the steel-reinforced door was equally full of files that were held together with cotton ribbon. They contained stories of investigations that had been dropped: they might be picked up in the future if new allegations came to light or new evidence surfaced. It was a bitter blow.

He had taken hits from supposed colleagues, was avoided in the corridors, no longer sought out by those who wished to rub shoulders with success. He would not go to the funeral, invite further humiliation. If *he* was there, and if the association charge could be proven, it would demean the prosecutor to have the uniformed men of the *carabinieri* wade into a throng of mourners, drag out an old man and cart him away. At the outset there had been great optimism, but failure was hard to embrace. The boys knew and were quiet, the banter gone. He would not stay late that evening – the death of the boy was insignificant, except that a successor had been eliminated. The crusader from Berlin was of no importance and his anger at it had been unnecessary.

He had smoked his last cigarette, and would have to scrounge from the boys again. There was a mirror by the door. He used it to tidy his hair and straighten his clothing, as if a prominent visitor was waiting to see him. He saw himself, saw the ravages, the price of the investigation.

He opened the door and they were up, shrugging into their coats, pistols in their holsters. 'Sorry, boys, just fags. Short of fags.'

He was happy to be alone.

Jago would watch for the dogs. If they were quiet, if they were inside the house, he would go down and excavate the cable, but later.

It was still too early. The light was going and the shadows lengthening, but the cars at the front had not yet thinned. He rolled the question in his head: Bernardo would not return to his bunker while the cars were still there, the drivers and bodyguards hovering, cigarettes glowing.

His mind was changed.

A hearse was bringing the coffin home.

Jago had a good view of it. Cigarettes were thrown down and caps came off men's heads. They formed an aisle, no instruction but natural respect, held their hands clasped low and ducked their heads as the coffin was carried past them. Men spilled out of the house and stood close together on the step. Like a guard of honour, but without overt ceremony. Jago looked for a glimpse of a face in the background. He saw Giulietta, who stood straight-backed. She had changed into a black dress, cotton, not silk, he thought, no jewellery, and behind her was the old lady. Teresa and a gaggle of children followed the coffin. It lurched on the step, was steadied, then taken inside and the doorway cleared. He had not seen him – no older man there had been accorded greater deference as master of his own home.

The aisle that the drivers and hoods had made disintegrated. The cigarettes came out, were passed and lit. The kid had the dogs on the hill but the line they took was higher than the cleft in which he lay. They tracked but without a scent, and were well away from him. Then, among the dogs, there was pandemonium. A small deer bounded clear of them, acrobatic in its flight over rock faces. They chased it for a bit, then lost heart, and the kid called them back. It was a listless search and Jago did not feel threatened.

He thought only of the old man, the bunker plunged into darkness and him groping for matches and candles, or a torch, fear gathering round him, pressing close on him. Images flashed in his mind: a girl taking off her clothing, a girl whose face bled or had just been stitched, a policeman who had left a laptop open, and the *FrauBoss* who would by now have sent dismissal details to Human Resources.

He had not seen the old man who could decide who lived and who died. He would know him when he saw him, would recognise the fear, smell it.

16

He stirred because of the cockerel.

Jago had only rarely seen it. The coop where it ruled was hidden from his view. It was young, had a fine comb on its head, mahogany feathers with red flashes. The cockerel was another friend he had acquired. He liked it, watched it and felt part of its brotherhood. The dogs did not worry it and he thought that the old woman and the handyman talked to it. In the half-light, he wondered what the cockerel knew of shipments and killings and investments. If it knew that a corpse was laid out in the house, it showed no respect – its crowing was as loud as it was on any other morning. The bird said that the day started.

The last day . . .

Lights came on in the kitchen and the door opened. The dogs bounded out and the cockerel ignored them. That was the routine.

He had the feeling, relentless, that it was the last day.

The old woman appeared. He had no name for her. There would have been a name in the file he had glanced at it, but she had not been a priority family member. He looked hard at her and wondered whether she was capable of kindliness, whether she had wept that night in her bed. She held herself erect and carried a bundle of sheets . . . At that time in the morning. It was confirmation.

It seemed inevitable to Jago that the last day had dawned. The target ahead of him – the ultimate worthwhile challenge – was the old man, and the weapon was a buried cable.

She turned, called, seemed almost to stamp her foot in impatience. She waited, perhaps half a minute. The birds chorused and a strange fly danced on the rock in front of him – wide-winged, camouflage colours, with a tail that suggested it might sting. The pigeons and crows were stirring above him, and the dogs followed her, close to her legs. She was by the chair she had sat on when the boy's life had bled away on the uneven concrete. She was only a few yards from where she had kicked the head of the injured wolf. She had not cried then, or shivered in grief. Her composure had been iron strong. He knew it was the start of the last day and was glad.

The handyman came to her and she cuffed him behind the ears. Jago saw it. He wasn't sure if it was offensive or friendly. A familiarity, but it had hurt the man – his head had flipped sideways. He was given the sheets. The ritual began. He unfastened the old ones from the line and folded them over his arm. He lifted the one handed to him and pegged it, checked the length so that the hem hung within a centimetre of the pathway. She hovered near to him, approved or made him adjust the peg. It was good that it was the last day, near the end. Jago was calm.

At this time of the morning, the old man would have gone with the bucket, water bottles and food to the cave. There had been a child – Jago knew because he had seen the dress – a prisoner, with a chain to hold her. The cave had been abandoned and the evidence left where it was. He assumed the child had died. He could judge her age from the size of the dress. He remembered himself at that age, a kid in Canning Town, not yet at St Bonaventure's. The streets around his home had been a kind of a jungle, but he had not been chained in darkness, alone and drifting towards death. At this time of day, the child would have heard the soft brush of footsteps on the ground – it might have lasted days or weeks, even months, and each morning the man would have come before the sun was up. He might have spoken and might not; he might have hit the child if she screamed and might not.

Those thoughts left Jago confused, so he moved on. He found new points on which to concentrate. The fly had deserted him. He would have liked something to eat, but could go without for a few hours longer. There was no warmth yet in the sun but the sky brightened slowly, the grey was softer and the haze thicker beyond the house and the small City-Van. Down the track and towards the slight bend the men had their fire in an oil drum. He had seen nothing unusual.

He was trained to observe clients, and credited with the knack of understanding their moods. The *FrauBoss* might talk to them and engage their attention while he watched and evaluated. They would find excuses for moments together out of earshot: most likely the client would need a comfort break or they would go to make coffee or bring fresh water. He would advise: a business approach, calculated and without eye contact, but with reference to the performance pamphlets. A softer approach to the client, a smile, understanding of what was needed, and empathy. He couldn't read the old woman, and didn't know how to interpret the smack she had given the handyman.

The sheets were up. He assumed that Bernardo would now return to the bunker – lit, heated, served by the cable that had been reburied, the join where the third sheet met the fourth – after a night in his own bed.

He thought it would be a busy day at the house because of the body.

Bernardo lay on his bed, facing the bright strip ceiling light.

He had been careless, which annoyed him. He had spent the night keeping vigil beside the open coffin, had stayed there after the old men had driven back to their own villages or down the hill to Locri. He had stayed too long. The men of the *cacciatori* team pulled victims from their beds at dawn. It was easier then for them to secure a building, and easier for the helicopter to make a safe landing. A target of importance, such as himself, would have warranted a helicopter flight – in handcuffs – to the barracks in Reggio on the far side of the mountains. He should have moved an hour earlier. Had they come, he would have been trapped in the old bed where he had been conceived and born, where he had made his sons and daughter – then given minutes to dress, yesterday's shirt, socks and underpants, and spirited out. If it had happened he could have guaranteed he would not die in that bed.

The end for Bernardo would have come in a prison cell, or a guarded room in a public hospital, a chain holding his ankle to the bed frame. He had overslept. They might well come that day. The clerk at the Palace of Justice was the provider of much information – all of it proving genuine. He was a necessity on the payroll but cheap: a hundred euros a week. But he would not have known whether a last-resort raid was to be launched. Bernardo shivered. Tomorrow would be different. He had the clerk's guarantees that, as matters stood, the surveillance would be lifted and the file slid onto a high shelf to be forgotten.

He shivered because he had overslept after the long night with the open coffin.

The bird had woken him – his fingers must have fumbled when he set the alarm clock, which hadn't roused him. And much would happen that day. He must be seen in his own home, scrutiny must be at its most intense and danger to his freedom constantly evaluated. He had made a list and briefed Giulietta on what was required of her.

So much to be completed that day – there always was when death came to a family – and other matters concerned him. So much to be done. The ceiling light flickered. It was newly installed – Stefano had done it – but it flickered. The annoyance fuelled his tiredness, but he couldn't rest.

The pigs were the product of Italian Large White sows and a Calabrese boar, noted for their size and the quality of the meat they produced. Also on that small farm, high beyond the foothills and at the edge of the most remote mountain ridges, there were specimens of the locally bred Black Pig. Their owner farmed some seventy of them. They were valuable to him when the slaughter man came and also when requests of a different nature were made – which also paid well.

The few boars were kept apart, but the sows had areas, when not farrowing, where they foraged among the scrub and thin woodland. They seldom found enough to gorge themselves but had to search for food and stayed lean. It was said that the meat they provided was the finest in that small area of the region. They were never bloated, always hungry. At all hours, such was the reputation of the farm, customers called to be sold meat – fresh or smoked – and visited for other services.

The kid arrived on his scooter.

The reason for his visit had not been explained to him but there was an envelope in his hip pocket. He thought the place was as lonely as anywhere he had ever been in his short life. He rejoiced in the trust placed in him. He was two and a half years younger than Marcantonio and had been regarded as a shepherd – good with goats and dogs – until the grandson of the *padrino* had travelled to Berlin. The kid had not been outside Italy, or the Calabrian region, and had been over the Aspromonte to Reggio only once, with a school trip to the museum to see the bronzes. He parked the scooter, put it on its stand. Two men came from a hut away from the main house, where washing hung and smoke spilled from a chimney. One wore a rubber apron stained with blood. They eyed him.

He told them, stammering, who had sent him, produced the envelope and passed it to them. A hand was wiped on the seat of its owner's trousers, then took the envelope. The man read what had been written on a small sheet of paper, then took from his pocket a cigarette lighter, set fire to the paper and held it until the flame was against his skin. Then he let it fall and ground his heel into it. What was asked of him would be ready, the kid was told. Nothing more.

Pigs were around him, big, comfortable and reassuring. They butted at his legs with their snouts and seemed no threat to him, broad enough for a child to ride on. He went back to his scooter, swung his leg across the saddle and fired it up. He started on the journey down the mountainside on the rough track. It was good to be trusted.

Massive concentration. Two men wholly focused. A plastic jar was held ready. The target was in front of them.

Fabio would respond first. His call, not Ciccio's. They had been talking about their wives. They would be out by the end of the day – not allowed to call ahead, of course not, from the stake-out site, but they would ring home when the transport brought them to the barracks and after the debrief. It might be midnight or into the small hours. The job had wreaked havoc on his marriage, on any relationship, and the surveillance teams were flooded with guys trawling foreign dating sites. He and Ciccio were from the same town, Cittanova, and their parents' homes were separated only by the park with the old trees in it, near to the war memorial and the school where they had been pupils. Fabio and Chiara never went back together to the town to see their families. She could; he could not. When he wanted to see his own parents a rendezvous had to be agreed in Cosenza or further north: he would don the disguise of a priest, or a crippled beggar, and all the time he'd watch for cars coming out of a steel-fronted gate. Chiara hated the job, and one day he'd have to choose. Fabio had the plastic jar, but it might be that he'd cede authority to Ciccio, who had the handkerchief.

The scorpion fly was beautiful. They had killed so many unnecessarily in the jar: they had been trapped, then died in the damp captivity.

His own situation was bad, but Ciccio's was worse. Ciccio was Fabio's best friend, only friend, his irreplaceable friend. Ciccio's Neomi had a degenerative condition of the hip or pelvis. The four use to ski together in the Alto Adige but that was not possible now. In the summers they would go together to the beaches up by Salerno, where the men would not be recognised, but Neomi hardly swam now and could not play beach games. The strain told on all of them. When they talked about women it was not their conquests but the value of being together, quiet and calm. Hard times. Enough stories circulated in their barracks about men coming off a surveillance duty, arriving home in the middle of the night to find a strange car parked outside the block, knickers on the stairs and chaos. There but for the grace of the good Lord . . .

Fabio murmured, 'Do you hate it?'

'Hate what?' Ciccio, puzzled, looked away from the scorpion fly but his hands were poised to sweep it up.

'Do you hate that insect?'

'Of course not. I love it.'

'Why condemn it for the benefit of an entomologist's study if it's done you no harm?'

Ciccio took the plastic jar from Fabio. He put it by his shoulder and let it slip. It rolled back to lodge between them. Both chuckled. They could laugh soundlessly, and rejoice. Better to have saved the life of a Scorpion Fly and have laughed than to have gone further with their analysis of the women. The insect stayed close. It was not afraid of them.

And Scorpion Fly, the operation originated by a prosecutor in the Palace of Justice on the far side of the Aspromonte peaks was running towards its conclusion.

They watched it – and watched the old woman, Mamma, bring out more washing, which would have been hers and her daughter's but, as always, nothing of her husband's. They watched Stefano feed the chickens, and Giulietta emerge from the front door to light her first cigarillo of the day. The sun climbed at leisure, and there was a babble of children's voices. They had an agenda: enjoy the Scorpion Fly, prepare a cold breakfast, look after their personal hygiene, then start the slow business of packing up what they had brought. It would be a long, hot day.

'Does it matter, Ciccio, if we fail in the mission and he stays free?'

'It matters no more than the last time we failed and the last time we won. It's the job. It's not personal.'

'The young man down there – that's personal.'

'Maybe he's already pulled out.'

'Did he kill Marcantonio?'

'Of course not. A bank clerk against a seasoned criminal? No. Don't forget, see, hear, know *nothing*. And survive.'

The children's voices were louder.

He felt a serenity in the woods and among the rocks, with the cool of the early morning. The school group added to the atmosphere of peace and dignity.

They came in a crocodile and wore brightly coloured bibs. Boys and girls, who looked, from a distance, to be six or seven. They were shepherded by a teacher at the front and another at the back. Two of the men from the block on the track escorted them. Their voices were shrill. Jago assumed that the coffin lid would be off and that the undertaker would have tried to clean up the boy's face after the basic autopsy had been done in the mortuary. The children were not cowed by where they were – they might have been going to play football in a park. Jago liked that. It would have been by arrangement. A dozen women, of different ages, all in neck-to-ankle black, had already arrived and now formed up at either side of the entrance to the house. Men had arrived in the last half-hour from the village but they stayed inside.

The moment was for the children. The old woman was on the step, with her daughter and daughter-in-law. The teachers propelled the children into a crescent, and they sang. It was hurriedly rehearsed but a flavour of spontaneity reached Jago in his vantage point. It might have been a hymn, one of the choral arrangements that were popular at St Bonaventure's. There was no accompaniment, just the sound of little voices. Jago wondered how difficult it had been to persuade the staff at the school to bring the children up from the village. Perhaps a new roof was being talked of, or a playing field. Perhaps they had come simply because the family ensured that the community under their control lived well and had the money they needed to survive. Fun for the little ones to miss a morning's lessons to sing at the home of the boss, whose words were law to their fathers, but who was hiding underground and had lost a grandson because Jago had thrown a tyre iron at him. One of their teachers was conducting them – too flamboyantly. Perhaps the school needed a new toilet block.

At a sudden gesture from the teacher, the children were silent for a moment, and the sound in Jago's ears was of the birds singing their own anthems. The children said a prayer, only a few lines, more hesitantly than they had sung. Jago wondered whether the old woman – confronted with so many small innocent faces, clean, unblemished cheeks and laundered clothes – would have a wet eye. He looked hard at her. He could see a profile of her face, but

no clenched hand, a wisp of a handkerchief held tight. He saw no
movement towards her eyes. Neither the daughter nor the
daughter-in-law wiped away a tear. He assumed it was how they
lived, that it was about power. A family imported scores of kilos of
cocaine and had produced an immature young man, who had
found his pleasure in beating the prettiness out of a girl who was
trying to establish a business in Berlin. The family's power showed
in the arrival of a class of schoolchildren to sing and pray. The
family owned the village. It was a brief lesson, and he assimilated
it. He doubted there were gold taps inside, and knew there was
only a Fiat City-Van at the front door, but he sensed the power
and would answer it. He knew where the cable join was.

The children waved. The old woman went back into the house.
The daughter-in-law followed her. The children, with their escorts
and teachers, skipped away down the track. In a few minutes they
would be back in the sanctuary of their classroom. Giulietta stayed
outside, lit her second cigarillo of the day and spoke to the handyman. A short exchange: her talking, him nodding agreement,
showing he understood. Jago had expected the priest to be there,
and noted his absence.

The sun had crawled a little higher. The dogs were quiet in the
sunlight, their bellies full of the food that had been put out for
them an hour earlier. More women came up the track.

There was a route down the hill, which seemed to lead from the
boulders towards the stone on which the wolf had rested. It had
tumbled directly down when shot, but Jago thought he saw a way
to the right where it would be possible to crab among ledges. He
would have to scramble the last twenty feet and would be behind
the derelict shed, on ground that was hidden from him now. He
would be within a minute of the sheets that hid the pathway.

He would have liked some coffee – strong, the coffee that the
Turks in Kreuzberg would drink. Something to stiffen his resolve.
There was no one to do that but himself.

He watched the dogs. It might take him hours to descend. They
were curled up, asleep.

It was a brotherhood. Carlo held back as Fred led with the hugging and the brush kisses. It wasn't how they did reunions at the Dooley Terminal, or how old friends met up at the Custom House on the Thames, but Fred knew what to do and did it well. They were in the back car park of the *carabinieri* building at Locri. They'd spent the night in a small hotel north of Siderno and dried out their clothes, set off at dawn and reached the barracks on the edge of the town. It was a fortified stronghold and, other than the road, looked out onto olive groves. Fred was their friend. A piece of paper confirmed Reggio's authorisation for the two men to intrude but the reunions did the job better. Word had passed from Brancaleone that had put them in crime-scene gear the previous day. When Fred had been down in previous years, topping up his 'Ndrangheta file, he had brought whisky and dropped money into the box for the dependants of dead or sick men and women in the force. The whisky went into Christmas raffles, but the thought counted. Laughter ripped round the canteen at the story of a swim in the sea and soaked clothes. But the conversation soon turned serious. Fred was lectured on what it was like to be a *maresciallo* living in the town, with a wife, and children at school, being shunned and having no friends. The posting would be for four years and was necessary if an officer had ambitions. Living alone, but for the company of colleagues, was bearable for men, but the women suffered from the isolation. The talk moved on, the *maresciallo* leading it.

Trust among brothers. The final day of an investigation. A surveillance point to be wound down. Limited roadblocks to be pulled out.

'He's there, for sure, but we can't wait for ever. He's a cruel man and an influential criminal. There are many who are similar or worse. We allocate resources where they show best results. Your man on the hill – we call him the *nomade* – we think he played a part. There was a metal object beside the body of the grandson. Did it cause him to shoot himself, an object hurled at him? Would anyone intervene when a wolf is to be killed?'

Fred said, 'I expected to hear from your people in Reggio that the banker had left in the night from Lamezia. Why would he stay longer?'

Carlo said, 'I think he has a bird's eye view and doesn't want to leave it.'

Neither man said that, in their understanding of the psychology governing Jago Browne's actions, he was driven, unable to turn his back on a challenge. It was obvious to both of them, though.

'If they find him, he'll disappear.'

Carlo said, 'I don't wish to cause offence but you should evaluate the washing line.'

Fred said, 'The washing line is the answer – we think.'

A shrug, 'Our surveillance has a view of it but has seen nothing.'

They were invited. No reason to refuse. A show of authority was to be mounted that day. Bravado and probably meaningless, but if they wished, they could attend. Fred accepted. Coffee was served.

He drove carefully, as always.

For Father Demetrio, the vehicle was neither a status symbol nor comfortable. It was to get him – dry and reasonably warm – between two points. He had been delayed.

Would he preside over the funeral? He had accepted the invitation and was loath to break his word. By then he would have betrayed them, damaged the family to an unparalleled level, but he had agreed to officiate at the funeral and he could not retract his promise. His housekeeper had taken a phone call. A family with a smallholding high above the village, who scratched a living in the forest from the mushroom crops, had sent a message saying that they needed *urgently* to see him on an important matter. They were on their way. He had waited, and had lost the chance of an early start, straight after his dawn devotions.

He checked frequently in the mirror and from time to time was aware of vehicles behind him – lorries, delivery vans and a dark HiLux. It was a difficult road, with few opportunities for overtaking and the queue built behind him. When a lorry, close to his back bumper, flashed its headlights at him, he would ease over

against either the cliff edge, where sometimes there was an accident barrier, or to a vertical wall of blasted rock, fashioned by
dynamite and sledgehammers. The passing drivers would look
down at him, ready to curse him for delaying them, then see his
collar, wave, smile, and give him a fanfare on the horn. The HiLux
did not pass him, but stayed tucked in. There was always a motorist
who didn't wish to lead and was happier when someone ahead
negotiated the hairpins.

Another message had come by hand – no explanation. The
family were not coming. Peculiar, but . . . Later that morning, the
old man's wife, a hard bitch, would be in the church in the village,
supervising the flower arrangements. There was always a grand
display when a dedicated criminal was laid to rest, usually white
lilies, which stained if the stamens fell on the altar cloth or a carpet.
He considered his address as he drove, often in low gear because
they had not yet come to a high point.

He might say, 'I have known Marcantonio for all of his cruelly
short life and have taken pleasure in the sharpness of his wit, the
profundity of his offerings, the depth of his concern for others
and, above all, for the sincerity of his faith.'

He could say, 'We have to believe that, on rare occasions, the
dear Lord who looks down on us determines that He will test us
and so allows into our midst a creature that is vile, almost totally
evil and without a redeeming feature. That was Marcantonio.'

Traffic surged past him because the road had widened across a
short plateau. There were tight bends ahead. Much went past him
but the big vehicle – black-painted, with privacy windows – did
not take its chance to leave him behind. It was close to him, but he
couldn't see the driver. He lowered his window and waved it on
– the road in front was clear and nothing had yet come up against
the tail of the HiLux. He saw no indicator light, and it did not
come up to pass him. It was a bad stretch, and the local authority
had promised a barrier but had not delivered one yet. He could
see far below a dry riverbed and rocks that were angled and sharp.

Father Demetrio might say, 'Young people, and we who are
older, in our community, could set themselves the challenge of

emulating Marcantonio. A scholar at his books, a devoted son and grandson to his family, a neighbour we would all want, a leader, and a young man who symbolised kindness to those less fortunate, care and generosity.'

Father Demetrio could say, 'Marcantonio goes to the cemetery unloved and unadmired by any person in our community who is not bonded to his family's criminal conspiracy. Perhaps he had no choice but to take the road he embarked on: the smuggling of narcotics, the use of extortion to fill his bank accounts, the peddling of immigrants half crazed with fear, of weapons of war, and of children to markets where they are bought and sold as slaves, then put to work in the filthy pornography trade.'

It was a bad drop and rock falls had dislodged any pine trees. There was nothing to check the fall of a vehicle if it went too close to the edge of the road, strayed over the warning line of faded white paint.

He might say, 'He lit all of our lives. He is now under the protection of Jesus. We are all better persons for having known him. We will not forget him and will cherish our memories of dear Marcantonio.'

Or, 'I suppose there were redeeming features in his life, but Marcantonio guarded them from me. I saw no sign, ever, of modesty or love, or of any desire to fulfil any task that he did not reason would bring advantage to himself.'

The vehicle behind was so close.

'An example to us all.'

'An example to us all of what happens to the young when they live, and are reared, in the hate-filled environment of a criminal family that permits no conscience, has no hesitation in inflicting pain, misery and dependency in the interests of personal gain. Good riddance and—'

He was jolted forward.

The impact was harsh and sudden, as if the driver behind him had hit the accelerator. He wore his belt but it was loose, and he hit the headrest, then swung forward and his temple cracked the top of the wheel. But he held on – he had to. He held the steering wheel with all his strength and kept the tyres on the road. He was nudged towards the cliff edge, but resisted – he felt himself going and thought the vehicle behind had insinuated its bonnet and front wheels between the rock wall and his own rear tyres. It was inexorable. He was driven towards the edge and—

He was supposed to be a man of God and was considered a reasonable priest, who did not flout the rules of his profession. He didn't know what he should say, so he said nothing. He did not beseech his God for help. He swore – which he never did, not even in the hearing of his cat – did not pray, and was answered.

A lorry came round the corner, braking and slewing across the road.

Father Demetrio hit his pedal and went clear. The space in front of him, between the rock wall and the lorry's giant wheels, was minimal. He went through the gap. Paint fragments flew and the contact screamed. He was free. Sweat poured off his body and his eyes were misted. He looked into his mirror. The vehicle behind him had not had room to skirt the lorry. He drove at full speed. He abandoned caution.

He knew where he would go.

Father Demetrio had sensed it would happen, but not when or how. He was past the turning to Montalto and was on the Reggio road. It would have been sensible to take a slower, more obscure route to the city, but he wanted speed to be his saviour. The high pines flowed past, and he saw the cars of the mushroom pickers. When he looked into his mirror, often, but he couldn't see the black HiLux. His hands shook as he held the wheel, and the enormity of his intended actions confronted him.

He had done something unusual during the early hours of the morning: he had unburdened himself to his wife. The prosecutor would be on course for new pastures when the guillotine blade came down on Scorpion Fly. He had left his bed, shaved hurriedly, kissed her cheek, then bawled something encouraging at the kids. He had shoved an apple into his pocket and been hustled to his car by the escort. Had he won the lottery? He had said, 'A new day, a new start,' to his chief guard, then explained his thinking. The prosecutor had watched his initial bemusement, then heard a chuckle, and finally saw them accept his view.

They were early in the building. It was not a place where people hurried – the wide staircase never doubled as a racetrack. He ran up the steps, a smile on his face, his guys chasing him. Their footfall echoed off the high ceilings and bounced off the bare walls. He clattered across the lobby, punched numbers at his door, waved to them and was inside, alone. He lit a cigarette, then turned on the coffee-machine and sank into his chair. He felt liberated.

When a light blinked at him, he got up and went to make his coffee, a harsh espresso, good for the start of a new day, a new target. He poured it into a dirty cup and swigged. He savoured it, then went to the floor safe.

At home his wife would be setting out breakfast for herself and the children. He had rarely talked to her about his work, but today she had given her opinion, then sunk back into the pillows.

He took the Scorpion Fly files from the shelf where they had been untidily wedged, and made certain that the strings binding them were fastened securely, carried them to the appropriate cupboard and opened it. A sight well known to any Italian government servant confronted him: layer upon layer of paper. A near lifetime's work was in front of him, crazily organised, the successes and failures of his career. Successes against 'Ndrangheta? A few – not many, but some. At that moment, he could have wallowed in the self-pity that had governed him over the last several days, or he could have flicked through the pages of those that had produced better results. One detailed the investigation, under his leadership, that had convicted Rocco and Domenico from that family of adders. It might have been labelled 'success', but their convictions had been based on the testimony of a turncoat, a *pentito*. They had not been able to safeguard the wretch's life: the man was barely cold in his newly dug grave. Did he and others at the Palace of Justice care sufficiently about the men and women who came forward, putting their lives on the line, to testify? He doubted it. He heaved the file into the cupboard and shut the door.

A new file welcomed the prosecutor. There were similar cupboards in every ministry of central and local government, in courthouses and police buildings – anywhere bureaucracy ruled: agriculture and forestry, tax, VAT and Customs, health, utilities . . . the Italian curse. The new file was slim; the family was based in Monasterace.

The Greek colonists had been to Monasterace and had called their settlement Caulonia. The town was built on a hilltop, once fortified, and holidaymakers came in the summer to use the beach and the marina. The case would involve alleged murder, extortion, narcotics trafficking, the sale of military weapons. Only the names would be different. Next week he would go there to walk on the esplanade by the marina, then drive up the hill into the town and stroll in the narrow medieval streets, sniff the air and test the atmosphere. He would regain the keen sense of the hunt that he had last felt when he had first gone to the village in the foothills of the mountains where the *padrino*, Bernardo Cancello, held court. He lit another cigarette, sat at his desk and thought they were mocking him. Sheets of paper, held together with string and cheap cardboard, surveillance photographs, a few witness statements: all mocked him. Freedom was short-lived. The ache in his mind returned.

The family were laughing at him, and Scorpion Fly was in its last hours. It was a failure. What else could he do?

When she stretched, her bones and joints creaked, the sound of branches cracking. She had food and water, but Consolata didn't eat or drink. Her back against a tree, knees hard up against her chest, she had slept after a fashion. In the distance a cockerel had crowed. Above her, birds had flapped and called, the wind had sung in the trees and a church bell had chimed, but she had been alone in a pit of misery. Above all she was insulted. The dent to her pride hurt more than rejection.

A punch or a kick would have been easier to bear. She might have kept some of her dignity if she had turned on her heel, left the wood, found the car and headed home, but she had reached for him and he had pushed her away. He had said nothing, just indicated that she was surplus to his requirements.

Consolata knew what she should have done. She had waited throughout the day, having convinced herself he would come back, then through the night. She had woken, expecting him to be sitting opposite, watching her. Consolata would go to look for him. She would find him on the hillside, slap his face, then hold him hard and . . . She stretched fiercely. She was from the city, the streets of Archi, and all she knew of the countryside was what a lover had taught her.

She would go slowly. How would she find him? She didn't know.

The kid came back.

There were *carabinieri* further down the track, on the far side of the men who kept the oil drum burning through the night. They monitored who came to the *padrino*'s house. Many were allowed through that morning, and all would have been photographed discreetly by the *carabinieri*.

His scooter tyres sprayed gravel when he turned sharply.

The women would be in one room. Teresa would bring them coffee and juice and they would sit with Mamma – who often fed the kid and might have been fond of him. The men would be in the room with the wide-screen television and the copy of *Scarface*. It was likely that the big man would be there now. The kid knew about the bunker: he had not been told but had realised where it was. Stefano came from the side of the house and greeted him. The kid thought Stefano took liberties, that he was over-familiar with the family – he didn't understand why. The man had no blood link with them, and no skills other than driving.

The kid reported what he had been told at the farm, and asked what he should do now. He always looked for more work because that was how he would gain the family's trust. There was a network of cousins and nephews, couriers who went to Gioia Tauro and were sent to the north, or Germany and Spain. One travelled twice each year to Venezuela, and two others went together once a year to Melbourne in Australia and Toronto in Canada. He thought that if he worked hard, the matter of his blood would be less important and the family would come to value him. The kid thought he might become a killer for the family, if he was trusted enough. He had been inside the house and had seen Marcantonio in the open-topped coffin, much of his face covered with white silk to hide the damage. He did not know what it would be like to kill. He felt no grief at the death of the old man's grandson.

Stefano told him to keep watch at the back of the house with the dogs. There was always juice for him in the fridge in the kitchen and he was permitted to go inside and take it. He did so now, and the dogs crowded against his knees. He knew all the paths, tracks and footholds on the steep slopes behind the house.

They had come through the village. A *maresciallo* – pale face, rimless spectacles, and a well-pressed uniform – explained the geography of the village, where the priest lived with his house-keeper, the shopkeeper, the butcher, and the collector of any produce that could be taken to Locri vegetable market. At a shut-tered building he had slowed and told the story of a dead *pentito*, a man who had been promised protection then denied it. He had served his purpose and was dumped as flotsam.

Carlo liked him – he thought he was at the level in the *carabinieri* where corruption, politics and watching your back were inappropriate. When they had come disguised as scenes-of-crime officers, they had been in the back of a van and had seen little. The village was a series of jerry-built homes; some had rusted scaf-folding poles round them. Many had outside walls that were not yet rendered, the window frames held in position by daubed cement, without paint. There was a football pitch near to the school but ponies grazed on it, and two male goats, tall and haughty, were tethered near the centre circle. The place seemed to him to exude rank poverty, with one exception. He did not need to remark on the sort of cars that stood outside the unfinished buildings: Mercedes saloons, BMW coupés' off-road Audis.

The *maresciallo* parked the jeep. They smoked and reflected . . .

Carlo asked himself, *What am I contributing? What is my good deed for the day? When did anyone here last change anything?* He was glad he wasn't required to give any answers. He did his job, didn't he? Same as Fred and the Italian – same as an army of men and women low on the promotion ladder in Britain, Germany and Italy. No rubbish on the street, expensive cars. Men at the junctions, where rough tracks led to the olive groves, wore grubby trousers and shirts, cupped their fags and watched. A big place for watching. The *maresciallo* said he'd appreciate it if his guests stayed low-key; they were not to take photographs or produce their phones.

Two jeeps were across the road, parked to make a chicane. Their engines idled. Carlo and Fred were invited to get out and did so. The sun's warmth flared back from the tarmac surface. Fifty or sixty yards ahead they could see an oil drum spewing smoke and half a dozen men. Carlo didn't doubt that firearms were readily to hand, and pickaxe handles. He and Fred were watched, impassively or indifferently. Tomorrow there would be a funeral but they would not be there. The *maresciallo* would, and the spotters with their telescopic lenses, but Carlo and Fred would be on their way, excuses to stay exhausted. They were told the approximate area where the surveillance post was in place, and the assumption was made that the intruder – they called him the *crociato*, the crusader – was nearer to the building, lower on the hill.

What was he doing? Why was he still there? Fred said a compulsion drove him. 'He was never been anywhere that is remotely a front line, never experienced close-quarters danger and may never have another opportunity to match this so he is reluctant to leave. What will he go back to? Driving a taxi? A factory bench? The work of a ledger clerk in an insurance company? Of course it is difficult for him to prise himself away from what he has here.'

But they and the guys on the hill were pulling out. He'd be on his own if he stayed, no friend within reach. Fred used his phone to check flights out, and book seats, to Rome together, then onwards separately. Carlo thought it would be fun to meet Bentley Horrocks on the leg to Heathrow – intimidating but fun.

Cars streamed from the house higher up the track, younger men driving, their elders beside them, their faces turned away from the *carabinieri* photographer. From what he could see of them, Carlo thought their expressions masked their feelings: there was no sign of hate, contempt, arrogance or humility. They didn't notice the men in uniform, and the cars travelled a respectful speed, slowing to go into the chicane, then accelerating out of it. Dust billowed after them.

The *maresciallo* said, 'The families have destroyed Calabria, with physical and moral vandalism. We can't break it. Is your man on the mountain so conceited that he believes it possible to alter the historical certainties of the region? To do what we cannot? Or is it a gesture?'

'I've never liked gestures,' Carlo said, 'but I'm not reading him too well.'

He had a quick look behind him.

Time to go: the sheets had rippled, as if something had brushed against them. He had not seen the old woman and imagined that she was entertaining those who had come to keep vigil with her. He had heard cars leaving, and when he'd lifted his head the obvious had been confirmed. The men had gone. Bernardo would have entertained them – the movement at the far side of the sheets had told him that the *padrino* was going to his bunker.

Jago pushed himself forward.

He had worn down the lichen on the stones under the boulders, compressed the moss and flattened the grass. There was a small bag that he had managed to push under the boulder on the left side so it was well hidden. The two lines he had scratched on the side of the opposite boulder were clear to see. He had done it with the penknife. Simple, like a signature. He had been there and left evidence as proof: only the young man who lay dead in an open coffin would have recognised the significance of two scratched lines. He would not linger on the way out.

It was the last time he'd see it. The gap into which he had wriggled seemed so narrow.

The kid was out, and so were the dogs. They were on the far side of the property, climbing. Jago had a good view of the kid and didn't feel threatened. He was confident that it was the right time, and he thought it best to be away and clear in daylight. His chance, he reckoned, of getting away up the slopes and over the rock falls, was good in daylight, and slight in darkness. That was his banker's training: an evaluation of risk.

He went down, trying to hug ground that was in shadow. He didn't know where Giulietta, the handyman or the daughter-in-law were, but he could see the men far down the track keeping watch there, and beyond them, near to the bend that was the start of the village, *carabinieri* trucks were parked across the road. They'd be too far away to save him. He went steadily and carefully, thinking of the pandemonium he would create when the power failed . . .

17

Jago did his best to be silent but he trod on dry twigs, which snapped, and scuffed dried leaves.

He had slipped twice. The first time he had gone down hard and broken the fall by clinging to a birch sapling growing from a crevice. On the second, his left foot had hit a level platform of rock that might have been three inches at the widest point. Pain had shot up his leg into his pelvis. Delusions gripped him. He thought he was closer to the family than to anyone sitting in judgement over him at the bank. His chair had been taken by someone else now.

His trainer soles scraped over rock surfaces and squealed as they slipped. Each time, Jago stopped. He froze and hugged the ground, tried to bury himself in rock, scrape a trench where the moss and earth were less than an inch deep, or to hide behind a tree trunk that was four or five inches in diameter. He had come halfway down. He hadn't been seen: no one had come out of the house. He believed that the head of the family had retreated to his bunker, that the kid and the dogs were on the far side of the valley, that the men stayed at the outer gate and the uniforms were further away, beyond earshot. When he stopped he worked hard to slow his breathing.

The chair in Sales was occupied. Jago could not see the occupant's face but he seemed to have strong shoulders and wore a white shirt with a tie. A suit jacket was draped on the chair back. He was close to the *FrauBoss*, and his blond hair, cut short, contrasted with her ebony. It had not taken Human Resources long to find a replacement. A few days – he was not sure how many, or what day of the week it was. That had little relevance when he was sliding on his backside down rock faces, or clinging by his fingertips to ledges. Below him was a patio and beyond that an open area in which the hard seat was still placed, the trellis of vines, and the line of sheets. He could see the shed better now, the walls and the damaged frame of what had once been a window. The chickens ignored him, and he couldn't see the cockerel.

He had not aroused an alert. The door was open and he could hear a radio playing sentimental music in the kitchen.

He looked closely at the next stage of his descent: he should track to his right. Below him he had seen a small cliff face, a drop of more than twenty feet. He searched to his right for places where his fingers could grip and others that would give a foothold.

A fly came. He hadn't seen one like it before. It was very near to him. There was a stone outcrop almost level with his eyes and nose and above it a cobweb, its mesh designed to trap. He couldn't see the spider that had made it, but he used a finger to dismantle the web so that it was no longer a threat to the fly. It seemed important. The fly had long antennae stretching from its head, six fine legs, and its wings, camouflaged with dark brown blotches, stretched beyond the length of its body, which was thin, as if it had been shaped on a potter's wheel. The tail had an orange tip that was like a scorpion's sting. He thought he had made it safe. That was where it had begun: a fly in a web. He had watched the fly's death, and the car had come. If he had been later, if the *FrauBoss* had not been delayed, if he had looked the other way and minded his own business, the fly would still have been killed and eaten, but Jago would not have joined a fight in which he had no stake.

The fly flew away. His mind cleared.

Jago looked for the route he would need to take, to his right, for the next leg of his descent, which would bring him to the line of sheets and a buried cable.

They packed their gear carefully into the bags. The camera's lenses and the image intensifier for the binoculars were worth thousands of euros, and their arses would be well kicked if the kit was not securely stowed and they dropped it, damaging the optics.

They had had glimpses of the boy going forward. To Ciccio, he was now a part of the scenery. The suit, tie and shaven cheeks in the photo that had seen sent to their communications hub were long gone. They had seen Jago Browne twice, maybe three times, moving down the hill towards the house. What to do?

Fabio had said, 'I didn't see or hear anything. What did you think you saw or heard?'

'I don't know.'

Better to be incompetent than devious. They had had no sight or sound of him. At their pay-grade, they would be thanked only for hard, clear information. He was 'a can of worms', and their intent was to get off the slope before darkness with everything they had brought in. Problem solved.

Ciccio swore.

She was no more than five metres from them.

She moved as he had taught her to.

Ciccio tilted his head and saw Fabio's face: incredulity. She went past them. They had the scrim net in front of them. It hid their hands and faces. She might, actually, have tripped over them and stayed ignorant of their presence. Ciccio's assessment of her: a good kid, a fair shag but intense. Her mind had been at war with the criminal classes of Calabria. Her conversations all ran along the same tracks and finished with the demand for detail of the families: that was all that concerned her. His own interest was based on her performance beneath him, and the matchless fun of tracking her hiding places and hunting her down, or reversing their roles, when he hid and she came after him. Always, when she'd got her breath back, she would ask questions. How many weeks? A few. How had it finished? It had run its course. Had he been fond of her? He'd sort of felt responsible – he'd thought her confidence was fake, that she was vulnerable.

'Did you see that?'

'A woman.'

'What in fuck's name is . . .' Ciccio's mouth was an inch from Fabio's head. She was gone. She didn't move badly but was still a novice. She had been a quick learner, but eventually he'd had enough, ignoring her texts and not returning calls. He added, 'She's called Consolata. She's an activist; anti-*pizzo* shit. I knew her.'

'For Christ's sake, you didn't— Ciccio, were you screwing her? What about Neomi?'

'It was before Neomi.'

They couldn't see her now, but heard her once when she must have kicked loose stones and a few had fallen. Ciccio had had a view of her face: she had looked close to breaking point. She had glanced around her, as if searching for something, then gone on.

'If you were cheating on Neomi, I'd—'

'I told you the truth.'

Silence clung between them. Repeat: hear, see and know *nothing*. They could justify it. They had a 'mission objective'. They were there to identify the hiding place used by Bernardo Cancello, *padrino* of a clan, locate it and report it. They liked the jokes: Q. Why do elephants paint their toenails red? A. So they can hide in cherry trees. Q. Have you ever seen an elephant in a cherry tree? A. No, so it works ... There was no humour now. They hadn't found him.

The thought of having to offer explanations, have his career examined, his liaisons subject to scrutiny, was unattractive. They made no call. It was sufficient for him to register that they had not seen the high-value target.

The light burned down on him and the television was loud. Bernardo remained on his back on the unmade bed, and time passed. And he pondered – he had much, that afternoon, to think about. His guests had gone and some had nodded in imitation of sincere condolence or had touched his arm in a private gesture. All were familiar with sudden death.

He had moved on from the death of Marcantonio. The clock could not be turned back. There was much that could not be halted. The funeral the following day would be a grand occasion: the coffin would be brought from the house to the church on a bier pulled by four black horses, plumed. He would not be there, but it would happen. His man, Stefano, would be on his way by now to a hotel in Brancaleone: another situation that would not be stayed. And somewhere on the road to Reggio, the capital city of the region, his daughter was tracking the car of the priest and might now have dealt with it where the hairpins were sharpest and the cliff edges steepest. Had she not already done so, then she had in her handbag the gift he had made her.

He was not dragged down by grief but was victim to a high level of aroused emotion – it was as if the good days, long gone, had returned, power with them. He had been told, and Giulietta had sworn it was on the word of the clerk in the Palace of Justice, that this would be his last full night in the bunker. He would not go to the funeral, but would be discreetly out of his gaol. The priest would have thought himself Bernardo's friend. He had no friends.

The kid saw her.

He had little formal education. His teachers had found him brightly intelligent, bored beyond salvation, almost impossible to motivate. They had told him to his face that his mind was sufficiently sharp for him to go far – they had meant he had the wit to move away from a village in the foothills of the Aspromonte and make a success of himself in any world beyond the boundaries of organised crime. Their advice had been decisively rejected. He had stayed and made himself useful.

Now he was tested.

No one in the village had the right to be on the steep, wooded slopes behind the family's home. No stranger would be there in innocence. No surveillance team from the Guardia, the Squadra or the *cacciatore* would be represented by a woman who wore no camouflage clothing, seemed to carry no weapon and was alone . . . Alone, but might represent a threat.

The kid belonged to the family. He had made his choice. If the family fell, he would go down with them. It was not possible to hold up a hand when the *padrino* lay in his own blood and suggest to a new family that he could switch allegiance without hesitation

and belong to those whom, a few hours before, he would have
helped to garrotte, strangle or shoot – not that he had been asked
to kill yet, but if the time came he didn't think he would fail. His
experience of taking life was confined to slitting the throat of a
goat when its foreleg was broken and of drowning an old dog that
was no longer of use.

He assumed her to be the reconnaissance of a rival family.
There was no love between the clans. The feuds were mostly
suppressed, but they didn't go away even after alliances of
marriage had been made. If the power of the family faltered,
others would come from the villages around or from Locri,
Siderno or Brancaleone and take control of their lives. He doubted
he would survive – so a movement on the hillside alerted him.

He thought the girl he had seen was in her twenties. She wore
jeans and a dark anorak. She might have a handgun, but he hadn't
seen it.

Three dogs worked with the kid. At his whistle they'd freeze,
raise their ears, listen for his next command, and he would guide
them with the calls used by generations of shepherds in the mountains. They had ground to cover – they had to get to the far side of
the valley where the trees grew thickest and the rocks were steeper.

The kid had had only a glimpse of her, but that was enough.

The sun was at its zenith, the heat as intense as it would be that
day.

Where the men were was hazy, but the light fell high on the
hillside, leaving it clear and easy to watch.

Fred saw Carlo mopping his forehead with a handkerchief and
there were sweat stains on the Englishman's shirt, across his back
and at the armpits. They had no hats. Most of the men had taken
refuge inside the vehicles but the doors were open to allow any
breeze to blew through. They stood together in the shade available
from a stunted oak, which offered little cover. They were surplus
to requirements but had half a day to kill. It was often like that.
Fred's superior officer, young, groomed, climbing, would have
forgotten he had sent a man to Calabria, the cliff edge of the

known world. If he had talked of his man's presence on the Ionian coast he would have justified it as 'someone else's problem, the Italians. We're giving them all possible support'. No great moral issue at stake.

Carlo was swaying on his feet, suffering. Fred prodded him.

'I was reflecting, my friend, on my senior officer's view of this affair. And you?'

'I was about asleep on my feet. My gold commander will be with a chum on a golf course. I won't figure among the bogies.'

'And nothing's happening.'

'My experience,' Carlo said, 'is that when nothing *seems* to be happening, all hell is about to break loose. Remind me to tell you a few old tales that prove it. It's confusing, sudden, chaotic and . . .'

Fred was no longer listening. The *maresciallo* was peering through his binoculars, not scanning and searching but focused and following. He slipped them towards Fred and pointed. Fred locked on the kid. Dogs barked far away, the sound they made when they'd found a scent or a target. The kid followed them, skipped between rocks, then was lost among trees that towered up behind the house. He was above the line of sheets to the right of the house. The binoculars were taken from him. He asked the *maresciallo* what his orders were. His response: to observe, monitor and have a presence, no more, until dusk. In the evening there would be a farewell gathering.

'Confusing, sudden and chaotic': when was it ever different? Where was their boy? Why was he there? When would he appear? The mood had changed, as if the sun had cooled. The lenses watched the hillside.

She drove well and was calm. The priest led and she followed on the Reggio road, past the Montalto turning, and past the place they called Serro Juncari. Her father liked to talk about it. He had not been there but her grandfather had. A great meeting of impor-tant men held in secret one misty morning on a high plateau, hidden from view by wild pine trees. An informer had betrayed them: *carabinieri* had crept close and attempted a mass arrest. Her grandfather had escaped but many had not. Those captured had spent a short time in the San Pietro gaol in Reggio. The combination of political influence, judicial complicity and well-targeted envelopes had ensured that life soon, in the mountains, regained normality. The role of the informer had hurt the families, the whispers of the *soffiato*; different from a *pentito*, more dangerous. The latter ended up in a police cell, then called for a prosecutor and appeared in court. The damage could be contained. The *soffiato* was the murmur in the wind, unknown and unsuspected, probably liked and certainly trusted. The leeching of information went on over months and even years; the details of arrests were muddied at the Palace of Justice and the role of the informer was hidden. When her father had used the word – *soffiato* – he had spat.

Her father thought that Father Demetrio, booked to conduct the funeral of Marcantonio the next day, might be about to betray the family. Good enough for her. She trailed the priest towards Reggio, staying two or three vehicles back. She had lost any opportunity to drive him off the road. It was against her leg, hidden from view.

If the Beretta was needed, and the chance came, she was experienced in its use.

Shaken, but more determined, Father Demetrio crossed a high point and could see the city below. A group of men and women were spread out close to the road, standing behind telescopes and tripods. He identified them as a group of the foreign birdwatchers who came to Reggio to monitor migrating species. They straggled along ground left rough after road widening, and would have been half suffocated by vehicle fumes. He had read about them in a newspaper: they complained persistently about the old sport of shooting as practised in Calabria. Enough. Calabrians did not need foreigners to dictate their behaviour. It should be done from within. The future was in the hands of persons such as himself, and conscience tore at him, leading him towards his ultimate destination that day. He saw the city and the brilliant blue of the sea, the hazy outline of Sicily and the massive shape of Etna, capped with a wisp of thick cloud. He was looking for the piazza that lay in front of the Duomo, his destination.

He left the bird watchers behind. The road dropped ahead of him. His hands shook and his leg muscles were wire tight. He glanced into the rear-view mirror several times but he didn't see the black vehicle again.

He drove down the steep, winding hill and accepted that his life had changed.

Jago heard the dogs before he saw them.

A sharp memory: a weekend of executive bonding in the Herefordshire countryside, on the edge of the Welsh Marches, when he had been slogging in the City. There had been hiking, zip-wire riding, paint-ball fighting and quad-bike racing. They'd been trying to cross the river with a ball of string and ten different egotists offering opinions when, out of the mist, on a Saturday morning, the hunt had cantered by. It jogged him now. Not the riders in fancy dress, or the big horses that probably lived better than their grooms, but the baying of hounds on a scent. At first he hadn't seen them, but he'd heard the cry. On a dark moonless night, the sound would have terrified him. Now, though, it was bright sunshine and the cries of the dogs rang in the air, bouncing off the rock walls.

It was not for him – Jago had that comfort. The dogs were headed, guided by whistles and calls, along a line that ran higher than where Jago was.

The kid slipped into view, then out of it, but took secondary place. The dogs held him. They did not race ahead and have to be called back. They worked at a steady pace, quartering the ground, prancing on rocks and diving into caves. The kid held them with his commands. Jago didn't know what or who they were tracking, but it was a form of sport. He assumed that the dogs had a line on the men who had fed him, but they'd have firearms and probably dog repellent – they'd be equipped to protect themselves. The dogs were almost as much a part of the family as any of the humans. He knew what their teeth could do because they had taken apart the wolf's body.

The kid directed them, and they must have been close to where he sent them. They seemed to have caught his mood because their cries were sharper. Then, at a final command, the noise was cut. Jago could see the outline of their ribcages, their spines, their flattened ears. The three dogs advanced in silence, their bellies hugging the ground. He thought they were closing on their target. He waited to hear shots fired.

The yard beyond the kitchen remained empty and the solitary chair threw a longer shadow. Again he could hear the radio playing inside. The kid went slower and more carefully. Jago thought they were close to the target but far above him.

She could no longer see the dogs.

It was a moment of fear, unique to Consolata.

Quiet cloaked the trees. She had not identified where the dogs were or the kid who was with them. She had frozen. She didn't know where to go, what to do, where to turn.

She looked around her, saw and heard nothing. She had come across the cleft between two great boulders. It was obvious that he had been there. She had found his rubbish and stayed too long. She thought of how he had been with her at the rendezvous, when he had taken the food but not her. The ground was squashed and she had found the poorly hidden rubbish – how had he come by food issued to the Italian military?

Consolata, looking down onto the back of the house, gave Jago credit for having found a perfect vantage point. The panorama offered a clear view of the back door. She saw a trellis, with ripe grapes hanging from it, a washing line, with sheets, towels and pillow cases pegged to it. She saw a chair, and a place where the yard had been scrubbed. She strained to hear. She was aware only of a radio playing light music. The silence unnerved her. The peace, she knew, was not real.

At the squat, as a campaigner, she was thought of as determined and without fear. Those traits – she knew – unsettled some.

She should have had a lover in the squat, but did not. Because she had no lover, Consolata had come in search of one. She had made her commitment: if she found him, she would drive him off the mountain and take him to Scilla. She would let the darkness fall and the moon rise, then lead him to the beach and would brook no argument. She hadn't found him.

The shadows were longer now, and dusk would come fast. She turned to look away from the house and wondered if he had spent his entire time in this place, where he was at the moment and what he was doing. Then she looked for a way to haul herself clear of the plateau and start back.

She cursed him, not aloud, and despised herself for following him. It had been easy to come down, find this ledge, sliding on the backside of her jeans the last two metres, but was harder to pull herself up. She had a grip with one trainer and a hold with one hand, fingers gripping a smooth rock surface, but her foot slid away and she lurched back. She tried again, but her fingers couldn't take the strain and, once more, she toppled back, and swore, then went at it yet again.

She was up off the ledge and had a good grip with foot and fingers when the dogs came. Not big ones, not the dogs the police used or the military. There had been dogs of that build, that aggression, round the bigger rubbish dumps in Archi. They would fight each other for food scraps, but the worst ferocity would be directed at anyone foolish enough to interfere with them. They had her legs and she lost the foothold, kicked to get them clear of her and fell over the edge.

The dogs went with her. Two leaped after her and one clung by its teeth to her jeans and held tight. She was shouting, near terror, and the dogs were snarling. She rolled and cannoned off a tree, then bounced into a rock face. She was dazed now, unable to help herself, and another dog had its teeth on her arm. The anorak was ripping. The kid was above her, crabbing sideways, sure-footed, managing the ground with ease. It was a snapshot moment, as if a camera had captured it: the coldness in the face, the absence of excitement, the lack of emotion. He was a teenager and had smooth cheeks. His eyes never left her and showed no pleasure at her fate but no sympathy either. Dead eyes. She rolled further, and the ground came up fast to meet her. She hit a chair on the slabs of the patio.

An old woman had come out with a broom, which she waved at the dogs. They backed off. Consolata saw a face that was lined with age and the skin sagging, and knew she was confronting the mamma of the family. First a cackle, then the face set. Aspromonte granite.

The old woman, ankle to throat in black, called, 'We have a little bitch, all bones, a little spy, watching us.'

They had a fine view of the yard, and the kitchen door.

Women spilled out of it. They seemed uniformed in black, the 'mourning squad', and came armed. Some were hideously skeletal, others grotesquely obese. They would have been roused from their vigil over the dead boy by the snarling of the dogs and the old woman's shout. From the kitchen, some had brought knives and one had a saucepan. Another brandished a meat cleaver, and the last gripped the handle of a lump hammer.

'Report or not?'

Fabio hissed, 'I have never been unprofessional and—'

The dogs were outside the circle of women, sniffing the backs of legs. The kid had come down from the rocks and had the wisdom to stay back. The low sunlight caught the steel of the knives, the pan, the cleaver and the rim of the hammer head. Fabio thought he might be sick. He could no longer see her. She was blocked by the women's backs. They bent. He heard no scream, and the dogs were quiet. The kid was at the edge of the yard and did nothing.

'Do we shoot?' Fabio asked.

A hoarse answer from Ciccio: 'We shoot only to preserve life, our lives or a victim's. We do not shoot to warn. If we shoot it is to kill. Do you need me to read you the regulations? We do not do warning shots. Ever.'

'Or shout?'

'We're not "intervention", we're "surveillance". We watch, we note.'

'She was your girl. You knew her . . .' Fabio let it tail off. It was a cheap shot. He couldn't see her. He hadn't met her. Ciccio had not brought her on a foursome outing for a meal, a drink, a movie. He had kept her to himself. It was difficult to work out what the women were doing. They were crouched now, but he didn't think the knives had been used, while the hammer and the saucepan were not raised high to strike. A card came up in a wizened hand. It was encased in cellophane, and would have been hung around Consolata's neck. Fabio had his pistol in one hand and a pepper spray in the other, but Ciccio held the binoculars. It was an ID card. It was passed among the women. Ciccio mouthed that it was the card for a member of the Addio Pizzo or the Reggio Libera. Gales of coarse laughter rose to them.

Fabio said, 'The camera! Use the camera.'

'Can't.'

'Use the camera! Record it!'

A hesitation. 'It's packed. It's in the fucking case. Lenses are off. Everything stowed.'

'You didn't tell me.'

'Fuck you, Fabio. You saw me pack it. We agreed. We were due to go – we had nothing to report, nothing to see. It was over, finished.'

Two good friends had fallen out. That was new in their relationship. It had damaged mutual fondness and respect, which might not be retrieved. They didn't shoot, shout or use the camera. The women were bent over the girl.

He could have intervened. Jago was close enough to use his fingers to root a stone from the ground – which wasn't hard after the rain – and hurl it at the bent backs of the women. Guaranteed a hit. They were, he thought, a colony of ants boiling over the girl: he couldn't see what they were doing. Had he thrown a stone, hit someone and caused her to squeal, the ants would have exploded in all directions, but Jago wouldn't do it.

If he deflected their attention from Consolata in any way, he would kiss goodbye to any chance he might have of reaching the cable. He would do nothing. He had only seen the cable from a distance but he could almost feel the smooth plastic that coated it. He was near enough to the washing line to see the different colours of the plastic pegs and distinguish the simple pattern on the sheets, autumn leaves on one and faded full-bloom roses on an other. Where they hung together, hiding the track, he would unearth the cable at the join. He would not give up the chance. It would come only once.

He barely moved, only the flicker of an eyelash. His heartbeat and breathing were regular. He could see what they were doing to her. There were many stones he could have used – they had fallen down long slopes, dislodged by heavy rain.

When he had sat on the bench, fresh off the train, and her poster had blown out of the overfilled waste-bin to snag against him, he had said to her, 'I think I know what winning is against them. I did it yesterday. It was only small but I won.' She had stopped and had asked him what 'winning' was. She had never managed it. He would win when he broke the cable, trapped the *padrino* in darkness and frightened him. The child chained in the cave would have been terrified, and the old man would be.

The knives were on the ground, with the saucepan, the cleaver and the hammer. The kid collected them, then was waved away by a gaunt, scrawny arm. Women's work, not for the kid to see. Jago was the witness. The laughter came more often, guttural. Sometimes shoulders shook because this was their joke. He couldn't see her but knew what they were doing. The kid was at the kitchen door, watching unnoticed. The clothing came off, to be flung over shoulders. An anorak, jeans, trainers, and the two T-shirts – everything she had offered to take off for him. The women broke apart.

She lay huddled in the foetal self-preservation posture. All that she wore was the ID card in its plastic holder, hung from her neck on its lanyard. He had seen it on the beach. They pulled her up. The sun, low-slanted, caught her skin. She was not given her clothes, which were left at the kid's feet, close to the door. They marched her round the side of the house. He thought her beaten, but was wrong.

She flailed with her arms and her hair flew, fighting free of the hands clawing at her and yelled to the skies, in his language: 'Jago, where are you? Jago, I need—'

A moment of defiance, which was gone as fast as it had come. The hands had her arms and one pulled at her hair, shaking her head hard.

They walked her to the side of the house, up past that wall and out to the front, then took her across the gravel, where the City-Van was usually parked. She would have walked over sharp stones but she no longer resisted. They took her as far as the gates that led onto the track. In the distance, ahead of her, was the block where the village men were and beyond them the *carabinieri* vehicles.

She was pushed, dismissed, and began the long walk.

Jago's target was the cable. He had not been compromised.

Ciccio said, 'We didn't have to shoot. Her life wasn't at risk.'

'Good-looking, all of her.'

Ciccio hit Fabio. With a clenched fist.

Stefano was a humble man, ran errands, said what he was told to say and played his part well. He had no language other than the dialect peculiar to the Ionian coast of the Aspromonte. The lawyer who lived in the near-deserted coastal development up the beach from Brancaleone, Humphrey, was the go-between. He could not have faulted Stefano, even to the way the man held his cap across his stomach, in counterfeit respect, and realised the seriousness of his own situation. Stefano had told him, and he had understood the implications, that two foreign policemen had been seen talking with Horrocks. He and a member of the family had witnessed it. Humphrey should be careful about the company he kept, whom he took money from. He had shivered and protested that he knew nothing of such a security breach. He hoped fervently that he was believed. He explained the situation to Horrocks and tried to smile.

'This chap is going to drive you to the meeting. You'll meet the top man – that's out of my league and I'm not invited. They're in mourning because of the death of the boy who came to see you, so they're making a big gesture by seeing you. A mark of respect, you might say. Jack will stay with me but you'll be fine. It's the big league, Bent, top-table stuff.'

Humphrey did his best. Bentley Horrocks was vain, not really a man of the world. The lawyer thought Stefano played it well. A smile and a wink, they said, was best when handling a man who had been condemned but was ignorant of it. He remembered seeing the two men with Bent outside the hotel – he had been in the lobby. Bent hadn't answered when Humphrey had asked who they were. Silly boy for being seen with them, and a dangerous boy for Humphrey to know too well.

Jack said, 'Where you deserve to be, Bent, top table and big league. Brilliant.'

Humphrey drove a big car, and assumed Bent had a Beemer or a Merc in London, perhaps even a Bentley *cabriolet*, so it had been a surprise for him to be ushered into the passenger seat of a Fiat mass-market, seen-better-days, City-Van. He went off, good as gold. They watched him driven round the corner and out of sight. He saw that Jack – no fool, Giacomo, a survivor, who put up with serious shit in the interests of comfort – was white-faced and his hands were trembling. He told Jack to clear their rooms, and pack the two bags: they'd be leaving for Lamezia in a half-hour.

'You know what's good for you, Jack? They've long arms, and not many places they don't reach to. Always gets awkward when anyone opens their mouth out of turn, pulls anything fast on them . . .'

'I do, Humphrey. I think I know it quite well – what's good for me. Yes.'

'Is that her?'
    'It is.'
Carlo's question, Fred's response.
She came towards them.
The *carabinieri*, same as the Customs man and the investigator,

would have 'seen it all' and were not often fazed. Heads dropped or eyes went to the skies, to the lowering sun, big, red and full of war, and the loose puffs of cloud. She walked as if in a dream, the ID card on her chest. Her arms hung slack at her sides. She made no attempt to cover herself, as if she were beyond modesty. At first the *maresciallo* had followed her with his binoculars but now he let them hang from the neck strap. The women would have resumed the vigil, something to chat about over the open coffin.

She was alone and walked in the centre of the track, with no protection for her feet. Sometimes the rhythm of her stride broke and she hopped – must have stepped on a sharp flint.

The men stood aside, ignored her. Backs were turned, shoulders offered. One, not meeting her eyes, offered her an old sack, hessian, which he'd picked up from the ground beside the oil drum, and held it out to her. She didn't take it so he let it fall.

She left them, looking straight ahead. From where they were, that far away, they had heard one long shout, an entreaty, but not her words.

Fred had said to Carlo, outside the communal house in Archi, when the door had been slammed on them, 'God protect us from crusaders, bigots, her and her crowd . . . She laughs at us because we are the little people.'

Hilde was his wife, and Carlo's woman was Sandy. That was established. They hadn't fished out photographs but had mentioned them on the long journey from the Tyrrhenian Sea to the Ionian coastline. He would not tell Hilde what he could see as he stood beside the bonnet of the *carabinieri* vehicle. None of the men were at ease, but he reckoned he and Carlo bore the heaviest responsibility. He would never speak of this walk to a living soul when he returned to his home and doubted that the Englishman would. It was because of him, because of the laptop left on a table in an interview room at the station in Bismarck-strasse. He could source it all back. She walked steadily, and he reckoned that her mind was numb. She hid nothing of herself, and nothing about her explained where Jago Browne was.

The *maresciallo*, at his elbow, said, 'It's about the power have.

You understand? You think Carlo understands? They have the power to hurt far beyond the inflicting of pain. Total humiliation is worse than anything physical. That is what they have done to her. I cannot see a mark on her body. No electrodes have been used, no cigarette burns. They have broken no bones. She has lost her clothing, which she can replace for a hundred euros. She is scarred, though. She may never be free of the experience. Maybe six or seven women took part in stripping her. Technically that is an assault, but if I try to put them into a courtroom with no witness, I'll be laughed at. Standing here, we are ignored. If I go closer, I risk a confrontation. They tolerate us here, but no nearer. On the eve of a funeral it doesn't suit them to kick us half to death. They make the rules. They have awesome power.'

Fred tried to look into her eyes, to offer solidarity – and thought Carlo would – but she sleep-walked past them. She was given a blanket from the tailgate of a vehicle. It was draped over her shoulder, lay on the soft skin, covering one nipple but not the other. She didn't wrap it closely around herself. A car door opened and she was helped inside. He considered, not seriously, going to the door and asking her if she had seen Jago Browne on the hill. If she had, how was he? Had he yet explained his intentions – and when was the silly fucker coming out and getting himself onto a plane? He could have asked all of that, but did not. He wondered, again, where the boy was and what he would do. He heard sobbing, quiet and not theatrical.

The *maresciallo* said, 'They do what they want. They buy who and what they want. It is difficult to win.'

Carlo, murmured, 'But we have to keep trying.'

Both men were sombre. Where was the boy and what would he do? And when would they have a chance to decide on his vision of victory, if ever?

Jago Browne went down the last few yards of the slope with almost excessive caution. The women were gathered in the kitchen, with a television on. The kid had lit a fire in an incinerator and Consolata's clothes had gone into it, all except the trainers. The kid had poked the fire, then called the dogs to him and now was on the high hillside. Why she had been there he had no idea, but it would have been ungrateful not to thank her – silently, fleetingly – for the diversion she had promised him. He didn't know whether she was still with the police at the block far down the track. The daughter-in-law was at the house, with the children, and he could hear their shrieks as they played inside. The open coffin was not enough to quieten them. He thought now was a good time. He was certain that the old man, the head of the family, was in his bunker, underground. He went towards the sheets.

He slid the last few feet. The chickens ran to him, but the cockerel was wary. They came near to his legs and pestered him. He kicked dirt at them and they pecked at it, looking for food. He came past the derelict shed and saw where the ground beyond it was subsoil, with no bed of rock. There was weed and thorn, and he registered that part of the shed's wall was of newer stone, freshly pointed. He went past a sheet where the motif was roses with wide stems. In front of him, almost under his feet, the earth was scuffed with footprints. He stood still and listened. He heard the sounds from the kitchen and the kid's whistle from up the hill. He wondered whether his new friends – the providers of food – had watched him come down the last short cliff face. They couldn't see him now, wouldn't know where he was and what he was doing. The earth was loose and had been stamped on but had not settled. No excuse. He thought it the supreme moment of his life. No excuse to delay.

He dropped to his knees.

He scraped hard with his hands, tore at the soil and scratched, as a cat would have. The earth came clear and he drove his hands into the soil and found where it was looser. The pile he made grew.

Jago opened the hole.

He had been accurate to a pinpoint. The cable was revealed, and the PVC insulation tape wrapped round the join. He scrabbled with his fingers under the tape and cleared a further section of the cable.

His fingers fastened on it. He had it in two hands and eased himself onto his haunches. The cable strained. He drew a deep breath.

18

He let the breath ease out, threw his bodyweight back and heaved. Jago had no knowledge of electricity, didn't know what would happen, but thought himself safe. He wrenched.

The cable leaped from the ground a few feet, then stuck fast. He pulled harder and saw the tape come loose. A last drag and it had parted. A flash of light dazzled him.

Jago clung to the cable end. He saw the short folded ends of the copper wire and threw it aside. There was a scorch mark on the grass and a few leaves were singed. He was on his back, and rolled.

The chickens came to him and he was surrounded by a clucking chorus, demanding corn or whatever they ate. He ignored them, his focus on the cable. He assumed it best to get the ends back into the little pit he had gouged and fill it again. He tossed in the dead end of the cable, and handled the live end with what he hoped was care. Each week in the *Newham Recorder* there were stories of fatalities caused by accidents linked to electricity. He kicked earth over the copper ends, covered them and stamped them down. The chickens had given up on him. He heard the kid and his whistles but they were high and far away from him.

It was done, finished. In the morning it would be clear that the ground had been disturbed, but not now that dusk was coming and the shadows were longer. The sheets hung still, and light from the kitchen doorway reached the grapes on the trellis.

Jago Browne was where he wanted to be, not in an air-conditioned office, not in front of a bank of screens, not looking up to see the big TV suspended from the ceiling that carried information from Bloomberg and CNBC, not wearing a suit and impressing a client who had made millions, not pounding on a bike in a gym or running on a treadmill. He thought the place raw, fresh, and felt no fear. He had a sense that it was where he belonged, and lingered for a few seconds, then was gone. There was still work to be done, more challenges in front of him.

He eased away, left the chickens disappointed. He went back past the shed with the broken window frame and sagging door, the stone wall, and the slope where the soil and stones were different and fewer weeds grew. There, Jago strained to hear a sound – evidence of his work – but heard nothing. He began to climb. As he went up small cliffs, traversed little gullies, and tried to find the ledges for his feet, he thought himself most vulnerable. His eyes were inches from rocks and foliage and he was unable to twist his neck to see what was behind him – the women from the house, or the kid and the dogs could have crept up behind him to snatch him when he could not defend himself. He went on until he thought himself out of sight of the kitchen door. Then he rested.

Jago had seen Consolata. Her appearance and capture had not involved him. He had seen Marcantonio, with the raised shotgun and the wounded wolf, and had hurled the tyre iron, then had seen the flash of light and smoke spurt from the barrel but had felt no involvement. Life and death moved on, and he went with the flow. He moved, did not rush to be back at the road and looking for a ride out. He had no torch, just his fingers to help him.

Dusk hurried on him, and the colours around him greyed. He blundered onto it. He thought that once, long ago, it might have been a man-made path – there were places where the slope had been cut away and it was level. It was narrow, wide enough only for one person, and wove around the bigger rocks. For the first fifty yards or so, he would have been in deep cover, hidden from the house and the yard. Not what he wanted: he had to see the shed, the sheets, the door and the yard.

There was a rock beside the path.

He could lever himself to the top by taking hold of a birch sapling and dragging himself up. He lurched onto it and looked down, panting. Deep tiredness gripped him. He lay on the rock and thought of the squat castle keep perched on the summit of the mass at Scilla, which dominated the beach below. He was rewarded. He had a gap between trees and foliage to peer through, a vantage point. He had a good view, better than the one from the cleft under the two boulders, from the shed to the kitchen door.

And what Jago couldn't see, he could imagine.

Pitch darkness. He couldn't see his hand.

He was off the bed. There were power cuts often enough in the winter when the storms came in off the Ionian Sea and when the poles carrying the electricity were undermined by subsidence, or when trees came down on the lines. Usually, then, there was warning – the power would go, come back, go again. This time there had been none.

He was Bernardo Cancello. He was the *padrino* of his *cosca*. He had authority over the village and responsibility for events far beyond it. If there was a power cut, the first house in the village to have its electricity restored would be his . . . but he had never been in the bunker when the power had failed, always in the house. Mamma knew where everything for such an emergency was kept.

The blackness was total.

His leg was bleeding. He could feel the moisture on his skin and the wound smarted. He had come off the bed and had not thought where he was going or where the torch was, but had stood, taken a step forward – a blind man – and hit a chair, scraping his shin against it. He hadn't bled since he and Stefano had changed a tyre on the City-Van. The jack had slipped and he had caught his hand on the mudguard. He had blamed Stefano, cuffed him hard and . . . He didn't know what to do. The power was never off for long unless there was a massive storm, as there had been three or four days ago. Then there had been no cut, not even a flickering of the lights.

He couldn't remember where the candles were or the matches. Stefano would have known where they were. Bernardo had an old watch, given him long before by a friend, who had been shot dead in the open market of Gioiosa Ionica. He had had it more than twenty years and it still told good time, but the luminous paint on the arms had faded. He could have had a Rolex, a Breitling, a Longines or an Omega for four or five thousand euros – he could have matched the watch Marcantonio had bought in Berlin. He could have had any watch, and the face would have been lit, the hands clear to see. Teresa had a good watch, and Marcantonio's was on the chest in his bedroom. Mamma would not part with the one he had given her for a birthday twenty-nine years ago, from a shop on Corso Giuseppe Garibaldi in Reggio. No watch with illuminated hands. No red light on the plug for the small fridge, or for the two-ring stove, or for the mini-boiler on the wall. No light at the heater on the floor or the air-conditioner.

If it had been midnight, and he had been in his house and the power had gone, he could have stood at the front door, while Mamma rooted out the candles, the hurricane lamp or the big torch, and looked down and to the east where he would have seen some of the streetlights on the coastal road. There might have been moonlight. Headlights on the roads below the village, and stars above. Some houses in the village had small generators. He had no light to look at. Nothing. It was as the cave had been – but not for Bernardo.

The inner door, if he could find it, led to the tunnel of concrete pipes and was power-assisted. He could open it by hand, but electricity made the job easier. The outer door could be opened only when the power was on. And he didn't know what he might trip over or blunder into next. The child in the cave had not been able to hurt herself in the darkness because the chain had held her. At the back of the cave, where she had been, where her mattress was and where water dripped from the rock above, there would have been the same black emptiness.

He had been told by Stefano that he might blow the fuse if he overloaded the system – but he had not. Nothing new was plugged in. He had to wait for Stefano – but his driver was far away. If not Stefano, he must wait for his daughter, but Giulietta was tracking the priest whom he had condemned. His daughter-in-law would have had the strength to open the far door from the outside, but she never came to the bunker. She did nothing that might spoil her clothes. Mamma would not come – and she was deaf: she wouldn't hear him if he shouted when she was next near to the door, feeding her chickens.

The dark was unique to him. He could see nothing. He didn't want to move for fear of hurting himself. There were times when the leader of a family, the *padrino*, must show courage, must lead his men of honour from the front, set the example. Now nobody was watching. Nobody cared to see his courage. He had begun to shake, and he couldn't suppress the tremor in his arms and hands. His legs felt weak. Silence clawed at him. When the child had been in the cave there had been the noise of dripping water, and she had told him tearfully she had heard rats moving. No water dripped in his bunkers and no vermin had found its way in.

He was surrounded by silence, in total darkness, and the shaking in his limbs was worse. He didn't know when anyone would come, or whether he was forgotten. He thought it pointless to shout: he would not be heard.

Jago sat on the flat surface of the rock, his back against a bank of sparse earth, stones and the network of roots from a birch tree; all of his body was in shadow and he thought himself well hidden.

He had a view he rated excellent – maybe that was what his life had come down to, the rating of a view, not the credit rating of a company or the wealth rating of a potential investor. He could see the porch roof at the front of the house, the parking area where the City-Van was usually left, and down the track to where the men stood guard. The oil drum was lit and threw up sparks; beyond it were the lights of the *carabinieri* vehicles. He could also see the kitchen door, the patio with the single wooden seat, the yard before the trellis blocked him, the line of sheets and the roof of the derelict shed. Nothing happened, no panic. Only the chickens scratched and fussed in the grit. He wondered how it was in the darkness, what the man was doing.

It might have been a total failure. The old boy could have slipped off his bed or out of his chair, found his way immediately to a shelf, a cupboard or drawer, picked up a power torch, and switched it on. The dark might have been only a minor inconvenience. Jago considered that unlikely. Chaos and confusion, in his limited experience, always accompanied a power-cut, as if the world was ending. Nobody stayed calm when the electricity failed. He expected that Bernardo would appear eventually, stressed, and breathless.

He did not consider his effort worthless. The picture in his mind was of the old man trapped in darkness, afraid. Jago had his knees up and his arms round them. At that moment, with the crows and the pigeons settled in the branches above him, and the light gone, he reflected that he held the power, not Marcantonio's grandfather. He had, he thought, more power and control than he had ever possessed in his life.

He thought it would play out in front of him that evening. The cool breeze was refreshing. Food would have been acceptable, but in comparison to what he had achieved, and where he was headed, that was a trivial concern. Below him, it would explode, he was sure.

The City-Van struggled on the steeper sections of the road. Stefano had to drive in a low gear when the little engine strained. When they had slowed right down and fumes billowed from the exhaust, he would smile sweetly at his passenger. They didn't talk. Because Stefano had no English and his passenger no Italian, he could hold a conversation only in sign language. He pointed to his watch to indicate when they would reach their destination. He offered cigarettes out of politeness, which were declined, and a fresh bottle of water, which was accepted.

It had been easier than Stefano had anticipated. That the Englishman would make this journey into the unknown, without the company of his associate, had surprised him. He thought the lawyer from along the coast, Humphrey, had understood and possessed the wisdom to give no sign of it. The associate had shown nerves, was Italian by birth, and might also have grasped what lay in the Englishman's future. It was not for Stefano to make judgements on what was planned and would happen.

But – *but* – he had seen the Englishman talking with two men, an hour before a scheduled meeting, who were obviously foreign law enforcement. They had made no attempt to disguise themselves. He had sat beside Giulietta and felt her ... He wondered where they were now, where they were waiting. They'd have a long wait. The Englishman's phone, of course, was off and it had been Humphrey's job to guarantee that basic security procedure. He pointed again to his watch – twenty minutes more on the road. He needed now to have his headlights on and the sole excitement of the journey – other than the bends and cliff faces – was a small deer rushing into the road and freezing in the headlights, then sprinting into the trees. When he pointed to the hands of his watch, he fastened his smile on the Englishman.

He saw the belt buckle, quite heavy, ornate. He saw the teeth and wondered how many were artificial. He saw the length of the fingernails.

The belt would come off – it was usually necessary – and then the Englishman's trousers would drop but that would not be important. Teeth were always a problem – few of Stefano's were his own but he was well looked after financially and the artificial ones were comfortable. Natural teeth were a problem because they didn't degrade. Neither did fingernails. Otherwise, little remained to be shovelled up and buried. He laughed. The Englishman looked sharply at him. There had been a man near to Cosenza, a businessman who had defrauded a significant *padrino*. The businessman, elderly and arthritic, had had hip-replacement surgery to regain his mobility and the metal – of course – had survived. It had been dangerous to retrieve it afterwards: not willingly given up by the pigs. Men always laughed when it was mentioned over shots of coffee.

Word would seep out. A very few would know. Neither Stefano's nor the Englishman's name would feature. But among the 'very few' Bernardo's prestige would be enhanced – as if that were important.

He laughed again. They were high in the mountains, on a plateau, with pine trees close to the road. He steered between deep ruts and potholes, and saw no other vehicle. Stefano thought the man ignorant – but that would make it easier when the time came.

Giulietta's devotion to the word of God might have matched that of Father Demetrio but did not compare with her mother's.

She had never been to a service conducted at the Duomo in Reggio. The cathedral was the largest house of God in the region. She found it neither enticing nor attractive – it had gone up hurriedly after the great earthquake. Because her target had led her there, Giulietta – on side lights and unnoticed – double-parked fifty metres from the priest's car. He had looked around him, seemingly anxious, maybe imagining himself already a fugitive. He had put money into the hand of a thin elderly parking attendant, a meagre gratuity, no doubt. The man who had baptised her had once been overheard to describe her as 'a sad creature, trapped by that facial aberration'. When Giulietta needed to leave the HiLux, with the distinctive dented front bumper, she would drop a twenty-euro note into his hand and hold a handkerchief across her face to hide her nose.

Her telephone, switched off, lay in her handbag. The Beretta pistol was under her thigh, hurting her flesh. She might leave him alive overnight if the opportunity to take him down didn't present itself, or until after he had conducted the funeral mass for her nephew. On the other hand, she might end his life in the next few minutes. She smoked. It was risky to light a cigarillo – she must not discard it in a gutter, thereby giving a chance to the forensics technicians, who would search for DNA traces – but she needed to smoke. It relaxed her.

He had gone to a side entrance, a discreet one, not used by the cathedral's flock, and rung a bell.

A man, tall and austere, had opened the heavy door for him. And that man, a fool, told Giulietta all she might need to know. The man glanced sharply to the right, to the left, then straight out into the poorly lit parking area. Then his arm went round Father Demetrio's shoulders and he was brought inside. The priest was not there to discuss a set of hymn books for the village school or the service to celebrate the next commemoration of the patron saint, Francis of Paola. It was an entry of stealth and guilt.

She waited.

'That's what I know.'

Two heads close together, almost touching.

'I cannot, Demetrio, make up your mind for you.'

A choir of children were practising without accompaniment, guided by the master.

'I've harboured the guilt for too many years.'

They were in a darkened corner of the cathedral, where few candles burned. 'You didn't have to come to me. You know the words of the Holy Father. "Blood-stained money, blood-stained power, you can't take it with you into the next life." That was what he said to the mafia leaders.'

They sat on hard seats, hunched.

'I'm getting old and want to leave this world in peace.'

'You must follow, Demetrio, the road that is clear to you. Conscience cannot be manipulated for convenience. The Holy Father also said, "Repent. There is still time not to end up in Hell, which is what awaits you if you continue on this path." His message was unequivocal.'

'A prosecutor at the Palace of Justice is investigating this family.'

'Don't ask me to be your messenger, Demetrio.'

'To see him would be a mockery of my whole professional life as a servant of God, a friend of that family. I believe I have little time.'

'Is your health not good, Demetrio?'

He could have mentioned then that he had almost been driven off the road. Had the tyres lost purchase, gone over the edge, there would have been a drop of forty or fifty metres into a dry riverbed. He supposed he had come to the cathedral to see a man he had known for many years – he was not a close friend – and had hoped his resolve would be strengthened.

'I'm reasonably well. Thank you for your support. I hope I have enough time.'

'Because of your unique position in relation to this clan, would you consider, Demetrio, an anonymous denunciation? An alternative if your courage fails you.' You might also consider the wider implications.

'No.'

'You would be aware of the potential for the embarrassment of the Holy Church, should a priest be required to testify in the *aula bunker* and be associated with a matter so sordid. Ponder the difficulty the Church might have to confront. Yes?'

'I'm grateful for your wisdom.'

'You'll consider it, then?'

He thought they would work late at the Palace each evening. The newspapers reported that they were always at their desks. He had looked up the number before leaving and would announce himself before he reached the building. He thought he had been offered an unworthy escape from responsibility and responded in time-honoured fashion. He squeezed the man's arm, a gesture redolent of comradeship and understanding. Demetrio was rewarded with a smile of complicity. Their cheeks brushed. It would be believed, as he left, that he would write a letter but not sign it, then post it, having wiped the paper and envelope to remove his fingerprints. He was told he was brave, that one day his courage might be known to a wider audience and that it was the task of all citizens to fight the evil of criminal conspiracy. He was asked if he would now drive back to the village, cross the range of mountains and prepare himself for the funeral mass in the morning. He smiled, turned and was gone.

His shoes clattered on the flagstones and he crossed the three great central naves, ducking his head before the principal altar. There, he crossed himself and went out through the door.

Near to the parked car, he made a call. He said whom he wished to speak to, and on what matter, then rang off. A great tiredness afflicted him, and fear.

'Is there a rhinoceros here?' Fred asked.

They were at the roadblock. The fire in the drum burned ahead of them. They could see the men's cigarettes glowing and some-times heard their voices. The lights of the house were up the hill before the wall of darkness that was the foothills of the mountains.

Carlo answered, 'I don't think so.'

A *carabinieri* van with women officers had come for Consolata. They'd brought a rucksack of assorted clothing and underwear, uncertain as to what would fit. She'd dressed in the back of the van – the women had put newspaper up on the windows.

'You cannot say for definite that there's no rhinoceros.'

'There is no rhinoceros here. I can say it with complete certainty. I am with Mr Russell and your German is a fantasist.'

From inside the vehicle she would have seen and remembered them. The clothing loaned her was too big, which seemed unim-portant. Now she peered at them – they were in front of the headlights. It was an intense stare, but she asked nothing. She would have had a list of questions: who was he? Why was he there? Who was controlling him? Neither Fred nor Carlo could have answered because as yet they had no idea of what motivated Jago Browne.

'You will not, Carlo, have heard of Ludwig Wittgenstein, a great thinker, a German. He argued with your Bertrand Russell, a British philosopher and a man of high intelligence. Was there a rhinoceros in the room? Russell said there was no rhinoceros in the room, but Wittgenstein would not admit to its absence. Russell searched the room, looked under the table, moved the chairs, but the German refused to accept the absence of the rhinoceros. It could be there, but not seen. Two fine men, blessed with huge reservoirs of intelligence, and that was the area of their dispute. I side with Wittgenstein.'

While she had dressed, Carlo had murmured to him that she'd have been more useful to her protest cronies if she'd had herself murdered, or at least maimed. 'Walking down the road stark naked is hardly the stuff of martyrs.' He had not disagreed.

'Where is the rhinoceros?'

'Behind the sheets. Would your mother have left out washing for that long, allowed it to dry until it's as stiff as a board?'

She had been driven away. He doubted, poor kid, that her ordeal would be kept secret for long. He hadn't seen a flash, but one of the men ahead would have a camera phone – any picture taken would go viral. He thought her brave, endowed with a rare nobility. The other girl, the one coming out of the hospital with stitches in her cheek, had had that stubborn defiance – and she'd have thought them two old men who'd lost the taste of the fight. She might have been right.

'My mother would not. She filled the backyard with sheets at dawn and shifted them at dusk. If it rained they were dried in front of the fire.'

'The rhinoceros is behind the sheets.'

'I'm not arguing.'

'It's staring us in the face.'

The moon was not yet up. The house would have been more than three hundred metres from them. He went to the *maresciallo* and asked to borrow his binoculars. He focused and peered, his eyes aching from the effort. He thought he could see the sheets. They masked a hideaway – he would have bet his shirt on it. He did not gamble – against his morals and his religion.

He turned to Carlo. 'Do we go with this?'

'Yes.'

'We're not looking for medals.'

'No medals, no citations, just a glass of beer.'

Fred went to the *maresciallo* and gave back the binoculars. It would be the young Italian's call. He explained briefly, handed over evidence and intuition. His face was studied hard, a search mounted for certainty. Fred had total confidence. It had been there in front of them, had beckoned them and been ignored. It was the elephant, the rhinoceros or the giraffe in the room. Big decision for the young man. He could fall on his arse or end up with the smell of roses in his armpits.

The *maresciallo* used his phone, had the secure link.

Women walked past them, all in black. Their fingers had pulled off the girl's clothing. Now they made no contact. They were going back to the village – Carlo, Fred and the uniforms might not have been there. They went on into the gathering night, with the shuffle of flat shoes on the track and little trills of laughter.

Carlo whispered, 'Watch this space, ladies.'

He was Bentley Horrocks, a man of status.

The vehicle was parked, and the driver – a fucking peasant – reached across him to unfasten the door and pushed it open. He gave that dumb smile. Bent stepped out, straightened his back and stretched. There wasn't much to see. They were off the metalled road, and had come up a track, passing a field with two rusted tractors and a collapsed cart. The air was cooler than it had been on the coast and a wind riffled his hair. Then the smell was in his nostrils.

A farmhouse stood in front of them. He assumed it was a farmhouse – a bungalow, built with cement blocks, no rendering or paint to finish the job. His home, the country one, a farmhouse in rural Kent, had half a dozen bedrooms, a tennis court, a swimming-pool and a few acres. It would fetch three or four million. And no one was there to meet him. He'd expected a big car and another for the goons to be waiting, and the main man to be there to welcome him. The smell was vile – it wouldn't have been tolerated in the part of Kent where his place was.

Bent snapped his fingers. It was what he would have done in a restaurant if the owner was slow with the drinks or the menus. He snapped them and shrugged – a 'What the fuck's going on?' gesture. The peasant grinned. There was the smell of animal shit, then the sound of them grunting, whatever pigs did.

Men came forward. Torches shone into his face.

Half a dozen men. One goon would come forward, do a fast frisk for a weapon or a wire, then the big fellow would walk out of the shadows and there'd be a handshake, maybe a kiss because it was that part of the world. The Turks liked a kiss, as did the Albanians. He tried to look confident. Always said, Bent did, and Jack would echo it, that the first responses were the ones that mattered. Going to do business with a man, a stranger, about to talk over four or five million euros' worth of stuff, and it was necessary to show you weren't fazed, took it in the stride . . . had gotten it wrong.

It was difficult for him to see properly because the torch beams were shining at him. No one welcomed him. He looked for the little fucker – the peasant – but couldn't see him. He'd seen two faces, never seen them before, at the front of the hotel, smiling through the introductions, in broad daylight where the rest of the fucking world could see . . . He could smell the pigs and hear them.

The men behind him did the pinioning. Something round his arms, then his wrists. The necessary violence to control him, but nothing more.

He started to kick out – waste of fucking effort. And started to shout – waste of fucking breath.

They hadn't bothered to hood him, or to stuff his mouth so he couldn't yell. Not one man reacted to his shouts. He would have started to jabber – in English, because he had nothing else – about what he could pay. How much his life was worth. Jewels, cash, bullion. More light blinded him, and he realised the headlights of the City-Van were full on him as the peasant drove past him, seeming not to notice him, and went off the way they had come. Then he was left with the torches and they took him forward. They brought him closer to the pigs' pen, which had a low wall round it, more cement blocks. The heads came up and one man stood beside the pen and poked at them with a stick, goading them. He would have angered and hurt them.

He wondered if Jack had known. Too fucking right the lawyer had known. Everyone had known, except Bentley Horrocks.

Only at the end did he shriek. He heard himself. He tried to thrash around and free himself but they were lifting him, like he was a bloody kid. He could hear the pigs and the frenzy of grunting. He was over the wall and, for a moment, they held him up, then dropped him. He saw nothing else, but the smell was with him, and the noise, and the pain.

Humphrey drove and didn't make conversation. Jack had nothing to say.

The radio was turned up loud, which was useful because they couldn't talk over it. Jack sat in the passenger seat and imagined unpleasant scenarios. They centred on whom he would have to provide with explanations as to why he had come home early and left Bent, his boss, to travel alone. Not much wriggle room, and he had Bent's bag with him, and the phones. There might be a problem over why he was carrying Bent's passports. He'd come up with one solution to his anxieties. He'd make sure that Bent's passports and phones stayed in the lawyer's car. Not quite sure yet where he would stuff them, but they'd be there. If it got nasty, and he ended up in an interview room at Old Street, then Humphrey's name would be bouncing off the walls all the time the recorder was doing its job.

They were onto the main road, dual carriageway, the really good earner for the Calabrian clans, all done with Brussels cash, among camper wagons and loaded cars. It was the fag end of the season. He wondered where Bent was, what they'd prepared for him, and if anything of him would ever be seen again. There'd be serious fighting round Peckham, Deptford and Rotherhithe when it became known that Bentley Horrocks was off his manor, not expected back, and some tidy little interests were going begging. He'd have to keep his head down while the territory was carved up. And detectives in the Crime Squad would be going short of the cash in the brown envelopes. Trace was about the only one who wouldn't blink, would just get a replacement and carry on, nice girl, not unintelligent. He'd never been accused of being *fond* of Bentley Horrocks, but Jack shivered a little, even in the heated car, at the thought of what they might have done with him.

As people often said, 'Some you win and some you lose.' Jack thought it a tidy old loss, but said nothing.

Giulietta had a good view of Father Demetrio. The village priest walked backwards and forwards, agitated. He had made just the one call, then had set off on the tramp that took him again and again round the car park. Twice he was nearly run down by motorists leaving. Once he had hopped back, and the other time the driver had hammered his horn at him. He smoked all the time, and lit each new cigarette from the end of the old one. When he was nearest to her she'd thought he was shaken. His eyes were staring at nothing. He would lead her. She would follow. To wherever.

The files were spread across his carpet. The prosecutor, on hands and knees, was in front of them. The cupboard was wide open and part of a shelf was empty. Now he pored over them. He had been working that afternoon and into the evening on new challenges, new targets, trying to ease the burden of a failed investigation, to move on. His coat had been hitched over his shoulders, his bag in his hand, and he had made the call to his wife that he was leaving – yes, he was, truthfully, he'd be home in a quarter of an hour – and the phone had rung. He could have let it ring and ignored it.

The escort boys had been on their feet, their magazines dumped in the chairs, radios at their ears, weapons at their hips. They would have thought themselves blessed that their principal's attention was diverted from failure. But he had turned and gone back in. He had heard a stammering, hesitant voice, words that spewed with a degree of incoherence. A name had been given – and the trumpets had blasted recognition – the location of the *padrino* and of his *cosca*, the place where he was hiding, and the *soffiato* was on his way, driving to the Palace of Justice. The call had been cut. What was the informant's name? Not given. What make of car was he coming in? Registration? No time to ask. He was no longer going home. He asked if two would go down to the main lobby. A car was on its way – unidentified. The driver would park, walk to Reception and ask for the prosecutor by name. He was to be brought to the office.

He went over the old files so that he could control an interview. The walk-ins were always the best. To turn a criminal, make him a *pentito*, was seldom satisfactory. But when a man came to the door, asked to come in, was willing to talk and lay his life on the line, he was a rare treasure.

He demanded fresh coffee. The leader of his team would telephone his wife and make the excuses.

They were out of their hide, with the canvas kitbags, the rucksacks and the plastic rubbish bag. It was dark and Fabio had the lenses over his eyes, which gave a watery image of what lay ahead. They were held by the sounds, wasted effort to fathom their source or what they meant.

The dogs patrolled at the door restlessly, the kid sat on the hard chair, listening, and Mamma had come to the door every three or four minutes, looked up the path past the sheets, then turned away. They had gear for enhancing sound but that was packed away now and neither had the inclination to root in the bags for it. They were ready to go. For them Scorpion Fly was over, but they hesitated.

Ciccio said it was the television. It was a muffled noise, faint, maybe distant shouting, or perhaps a poor soundtrack on whatever programme was on. They wanted out. It was always difficult to walk away from failure, but it wasn't the first time and wouldn't be the last. Both were more familiar with failure than success.

Fabio slapped Ciccio's arm. Enough. They had authorisation to quit. Ciccio nodded. He punched in the code and was poised to transmit. A message on the screen blocked his own. *Maintain location. Observe and report.*

They went back to the entrance to their shallow hole, lay down and seethed.

Carlo watched the *maresciallo*. A little fellow, unlike most of the unit. He lacked their physique, and his spectacles were high magnification. He was giving someone serious stick on the phone. Carlo had the impression that he was being fobbed off. They'd all experienced it: the greatest revelation ever in law enforcement came into a control room, but the bastards were all too busy, or hadn't the sense, to react. He wasn't winning.

'I can tell you where the fugitive is lying up. Have I seen him? No, I have not. Have I a direct informant? No. What I have are my eyes and my instinct. Isn't that good enough?'

No. The phone was snapped off. The little guy came to them. They had new information at the Palace of Justice. An informant was coming in. The *maresciallo* was surplus to requirements.

'Their privilege,' Carlo said. 'We'll see what shows. That's where the *padrino* is, don't doubt it.'

He had fallen over. His head had caught on the table where the TV sat. Blood ran from his nose. He hadn't found the torch, the matches or the candles. The nightmare played out. When he had been with the other older men Bernardo had shown, he thought, composure and dignity in the face of disaster. The loss of his heir had weakened him, left him adrift. He had met their eyes as they observed him, searching for signs of a loss of willpower. Not now.

He howled. He had found the door and tried to open it, but had failed. He was trapped, like a man laid in a coffin who recovers his senses and can hear the blows as the lid is nailed down but cannot move or make himself heard. He was on the floor, on thin carpet, and he screamed towards the ceiling. Nobody was listening and his voice was hoarse. Mamma wouldn't come – she never did. Stefano would, but he'd gone to the place where the pigs were bred. Giulietta was tracking the priest, the bastard Demetrio, whom he had identified as a traitor. The kid, who was around the house, did not know the workings of the bunker. Marcantonio did, but he was cold in a box on trestles. His nose bled freely. The shouts had become a scream. An old man's call, pathetic.

No one came. He couldn't see his hand. When he moved he hit himself. Each movement seemed to Bernardo to show his growing weakness.

When the child had been in the cave, at the start, they had left a candle to burn during the night in a jar that had once held jam. They had come one morning and it had toppled over. The flame had scorched part of the bedding. If it had caught seriously alight, the child might have been burned alive. She could not have escaped from the flames because the chain secured her leg to the wall at the back of the cave. They had not lit it again. The child had been left in darkness. It would have been the same total darkness in the cave as it was now in the converted container. No glow from distant streetlights or car headlights. No light. The child would have cowered on the bedding they'd brought her. He was as frightened as the child would have been.

He had watched on the television in the kitchen – many years before – a programme made by the RAI featuring the 'kidnap industry', as they had called it. The parents had been interviewed. The father had said a few words, tears streaming down his face, but the mother had cursed him: the money had been paid six months or more after the child had been buried on the hillside, higher than the cave. The mother had hurled abuse at them because the money had been paid and the child had not been returned. Then he had been unmoved by her voice. All had changed now.

His voice was failing so his cries were weaker. No one came. He went unheard. The blood dribbled from his nose and he lay on the floor.

It involved a man he had never met. Jago Browne thought he knew how it would play out. He felt strong.

There had been shouting and Jago assumed there was a vent near to him, for fresh air, that the noises from inside the bunker were funnelled up to him. They had started as inconsistent, deep-pitched yells, part impatience and growing annoyance. Later they had become angry, aggressive, but with an element of self-control. Last, the breakdown: screams and what he thought might be whimpers. Jago had felt good. He had thought himself close to achieving his objective. Now there was no sound.

He would stay long enough to see him.

The climax would come when he looked into the eyes of the man, whose chin would shake. He did not think himself in danger, did not consider that he had been there too long, putting his life at risk.

Jago had folded the coat and sat on it, making himself as comfortable as possible, hidden on the rock. He didn't know how long he would have to wait, and didn't particularly care. His mission was in its last hours. That he knew.

19

Something to watch, at last, other than the chickens.

The lights were feeble in front of the house, but headlights approached and threw a fiercer beam. Jago saw it from his vantage point – it was a while now since he had last heard the distant sounds of yelling, then crying. The dogs bounded round the side of the house and the kid strolled after them, smoking. Jago noted that some of the men from down the track had moved closer to the house. The handyman parked the car and killed the engine. He called the kid and dismissed him.

It was nearly over. Jago wanted to put a living face to the photograph he held in his mind. He wanted to see the man collapse, and be able to tell himself that *his* work had achieved it. He cut out the role of the girl in Charlottenburg and on the beach in the moonlight. *He* had done it.

This was his territory. He didn't know anywhere else as well as he knew the narrow panorama in front of him. Not the street in front of the one-parent family home in Canning Town, not the walk from the bus stop in Barking Road, or the stretch from St Paul's Underground station to a tower block in the City. The hike to the bank in inner Berlin was already a faded glimpse. He knew everything about this place. He had absorbed each sprouted shrub in the apology for a garden, the trees and grass. He knew how many paving slabs made up the patio and how many struts held the hard chair's legs in place. He knew the volume of the grapes on the trellis, the colours of the dogs' coats and their pecking order. He could smell what they cooked in the kitchen. He could assess the old woman's hip or pelvic problems. He knew the range of the sheets used on a bed in the house. He felt a sense of belonging to this place, was reluctant to leave it . . . and the time had run its course. Like a curtain coming down. People walked urban streets often enough to know where they could stand, see into a lit window, watch the life of a family with children and become a part of it in loneliness. Jago hated the thought of leaving. Here he viewed extreme power and excessive wealth.

The kid came back with a steaming bucket and cloths. He had an extension lead, too, which ran from an outside power point, and a vacuum cleaner. Under the older man's direction, he was to clean the City-Van. It might have been fifteen years old, Jago thought, and they worked hard. It was easy enough for the one-time banker to fathom. The vehicle was being cleansed of clues left by a passenger sitting in the front. A murder – not a wounding or an assault. The handyman had been the driver and Jago saw nothing different in his bearing from the other times he had seen him. It shouted at him that a killing was no big deal and was rounded off with a methodical car wash. He watched it all, and waited. He should have been on his way up to the road.

They were thorough. The bag from the vacuum cleaner went into the incinerator at the back, and sparks flared up. The interior surfaces were washed carefully, the cloths frequently rinsed. The water went down a drain. Then, the kid was sent for a hosepipe, which was plugged into a tap on the patio. The wheels were jet-sprayed. There would have been evidence on them of where the City-Van had been driven to and from. Jago wondered how often they needed to clean the vehicle, and why a man with the affluence of the *padrino*, and the authority, denied himself a better set of wheels. He had much to learn, but the course was nearly run.

He thought, when the work was done, that the handyman might be sent to bring the family leader out from his hole. He wanted to see it and would hold his position until he did.

He'd have to wait longer. The old woman had come out of the front door with a scrap of paper. The kid had gone to feed the dogs.

There was a moment when the handyman and the old woman were together. Jago saw it. A little gesture – fingers on an arm. He hadn't seen it before. A girl from Sales might have stayed in the pub with a guy from Investments after the others had left. The next morning the gestures and the eye contact would tell the story: his place or hers. Everyone knew. He'd learned more about the family and their home – the handyman and the wife of the *padrino*. They'd taken a massive risk.

He thought she had given the handyman a short shopping list. Now he drove away to fetch what was wanted, which meant he would not go into the bunker yet. Jago had to wait, but could revel in imagining the degree of torture he had inflicted.

He had given up.

His father never had. He had fought right up to the moment when they had taken his life in the open-air market. His uncles had been fighters, too, and his brothers – one knifed in gaol, the other bound and thrown into a ravine – would have struggled until they had drawn their last breath. In their own ways, his sons in their northern gaols would fight to maintain their pride. They would never capitulate. Bernardo almost did.

No one saw it. When men looked at him they assessed his strength by his posture, whether his hands shook as tension mounted, if he blinked too much. The men with him at the vigil beside his grandson's coffin would have watched him to see if he had a grip on his future.

Now he was not watched. He was not seen or heard. Bernardo didn't know if anyone would come soon or whether they would leave him until morning.

He was on the floor. Each time he moved he hurt himself. He had found a chair and lifted himself up but the chair had turned over under his weight and he had cracked his head. He had groped to the side of the container, close to the sink. He had taken hold of it and was dragging himself up, but his hands had shifted and one had landed on the soap – scented stuff that Teresa had bought. He had toppled, twisting his knee.

He could make no sound other than a croak. His sense of combat was gone because he couldn't imagine which enemy faced him. He felt abandoned. He did not know where Mamma, Stefano and Giulietta were. He wallowed in self-pity and the darkness wrapped around him. He hurt himself each time he tried to move. He lay still, his strength dribbling away. He waited, as the child in the cave had waited. Everything that Bernardo was, all that he had achieved in power and wealth, was off the back of that child who had been in darkness.

No one came.

The Palace of Justice was lit. Floodlights bathed the high walls. More shone over the wide car park. But it was evening and the majority of those who worked in the justice system had gone home or to restaurants. Two SUVs in army camouflage stood in one corner and a knot of troops huddled close to them, automatic weapons slung on their chests or handguns in holsters.

Walking forward briskly, Giulietta held the Beretta close to her thigh. She hadn't fired at a man before. She was accurate in target practice – against bottles, cans or a ripe melon – which would explode dramatically. She had followed the car into the parking area and it suited her that he had stopped in shadow. There were trees among the marked parking spaces that provided good cover. She had seen him get out of the car, not bothering to flash his keys at it. Then he had wavered and lit a cigarette. That he had brought her there confirmed her father's suspicion. Beyond him men lounged at the main doors. She sensed they had been alerted and were there to meet a new prize. He would soon, a few more paces, be within their orbit. She closed on him.

She had left her keys in the HiLux and the engine idled softly behind her.

He was under trees, about to enter a row of empty bays where the light fell brightly. Giulietta did not dither: a job to be done. She lifted her headscarf to cover her nose, mouth and chin. She called his name softly. 'Father Demetrio, a moment, please.'

He stopped. Turned. She saw his ravaged features. He might have forgotten himself and noted that, at a Calvary moment, he could see a familiar face, which smiled warmth at him. He gave her enough time. A full second, two seconds, no more. Realisation was coming but his brain worked faster than his limbs. She had the pistol up. He had two options: he could spin and run for his life or charge her, arms swinging, and try to knock the pistol aside. She saw only something craven. It was just a few days since he had been an honoured guest at her mother's birthday celebration, the lone outsider. She loved her father, mourned his ageing, but believed in his judgement. The man before her had headed from the cathedral to the Palace of Justice, and was expected. He was statue still, and seemed to plead with his eyes.

As Stefano had taught her, Giulietta did the Isosceles stance. She knew the Weaver stance and the Chapman, but had always preferred Isosceles. Feet apart, knees fractionally bent, weight forward, her arms were outstretched, her right hand held the butt and her index finger was beside the trigger's guard. Her left fist was locked across the right and held it steady. One in the breach and safety off.

She had known Father Demetrio all of her life. He had lectured her on the Church's teachings, had heard her teenage confessions, and she had walked behind him in saints' days' processions through the village. It was thought he favoured her because of his friendship with her father. Old friendships, past kindnesses were of little value. Her finger groped for, then found, the trigger.

She thought, in the last moment of his life, that he still did not believe what confronted him. His chin shook and his throat wobbled, as if words were blocked there. The men behind him at the door had looked around but not seen him. They were beside the main entrance to the parking area.

She fired.

Better, of course, if the weapon had been fitted with a silencer, but it was not. The second shot was immediate. Not chest shots, when a man might be saved by the immediate skill of a surgeon practised in dealing with bullet wounds, but the head. There would be several medics at the Ospedale Riuniti in the city who were used to handling gunshot injuries. Two shots to the head, so fast that it barely had time to sag and she had not needed to adjust her aim. The recoil was hard on her rigid arms and spent itself in her shoulders. The smell was in her nostrils. He slumped.

She crouched, looked for and found the shiny cartridge cases ejected from the Beretta, picked them up and dropped them into her pocket. A plastic bag would have been better: her good suit trousers, from the new mall outside Locri on the Siderno road, were contaminated now, as was her top. She noted that blood trickled from his head, and that there were no convulsions nor gasped breathing.

She thought it had been easy, but she did not feel elated or excited. A job had been satisfactorily completed. She had to step over him – a wide stride because of his size and she had to avoid the blood.

Rifles and handguns were armed. She heard shouts. Inside the HiLux, she jammed it into gear, then swung into the oleanders, planted to separate the rows of bays, bumped over them and reached the far side of the parking area. She used an emergency entrance, designed for fast access to ambulances or police vehicles, and was gone.

Giulietta might have congratulated herself, but did not. She went into the city and cut down onto Corso Vittorio Emanuele. She thought she had left chaos behind her, which was good, and with it stark confusion, which was better. She wanted to get home and tell her father what she had achieved. She wanted to see his smile spread, feel his hand on her shoulder or cheek. He never looked at her nose or spoke of it. She heard sirens but they were far away. She felt confident because the Blocker spray, purchased in Locri, would reflect off the registration plates and disable any cameras efforts. Giulietta accelerated. She thought her father would be proud of her and praise her.

Pandemonium spread clumsily at the Palace of Justice. The police, *carabinieri*, soldiers and the prosecutor's escorts, who had waited at the door, were hit by the depth of the failure.

The medical team came, and the blame game began before the body was cold. Whose fault was it? Everyone's, except each accuser's. Some claimed to have seen the taillights disappearing and there were CCTV cameras. How many were working? Some. There would be a few images. They would show a woman with a face mask and a handgun, a HiLux but the registration would have been tampered with to prevent the number being read. There had been hopeless efforts to revive the victim. It was agreed that the assassin had been trained, expert and was formidable. The priest was identified from his wallet. One of the escorts made the call on his mobile to the office high in the Palace.

He came, ashen-faced. The prosecutor had dared to hope. All he had been told in the priest's phone call was his name and his village, which had been enough to whet the appetite of a starving man. His joy had been huge, but short-lived. The ambulance had arrived. He had been promised that roadblocks were in place around the city on all principal routes to north and south, and on the main road heading up into the mountains. Useless. Why? Myriad routes led from the outskirts of Reggio towards the high villages of the Aspromonte.

When he arrived beside the body, the recriminations ceased. A man of dignity, wedded to his work, had been dealt a crushing blow. He was handed the contents of the pockets and a phone, and saw that the last call made was to himself. It was the nature of his work: the Lord in his wisdom gave and the same Lord with the same wisdom took. The flashes were from the photographer. The forensics and scenes-of-crime people were impatient to collect what was left in the way of evidence that had not been trampled over. The prosecutor saw, under arc lights, the face of the priest. The colour had drained from it and the jowl hung slack. He reflected that death had not treated the corpse kindly. He had not met but had known of him, and would have regarded him as one of the professionals who wormed close to the families and facilitated respectability.

His guards hovered close to him. The phone vibrated in his shirt pocket. They closed round him, feeling his frustration. He noted the number, answered it, then listened to what he was told from the control room. He thought himself a man who clutched at dreams. It was a calm voice, without the emotion of the chase, and he could gain no impression of whether he was offered a good chance, an average chance, or a chance with no provenance. He was told of a young man of above average intelligence, but of junior rank and limited experience. He could have demanded answers to a cascade of questions. He stood within two or three metres of the body of the priest, who might have resurrected an investigation and had been silenced. He was nudged aside and the ambulance team began to heave the cadaver onto a gurney. He thought one question important.

'Is he sure?'

Carlo said, 'What you have to understand, Luca, is that – to quote – 'There is a tide in the affairs of men . . .' You have to jump on it and ride the wave up the beach. Know what I mean?'

Fred said, 'It was their beloved Shakespeare, writing about Rome, and it is from one of Caesar's killers, from Brutus, "Omitted, all the voyage of their life is bound in shallows and in miseries". In other words, don't think me impertinent, you get off your arse and get on with it or spend a long time regretting the inaction. Are you with me, Luca?'

Luca, the *maresciallo*, shrugged, betraying nervousness. 'I take a huge chance. I was very definite. Apparently the prosecutor was about to receive the priest from the village. He was walking across the car park at the Palace of Justice, and had requested a meeting. A confession? What else? He was shot dead. The killer escaped and the chance was lost. He was told what I said. He tries to grasp it, the last throw. He asked Control one question, about me. 'Is he sure?' Am I sure, Carlo, Fred? They'll flay me if my intuition falls short.'

Carlo said, 'You'll be good, Luca, and you're riding with the A Team, the best.' Then, shit, do I believe that? A confident blow on the back followed.

Fred said, 'It'll take you onwards and upwards, Luca, and when you're at the top you'll remember two old men who gave you a push in the right direction.' He thought that if it failed, and the line of the sheets was irrelevant, he and Carlo would be long gone, not facing the brickbats. He clasped the *maresciallo*'s arm and squeezed confidence into it.

A helicopter was tasked. The *cacciatore* would be deployed, and the local *carabinieri* would have a role. A senior prosecutor was coming from Reggio, and there would be tracker dogs. The *maresciallo* had said it was the last chance. It was Carlo's work, and Fred's. They had opened their mouths, woven a skein of trust and now had to wait.

The clerk sat in his office, but only the observant would have noticed his door was not quite shut. He worked on expenses claimed, and was often late at his desk. It was assumed by those who dealt with him that he was deaf because he wore a hearing aid. He often reflected that much of critical sensitivity was said between men hurrying across the lobby. He heard the prosecutor come back to his office and rap out the combination on the door lock. Then he had held a staccato conversation with the leader of his escort: how long would the Bell Agusta take to be readied, then to fly to the location, and how long it would take for the prosecutor to be driven there? He heard it all; as he had heard much over many months.

He would need to wait until the building quietened, feet no longer sounding on the staircase. His attention seemed locked on his screen and the lists of items for which staff charged. The clerk received little reward for his work. The family paid him only five hundred euros a month, but it was never late; whether he had information or nothing to report, the envelope turned up without fail. He gave it to his wife, who sent it by registered post to an aunt in the Friuli district of the north-east, and she banked it. The money lay untouched in the account.

Hatred governed him. He was poorly treated at the Palace, regarded as incompetent and useless, good only for filling in the electronic ledger, nothing else. He could recite the date and the hour at which each perceived insult had been lobbed at him. If any had suggested that greed motivated him, he would have denied it. Such an accusation would be made only in a police cell, or an

interview room when disgust confronted him. The risk he took
was invigorating. The staircase was quiet. He used his phone to
call a friend in a coastal town south of Pellaro. He dictated a
message, succinct and clear.

It was the first leg of the cut-off calls. Four more would be
needed before the message reached a destination.

A girl came to the checkpoint.

She would have seen Carlo, Fred and the young *maresciallo*,
who paced and smoked. She was a teenager and rode an old
scooter. She had come up from the village, with a packet of Rizla
cigarette papers in her pocket. The message was in a code of old
dialect words. She was waved through. Why should she not be?
Stefano came after her and had to produce identity papers, then
was permitted to pass. Control's instruction was that the community close to the family should not be alerted by a new level of
security: calm must prevail.

The girl on the scooter, followed by the City-Van, reached the
second block. Everyone knew from the radio that there had been
a fatal shooting at the Palace of Justice and that the corpse had
been identified as Father Demetrio, their priest. He was not
mourned. Had he been alive, the men beside the oil drum would
have ducked their heads in his presence, but he was dead. More
activity: Giulietta had returned, driven by Teresa, Stefano had
been to the mini-mart, and Giulietta had shopping bags.

Beyond the block, short of the house, Giulietta was shown the
message that covered one side of a single cigarette paper. She gave
no sign of thinking it important and went inside through the front
door. Stefano knew his place and went with his bag to the kitchen
door. All appeared normal in their lives – and nothing was as it
seemed.

He had a good view of her. She came out with the handyman, and
the old woman hovered by the kitchen door. Jago thought the
entertainment had begun.

He felt the excitement he'd known as a child when he was taken to see a film or to a show in the West End, the anticipation of hearing an orchestra tuning or sitting forward as the lights dimmed.

The old woman held some clothes while the handyman had a newspaper and a small plastic container for petrol. Giulietta kicked off her shoes, then dropped her suit trousers – her legs were pale, not browned by the sun – and snatched the pair of jeans her mother held out to her. She had on a different blouse from the one she'd worn when coming to the front of the house. There was no panic, but she was quick, which told Jago that time was short. He thought that traders could move fast when the markets needed a reaction, but didn't panic, not even at the cliff edge of a crash. They kept their cool, as did she. He didn't know why the clothes had to be destroyed. They went into the oil drum where the trash was incinerated, and the fuel was splashed on top. The women stood back as the handyman did the business with a spill of rolled paper and a match.

Jago's mind leaped – it wasn't too great a chasm to cross. Clothes for destruction had been in up-close-and-personal contact with a killing. The flames climbed higher. Easy for Jago to see that Giulietta had fastened her jeans and was ready to take the small pistol her mother offered. It went into her waistband. A car cleansed and clothing burned. Evidence of a murderous few hours, Jago thought.

Giulietta led; the handyman followed.

The old woman was back inside. The kid now loitered and the dogs picked up the mood, were poised, but didn't know where the threat lay. The grandson would still be in the coffin in the house – maybe the lid had been screwed down. Jago had seen Marcantonio's confidence, had watched him strut about, as if he thought it his right to do so. Now he was forgotten. She had control. Giulietta had sent her mother inside and the handyman was following in her wake, a bag carrier . . . She was behind the trellis now, and he saw the ripple of the sheets as she passed behind them.

A little light fell from the kitchen, a little more from the fire in the oil drum, a fraction of moonlight from between the trees. He saw her crouch and fiddle with something. She must have found a switch or a catch that was controlled by electricity. It had been pretty obvious to Jago that the doorway was electrically powered: logical because of the weight of the stones in the wall. She was scrabbling, and must have failed. She whistled. He knew the sound, had learned its pitch. It was the whistle the kid gave when he directed the dogs. The kid ran towards her, and she must have made a gesture he recognised but that Jago couldn't see. He sprinted behind the sheet, under cover of the trellis, and was lost. The dogs scampered about, confused. The television or radio was loud in the kitchen. She was still struggling, trying to use her weight to open the door. Stones had come loose from the wall and she scrabbled, like people did on news bulletins when there had been an earthquake and victims were buried. The kid came back.

Jago saw the hammer.

She belted at something. The handyman tried to push her aside and do the job himself. She wouldn't have it. She hit again. Her calm was replaced now with frantic hammering . . .

Stone-faced, pissed off, they were in their cave and had taken out the bare minimum of the kit they had packed. The messages on the screen had been pithy, unpleasant. For days they had been on top of the sheets hanging on the line, for days they'd had the view of part of a derelict shed's roof and of the ground where the chickens scratched. They had been upstaged by a *maresciallo* at a roadblock, who was two hundred and fifty metres back from them and claimed to have identified the bunker where the head of the clan had his refuge. They didn't know where the Englishman was. Now they could hear but not see. They could hear hammering, the wrenching of metal and stones landing on the ground, but they couldn't see what was happening.

Fabio had muttered, 'If that's where he is, they won't believe we had no idea of it. We'll be accused of collaboration.'

Ciccio had said, 'Life isn't fair. If it was, everyone would be a hero, not washed up, like we are.'

The hammering reached fever point.

*　　　*　　　*

She pulled. The door hatch creaked, shrieked and came loose.

There should have been lights in the tunnel but there was darkness. She told the kid what she wanted. He scuttled off to fetch it. She led into the hole and Stefano followed. She called her father, at first softly, then louder but there was no response. She was at the inner door and Stefano was jabbering in her ear about the mechanism, the power needed and the override. The kid was back. He seemed frightened to enter the tunnel – and had cause to be because he was privy now to the family's greatest secret – but Stefano turned on his haunches, spat an instruction and the kid rolled the torch down the tunnel. Stefano issued more orders and the kid fled.

Giulietta took the torch.

She had seen the small intimacies between Stefano and her mother. They might once have slept together, but long ago. She had wondered whether she might be the bastard daughter of the family's driver. She had taken comfort in the evidence that she was not. She was her father's. If she had not been his, he would have registered the signs and Stefano would have gone into the acid or down a cliff, been fed to the pigs or shot and left in a ditch. She was her father's and would fight with her life for him and— Stefano knew the catch better than she did. He used the reverse of the hammer end, inserted it behind a lever and broke it.

More darkness, and faint moaning. She snatched the torch.

Giulietta went through the entrance, dropped to the floor and found him. She shone the torch and saw the blood. She came only rarely to the bunker, which had been built by her brothers who had expected to use it for their own safety from arrest. She hated the place and the smell. She tried to block out the stench of old sweat, fresh blood and stale food. It was cold in there and damp. She saw where his nose had bled and more dark stains on his trouser leg. There were no lights and she had no idea why the system had failed – the power was on in the house. She remembered.

She lifted her father's head. He seemed not to recognise her – but she was his daughter. She slapped his face. It was a punishing blow, calculated. His head jerked back and anger soared in his eyes. She dragged him up.

She didn't tell him. It wouldn't help her father, as the minutes fled, to know that the English player, travelling with an escort of foreign police, was now inside the bellies of pigs, or that Father Demetrio would by now be on a mortuary slab. Neither did he need to know that a helicopter was flying at speed towards their village, carrying *cacciatore*, or that a prosecutor was being driven in an armoured limousine, hemmed around by his escort, along the mountain roads. She remembered.

Marcantonio's return: a story told of a *pizzo* collection in a fashionable corner of Berlin, the intervention of an *idiota*, and a girl's face cut. She remembered that Marcantonio's car had been scratched, then the City-Van – the vehicle was worthless but not the gesture. She remembered that Francesco, the village butcher, had picked up a tyre iron beside Marcantonio's body. She remembered that the power was off, leaving her father imprisoned in the dark without explanation. And she remembered the message from the Palace of Justice, the imminence of a raid, that they'd know where to search for him. She remembered it all.

Between them, they were able to get him to his feet, to the hatch, then into the tunnel. No time to collect anything. If she hadn't slapped him he would have been a dead weight. He had, in part, recovered. They dragged him down the tunnel, metre by metre, and she remembered all that had happened in the few short days since Marcantonio's return. She wondered who he was – and why.

There was one place she could go, just one. She had never made a judgement on the funds that had launched the family towards success, affluence and a position of respect among the leaders of the mountain villages and coastal towns. She had never asked questions or interrogated her father. There was only one place. She had found it a few days after her thirteenth birthday, had understood why the chain was there, with the bucket and the child's dress. The place had fascinated and hardened her. She had made no judgement on the long-ago death of a little girl, or on the killing of Annunziata and her lover, or on why men were fed to the pigs. She had made no judgement on killing the priest, who was the family's friend. They came out into the night and the torch was off. He had regained the use of his legs but his arm was over her shoulders. She hissed to Stefano what he should do.

The kid watched them go, the dogs beside him, and they seemed to hear – a long way off – the throb of a helicopter's engines.

The path went from the back of the building and climbed.

They came past Jago. The path was below but close to the rock he sat on.

They were two dark shapes, seeming joined at the hip and shoulder. She was supporting him. They had no torch so would barely have been able to make out the path and might have fallen off it. He heard the woman curse, and a moan from the man. Again he heard her voice, soothing now.

He knew it was them.

Jago couldn't see the face. He hadn't seen it when they'd come out of the hole in the wall. He had known where it would be and had focused on it, but the handyman had blocked his view at the critical moment. He had seen her – there had been a moment before the torch was doused when it played on her features. Calm, in control. Jago had seen the man's shoulders and then they had ducked to the side. He had not seen them again until they were almost upon him. The moan told him the punishment he'd inflicted. It was time to be gone. He knew each footstep he must take, each sharp escarpment he'd scramble up, and each sapling strong enough to bear his weight when he levered himself higher up the slope towards the road. There was the airline equivalent, out of Lamezia, of the milk train – they'd find a seat on it for him. He'd get to a bar on the road back to the west side of the peninsula and call Consolata. She'd meet him, and give him back the last of his possessions. It had not been Jago Browne's fault that she had been on the hill – she'd had no call to be there – had been found, driven down and stripped. He could not have intervened. He would call and she'd drive him to the airport. There was a way up the slope if he caught at the saplings above and used them to lever himself to the next level. He would go fast then and . . .

But Jago hadn't seen the face. He hadn't completed what he had promised he would do. He did not consider that madness governed him, or that he was a changed man from the one who had sat in a park, killing time, watching the death of a fly in a spider's web not a week ago. He had mapped the way out. He stretched, felt the stiffness in his joints, the tiredness in his legs and jumped off the rock. He sprawled on the path, then pushed himself to his feet.

They led him.

Jago understood where the refuge would be. He had been there. The path was overgrown and stones that had once been steps had slipped askew in rain torrents. There were places where trees had fallen and he had to crawl, steep banks to his right and a drop to a stream bed on his left. Years before – twenty, thirty or even forty – the path had been dug so that it could be used in daylight or at night, in summer or winter. They would have come at least once in every twenty-four hours to visit the child. The helicopter was louder, no longer a faint rumble in the night sky. They made more noise in front, which was good for Jago. He thought the girl had brought the old man as fast as he could manage, but they dared not use a torch and it would have been hard going for them. They were like the wolf, lost, vulnerable and hunted . . . At the bank they would have been on the way home, or already there, paying off the nanny and feeding children, working out in the gym, jogging along the circuits of the Tiergarten or shovelling bundles into a washing-machine. Or worrying whether an old woman had a good return on her investments and wondering what the bonus might be after a half-yearly assessment. None of them knew where he was or what he was doing.

The helicopter circled. Ahead, they went faster, needing the sanctuary of the cave. Any teenager from Canning Town knew what gear was slung underneath a police helicopter. After thieving or a mugging, they knew the helicopter would be up and would carry on its belly a thermal-imagery camera that located body heat, and a NightSun searchlight, with a grotesquely powerful beam. The body-heat job was what they needed to avoid: the cave would do it.

He followed. She went faster. The engine roar was closer. The helicopter had started to circle the house.

The 'big bird' in the air always made Fred feel warm. He and Carlo were in need of the comfort factor. The young man with them, Luca, would either be well on the way to *colonello* in five years, or sewing blankets at some remote outpost, probably Sicily ... They were all smoking. Luca was between Carlo and Fred, holding the little screen. It showed the images from the helicopter.

Not promising.

They saw Mamma, slow on her feet, taking down the washing from the line, holding the pegs in her mouth, like shark's teeth. It seemed far below her dignity to look up and acknowledge the pounding rotor blades of the Bell Agusta. She took down her washing and replaced it, showing no sign of the crisis around her: a grandson's body in a coffin, a village priest, her friend, shot dead, a husband in flight, a daughter-in-law disappeared, and a form of vengeance carried out by a stranger. She held the pegs and folded the sheets.

Nothing justified the comfort factor.

The screen showed Stefano – identified by the *maresciallo* – playing football on the gravel in front of the house. The children with him, they were told, belonged to Annunziata who was a 'disappeared', buried or cut into pieces and scattered – who had taken a lover while married to one of the family's men.

They looked for a sign, a moment of significance, and didn't find it. The woman named Teresa, dressed for a promenade along the shore at Naples or on the Via Veneto in Rome – anywhere that wasn't up a track from a mountain village – watched the football from the front door, smoking and holding a wine glass.

Nothing that was any good.

The men by the oil drum, between the *carabinieri* and the house, had left the warmth of the fire. Some had gone along narrow paths across the olive groves and others had walked down the road, through the chicane that the vehicles made, talking quietly among themselves. They didn't spare a glance for the guns of the cordon, Carlo or Fred. Luca pointed out one, in big glasses with a cyst on his nose, and said he was the close cousin of a *pentito* executed that week in Rome; he had to work hard to demonstrate that he was no threat or he would himself be shot.

The screen showed the kid, the scooter boy, with the dogs around the chicken coop. They saw the heap of dumped stones at the side of the building and beyond the washing line. The dogs ran around the kid. Carlo and Fred didn't need to be told, but Luca said it: the scent was confused, the trail muddied. But there was the pile of stones, which was precious. It was all they had to cling to.

'Did we screw up, Fabio?'

'Maybe, maybe not.'

'Because we packed too early?'

'We took out the batteries, too, Ciccio, and the lenses.'

'What did you see?'

'Nothing. Was it Scorpion Fly?'

'That's what it was called, Fabio.'

'Significant about the scorpion fly, Ciccio, is that it appears to have a sting in the tail but doesn't. It's harmless. I might get a badge made that shows it. Time for the pretty boys to deploy.'

The 'pretty boys' were the *cacciatore*. They packed again. If they were challenged they would claim 'communications malfunction'. They had done their job to the best of their abilities and reckoned themselves above the dross but below the elite of the army that fought the long war. It hurt to fail but success was rare.

Carlo had the sense that his water told him the truth. Men like him, with his professional experience of hitting targets in the small hours, knew when success was guaranteed or failure beckoned.

Ahead of them were the *cacciatore*, off the helicopter now. Good guys. Berets worn jauntily, camouflage fatigues and pistol holsters slapping their thighs, grenades on their belts and machine guns carried warily, balaclavas over their faces, they'd sprinted up the track. The football was over and the washing hadn't been replaced. The dogs barked round them and were kicked away. Carlo was with Fred, the *maresciallo* and some of his people. They were Wave Two, the back-up. The older man, Stefano, faced the wall, his hands on his head, the kid beside him, his hands at the back of his neck. Teresa was with them too, and they had brought a chair for Mamma – the one that had been on the patio. The crack guys had gone ahead and Wave Two followed. To Carlo it was always obvious when the cogs of a mission didn't mesh.

They reached the house. The old woman stared defiantly ahead, appeared undisturbed by the crisis. Carlo's experience told him that the women were always the bellwether of a win or a loss, of whether the handcuffs would be used or the target was clear of the location. The kid and the older man gazed at the wall. They gave no sign of interest but were not cocky. Carlo and Fred walked past the yard, skirted the patio and went under the trellis. Fred reached up and plucked a bunch of grapes—

The first explosion. The chickens squawked. It shook Carlo, and Fred choked on the first of his stolen grapes.

A second flash-bang. Carlo counted. He liked them because they disoriented the opposition – better than gas in the eyes when a doctor had to give clearance. They usually made a bollocks of their first statement: always a good one to get in the bag before the lawyers were on the scene. He and Fred went past the washing-line, Luca with them. He saw the derelict shed, the stone wall, the heap of rocks and the hole that gaped in front of the *cacciatore* boys. He heard a shout behind him, shrill with warning. He turned.

The boot had a shiny toecap but the instep was coated with dirt. It was Luca's, and he had used it to scrape out loose earth where it had been disturbed. Bloody lucky he wasn't up there with the angels singing anthems. Among the earth in the little exca-vated pit were the ends of two sections of wire. Fred was at his side.

'There's a bunker, but no power in it. The entrance is an electric-controlled door, but it's dead. Back here, the wire's broken. Who did that?'

'Are you asking or telling?'

'He's quite a lad, your young man . . .'

He thought again of what the woman had said, in the kitchen of a small home in Canning Town, about her son – who had a brother working in the street market and a shop-assistant sister in the West End. He'd thought her strangely rude, and reckoned her opinion inappropriate. Nothing she had said would indicate why the boy, who should have been her pride and joy and had no link to the region, had decided on waging warfare on a criminal clan he didn't know and with whom he had little argument. Two flash-bangs had been rolled the length of the tunnel. Anyone lingering inside would have been deafened and temporarily blinded.

'Do you understand?' Fred jabbed the question.

'I don't.'

They waited and watched. The tunnel was filled with searchers.

One came back. A head shaken, a gesture with a hand. He thought young Luca, beside him, drooped, like a guy who thinks he's won the lottery and has spent the money twice, then finds he forgot to buy the coupon. A savage moment.

Carlo asked, 'Do you think we might have overstayed . . .?'

'Maybe the only useful thing we did was scratch our names on that tree.'

'Let's get the fuck out – after our comprehensive exercise in learning the perils of shoving a snout where it has no right to be.'

They turned their backs. Another day, another dollar. Carlo sniffed. He thought it looked, again, like rain – and, again, like he hadn't changed the world.

He'd known where to go.

They had led him.

It was a low entrance. He had to duck and his knees brushed the dried leaves that had accumulated at the mouth. Jago had the torch in one hand and in the other he gripped the penknife. The helicopter was still up but over the approach to the house, where the olives were grown, and towards the village. He thought it would come back, do more sweeps, but doubted that the thermal-imagery kit could penetrate the deep granite roof. There had been a little moonlight to help him find the hole, but instinct had told him where to look. They had gone quiet, off his radar, but the entrance was easy to find. He had relied on his memory – his lecturers at Lancaster had noted it, as had his line manager in the City and the *FrauBoss*. They had all remarked on it and his ability to retain what he had seen or been told once. The floor of the cave was compacted earth. He had a hand in front of him so that he did not snag an obstruction – there had been none when he had seen the cave's interior. He could hear them.

The old man was breathing harshly. Jago sensed his ordeal. Alone, in pitch blackness, unable to communicate because no one had come for him. Maybe on the floor and hurt – a new experience for him. He assumed Bernardo, the *padrino*, had once been as young, as arrogant, as Marcantonio. As he had aged, he would have become more cunning, wary, determined to cling to power. Those hard hours, because of Jago Browne, were the price of his having sent his grandson to Berlin. The old man's chest would be heaving, his heart pounding. She was quieter, but she must have shifted because he heard movement.

And he heard the firearm being cocked. The scrape of metal on metal.

A powerful torch was switched on and shone straight into Jago's face. He could see nothing and it hurt his eyes, which watered. He mustn't show fear. Fear was a killer in the alleys around Freemasons Road, behind the Beckton Arms or in any part of Kreuzberg. Consolata had shown no fear. If he showed fear, he was dead. They would read fear. He thought they didn't know who he was but were aware of what he had done. He had time.

Lower down the hill there were still occasional shouts from the troops, and the helicopter stayed overhead. He didn't think he would be shot, with the noise reverberating in the small space, before the search had finished.

He kept his face devoid of expression. He thought the family, for its survival, had snuffed out many lives. He neither smiled nor cringed. He thought they would be at the end of the cave, where the ring for the chain was. Jago waited to see the face of the old man. He would wait as long as he had to. The light never left his face, and he didn't turn away.

20

The light hurt his eyes but he stared straight into it. He thought it was the same torch that had been used to illuminate the wolf's head. Then he had seen the pain in the beast's features, but it hadn't flinched. As his example, Jago took a young wolf, with a wounded side. The animal had not backed down. He had his own torch and penknife.

He moved very slowly. It might have been a spider on a single strand of web that had come down from the ceiling and brushed the back of his neck, or a scrap of soil that had been dislodged. It irritated the skin at the gap where his hair and shirt met. It had been good of Consolata to bring clean clothing for him, but it was the food he had wanted – anything more from her? He didn't think so. He hadn't asked for her involvement. He laid the penknife in front of his crossed legs and showed that his hand was empty. He held it up, as if he was making an oath. He thought it would be Giulietta who held the pistol he had heard being armed. Unlikely that the old man would have been able – from his breathing – to hold it steady.

Her breathing was calm. The shouts far beyond the cave entrance were rarer and more distant. The drone of the helicopter placed it further away – he thought it was now over the village, searching there. Sometimes he heard the kid whistle for the dogs, but not close.

After he had shown his hand, and hadn't blinked in the power of the beam, he reached behind his head, found where the spider or the soil had touched him and scratched. He brought his hand back to the front, showed his empty palm, then rested it on his knee, leaving the penknife, blade open, on the cave floor. A flattened cigarette packet lay near to the knife, saved from decay by its plastic wrapping, and there were slivers of silver foil from chewing-gum. He must show neither fear nor impatience.

They couldn't come out of the cave without passing him, dead, incapacitated or alive. He didn't smile at the torch beam when he had eased the discomfort on his neck because to try to make easy contact would demonstrate weakness. He didn't play poker, had never sat in a smoke-filled room with a tumbler of Scotch and gambled with cards. It was about bluff. He would wait and however long it took, he would see the face of the old man and learn how greatly he had taxed him. It seemed that nothing was more important to Jago than seeing the jaw, cheeks, mouth and eyes of the *padrino*, and moving on from the monochrome image. When he had seen the face, learned the damage he had done, the power would have been transferred to him. He could wait.

The wind had freshened behind him. Jago fancied that old leaves danced. He heard the first patter of rain.

Jago had come of his own free will to a far corner of Europe and sat in a cave. He was sheltered from the coming storm and outside – in the mountains, coastal towns and hard-to-locate villages – were the organisers of the greatest criminal clans anywhere in the world as he knew it. The heat of the day had gone and the chill had settled under the low ceiling. The rain would soon surge and the drips would fall. When he put on his torch he would look into the face of the old man who was responsible for what had happened in the cave – and much else. He could have smiled at the thought of it, seeing the pain he had caused, the confusion he had brought down on the clan, but he kept his expression wooden and passive.

He no longer heard the helicopter. The shouts had died. The wind blew more fiercely and would scatter a carpet of leaves over the path they had taken, where their footprints might have shown. The rain would further degrade the scent they had left. He waited, the torch loose in his hand. He thought the old man's breathing had regained a regular rhythm. Perhaps he was over the experience of darkness in the dungeon. Jago wondered how long she could hold the pistol's aim.

*   *   *

Consolata came back to the squat. It was late but another meeting was in progress.

She stood at the door and watched them for a moment. Then Pietro gave her the dismissive wave that meant he had seen her, but that she should not interrupt – and that she had no part to play in their deliberations. She felt wretched, awkward in the clothing that had been wished on her, which was too large. She would tell no one. She went down the stairs and into the basement storeroom. Her bed was in the corner, beside the line of filing cabinets. Her pillow was under a poster of the group holding a big anti-Mafia banner when they had marched in Rosarno. She saw her bag. She didn't think it had been searched: they had ignored her. She wouldn't tell them of going to a park, dumping leaflets and finding a boy, or of taking him to a place of danger, or of facilitating the killing of a family heir, or of being rejected, humiliated. Her secret.

She stripped. At that time of night, to save money, the water was cold and the heater off. She took a cold shower, shivering and flinching under the spray.

Consolata dressed. She saw the radio she had once left on so that she could monitor every news bulletin. She put it into a cupboard. She went upstairs and found a computer still switched on in the room next to the one where the meeting continued, and began to fill in the electronic diary with events in the coming days that supporters could attend. She thought she had leaped for the stars, but had fallen into the gutter. Nothing had altered. She felt broken by the power she had confronted, but would go back to war, armed with leaflets: someone had to.

They were the last to board. They sat together, the engines gained power and the plane started to taxi. The storm was close and the pilot wanted to be airborne.

It was rare for Carlo to engage in small-talk, but he asked, 'Much on this weekend?'

'I've a boy at college in Dresden. We're due to go down and help him move to a new student hostel.' Fred grimaced. 'And I've papers to look at for a court appearance on Monday, vehicle theft. And you?'

'Nothing much. My partner's bought a new greenhouse, self-assembly from a flat pack. I hate them. And I'm behind with my expenses, not that they'll add up to much. Also there's a training course, ethnic diversity, on Monday that I have to read up on. I'm knackered, a bit vintage for all this. But it's been fun.'

The surveillance team checked into Control.

They were not asked how they were, what they had achieved, whether they'd enjoyed the ready-to-eat rations, whether they'd fucked up or were heroes of the republic. They dumped their kit, were told where to go on Monday morning. There was a whiteboard on the wall, and they saw their names on it, beneath 'Scorpion Fly'. That would have been cleaned off by the morning. Some of the kit went into the store, the weapons to the armoury . . . They'd drive together, find a beer somewhere, talk about something else.

The prosecutor had been to see the place, the hole leading into the bunker, and had declined to crawl inside. He was driven home and would be fresh in the morning to start his investigation into a family in Monasterace.

The aircraft had not been up for long. The flight path would take it north along the coast, then over the Bay of Naples and into Rome's airport, Leonardo da Vinci.

Jack, or Giacomo, had been hustled on board by the lawyer.

There was a party of bird-watchers behind him and behind them the two men he had seen talking to his boss, Bent Horrocks, who had brought – according to the lawyer – catastrophe to the venture. He would ask few questions and would strenuously attempt to answer none. He assumed he would be met by the Flying Squad or the Crime Agency and would dedicate himself to seeming stupid, ignorant and amnesiac. He listened. Always one loudmouth on a plane who thought any opinion he held was valuable and wanted to share it. Jack couldn't help but listen.

'. . . I'm very pleasantly surprised . . . Did I say that on the bus? Well worth repeating, don't you know? It seemed quieter, less hassle, in Reggio than usual. I didn't feel threatened in any way. Maybe they've got things under control, the authorities, and the criminals are on the run. Not before time. It all looked pretty normal to me, just like anywhere . . . and the birds were wonderful. I'm thinking, and I'm never afraid to admit, I'm wrong, that all this talk of organised crime, corruption, violence may be over-stated. Bloody newspapers – you know what I mean. Maybe it's a myth . . . It's been some of the best migratory birding I've ever known. That's what's important.'

He thought of Bent climbing awkwardly into the front passenger seat of the City-Van, touching his hair because he was off to an important meeting and wanted to look his best, and shivered. He looked behind him. The man with the mouth was quiet, eating a sandwich. The heads of the two guys behind the tripod crowd were lolling. He wondered how they could sleep, after what they'd done.

Water dripped from the roof of the cave.

The wind blustered outside. The damp clawed at his skin. He sensed the waiting was over. Thunder burst around them, funnelled through the cave entrance – the storm must have edged closer. The lightning flash lit them: he saw the girl and her father – one of her arms was around her father's shoulders and the other was at her side, the hand in her lap. The pistol was beside her but she wasn't holding it. The cave was in darkness again, except for the light of the torch, thrown on him and hiding them.

Jago wondered how long he had sat there, with the full beam in his face, since she had put down the weapon.

He held up his own torch, the bulb and the glass facing the roof of the cave, and switched it on. It would have to compete with the flashlight that was balanced on the stone floor beside her hip. The two of them were at the very back of the cave, close to the old mattress. He thought it would have split years before, its innards used by mice and rats for their nests. He thought he had seen the chain but was sure he had spotted the bucket.

He did it slowly. Jago was not some explorer landing on a beach of what would become a French territory in the Pacific Ocean, an Australasian coast or the edge of any part of the unknown world. He didn't need to say that he carried no weapon, had only beads and a Bible in his pocket. He thought they would have judged him because the pistol was down. He did it slowly, but with purpose. It was all about bluff. If his were called he would be shot – acceptable risk. The sort of risk that the traders lived with, not the investment analysts. The alternative? Perhaps the civil service – Environment, Food and Rural Affairs or Work and Pensions. Or industry, if he was lucky. He might open a tea room in the Cotswolds or trek off after water sources for the nomads of the sub-Saharan deserts of Africa. The torch edged across the roof of the cave and the wetness glistened. He saw more drips forming after others had fallen. His beam, fainter, came down behind them. They were where the child had been. And there was the ring. The beam wavered as he adjusted it. It caught the old man first.

Nothing special. Rather ordinary. It seemed a pasty face, not the deep colour of old stained wood. There were bags under the eyes, the lips were thin and the stubble was sparse, irregular. There was no indication of wealth and confidence, or of an old man who looked after his appearance, his health, except in the eyes. Jago thought the eyes betrayed him. They were dull. He wondered what would make the man laugh and bring a sparkle to those eyes. He had a long, hard look at the face. If he'd sat next to the man on the U-bahn or a Central Line train in London, he wouldn't have considered him worth engaging in conversation, giving the spiel of the sales team, dropping a card into his hand. The lack of lustre in the eyes told the truth. The old man, head of his family, wouldn't have cared if Jago Browne was dead or alive, would have stepped right over him, then forgotten him. The eyes said it.

He shifted the torch beam. She had the pistol in her hand now. Jago didn't know whether it was cocked, whether the safety was on. She didn't aim it. His light, poor by comparison with theirs, caught two small blemishes on her skin, one at the centre of her forehead and one on the left side of her chin. He assumed them to be blood spatters, that she had killed someone at close range and that most of the blood had soaked into her clothing, which had been burned. Her face was different from her father's. There was life in it, and interest. A strong face, with a hint of a mocking smile. She raised the pistol. Two hands on it. He thought the searchers had gone and the helicopter was far away. He switched off his torch and lost sight of her.

Jago didn't know whether she was playing with him, teasing or taunting him or whether she still had the aim, if a finger was against the trigger and if she had started to squeeze. The torch-light burned his eyes, and he saw nothing. The storm built to a frenzy.

He didn't know if he would register the flash before the bullet hit him. But Jago dared to hope, and waited to be answered.

After the autumn gales and deluges, it was a hard winter in the Aspromonte. Local people, the elders in the communities, said it was the harshest in living memory. Small villages, towards the peaks, were cut off by blizzards, and several farmers lost pigs because they couldn't feed them. But, with wonderful inevitability, spring followed the thaw, and wild flowers proved their ability to survive deep frosts. The trees sprouted blossom and foliage, the vines prospered and the olive groves showed promise of a fine harvest.

The winds from the east had been vicious and the snow had come from leaden skies across Berlin. A park near Bismarckstrasse had been carpeted, and each day the employees of a private-wealth section at a bank had struggled to get to work. There was a new favourite among the girls, a Norwegian-born young man, who had settled effortlessly into the foreign-exchange programme. Spring broke, and the crocuses were blooming in the beds in front of the iron benches in a small open space.

In autumn, winter or spring, the same criminality taxed the HMRC people working out of Dooley Terminal at the British container port of Felixstowe. Drugs came in, and the trafficking of

weapons and children, for paedophiles, continued with few inter-
ruptions. Foul weather blew in off the North Sea, and those
rummaging through Continental lorries and trailers were cut to
the bone by the cold in the open-ended hangars. Going to work
required commitment – but a driven man required no nudge. He
pursued a target through days of rain, sleet and ice into the first
days of the new optimism that came with the warmth.

A café where the open-air chairs and tables were bathed in
strong sunshine was a good place to meet for two irregular
colleagues, associates in kind. The prospect of such an occasion
could be said to have sustained the pair through five and a half
harsh months.

'Looks to me like she's had a nose job.'

'We say "rhinoplasty",' Fred answered.

'I'd call it an improvement,' Carlo said.

They were on the Boulevard du Midi Jean Hibert on the water-
front at Cannes. Not a bad place for a German investigator and an
unpromoted Customs officer from Britain to find themselves on
an April morning. They had a pocket-handkerchief table and two
grimly uncomfortable chairs. The German had a *citron pressé* in
front of him and the Briton bottled mineral water. Because the
table was against the road that divided the buildings from the
beach and the sea, the drinks would normally have cost fifteen
euros, but for them the question of payment had been waived.

'I'd call it a match made in Heaven – would you challenge that?'
Carlo asked.

'What else? Lovely couple. Makes you feel good just to look at
them.'

Which was possible. Beyond the pavement and the palm trees,
the road and the beach – far out to sea – a cruise liner edged
calmly along, heading west, and a tall ship, triple-masted, lay at
anchor. Sailing boats, under power, skipped in loose circles
across the water and motor launches made bow waves. Residents
walked at the edge of the beach and let toy dogs romp. The two
men were not looking at the sights that made the resort so famous

and expensive, so sought after. The couple inside, close to the window, had their attention. The two watchers exuded raw pleasure at being close to what Carlo would have called 'fingering a collar'.

'She's wearing a decent ring.'

'Only what she deserves.'

Each, in his home city, had made a dawn start. Fred had been at Tempelhof at first light, having crawled out of bed to the shriek of the alarm. He had pecked his wife's cheek and thought he would be back in time for a late supper. Carlo had struggled out of Sandy's bed, then left in darkness for Stansted and a bucket flight to the South of France. The French had shown willingness, by their standards, to co-operate.

The previous day the couple had followed their briefly estab-lished routine and walked from the apartment he rented to this café-bar and had ordered. Coffee had been brought, and glasses of bottled water. The man had picked up the water when a waiter had intervened, apologising for the dirty glass he had been given, whipped it away and produced another. In a van behind the prem-ises the locals had equipment to check the print on the glass with the one transmitted from Berlin. The match had left no room for doubt.

Carlo and Fred had wanted to be there at the end – probably unnecessary, but good for their morale.

'She's a nice-looking woman, now they've straightened her face up.'

'A bit old for him.'

'Think of the baggage she brings to the marital bed.'

They knew what the marital bed looked like – they'd seen it that morning. The Cannes-based detectives had met them at the airport and driven them into town. The concierge had told them that the couple had left the apartment. The door had been easily opened, the alarm disabled, and they had wandered round the rooms and seen what magazines the newly wed couple were reading. He was learning Italian from books and CDs and she was trying to improve her English. The bed was unmade and her clothing, some of which lay on the floor, was new and like nothing she'd worn in the village last autumn. He was smart-casual and left behind him the signs of new affluence. They'd have thought themselves safe.

'You satisfied, Fred?'

'Just like to finish my drink. Have you been busy?'

'A bit of this and a bit of that. Doing what I do best, the stuff no one notices.'

'I'll finish my drink and then we'll let loose the hounds.'

A month before, Fred had said, he'd been in the small square as the last of the snow was being cleared and he'd seen the girl from the pizzeria. She might have recognised him because she'd ducked inside quickly. He'd noted that the scar had knitted but not well. The man had come out. Fred had made some remark about the girl's wound and had been told she was due to see a quality plastic surgeon next week. They couldn't have afforded it, but an envelope had been delivered: ten thousand euros, in large-denomination notes. No letter, no explanation. A bank had been instructed to make the delivery by hand. Fred had found the bank, based in Liechtenstein, but had been blocked by its secrecy culture. Carlo's turn. He'd handed it to Vauxhall Bridge Cross, the spooks, where it had been used as a training exercise for the 'best and brightest' of a new intake. The big computers had been set to work and had located the origin of a telephone call. Simple.

Fred said, 'It was flawed, sending the money to the girl to have her face fixed. Idiotic.'

'He's soft. He'd think himself hard but he isn't.'

'You can't grow into them. They're unique, those families. They're successful because others can't equal them. No one from inside such a family would show such weakness, sentimentality. It was an outsider's error.'

Fred voiced the opinion that she was radiant, a woman on the edge of middle age who had lately found love.

Carlo thought he seemed confident, calm. His shades were over his eyes, and a gold chain hung round his neck.

'They've done a good job on her nose.'

'I never saw her smile when we were there . . . They'll do her for murder and bang him up for "association". She dropped a chap who was about to turn state witness. Made a good clean job of it.' Carlo shrugged.

The French police could make the arrest and the Italians would swamp the town with a legion of government lawyers to hack through the extradition process. But it was a pleasure for Carlo and Fred to be there. It would happen with a degree of theatre. Carlo reached into his pocket and took out a scarlet handkerchief that Sandy had given him the previous Christmas. At last it had a use.

They could see Jago Browne and Giulietta Cancello easily from where they sat. What stuck in Carlo's craw was that he had, at first, admired the bloody-mindedness of the young man who had dared to confront the family. In time he might find out, from interrogation reports, when the transfer of loyalty had happened, who had conjured it up, him or her.

'Would you call it greed, Fred?'

'I would quote to you from Friedrich Nietzsche. "For every man there exists a bait which he cannot resist swallowing." You accept that?'

'I looked it up. It bothers me – the ease of corruption. We had Robert Walpole. He said, "Every man has his price." Takes the gilt off the day.'

Fred said, 'From George Washington, "Few men have virtue to withstand the highest bidder." But it hurts. The young woman who did the driving for him, she's gone to Milan and works in an orphanage. She hasn't lost faith – didn't look for a pay-off.'

Carlo had the handkerchief in his hand. He said, 'Sir Walter Raleigh was a buccaneer and a pirate four hundred years ago, a man of letters, too, a poet. "No mortal thing can bear so high a price, But that with mortal thing it may be bought." Time to hit the road.'

'Right.'

'A good result.'

'Very good. An alright result. Yes.'

Carlo took a last look at them. They were laughing together, holding hands. Unremarkable and unexceptional, just two affluent people in a sea-front café-bar facing the promenade at Cannes, a playground for the well-heeled. It was unlikely he would go back, for work, to Calabria. He had been left with many loose ends, and few would be tied. He might never know whether the old man, head of the family, was still living like a rodent, buried underground and on the run, or how well the old woman had survived the upheaval. He remembered the handyman who drove the little City-Van, and the kid who was good with dogs. He might never know if the wedding had taken place at that house, a clean damask tablecloth over a dresser to double as an altar, the new priest officiating, or whether they had used the church and relied on the community's obedience and silence. He would never know whether the wedding night had been spent in the bed of the *padrino*, or how much expertise had been brought to the field of investment. Neither did he know whether Luca, the *maresciallo*, had gained entry to the fast track programme, or whether the prosecutor had prospered or not at the end of what they had called 'Scorpion Fly'. He hadn't learned much about the young man who had joined the family.

He made few judgements on the behaviour of others, and now was not a particularly rewarding time to slough off the habit. He would never forget the village and the hillside above it, the remote house with mountains as a backdrop, or forget Jago Browne. The German hadn't asked about the aftermath of Bentley Horrocks. If he had, the answer would have been economical because little of that was written up in his mission report: best buried, with a missing-person file. Carlo, punching Fred lightly on the arm, did his job as a plodder. He waved the handkerchief.

The gesture would have alerted the link. A radio call was made. A few seconds of peace, calm – the pavements were filling as the lunch-hour approached, the cruise liner had drifted further along the coast, more yachts had taken to the water and the sea vista had hazed. Some, Carlo reflected, would have been about to rise to their feet, push aside the table and lift a clenched fist of triumph, as the arrest squad went in. Damn it, he felt suddenly empty. Carlo didn't need to say it, but it would have been about 'belonging'. The young man had never been in a tribal reserve, like the squads at HMRC, which hunted up Green Lanes or any investigator in the KrimPol. With belonging came power, the proof of which was money. The noughts floated in his mind. He'd gone philosophical in search of an answer but it was not his business to understand, just to do his job.

He looked from the couple, still chuckling, to Fred. The gaze returned to him was stonily impassive. No mortal thing would find himself, herself, proof against the big bucks when they were wheeled out.

Two cars pulled up fast at the kerb, brakes and tyres squealing. The men were out running, jeans, T-shirts and pistols. The heads jerked up inside the café-bar and the laughter died. Shock spread, as it always did. Mouths sagged, eyes bulged, hands froze together, and the ring, still bright and new, was hit by the sunshine. No ceremony. Both on the floor, down among the chair legs, the expert, unemotional search, then the handcuffs. They were brought out, frogmarched close to where Fred and Carlo sat. Were they recognised? Maybe.

Fred said, 'What nailed him, gave him to us, was that he sent the money to the girl from the pizzeria where it all started. Tainted money. Money taken from the rinsed profits of cocaine trafficking. If I were to go and see her tomorrow, and tell her the origin of the money that would repair her face, she would reject it. Shall I tell her?'

Carlo said, 'If you don't, and she uses the money, you've compromised the truth. We're not archangels. We do what is best for the moment and causes least hassle. We don't stand in judgement . . . Is there time for a beer?'

The chairs were rearranged and the table was cleared.

It was at that moment, when the car's rear door was open – Giulietta was inside the other vehicle – that Jago Browne had seemed to catch his eye, then looked away and allowed himself to be pushed into the seat. He might have remembered Fred, beside him, and wondered where the mistake had been conceived. He might have wondered, too, why he hadn't stayed at the bank to live in the slow lane.

The cars left, and sirens yelled on the road. Fred and he would be driven to the airport. It was likely that, on the way, they'd talk expenses, kit, pensions or anything else that gave grief. Mutual congratulations would be *verboten*, forbidden. They had enjoyed a snapshot moment, handcuffs, arrests, the wave of disbelief that clouded young faces. That was enough. Would they meet again? Perhaps, perhaps not. Would they have time for a beer in the lounge before their separate flights? They'd make time.

'Did we win, Carlo?'

'I think so, Fred, but I'm not sure. In that corner of nowhere, it could be that *they* won because they can buy anybody, which is serious. Why doesn't anyone try to buy us? Or at least make an offer?'

'We're not worth the investment. Find a mirror. Look at yourself and me.'

They hugged. They laughed. Their transport was waiting for them.